JADE CITY

JADE CITY

FONDA LEE

orbit

www.orbitbooks.net

Cover design by [TK]
Cover illustration/photo by [TK]
·Cover copyright © 2017 by Hachette Book Group, Inc.

Orbit
Hachette Book Group
1290 Avenue of the Americas
New York, NY 10104
orbitbooks.net

First Edition: November 2017

Orbit is an imprint of Hachette Book Group.
The Orbit name and logo are trademarks of Little, Brown Book Group Limited.

The publisher is not responsible for websites (or their content) that are not owned by the publisher.

The Hachette Speakers Bureau provides a wide range of authors for speaking events. To find out more, go to www.hachettespeakersbureau.com or call (866) 376-6591.

Library of Congress Cataloging-in-Publication Data has been applied for

[TK]

ISBNs: 978-0-316-44086-8 (hardcover), 978-0-316-44089-9 (ebook)

Printed in the United States of America

LSC-C

10 9 8 7 6 5 4 3 2 1

• Chapter One •
THE TWICE LUCKY

The two would-be jade thieves sweated in the kitchen of the Twice Lucky restaurant. The windows were open in the dining room and the on-set of evening brought a breeze off the waterfront to cool the diners, but in the kitchen, there were only the two ceiling fans that had been spinning all day to little effect. Summer had barely begun and already the city of Janloon was like a spent lover—sticky and fragrant.

Bero and Sampa were sixteen years old, and after three weeks of plan-ning, they had decided that tonight would change their lives. Bero wore a waiter's dark pants and a white shirt that clung uncomfortably to his back. His sallow face and chapped lips were stiff from holding in his thoughts. He carried a tray of dirty drink glasses over to the kitchen sink and set it down, then wiped his hands on a dish towel and leaned toward his co-conspirator, who was rinsing dishes with the spray hose before stacking them in the drying racks.

"He's alone now." Bero kept his voice low.

Sampa glanced up. He was an Abukei teenager—copper-skinned with thick, wiry hair and slightly pudgy cheeks that gave him a faintly che-rubic appearance. He blinked rapidly, then turned back to the sink. "I get off my shift in five minutes."

"We gotta do it now, keke," said Bero. "Hand it over."

Sampa dried a hand on the front of his shirt and pulled a small paper packet from his pocket. He slipped it quickly into Bero's palm. Bero tucked his hand under his apron, picked up his empty tray, and walked out of the kitchen.

At the bar, he asked the bartender for rum with chili and lime on the rocks—Shon Judonrhu's preferred drink. Bero carried the drink away, then put down his tray and bent over an empty table by the wall, his back to the dining room floor. As he pretended to wipe down the table with his towel, he emptied the contents of the paper packet into the glass. They fizzed quickly and dissolved in the amber liquid.

He straightened and made his way over to the bar table in the corner. Shon Ju was still sitting by himself, his bulk squeezed onto a small chair. Earlier in the evening, Maik Kehn had been at the table as well but to Bero's great relief, he'd left to rejoin his brother in a booth on the other side of the room. Bero set the glass down in front of Shon. "On the house, Shon-jen."

Shon took the drink, nodding sleepily without looking up. He was a regular at the Twice Lucky and drank heavily. The bald spot in the center of his head was pink under the dining room lights. Bero's eyes were drawn, irresistibly, further down, to the three green studs in the man's left ear.

He walked away before he could be caught staring. It was ridiculous that such a corpulent, aging drunk was a Green Bone. True, Shon had only a little jade on him, but unimpressive as he was, sooner or later someone would take it, along with his life perhaps. *And why not me?* Bero thought. Why not indeed. He might only be a dockworker's bastard who could never be admitted to a martial school like Wie Lon Temple or Kaul Du Academy, but at least he was Kekonese all the way through. He had guts and nerve, he had what it took to be somebody. Jade made you somebody.

He passed the Maik brothers sitting together in a booth with a third, younger-looking man. Bero slowed a little, just to get a closer look at them. Maik Kehn and Maik Tar—now *they* were real Green Bones. Sinewy men, their fingers heavy with jade rings, fighting talon knives with jade-inlaid hilts strapped to their waists. They were dressed well: dark, collared shirts and tailored tan jackets, shiny black shoes, billed hats. The Maiks were well-known members of the No Peak clan, which controlled most of the neighborhoods on this side of the city. One of them glanced in Bero's direction.

Bero turned away quickly, busying himself with clearing dishes. The last thing he wanted was for the Maik brothers to pay any attention to him tonight. He resisted the urge to reach down to check the small caliber pistol tucked in the pocket of his pants and concealed by his apron. Patience. After tonight he wouldn't be in this waiter's uniform anymore. He wouldn't have to serve anyone anymore.

Back in the kitchen, Sampa had finished his shift for the evening and was signing out. He looked questioningly at Bero, who nodded that the deed was done. Sampa's small white upper teeth popped into view and crushed down on his lower lip. "You really think we can do this?" he whispered.

Bero brought his face near the other boy's. "Stay cut, keke," he hissed. "We're already doing it. No turning back. You've got to do your part!"

"I know, keke, I know. I will." Sampa gave him a hurt and sour look.

"Think of the money," Bero suggested, and gave him a shove. "Now get going."

Sampa cast a final nervous glance backward, then pushed out the kitchen door. Bero glared after him, wishing for the hundredth time that he didn't need such a doughy and insipid partner. But there was no getting around it—only a full-blooded Abukei native, immune to jade, could palm a gem and walk out of a crowded restaurant without giving himself away.

It had taken some convincing to bring Sampa on board. Like many in his tribe, the boy gambled on the river, spending his weekends diving for jade runoff that escaped the mines far upstream. It was dangerous—when glutted with rainfall, the torrent carried away more a few unfortunate divers, and even if you were lucky and found jade (Sampa had bragged that he'd once found a piece the size of a fist), you might get caught. Spend time in jail if you were lucky, time in the hospital if you weren't.

It was a loser's game, Bero had insisted to him. Why fish for raw jade just to sell it to the black market middlemen who carved it up and smuggled it off island, paying you only a fraction of what they sold it for later? A couple of clever, daring fellows like them—they could do better. If you were going to gamble for jade, Bero said, then gamble big. After-market gems, cut and set—that was worth real money.

Bero returned to the dining room and busied himself clearing and setting tables, glancing at the clock every few minutes. He could ditch Sampa later, after he'd gotten what he needed.

"Shon Ju says there's been trouble in the Armpit," said Maik Kehn, leaning in to speak discreetly under the blanket of background noise. "A bunch of kids shaking down businesses."

His younger brother Maik Tar reached across the table with his chopsticks to pluck at the plate of crispy squid balls. "What kind of kids are we talking about?"

"Low-level Fingers. Young toughs with no more than a piece or two of jade."

The third man at the table wore an uncharacteristically pensive frown. "Doesn't matter. Even the littlest Fingers are clan soldiers. They take orders from their Fists, and Fists from their Horn." The Armpit district had always been disputed territory, but directly threatening establishments affiliated with the No Peak clan was too bold to be the work of common hoodlums. "It smells like we're being pissed on."

The Maiks glanced at him, then at each other. "What's going on, Hilo-*jen*?" asked Kehn. "You seem out of sorts tonight."

"Do I?" Kaul Hiloshudon leaned against the wall in the booth and turned his glass of rapidly warming beer, idly wiping off the condensation. "Maybe it's the heat."

Kehn motioned to one of the waiters to refill their drinks. The pallid teenager kept his eyes down as he served them. He glanced up at Hilo for a second but didn't seem to recognize him; few people who hadn't met Kaul Hiloshudon in person expected him to look as young as he did. The Horn of the No Peak clan, second only in authority to his elder brother, often went initially unnoticed in public. Sometimes this galled Hilo; sometimes he found it useful.

"Another strange thing," said Kehn, when the waiter had left. "No one's seen or heard from Three Fingered Gee."

"How's it possible to lose track of Three Fingered Gee?" Tar wondered. The black market jade carver was as recognizable for his girth as he was for his deformity.

"Maybe he got out of the business."

Tar snickered. "Only one way anyone gets out of the jade business."

A voice spoke up near Hilo's ear. "Kaul-jen, how are you this evening? Is everything to your satisfaction tonight?" Mr. Une had appeared beside their table and was smiling the anxious, solicitous smile he always reserved for them.

"It's all excellent, as usual," Hilo said, arranging his face into the relaxed, lopsided smile that was his more typical expression. The owner of the Twice Lucky clasped his kitchen-scarred hands together, nodding and smiling his humble thanks. Mr. Une was a man in his sixties, bald and well-padded, and a third-generation restaurateur. His grandfather had founded the venerable old establishment, and his father had keep it running all through the wartime years, and afterward. Like his predecessors, Mr. Une was a loyal Lantern Man in the No Peak clan. Every time Hilo was in, he came around personally to pay his respects. "Please let me know if there is anything else I can have brought out to you," he insisted.

When the reassured Mr. Une had departed, Hilo grew serious again. "Ask around some more. Find out what happened to Gee."

"Why do we care about Gee?" Kehn asked, not in an impertinent way, just curious. "Good riddance to him. One less carver sneaking our jade out to weaklings and foreigners."

"It bothers me, is all." Hilo sat forward, helping himself to the last crispy squid ball. "Nothing good's coming, when the dogs start disappearing from the streets."

Bero's nerves were beginning to fray. Shon Ju had nearly drained his tainted drink. The drug was supposedly tasteless and odorless, but what if Shon, with the enhanced senses of a Green Bone, could detect it somehow? Or what if it didn't work as it should, and the man walked out, taking his jade out of Bero's grasp? What if Sampa lost his nerve after all? The spoon in Bero's hands trembled as he set it down on the table. *Stay cut, now. Be a man.*

A phonograph in the corner wheezed out a slow romantic opera tune, barely audible through the unceasing chatter of people. Cigarette smoke and spicy food aromas hung languid over red tablecloths.

Shon Ju swayed hastily to his feet. He staggered toward the back of the restaurant and pushed through the door to the men's room.

Bero counted ten slow seconds in his head, then put the tray down and followed casually. As he slipped into the restroom, he slid his hand into his pocket and closed it around the grip of the tiny pistol. He shut and locked the door behind him and pressed against the far wall.

The sound of sustained retching issued from one of the stalls and Bero nearly gagged on the nauseating odor of booze-soaked vomit. The toilet flushed and the heaving noises ceased. There was a muffled thud, like the sound of something heavy hitting the tile floor, then a sickly silence. Bero took several steps forward. His heartbeat thundered in his ears. He raised the small gun to chest level.

The stall door was open. Shon Ju's large bulk was slumped inside, limbs sprawled. His chest rose and fell in soft snuffling snores. A thin line of drool ran from the corner of his mouth.

A pair of grimy canvas shoes moved in the far stall, and Sampa stuck his head around the corner where he'd been lying in wait. His eyes grew round at the sight of the pistol, but he sidled over next to Bero and the two of them stared down at the unconscious man.

Holy shit, it worked.

"What're you waiting for?" Bero waved the small gun in Shon's direction. "Go on! Get it!"

Sampa squeezed hesitantly through the half-open stall door. Shon Ju's head was leaning to the left, his jade-studded ear trapped against the wall of the toilet cubicle. With the screwed-up face of someone about to touch a live power line, the boy placed his hands on either side of Shon's head. He paused; the man didn't stir. Sampa turned the slack-jowled face to the other side. With shaking fingers, he pinched the first jade earring and worked the backing free.

"Here, use this." Bero handed him the empty paper packet. Sampa dropped the jade stud into it and got to work removing the second earring. Bero's eyes danced between the jade, Shon Ju, the gun, Sampa, again the jade. He took a step forward and held the barrel of the pistol a few inches from the prone man's temple. It looked distressingly compact and ineffective, a commoner's weapon. No matter; Shon Ju wasn't going to be able to Steel or Deflect anything in his state. Sampa would palm the jade and walk out the back door with no one the wiser. Bero would finish his shift and meet up with Sampa afterward. No one would disturb old Shon Ju for hours; it wasn't the first time the man had passed out drunk in a restroom.

"Hurry it up," Bero said.

Sampa had two of the jade stones off and was working on the third.

His fingers dug around in the fold of the man's fleshy ear. "I can't get this one off."

"Pull it off, just pull it off!"

Sampa gave the last stubborn earring a swift yank. It tore free from the flesh that had grown around it. Shon Ju jerked. His eyes flew open.

"Oh shit," said Sampa.

With an almighty howl, Shon's arms shot out, flailing around his head and knocking Bero's arm upward just as Bero pulled the trigger of the gun. The shot deafened all of them but went wide, punching into the plaster ceiling.

Sampa scrambled to get away, nearly tripping over Shon as he lunged for the stall door. Shon flung his arms around one of the boy's legs. His bloodshot eyes rolled in disorientation and rage. Sampa tumbled to the ground and put his hands out to break his fall; the paper packet jumped from his grasp and skittered across the tile floor between Bero's legs.

"Thieves!" Shon Ju's snarling mouth formed the word but Bero did not hear it. His head was ringing from the gunshot and everything was happening as if in a soundless chamber. He stared as the red-faced Green Bone dragged at the terrified Abukei boy like a grasping demon from a pit.

Bero bent, snatched the crumpled paper envelope, and ran for the door.

He forgot he'd locked it. For a second he pushed and pulled in stupid panic, before turning the bolt and pounding out of the room. The diners had heard the gunshot and dozens of shocked faces were turned toward him. Bero had just enough presence of mind left to jam the gun into his pocket and point a finger back toward the restroom. "There's a jade thief in there!" he shouted.

Then he ran across the dining room floor, weaving between tables, the two small stones digging through the paper and against the palm of his tightly fisted left hand. People leapt away from him. Faces blurred past. Bero knocked over a chair, fell, picked himself up again, and kept running.

His face was burning. A sudden surge of heat and energy unlike anything he had ever felt before ripped through him like an electric current. He reached the wide curving staircase that led to the second floor where diners were getting up, peering over the balcony railing to see what the commotion was. Bero rushed up the stairs, clearing the entire expanse in a few bounds, his feet barely touching the floor. A gasp ran through the crowd. Bero's surprise burst into ecstasy. He threw his head back to laugh. This must be Lightness.

A film had been lifted from his eyes and ears. The scrape of chair legs, the crash of a plate, the taste of the air on his tongue—everything was razor sharp. Someone reached out to grab him, but he was so slow, and Bero was so fast. He swerved with ease and leapt off the surface of a table, scattering dishes and eliciting screams. There was a sliding screen door ahead of him that led out onto the patio overlooking the harbor. Without thinking, without pausing, he crashed through the barrier like a charging bull. The wooden latticework shattered and Bero stumbled through the body-sized hole he had made with a mad shout of exultation. He felt no pain at all, only a wild, fierce invincibility.

This was the power of jade.

The night air blasted him, tingling against his skin. Below, the expanse of gleaming water beckoned irresistibly. Waves of delicious heat seemed to be coursing through Bero's veins. The ocean looked so cool, so refreshing. It would feel so good. He flew toward the patio railing.

Hands clamped onto his shoulders and pulled him to a hard stop. Bero was yanked back as if he'd reached the end of a chain and spun around to face Maik Tar.

• Chapter Two •
THE HORN OF NO PEAK

The muffled gunshot went off on the other side of the dining room. A second or two later, Hilo felt it: the sudden shriek in his mind of an uncontrolled jade aura, as grating as a fork being dragged across glass. Kehn and Tar turned in their seats as the teenage waiter burst from the restroom and ran for the stairs.

"Tar," said Hilo, but there was no need; both the Maiks were already moving. Kehn went into the restroom; Tar leapt to the top of the stairs, caught the thief on the patio, and threw him bodily back through the broken screen door. A collective gasp and a number of screams broke out from the diners as the boy came flying back inside, hit the ground, and skidded to the top of the staircase.

Tar stepped into the building after him, stooping to clear the wreckage of the entryway. Before the boy could scramble to his feet, Tar palmed his head and forced it to the floor. The thief reached for a weapon, a small gun, but Tar tore it from him and hurled it through the broken door, flinging it far out over the water like a skipping stone. The thief gave a carpet-muffled cry as the Green Bone's knee ground down on his forearm and the paper packet was ripped from his white-knuckled grip. All this occurred so fast most of the onlookers did not see it. Tar stood up, the teenager at his feet spasming and moaning as the jangling jade energy crashed out of his body, taking with it the angry buzz in Hilo's skull.

Tar hauled the thief to his feet by the back of his waiter's shirt and dragged him back down the staircase to the main floor. The excited diners who'd left their tables backed silently out of his way. Kehn came out of the restroom, hauling a quietly whimpering Abukei boy along by the arm. He pushed the boy to his knees and Tar deposited the thief next to him.

Shon Judonrhu wobbled forward after Kehn, steadying himself on the backs of the chairs he passed. He didn't look entirely sure of where he was or how he had gotten there, but he was lucid enough to be enraged. His unfocused eyes bugged out from his skull. One hand was clapped to his ear. "Thieves," he slurred. Shon reached for the hilt of the talon knife sheathed in a shoulder holster under his jacket. "I'm going to gut them both!"

Mr. Une ran up, waving his arms in protest. "Shon-jen, I beg you, please, *not in the dining room!*" He held his shaking hands out in front of him, his jowly face white with disbelief. It was terrible enough that the Twice Lucky had been shamed, that the restaurant's kitchen had harbored jade thieves, but for the two boys to be publicly slain right next to the buffet dessert table—no business could survive the stain of such bad luck. The restaurant owner cast a fearful glance at Shon Ju's weapon, then at the Maik brothers and the surrounding stares of frozen customers. His mouth worked. "This is a terrible outrage, but gentlemen, *please*—"

"Mr. Une!" Hilo got up from his table. "I didn't realize you'd added live entertainment." All eyes turned as Hilo crossed the room. He felt a stir of understanding go through the crowd. The nearest diners noticed what Bero, in his initial cursory glance, had not: underneath Kaul Hilo's smoke-colored sport jacket and the unfastened top two buttons of his baby blue shirt, a long line of small jade stones was embedded in the skin of his collarbone like a necklace fused into his flesh.

Mr. Une rushed over and walked alongside Hilo, wringing his hands. "Kaul-jen, I couldn't be more embarrassed that your evening was disturbed. I don't know how these two worthless little thieving shits wormed their way into my kitchen. Is there anything I could do to make it up to you? Anything at all. As much food and drink as you could want, of course..."

"These things happen." Hilo offered up a disarming smile, but the restaurateur did not relax. If anything, he looked even more nervous as he nodded and wiped at his damp brow.

Hilo said, "Put your talon knife away, uncle Ju. Mr. Une has enough to clean up already without blood in the carpet. And I'm sure all these people who are paying for a nice dinner don't want their appetites ruined."

Shon Ju hesitated. Hilo had called him uncle, shown him respect despite his obvious public humiliation. That was not, apparently, enough to mollify him. He jabbed the blade in Bero and Sampa's direction. "They're jade thieves! I'm entitled to their lives and no one can tell me otherwise!"

Hilo held his hand out to Tar, who passed him the paper packet. He shook the two stones out into his palm. Kehn held out the third earring. Hilo rolled the three green studs in his hand thoughtfully and looked at Shon with eyes narrowed in reproach.

The anger went out of Shon Ju's face and was replaced with trepidation. He stared at his jade, cupped in another man's hand, its power now running through Kaul Hilo instead of him. Shon went still. No one else spoke; the silence was suddenly charged.

Shon cleared his throat roughly. "Kaul-jen, I didn't mean my words to suggest any disrespect to your position as Horn." This time, he spoke with the deference he would've shown to an older man. "Of course, I'm obedient to the clan's judgment in all matters of justice."

Smiling, Hilo took Shon's hand and dropped the three gemstones into his palm. He closed the man's fingers around it gently. "Then no serious harm's been done. I like it when Kehn and Tar have a reason to stay on their toes." He winked at the two brothers as if sharing a schoolyard joke, but when he turned back to Shon Ju, his face was devoid of humor. "Perhaps uncle," he said, "it's time to be drinking a little less and watching your jade a little more."

Shon Ju clutched the returned gemstones, bringing his fist close to his chest in a spasm of relief. His thick neck flushed red with indignity but he said nothing further. Even in his bleary, half-drugged state the man wasn't stupid; he understood he'd been given a warning and after his pitiful lapse tonight he remained a Green Bone only on account of Kaul Hilo's say-so. He backed away in a cowed stoop.

Hilo turned and waved his arms to the transfixed crowd. "Show's over, everyone. No charge for the entertainment tonight. Let's order some more of Mr. Une's delicious food, and another round of drinks!"

A nervous ripple of laughter traveled through the dining room as people obeyed, turning back to their meals and companions, though they kept stealing glances at Kaul Hilo, the Maiks, and the two sorry teens on the floor. It wasn't especially often that ordinary, jadeless citizens were witness to such a dramatic display of Green Bone abilities. They would go home and tell their friends about what they'd seen: how the thief had moved faster than any normal human being and plowed through a wooden door, how much faster and stronger still the Maik brothers were in comparison, and how even they deferred to the young Horn.

Kehn and Tar lifted the thieves and carried them out of the building.

Hilo began to follow, Mr. Une still scurrying along beside him, stammering quietly, "Once again, I beg your forgiveness. I screen all my wait staff carefully; I had no idea…"

Hilo put a hand on the man's shoulder. "It's not your fault; you can't always tell which ones will catch jade fever and go bad. We'll take care of it outside."

Mr. Une nodded in vigorous relief. He wore the expression of someone who'd nearly been hit by a bus only to have it swerve out of the way and drop a suitcase of money at his feet. If Hilo and the Maiks had not been present tonight, he would have had two dead boys and one very angry, drunken Green Bone on his hands. With the Horn's public endorsement however, the Twice Lucky had escaped being disastrously tainted and instead gained respect. Word of tonight's events would spread and the publicity would keep the restaurant busy for some time.

The thought made Hilo feel better. The Twice Lucky wasn't the only No Peak business in the neighborhood but it was one of the most successful and profitable; the clan needed its tribute money. Even more importantly, No Peak couldn't afford the loss of face if the place failed or was taken over. If a loyal Lantern Man like Mr. Une lost his livelihood or his life, the responsibility would fall on Hilo.

He trusted Mr. Une, but people were people. They sided with the powerful. The Twice Lucky might be a No Peak establishment today, but if the worst came to pass and the owner was forced to switch allegiance in exchange for keeping his family business and his head on his shoulders, Hilo held little illusion as to what choice he would make. Lantern Men were jadeless civilians after all; they were part of the clan and crucial to its workings, but they would not die for it. They were not Green Bones.

Hilo paused and pointed up at the destroyed screen door. "Send me the bill for the damage. I'll take care of it."

Mr. Une blinked, then clasped his hands together and touched them to his forehead several times in respectful gratitude. "You are too generous Kaul-jen. That's not necessary…"

"Don't be silly," said Hilo. He faced the man. "Tell me, my friend. Have you had any other trouble around here lately?"

The restaurant owner's eyes jumped around before landing nervously back on Hilo's face. "What sort of trouble, Kaul-jen?"

"Green Bones from other clans," Hilo said. "That sort of trouble."

Mr. Une hesitated, then drew Hilo aside and lowered his voice. "Not here in the Docks, not yet. But a friend of my nephew, he works as a bartender at the Dancing Girl, over in the Armpit district. He says he's seen men from the Mountain clan coming in almost every night, sitting down where they please and expecting their drinks to be free. They're saying it's part of their tribute, now that the Armpit is Mountain territory." Mr. Une took a sudden step back, unnerved by the expression on Hilo's face. "It might be nothing more than talk, but since you asked…"

Hilo patted the man's arm. "Talk is never just talk. Let us know if you hear anything else, won't you? You call if you ever need to."

"Of course. Of course I will, Kaul-jen," said Mr. Une, touching his hands to his forehead once more.

Hilo gave the man a final, firm pat on the shoulder and left the restaurant.

Outside, Hilo paused to pull a packet of cigarettes from his pocket. They were expensive Espenian cigarettes; he had a weakness for them. He put one in his mouth and looked around. "How about over there," he suggested.

The Maik brothers hauled the teenagers away from the Twice Lucky and pushed them down the gravel slope to the edge of the water, out of sight from the road. The pudgy Abukei boy cried and struggled the whole way; the other one was limp and silent. The Maiks threw the thieves to the ground and began to beat them. Heavy, rhythmic blows to the torso, pounding the ribs, stomach, and back. Smacks to the face until the boys' features were swollen almost beyond recognition. No strikes to the vital organs, the throat, or the back of the skull. Kehn and Tar were good Fists; they were not careless, and would not be carried away by bloodlust.

Hilo smoked a cigarette and watched.

Night had fallen completely now, but it was not dark. Streetlights blazed all along the waterfront and the headlights of cars driving by bathed the road in pulses of white. Far out on the water the slowly-traveling lights of shipping vessels were smeared into blotches by sea fog and the haze of pollution from the city. The air was warm and heavy with fumes, the sweetness of overripe fruit and the stink of nine hundred thousand perspiring inhabitants.

Hilo was twenty-seven years old, but even he remembered a time when cars and televisions were a new thing in Janloon. Now they were everywhere, along with more people, new factories, foreign-influenced street foods like tempura meatballs and spicy cheese curd. The metropolis strained at its seams and it felt as if all the people, Green Bones as well, strained with it. There was an undercurrent, Hilo thought, of everything running a bit too dangerously fast all the time, as if the city were an oily new machine cranked to its highest setting, teetering just on the edge of out-of-control, disrupting the natural order of things. What was the world coming to, that a couple of clumsy, untrained dock brats could figure on stealing jade off a Green Bone—and nearly succeed?

In truth, it would serve Shon Judonrhu right to lose his jade. Hilo could have claimed the three studs for himself, as justifiable punishment for Shon's ineptitude. He'd been tempted, certainly, by the energy that had radiated like liquid warmth through his veins when he'd rolled the stones in his hand.

But there was no respect in taking a few gems from a sorry old man. That was what these thieves didn't understand—jade alone didn't make you a Green Bone. Blood and training and clan made you a jade warrior; that's how it had always been. Hilo had both personal and clan reputation to uphold at all times. Shon Judonrhu was a drunkard, an old fool, a comical has-been of a Green Bone, but he was still a Finger in the employ of No Peak, and that made an offense against him Hilo's concern.

He dropped his cigarette and ground it out. "That's good," he said.

Kehn stepped back at once. Tar, always the more industrious of the two, gave each boy a final kick before following suit. Hilo studied the teenagers more closely. The one in the waiter's shirt had the classic Kekonese islander look—the leanness, the long arms, the dark hair and dark eyes. He lay half-dead, though it was hard to say if the jade fallout or the beating had done more to make him that way. The round-faced Abukei boy sobbed quietly through a constant stream of pleading: "It wasn't my idea, it wasn't, I didn't want to, please let me go, please, I promise I won't, I won't…"

Hilo considered the possibility that the boys were not the imbeciles they seemed, but spies or hired criminals working for the Mountain or perhaps one of the smaller clans. He decided the odds of it were low. He squatted down and pushed the hair off the Abukei boy's wet brow, causing him to flinch back in terror. Hilo shook his head and sighed. "What were you thinking?"

"He promised me we could make a lot of money," the teen wept, sounding more than a little wronged. "He said the old man was so drunk he wouldn't even notice. He said he knew a buyer, a reliable one, someone who would pay the highest rates for cut jade without asking questions."

"And you believed him? No one crazy enough to steal jade off a Green Bone means to sell it." Hilo stood up. There was nothing to be done for the Kekonese boy. Angry young men were prone to jade fever; Hilo had seen it plenty of times. Poor and naive, full of feral energy and ambition, they were drawn to jade like ants to honey. They romanticized the legendary hero-bandit Green Bones that filled comic books and movies with their exploits. They noticed how people said *jen* with respect and a little fear and they wanted that for themselves. Never mind that without the years of strict martial training, they weren't capable of controlling the powers jade conferred. They flamed out, went mad, destroyed themselves and others.

No, that one was a hopeless case.

The Abukei boy, though, was merely stupid. Fatally so? You could forgive stone-eyes for playing the lottery by river diving; you couldn't forgive a gross offense against the clan.

As if sensing Hilo's thoughts, the teenager sped up his verbal torrent. "Please, Kaul-jen, it was stupid, I know it was stupid. I'll never do it again, I swear. I've only ever taken jade from the river. If it wasn't for the new carver taking out Gee, I wouldn't have even thought about doing anything else. I've learned my lesson, I swear on my grandmother's grave. I won't touch jade again, I promise—"

"What did you just say?" Hilo crouched back down and leaned in, eyes squinted.

The teenager raised his eyes in fearful confusion. "I—What did I—"

"About a new carver," Hilo said.

Under Hilo's insistent gaze, the boy quailed. "I—I used to sell whatever I found in the river to Three Fingered Gee. For raw jade he paid on the spot in cash. Not a lot, but still pretty good. Gee was the carver on this side of town that most of us—"

"I know who he is," said Hilo impatiently. "What happened to him?"

Slow, shrewd hope crawled into the boy's eyes in realization that he had information the Horn of the No Peak clan did not. "Gee's gone. The new carver showed up last month, said he would buy as much jade as we could bring him, raw or cut, no questions asked. He offered to join up with Three Fingered Gee, but Gee didn't see the point of splitting his business with a newcomer. So the new guy killed him." The boy wiped snot and blood from his nose onto his sleeve. "They say he strangled Gee with a telephone cord, then cut off the rest of his fingers and sent them to the other carvers in the city as a warning. Now anything we find in the river goes to him, and he only pays half of what Gee used to pay. That's why I tried to get out of diving—"

"Have you seen this man?" Hilo asked.

The teenager hesitated, trying to decide which answer would save him and which would get him killed. "Y-yes. Just once."

Hilo exchanged a glance with his Fists. The Abukei boy had solved one vexing mystery for them, but raised another. Three Fingered Gee might be a black market jade carver, but he was a familiar one, a known entity, the stray dog in Hilo's yard that stole from garbage cans but was not troublesome enough to be worth killing. So long as he confined himself to buying raw jade from the Abukei, the clans left his little smuggling business alone in exchange for occasional tip-offs on bigger fish. Who would flout No Peak authority by killing him?

He turned back to the boy. "Could you describe him—this new carver?"

Again the hesitation. "Yes. I—I think so."

When the boy had stuttered through a description, Hilo stood up. "Bring the car around," he said to Kehn. "We're taking these boys to see the Pillar."

• Chapter Three •
THE SLEEPLESS PILLAR

Kaul Lanshinwan could not sleep. He had once been a reliable sleeper, but at least once a week for the past three months he'd found himself unable to drift off. His bedroom, which faced east from the upper floor of the main house on the Kaul property, felt obscenely large and empty, as did his bed. On some nights he stared out the windows until the glow of dawn crawled its tepid way across the view of the city's skyline. He tried meditating to calm himself before bed. He drank herbal tea and soaked in a salt bath. He supposed he ought to consult a doctor. Perhaps a Green Bone physician could determine what energy imbalance he had, unclog whatever flow was blocked, prescribe the right foods to restore equilibrium.

He resisted. At the age of thirty-five he was supposed to be in the prime of his health and at the peak of his power. It was why his grandfather had finally consented to cede leadership to him, why the rest of No Peak accepted that the mantle had passed from the legendary but old and ailing Kaul Seningtun to his grandson. If word got out that the Pillar of the clan was suffering health problems, it would not reflect well on him. Even something as mundane as insomnia might arouse speculation. Was he mentally unstable? Unable to carry his jade? Being perceived as weak could be fatal.

Lan got up, put on a shirt, and went downstairs. He slipped on his shoes and went into the garden. Being outside made him feel better at once. The family estate sat near the heart of Janloon—one could see the red roof of the Royal Council building and the tiered conical top of the Triumphal palace from the upstairs windows of the house—but the buildings and landscaped grounds of the Kaul property sprawled across five acres and were enclosed by high brick walls that sheltered it from the surrounding urban bustle. To a Green Bone, it was not quiet—Lan could hear the rustle of a mouse in the grass, the whirr of a small insect over the pond, the crunch of his own shoes along the smoothed pebble path—but the ever-present hum of the city was faint. The garden was an oasis of peace. Alone in this small patch of nature, away from the heady swirl of other jade auras, he could relax.

He sat down on a stone bench and closed his eyes. Settling into his own heartbeat and breath, into the steady churn of blood through his veins, he explored unhurriedly. He followed the wingbeats of a bat overhead as it darted this way, then that, snatching insects out of the air. From the breeze skimming across the small pond he picked out the scent of blooms: orange, magnolia, honeysuckle. He searched along the ground for the mouse he'd sensed earlier and found it—a hot spot of thrumming life, stark and bright in the darkness of the lawn.

When he'd been a student at Kaul Du Academy, he'd spent a night locked in a cavernous pitch black underground chamber with three rats. It was one of the tests of Perception administered to initiates at the age of twelve. He'd groped blindly along the cold stone walls, listening for the inaudible *scritch* of tiny claws, questing for blood heat like a snake, keenly aware that the exam ended if—and only if—he caught and killed all three of the sharp-toothed rats with his bare hands. Lan's back tensed at the memory.

A sharp nudge in the periphery of his awareness: Doru was approaching, crossing the garden, the invisible but distinctive jade aura that surrounded him parting the night like thin red light cutting through smoke.

Lan let out his breath and opened his eyes, a grimace of a smile tilting his mouth. If Doru found him catching mice in the garden at night it would be a far greater symptom of instability than mere insomnia. He was irritated, though, at having his solitude interrupted and did not get up to greet the man.

Yun Dorupon's voice was soft and raspy. It smelled medicinal and sounded like gravel being sloshed in a pan. "Sitting out here alone? Something the matter, Lan-se?"

Lan frowned at the man's use of the familial endearment; it was a suffix to be used with children and the elderly, not one's superior. For a Weather Man to use the term with his Pillar suggested a subtle insubordination. Lan was sure that Doru meant no disrespect; old habits were simply hard to break. Doru had known him since he was a boy, had been a fixture in the clan and in the Kaul household for as long as Lan could remember. Now, however, the man was supposed to be his strategist and trusted advisor, not his minder and uncle figure.

"Nothing," Lan said, finally standing up and turning to face the man. "I like it out here in the garden at night. It's important to be alone with your thoughts sometimes." A mild rebuke for the intrusion.

Doru did not seem to notice. "I'm sure you have a lot on your mind." The Weather Man was a rail-thin figure with an egg-shaped head and tapered chin, who wore wool sweaters and dark blazers that padded him up even in the oppressive heat of summer. His stiff manner gave him the air of an academic, but that was grossly misleading. Decades ago, Doru had been a Mountain Man—one of the indomitable rebels led by Kaul Seningtun and Ayt Yugontin, who resisted and ultimately ended foreign occupation of the island of Kekon. Doru had spent the final year of the Many Nations War in a Shotarian prison, and rumor had it that underneath his dowdy clothes he was missing plugs of flesh from his legs and arms, along with both his testicles.

Doru said, "The KJA is due to decide on the latest round of proposed exports by the end of the month. Have you considered whether you'll be lending your approval in the final vote?" The debate within the Kekon Jade Alliance over whether to increase the national sale of jade to foreign powers—namely Espenia and her allies—had been going on all spring.

"You know what I think," Lan said.

"Have you spoken about it to Kaul-jen?" Doru meant Kaul Seningtun of course. No matter the three younger Green Bones in the family—for Doru there was only one Kaul-jen.

Lan hid his annoyance. "There's no need to bother him when it's not necessary." Perhaps Doru wasn't the only member of No Peak who expected Lan to consult his grandfather on all major decisions, but that could not go on. It was past time to start sending the message that he was the one who held sole responsibility as Pillar. "The Espenians ask too much. If we bow down to them every time they want something of us, it wouldn't be long before every last pebble of jade on the island finds itself into an Espenian military vault."

The Weather Man was silent for a moment, then inclined his head. "As you say."

The thought came to Lan unbidden: *Doru's getting old, too old to change. He was grandfather's Weather Man and will always think of himself that way. I'll need to replace him soon.* He cut off his unkind train of thought. A good sense of Perception didn't enable a Green Bone to read minds, but those with a honed ability could pick up on the subtle physical changes that laid bare emotion and intent. The only visible green on Doru were the understated rings on his thumbs, but Lan knew the man wore most of his jade out of sight and was more skilled than he appeared; he might Perceive the sudden turn in Lan's mind even if there was no sign of it on his face.

He masked any possible slip as impatience. "You didn't come out here just to badger me about KJA business. What else is it?"

The floodlights at the gate switched on, bathing the front of the house and the long driveway with yellow light. Doru said, "Hilo just arrived. He's asking to see you right away."

Lan crossed the garden and walked quickly toward the shape of Hilo's unmistakable, oversized white sedan. One of his brother's lieutenants, Maik Kehn, was leaning against the driver side door of the Duchesse Priza, checking his watch. Maik Tar stood off to the side with Hilo. At their feet were two lumps. As Lan drew near he saw the lumps were a pair of teenage boys, slumped forward over their knees, foreheads to the asphalt.

"Glad I caught you before you went to sleep," Hilo teased. The younger Kaul often prowled the streets until dawn; he claimed it was all part of being a good Horn, the threat of his nocturnal presence tempering the agents of vice that plied their trade in clan territory when darkness fell. No one could say Kaul Hilo was not dedicated to his job, particularly when it involved food and drink, pretty girls and loud music, bars and gambling dens, the occasional incident of explosive violence.

Lan ignored the jibe. He looked down at the two boys. They had been badly beaten before being driven here in the car and deposited on the pavement. "What is this about?"

"That old boozehound Shon Ju nearly lost his measly bit of jade to these clowns," Hilo said. "But it turns out this one," he nudged the heavier-set boy with his foot, "has some interesting news I thought you ought to hear in person. Go on kid, tell the Pillar what you know."

The teenager lifted his face. Both of his eyes were black and his lip was split. His blood-plugged nose made his voice nasal as he told Lan about the sudden takeover of Three Fingered Gee's raw jade business. "I don't know the new guy's name. We just call him The Carver."

"He's Abukei?" Lan asked.

"No," slurred the boy through puffy lips. "A foreign stone-eye. He wears an Ygutan-style coat and one of those square hats." He glanced over nervously as his companion stirred and moaned.

"Tell him what The Carver looks like," Hilo demanded.

"I only saw him for a few minutes this one time," the boy hedged, frightened anew by Hilo's sharp tone. "He's short, a little heavy. He has a mustache, and spots on his face. He dresses like an Ygutanian and carries a gun, but he speaks Kekonese with no accent."

"What territory does he work?"

The Abukei teen was sweating under the interrogation. He lifted his bruised eyes to Lan, begging. "I—I'm not sure. Most of the Forge. Parts of Paw-Paw and the Docks. Maybe up into Coinwash and Fishtown." He dropped his forehead to the ground and his voice became muffled. "Kaul-jen. Pillar. I'm nothing to you, nothing at all, just a stupid kid who made a stupid mistake. I've told you everything I know."

The other boy was conscious now, though he remained silent except for his labored breathing. Lan said, "Look at me." The teenager raised his head. The whites of his eyes were red from burst capillaries. His expression was sunken and haunted—not the face of a boy at all, not anymore, but the face of someone who'd tasted jade the wrong way and was ruined because of it. He must be in terrible pain but he still radiated an inner rage that burned like a gaslight.

Lan felt a small knot of pity for him. The boy was a victim of confusing times. The laws of nature used to be clear. The Abukei were immune to jade. Most foreigners were too sensitive to it; even if a Shotarian or an Espenian learned to control the physical and mental powers, he would almost certainly fall victim to the Itches. Only the Kekonese, an isolated race descended over centuries from the hybridized bloodline of the Abukei and the ancient Tun settlers to the island, possessed a natural ability to harness jade, and even then, only after years of extensive preparation.

Unfortunately, these days, exaggerated stories of supposedly self-taught foreigners wearing jade gave impoverished Kekonese kids the wrong idea. It made them think that all they needed were some street fighting lessons and maybe the right chemical aids. Lan said, "Jade is death for people like you. You steal it, you smuggle it, you wear it—it all ends the same way: with you feeding the worms." He fixed the boy with a deadly stern gaze. "Get off my property, both of you, and don't let my brother see you again."

The Abukei boy clambered to his feet; even the other one got up faster than Lan would have thought him capable of. Together they limped hurriedly toward escape without looking back.

Lan said to Maik Kehn, "Tell the guard to open the gate." Kehn glanced at Hilo for his approval before doing as Lan ordered. The tiny gesture annoyed Lan. The two Maiks were slavishly loyal to Hilo. They eyed the two fleeing boys carefully, remembering their faces.

Hilo's smile was gone. Without it he looked his real age, instead of barely older than the teenagers he'd brutalized. "I would have let the Abukei boy live," he said, "but the other one—you made the wrong call. He'll be back, he has that look. I'll only have to kill him later."

Hilo might be right. There were two types of jade thieves: most wanted what they believed jade could give them—status, profit, power over others—but for some, the desire for jade itself was a rot in the brain, an obsession that would only grow. Hilo might be comfortable judging and executing for a first offense, but Lan was not ready to say there was no hope for the boy to find some other outlet for his ill-conceived ambition. "You taught them their lesson," he said. "You have to give people a chance to learn. They're just kids after all—stupid kids."

"I don't remember stupidity being an excuse around here when I was a kid."

Lan regarded his brother. Hilo's hands were stuffed into his pockets, his elbows jutted out and his shoulders curled slightly forward with casual insolence. *You're* still *a kid,* Lan thought ungenerously. The Horn was second in the clan and of equal rank to the Weather Man; he was supposed to be a seasoned warrior. Hilo was the youngest Horn anyone could remember, but despite this, no one seemed to question his position. Either because he was a Kaul and carried his jade well, or perhaps because, when the old Horn had retired a year and a half ago, grandfather had approved Hilo's appointment with no more than a shrug. "What else would he be any good for?" Kaul Sen had said.

Lan changed the subject. "You think the new carver is Tem Ben." A statement, not a question.

"Who else could it be?" said Hilo.

The Tems were part of the powerful and sprawling Mountain clan. They were a proud family of Green Bones, but Tem Ben was a stone-eye. It happened sometimes—recessive genetics combined to produce a Kekonese child as unresponsive to jade as any Abukei native. Being an embarrassment to the bloodline as well as a brutal lout, Tem Ben had been shipped off by the family years ago to study and work in desolate northern Ygutan. His sudden return to Kekon and his savage entry into the unpolished jade dealing business made a certain degree of sense. Only a jade-immune stone-eye could buy, hoard, cut, and sell street jade. As for what his activities implied—that was more disturbing.

"He wouldn't be back here without family say-so," Hilo concluded. "And the Tems wouldn't do anything without approval from Ayt." Hilo made a noise in his throat, then spat into the bushes. Clearly, he referred to Ayt Mada, adopted daughter of the great Ayt Yugontin, and now the Pillar of the Mountain clan. "I'll wager my jade that grasping bitch not only knows about this but had a hand in arranging it."

Doru had been hovering in the background the entire time and now glided forward like a wraith to join the conversation. "The Pillar of the Mountain clan concerning herself with carvers of black market jade scrap?" He did not hide his skepticism. "That's quite a leap to make based on the word of a frightened Abukei boy."

Hilo turned a thinly-veiled look of disdain on the older man. "He might be a drunken fool, but Shon Ju keeps his ear to the ground. He says our Lantern Men in the Armpit are getting their businesses squeezed. The owner of the Twice Lucky told me the same story and said it's Mountain Fingers doing the squeezing. If the Mountain's trying to muscle us out of the Armpit, is it so hard to believe they'd want someone they control working inside our districts, feeding them information? They're gambling we'll leave the new carver alone and not risk antagonizing the Tems over a little smuggling."

"You're jumping to a number of conclusions, Hilo-se." Doru's voice was a calm counterpoint to Hilo's. "The names Ayt and Kaul go back a long way together. The Mountain would not move against your grandfather while he still lives."

"I'm telling you what I know." Hilo paced in front of the two older men. Lan could sense the agitation running off of him freely. Hilo's jade aura was like bright liquid next to Doru's thick smoke. "Grandda and Ayt Yugontin respected each other even when they were rivals, but that's all in the past. Old Yu is dead now and Mada is making her own moves."

Lan looked up at the grand, sprawling Kaul house as he considered his brother's words. "No Peak has been growing faster than the Mountain for years," he conceded. "They know we're the only clan that's a threat to them."

Hilo stopped his pacing and took his brother by the arm. "Let me take five of my Fists into the Armpit. Ayt is testing us, sending her littlest Fingers to cause trouble and see what we'll do. So we cut a few of them off and return them to her in body bags. Send the signal that we won't be messed with."

Doru's thin lips pulled back as if he'd bitten into a lime. His wedged head swung around to pin the younger Kaul with disbelieving scorn. "Have they killed any of ours, either Green Bones or Lantern Men? Are you saying we should be the first ones to spill blood? To break the peace? A certain amount of savagery is to be expected in a Horn, but such childish overre-action is a disservice to your Pillar."

Hilo's aura flared like a wind-licked flame. Lan felt it buffet him like heat a second before Hilo said, in an incongruously chilled voice, "The Pillar can decide for himself when he's being badly served."

"That's enough," Lan growled at both of them. "We're here to make decisions together, not get into cock waving contests."

Doru said, "Lan-se, this sounds like a case of a few overeager and quar-relsome youths in the Armpit, which has always been a troublesome part of town." The Weather Man's jade aura glowed evenly like smoldering old coals, the slow-burning residual energy of a man who'd survived many fires and was not eager to start them. "Surely a peaceful solution can be found, one that preserves the old respect between our clans."

Lan looked between his Horn and his Weather Man. The two roles existed to be the right and left hand of the Pillar, responsible for the military and business arms of the clan, respectively. The Horn was visible, tactical, the clan's most formidable warrior, leader of the Fists and the Fingers who patrolled and defended clan territory and the residents within from rivals and street criminals. The Weather Man was strategic, operational, the brain working behind the scenes through an office full of capable Luckbringers, managing the clan's substantial flow of tribute money, patronage, and investments. A certain amount of conflict between these two critical roles was hardly surprising—expected, even. But Hilo and Doru were starkly opposed in nature as well as position. Looking at the two men, Lan questioned what to rely on: Hilo's strength and street instincts, or Doru's experience and caution.

"See if you can find out whether the Ayts are backing Tem Ben," Lan said to Hilo. "In the meantime, send some of your Fists into the Armpit, but only—" he shook his head at his brother's expectant look, "to reassure our Lantern Men and protect their businesses. No attacks, no retaliations, no whispering of names. No one sheds blood without family approval, not even if they're offered a clean blade."

"A prudent decision," Doru said, nodding.

Hilo grimaced but seemed partially appeased. "Fine," he said. "But I'm telling you, this will only get worse, not better. We won't be able to ride on grandfather's reputation much longer." He tugged his right earlobe in the customary gesture to ward off bad luck. "May he live three hundred years," he grumbled dutifully but without feeling. "The fact is, Ayt is making a point of parading her power as Pillar, and if No Peak is going to hold our own, you're going to have to do the same."

Sharply, Lan said, "I don't need my little brother to lecture me like an old man."

Hilo tilted his head at the reprimand. Then he smiled broadly, his face transforming, regaining its open boyishness. "True; you have enough of that around here already, don't you?" He turned away with an affable shrug and strolled back to the monstrous white Duchesse, where Maik Kehn and Tar stood sharing a smoke and waiting patiently for their captain to return. His warm jade aura receded with the smoothness of a summer river; Hilo was not one to stew in a grudge after a confrontation. Lan marveled that a childhood of ruthless training at Kaul Du Academy had not dented the younger Kaul grandson's relentlessly cheerful ego, the way he sauntered through the world as if it were a set piece built around him.

Doru said quietly, "You must excuse my rudeness to him tonight, Lanse. Hilo is a fearsome Horn—he just needs to be kept on a short leash." His pinched mouth curled up, as if he knew Lan had been thinking the same thing. "Do you need me for anything else tonight?"

"No. Good night, Doru."

The old advisor inclined his head and retreated silently down the side path that led to the Weather Man's residence.

Lan watched Doru's figure recede, then walked up the driveway to the Kaul house. It was the largest structure on the estate and the most impressive—clean, modern symmetry, classic Kekonese wood paneling and green tile roof, concrete pavers glinting with crushed seashells. The white columns were a bit of an ostentatious foreign accent that lent grandeur but that Lan would probably not have included if the decision had been up to him, which it had not. Grandfather had spent a good part of his fortune designing and building the family home. He was vain about its symbolism too, said it was a sign of how far Green Bones had come that they now lived in open wealth when only a generation ago they had been hunted fugitives hiding in secret jungle camps in the mountains, surviving only on their wits and stealth and the help of civilian Lantern Men.

Lan raised his eyes to the upper, leftmost window of the house. It was lit behind the silhouette of a man sitting in a chair. Grandfather was still awake, even at this time of night.

Lan let himself into the house and hesitated in the foyer. As much as he disliked to admit it, Hilo was right—he needed to more firmly wield his power as Pillar. It was his responsibility to make the hard decisions, and seeing as he wasn't able to sleep tonight, he might as well handle one of them now. With more than a little misgiving, he climbed the stairs.

• Chapter Four •
THE TORCH OF KEKON

Lan walked into his grandfather's room, which was furnished with beautiful furniture and art: rosewood tables from Stepenland, hanging silks from the Five Monarchs period of the Tun Empire, glass lamps from southern Ygutan. Most of the available wall space was covered with photographs and mementos. Kaul Seningtun was a national hero, one of the leaders of the fierce Green Bone-led uprising that had, more than a quarter of a century ago, finally ended the Empire of Shotar's control over the island of Kekon. After the war, humbly expressing that he had no appetite for politics nor desire to rule, Kaul Sen become a prosperous businessman and towering civic figure; photos of him shaking hands and posing at various official state functions and charitable events vied with certificates of honor on the wall.

The old man who had once been called the Torch of Kekon did not appear to dwell on the evidence of his accomplishments or the luxurious things he had acquired. Instead he spent most of his time gazing out past the city skyline to the distant green mountains covered in jungle and shrouded by clouds of mist. Lan wondered if, in the twilight of his life, that was where his grandfather's heart lay: not in the city he had helped to build up from the ashes of war to the swarming metropolis it now was, but deep in the interior of the island, a place the ancient Kekonese had considered sacred and foreigners had believed to be cursed, where young Kaul Sen had spent his glory days with comrades as a rebel and a warrior.

Lan stopped warily a short distance from his grandfather's chair. It was hard to predict the old man's moods these days. Kaul Sen had always been an unrelentingly energetic and formidable man—quick to praise, equally quick to criticize, effusive with both. He never minced words, never settled for the small gain when more could be risked for outright victory. Now, even at the age of eighty-one, he still radiated a dense and powerful jade aura.

He was not as he had been, though. His wife—let the gods recognize her—had passed away three years ago, and four months later Ayt Yugontin had died from a sudden stroke at the age of sixty-five. Some vital aspect of the Torch's indomitable will had slowly drained away since then. He'd handed clan leadership over to Lan with little ceremony and was now often pensive and withdrawn, or volatile and cruel. He sat without moving; a blanket was draped over his thin shoulders despite the summer heat.

"Grandda," Lan said, though he knew announcing his presence was unnecessary. Age had not dulled the patriarch's senses; he could still Perceive another Green Bone from across a city block.

Kaul Sen's gaze was fixed on some middle distance; it was difficult to tell whether or not he was paying any attention to the program that was playing on the color television that had recently been installed in the corner of his room. The volume was turned down on the set but at a glance, Lan saw that it was a documentary on the Many Nations War, in which Kekon's fight for independence had been but an ancillary part. A burst of light from an onscreen explosion flickered off the many squares of framed glass around the walls.

"The Shotarians, they used to drop bombs on the mountains," Kaul Sen said, his voice slow but still resonant, as if he were addressing a rapt assembly of people instead of the dark window pane. "But they were afraid of creating too many landslides. They would advance through the jungle in a line, those Shottie soldiers. They all looked the same, like ants. Clumsy. We were like panthers. We'd pick them off, one at a time." Kaul Sen jabbed the air with his finger as if marking invisible Shotarian soldiers around the room. "Their guns and grenades against our moon blades and talon knives. Ten of them to one of us, and still they couldn't crush us, no matter how they tried. Ah, how they tried."

This again. The same old war stories. Lan steeled himself to be patient.

"So they went after the Lantern Men, the ordinary people who hung green lanterns in their windows for us night after night. Man, woman, old, young, rich, poor—it didn't matter. If the Shotties suspected you of being in the One Mountain Society, there wouldn't be any warning. You would just disappear." Kaul Sen shifted back in his chair. His voice took on a grave, musing quality. "There was a family that hid me and Yu in their shed for three nights. A man, his wife, and their daughter. Because of them, we made it back to camp alive. A few weeks later, I went back to check on them, but they were gone. All the dishes and furniture still in place, the pot still on the stove, but they were gone."

Lan cleared his throat. "That was a long time ago."

"That was when I showed you what to do if you needed to—how to cut into your neck with your talon blade. Quick, like—" Kaul Sen mimed a vicious motion against his own jugular. "You were maybe twelve years old at the time, but you understood perfectly. Do you remember, Du?"

"Grandda." Lan winced. "I'm not Du. It's me—your grandson, Lan."

Kaul Sen turned to look over his shoulder. He seemed confused for a moment; it was not the first time Lan had caught him speaking aloud to the son he'd lost twenty-six years ago. Then his eyes cleared of their fog. His mouth flattened in disappointment and he sighed. "Even your aura feels like his," he grumbled. He turned back to the window. "Only his was stronger."

Lan closed his hands behind his back and looked away to hide his irritation. It rankled enough to come in here and see the photographs of his father rivaling the number of honors on the wall, without also having to endure his grandfather's increasingly frequent and offhanded insults.

As a child, Lan had treasured the photographs of his father. He'd spent hours looking at them. In the largest of the black-and-white images, Kaul Du was standing between Kaul Sen and Ayt Yugontin inside a military tent. The three of them were examining a spread-out map. They had talon knives at their waists and moon swords slung over their shoulders. Dressed in the loose green tunic of a One Mountain Society general, and looking straight into the camera, Kaul Du radiated revolutionary zeal and confidence.

Now, though, Lan saw the mounted photos as frustrating relics. Looking at them was like looking at an impossible photograph of himself trapped in a bygone time and place. He was the spitting image of his father—the same jawline and nose, even the same expression of concentration, left eye narrowed. Comments on their likeness had filled him with pride as a boy: "He looks just like his father! He's destined be a great Green Bone warrior." "The gods are returning the hero to us through his son."

Now, both the photographs and the comparisons were merely galling.

He turned back to his grandfather, determined to steer both of them back to the present. "Shae's coming home this week. She's arriving on Fourthday evening to pay her respects."

Kaul Sen swiveled around in his chair fast. "Respect?" He drew himself up in fierce indignation. "Where was her respect two years ago? Where was her respect when she turned her back on her clan and country and sold herself to the Espenians like a whore? Is she still with that man, that Shotarian man?"

"Shotarian-Espenian," Lan corrected.

"Whatever," said his grandfather.

"She and Jerald aren't together anymore."

Kaul Sen settled back into his chair a little. "Good news, at least," he grumbled. "It would never have worked. Too much bad blood between our peoples. And her children would've been weak."

Lan bit back a reply in Shae's defense; it was better to let the old man voice his grievances and be done with them. He wouldn't be so angry if Shae had not always been his favorite as a child. "She's coming back to stay, at least for a while," Lan said. "Be kind to her, Grandda. She wrote to me, sending you her love, and prayers for your long life and health."

"Huh," grunted the elder Kaul, but he seemed somewhat placated. "My long life and health, she says. My son is dead. My wife is dead. Ayt Yu is dead too. They were all younger than me." On the television screen, lines of running soldiers were falling under silent gunfire. "How am I still alive when they're all dead?"

Lan smiled thinly. "The gods love you, Grandda."

Kaul Sen snorted. "We didn't end it right, me and Ayt Yu. We fought side by side in the war, but in peacetime we let business come between us. *Business.*" Kaul spat the word. He waved one gnarled hand at the room, indicating all he had built with an air of scorn and resignation. "The Shotties couldn't break the One Mountain Society, but we did. We split our clans. I didn't even get a chance to speak to Yu before he died. We were both so *stubborn.* Curse him. There will never be anyone like him. He was a true Green Bone warrior."

It had been a mistake to come up here. Lan glanced back at the door, debating how best to excuse himself. Grandfather was too caught up reminiscing about the days when Green Bones had been united in nation-alistic purpose; he wasn't going to want to hear about how, if Hilo was to be believed, his old comrade's clan and successor were now the enemy. "It's late, Grandda," he said. "I'll see you in the morning."

He started to go, but Kaul Sen raised his voice. "What did you come for at this hour anyways? Spit it out."

Lan paused with a hand on the door. "It can wait."

"You came to talk, so talk," his grandfather ordered. "You're the Pillar! You don't wait."

Lan blew out sharply, then turned around. He strode to the television and shut it off, then faced his grandfather. "It's about Doru."

"What about him?"

"I think it's time he retired. Time I appointed a new Weather Man."

Kaul Sen leaned forward, fully present now, his eyes tight. "Is he failing you somehow?"

"No, it's not that. I want someone else in the role. Someone who could bring a fresh perspective."

"Who would that be?"

"Woon perhaps. Or Hami."

The senior Kaul frowned, the map of wrinkles on his face shifting into a new constellation of displeasure. "You think either of them would be as capable and loyal a Weather Man as Yun Dorupon? Who has done as much for this clan as he has? He's never led me astray, never failed me in war or business."

"I don't doubt that."

"Doru stuck with me. He could have gone over to the Mountain. Ayt would have welcomed him in a heartbeat. But he agreed with me that we needed to open ourselves up to the world. We fell to the Shotties in the first place because we'd been closed for too long. Doru stuck with me and he never wavered. Smart man. Smart and far-sighted. Calculating."

And still your man through and through. Lan said, "He served you well for more than twenty years. It's time he retired. I'd like him to step down grace-fully, with all respect. No hard feelings at all. I'm asking you as his friend, to talk to him."

His grandfather stabbed a finger in his direction. "You need Doru. You need his experience. Don't push change just for the sake of change! Doru's steady, reliable—not like that Hilo. You'll have enough on your hands with that loose screw for a Horn. While Du was off fighting for his country, who knows what swamp demon snuck into your mother's bedroom to spawn that boy."

Lan knew his grandfather was being cruel to throw him off, distract him from his original purpose. Misdirecting opponents was something he'd always excelled at, on the battlefield and later in the boardroom. Still Lan was unable to help himself. "You've outdone yourself, managing to disparage half of your own family in one go," he said harshly. "If you think so little of Hilo, why did you approve when I named him Horn?"

Kaul Sen sniffed loudly. "Because he has fire and thick blood. I'll give him that. A Weather Man should be respected, but a Horn needs to be feared. That boy should have been born fifty years ago; he would have struck terror into Shotarian hearts. He would've been a fearsome warrior, just like Du."

The patriarch's eyes narrowed and his stare turned scrutinizing. "Du was thirty years old when he died. He was a battle-hardened leader of men. He had a wife and two sons and a third child cooking in the womb. Carried his jade light as a god. You might look like him, but you'll never be half the man he was. That's why the other clans think they can disrespect you. That's why Eyni left you."

Lan was speechless for a second. Then a dull rage broke and pounded behind his eyes. "Eyni," he said, "is not part of this conversation."

"You should have killed that man!" Kaul Sen threw his arms up into the air and shook them in disbelief of his grandson's stupidity. "You let a jadeless foreigner walk off with your wife. You lost face with the clan!"

A fleeting and horrible desire to shove his grandfather out of the second-story window crossed Lan's mind. That was what the old man wanted after all, wasn't it? Flagrant egotistical violence. Yes, Lan thought, he could have challenged Eyni's lover—fought and killed him in the way any self-respecting Kekonese man would feel entitled. Perhaps it would have been a more fitting way for a Pillar to act. But it would have been pointless. An empty gesture. He wouldn't have kept Eyni; she was already determined to go. All he could have done was trample out her happiness and make her hate him. And if you loved someone, truly loved them, shouldn't their happiness matter, even more than your honor?

"How does not killing a man in a romantic dispute make me an un-worthy Pillar?" Lan demanded, his voice clipped. "You named me your successor, but you've yet to show me support or respect. I came only to ask for your help with Doru, and instead I get ramblings and insults."

Kaul Sen stood up. The move was sudden and unexpectedly fluid. The blanket around his shoulders slid to the ground. "If you're a worthy Pillar, then prove it." The old man's eyes were like obsidian, and his face was a dry, harsh desert. "Show me how green you are."

Lan stared at his grandfather. "Don't be ridiculous."

Kaul Sen crossed the short space between them in a heartbeat. His body rippled like a serpent's spine as he slammed both hands into Lan's chest. The whip-like blow sent Lan stumbling backward. He barely managed to Steel himself; the shock reverberated through his frame with concussive jade-fueled power. Lan dropped to one knee and gasped. "What was that for?"

His grandfather's reply was to launch a bony fist at his face.

Lan rose and deflected the strike easily this time, as well as the three others that followed in quick succession. Lan felt the air hum with the clash of their jade energies.

"Grandda," Lan snapped. "Stop it." He backed away until he bumped into a table, still fending off a volley of blows. Lan grimaced at the old man's nearly out-of-control speed. *It's really time he stopped wearing so much jade.* Like automobiles and firearms, jade was not something that deteriorating elderly folks ought to possess. Not that Kaul Sen would ever willingly relinquish even the smallest pebble from the bracelets or heavy belt he wore at all times.

"You can't even beat an old man." The elder Kaul was like a badger, all sinew and bone and oversized bad temper. His lips were pulled back in a taunting leer as he jabbed and weaved. Lan moved to avoid him and knocked over an antique clay bowl; it landed on the hardwood floor with a heavy thud and rolled. "Come on, boy," his grandfather wheezed, "where's your pride?" He slipped a strike under Lan's arm and drove his middle knuckle between his grandson's smallest ribs.

Lan grunted with surprise and pain. Reacting without thinking, he cuffed his grandfather across the head with a cupped hand.

Kaul Sen staggered. His eyes rolled; he folded to the ground with a look of child-like bewilderment.

Lan was mortified. He caught his grandfather around the shoulders. "Are you all right? Grandda, I'm sorry—"

His grandfather drove two extended fingers, stiff as nails, into a pressure point at the center of Lan's chest. Lan collapsed, coughing violently as Kaul Sen rolled over, got to his feet, and stood over him.

"To be Pillar, you have to act with full intention." For a moment Kaul Sen's age fell away and he was once again the towering Torch of Kekon. His back was straight, his face was hard, every piece of jade on his body bespoke strength and demanded respect. Briefly, Lan saw through a haze of anger and humiliation, the war hero his grandfather had once been.

"Only full intention!" Kaul Sen barked. "Jade amplifies what you have inside you. What you *intend*." He tapped his own chest. It made a hollow sound, like a gourd. "Without intention, no amount of jade will make you powerful." He walked back to his chair and sat down. "Doru stays."

Lan got to his feet without a word. He picked up the fallen bowl and placed it back on the table, then leaned a hand heavily on the wall in a moment of epiphanic sorrow. Only in this, just now, had his grandfather truly made him Pillar—by proving to him beyond a doubt that he was alone.

Silently, Lan left the room and closed the door behind him.

• Chapter Five •
THE HORN'S KITTEN

When Kaul Hilo got behind the wheel of the Duchesse, Tar leaned his forearms through the open passenger side window. "So what did he say?"

"We're shoring up the Armpit," Hilo said. "No killing," he added. "Just protect what's ours. Our Lantern Men, our businesses."

"And if they challenge us? You okay with holding back?" Tar asked, in a skeptical tone that implied he knew his boss better than that. Hilo suppressed a sigh; Kehn rarely questioned him but Tar had been his classmate at Kaul Du Academy and talked back sometimes. The younger Maik never made it any secret that he thought Lan was too conservative, that Hilo was the stronger of the two Kaul brothers. Of course, it was self-serving of him, and Hilo did not appreciate it as much as he suspected Tar thought he did.

"No killing," he said firmly. "I'll talk to you both tomorrow." He started the Duchesse, circled the roundabout in front of the house, and rolled back down the long driveway.

He did not turn before the gates, up the narrower drive toward the house behind his brother's, the one appointed for the Horn of the clan. The previous Horn had been a grizzled general of his grandfather's and his taste in decor left much to be desired. When Hilo had moved in, the house had smelled of dogs and fish stew. The carpet was green and the wallpaper was checkered. A year and a half had passed and he had still not renovated the place. He meant to but could not be bothered. It was not as if he spent much time there. He was not the sort of Horn to issue orders from behind high walls and closed doors and leave the work to his Fists. So the house was a place to sleep, that was all.

As he drove away from the Kaul estate, Hilo rested an arm out of the open window and drummed his fingers in time to the beat from the radio.

Shotarian club music. When it wasn't Espenian jiggy or worse, Kekonese classical, it was Shotarian club. Many people of an older generation still refused to buy Shotarian-made products, listen to Shotarian music, or watch Shotarian television shows, but Hilo had been less than a year old when the war had ended and he was not one of them.

He was in a better mood now. He hadn't been granted all the leeway he'd asked for but he'd spoken his mind and knew what he had to do next. The thing Tar didn't understand was, Hilo did not envy his brother's position in the least. Handling bitter old Grandda, that freak Doru, KJA politics and the Royal Council...perhaps Lan had the patience for all that, but he, Hilo, certainly didn't. Life was short. He understood and embraced the simplicity of his role: lead and manage his Fists, protect his family's territory, defend No Peak from its enemies. Enjoy himself along the way.

He drove for twenty minutes, leaving behind the moneyed outskirts of the Palace Hill area around the Kaul home, speeding first down the wide boulevard of the General's Ride, then turning onto a two-lane avenue, and finally navigating increasingly narrow streets as he entered Paw-Paw, an old, working-class neighborhood crammed full of small shops, questionable street food vendors, and twisty alleyways that trapped careless rickshaw drivers, mopeds, and stray dogs. Paw-Paw had stood nearly untouched during the war and changed little in the time since, largely ignored by both questing foreigners and the pace of progress. At night, the streets were particularly labyrinthine; the Duchesse's side mirrors barely cleared the space between the far smaller and rustier parked vehicles on either side of a street of brick apartment buildings, built so close together a person could lean out the window and nearly touch his neighbor's wall.

Hilo parked his car five blocks away from his intended destination. He was not worried; he was deep inside Kaul territory. But he did not want his recognizable car to be noticed in the same place every night. It made his movements appear too routine, and it was important for his presence to be unpredictable. Besides, he liked to walk. The temperature had finally come down and it was a fine night. He left his jacket in the car and ambled leisurely, enjoying the peace found in that space between hours considered late and those considered early.

He ignored the front door and climbed the rickety fire escape to the fifth floor. There was a light on in the apartment. The window was un-latched and cracked wide open because of the heat. Hilo let himself in, swinging his legs across the chipped sill and treading silently across the carpeted floor toward the light in the bedroom.

She was asleep, an open book on her lap. The bedside lamp cast a veil of orange light across the side of her face. Hilo stood in the doorway, watching her chest rise and fall in gentle, undisturbed breaths. The bedcovers came up to her knees but no further. She was wearing a sleeveless cotton top with thin straps, and blue panties with white lace trim. Her dark hair was spread against the whiteness of the pillow, tendrils of it curving across the paleness of her smooth, unblemished bare shoulders.

Hilo admired her until the waiting became too much to bear. He crossed the room and took the book from her fingers, marked the page, and set it on the bedside table. She didn't stir; he marveled at this: at her utter deafness to possible danger. She was so unlike a Green Bone she might as well have been another sort of creature from him entirely.

He switched off the light, plunging the room into darkness. Then he climbed on top of her, pinning her body and covering her mouth with his hand. She came awake in a start; her eyes flew open as her body jerked under his weight. She let out a muffled scream before he laughed softly and whispered into her ear, "You should be more careful, Wen. If you leave the window open at night, men with bad intentions might come through it."

She stopped struggling. Her heart still pattered against his chest, excit-ing him, but her body relaxed. She pulled his hand from her mouth. "It's your fault," she snapped. "I fell asleep waiting up for you, and in return you scare the shit out of me. Where were you?"

He was pleased that she'd stayed up for him. "I was at the Twice Lucky, dealing with some trouble."

She raised her eyebrows. "Trouble involving gambling or strippers?"

"Not anything so fun," he promised. "Ask your brothers if you don't believe me."

Wen squirmed provocatively underneath him, her bare shoulders and thighs rubbing against his clothes. "Kehn and Tar wouldn't tell me a thing. They're too devoted to you."

"Give them some credit." Hilo pulled her earlobe into his mouth and sucked as he worked his belt and pants off. "I'm sure they conspired to kill me. When they saw how I looked at you? They knew right away I was planning to pop their little sister." He pulled her panties down and stroked between her legs, then slid his first two fingers inside her. "I had to make them my closest Fists or they would've gutted me."

"You can't blame them," she said, moving her hips encouragingly. His fingers glided in and out, slippery and warm. She undid the next three buttons of his shirt and pulled it over his head. "What could a son of the great Kaul family want with a stone-eye—especially from a disgraced family like mine—besides an easy lay?"

"Many easy lays?" He kissed her hard, impatiently, attacking her mouth with his lips and tongue. His cock was excruciatingly stiff against the inside of her thigh. Wen reached up to bury her hands in his hair. She ran her fingertips down his neck and chest, mapping the jade pieces studded all along his collarbone and through his nipples. She touched and licked them utterly without fear, envy or want, appreciating them only as a beautiful part of him, nothing more. He'd never let any other woman touch his jade, and it made him wildly aroused, this fearless intimacy he had with her.

He pushed inside her, all at once. She was delicious—a riot of sensation. Sunlight and ocean, summer fruit and musk. Hilo growled with pleasure and seized the headboard of the bed, wanting even more. His jade-sharp senses roared with blinding intensity: the crash of her heartbeat, the thunder of her breath, the fire of her skin on his own. He regretted turning off the light; he wished he could see her better, drink in every detail of her body.

Wen lifted her hips off the mattress, clenching him, her eyes fixed on his, two tiny motes of reflected streetlight like candles floating in a pool. Her intense adoration pushed him higher. He sucked her cherry nipples. He dove into the valley of her breasts and drowned in her incomparable perfume. Wen grabbed his hips and drove him relentlessly, and he came, careening delightedly out of control.

He lay on top of her, consciousness dancing away from him, breathing into the soft crook of her neck. "You're the most important thing in the world to me."

When he awoke, it was dawn. The sun was forcing its way into the crevices between the buildings, seeping into the windows. It would be another hot day.

Hilo gazed at the beautiful creature lying asleep beside him and an intense urge rose and took hold of him: he wanted to seize and envelop her, and through some magic, pull her into himself, so he could hold her nestled safe inside him wherever he went. Before Wen, he'd enjoyed women and experienced warm, even tender, feelings for them. But that was nothing compared to what he felt for Wen. The desire to make her happy was like a physical ache. The thought of anyone harming her or taking her from him filled him with feverish rage. She could ask anything of him and he would do it.

True love, Hilo mused, was sensual and euphoric, but also painful and tyrannical, demanding obedience. It was clearly altogether different from the rebellious infatuation Shae had had for that Espenian, or the sensible affection that had existed between Lan and Eyni.

Being reminded of Eyni deflated him a little. It had taken a few weeks, but he'd finally tracked down that whore and the man who'd so grievously insulted his brother. They were living in Lybon, in Stepenland. He considered hiring someone to do the job, but a clan insult ought to be handled directly by the clan. So he asked Tar to book an airplane ticket using a fake name and passport, but when he told Lan his plans, the Pillar had been ungrateful, angry even.

"I never told you do that," Lan had snapped at him. "If I wanted their names whispered, I would've done it myself, so it should've been obvious to you that I don't. Leave them alone, and from now on stay out of my personal life."

Hilo had been greatly irritated at the wasted effort. That's what he got, for trying to do his brother a favor. Lan always played his feelings so close to the chest, so how was Hilo supposed to know?

Wen stirred and made a delightful sleepy sound. Hilo forgot his rumination and crawled under the sheets to wake her with his mouth and fingers. He worked on her patiently, was gratified when he brought her to a shuddering climax, then made love to her again, more slowly and leisurely this time.

Afterward, as they lay in a sticky tangle, he said, "What you said last night—about your family—you shouldn't think that. What happened with your parents was years ago, and no one doubts Kehn and Tar. The Maik name is good with the clan now."

Wen was silent for a moment. "Not with all the clan. What about your family?"

"What about them?"

She rested her head on his shoulder. "Shae has never trusted me."

Hilo laughed. "Shae ran away with an Espenian naval brat and now she's crawling back like an apologetic puppy that pissed on the carpet. She's hardly in a position to judge. Why would you worry about what she thinks?" From the unkind tone of his own voice, he realized with some surprise and disappointment that he still hadn't entirely forgiven her.

"She's always had your grandfather's ear. I don't think he'd approve of me even if I wasn't a stone-eye."

"He's a senile old man," Hilo said. "Lan is Pillar now." He gave her a reassuring kiss on the temple, but his demeanor changed; he rolled over and lay staring pensively at the yellow ceiling fan as it spun around and around.

Wen rolled to her side and looked at him with concern. "What's wrong?"

"Nothing," he said.

"Tell me."

When he told her about the previous evening's events at the Twice Lucky and the conversation in the driveway of the Kaul estate, Wen propped herself up on one elbow and pursed her lips in concern. "Why did Lan let the boy go? A jade thief at such a young age; he's incurable. He'll only be more trouble for you later."

Hilo shrugged. "I know, what can I say? Lan is an optimist. How did he become so soft-hearted, my tough big brother, who always used to put me in my place? He's green enough but he doesn't think like a killer and Ayt is a killer all right. It's obvious war with the Mountain is coming—can't he see that? That self-important old ferret Doru isn't steering him right."

"Surely Lan ought to listen to you over Doru."

"Doru is like an old vine in the clan; there's no getting around him."

Wen sat up. Her glossy black hair tumbled over her back and the morning light illuminated the flawless curve of her cheek. She said to him, "You have to start preparing to defend No Peak on your own, then. Doru has his connections, his informers, his sneaky ways. But all the Fists, and the Fingers under them, are yours. Green Bones are warriors first, businessmen second. If there's a war to come, it'll go to the streets—and the streets belong to the Horn."

"My kitten." Hilo wrapped his arms around Wen's shoulders and kissed her neck from behind. She put some of his Fists to shame. "You have the heart of a jade warrior."

"In the body of a stone-eye." Her sigh was lovely even though her voice was bitter. "If only I was a Green Bone, I could help you. I would be your most dedicated Fist."

"I don't need another Fist," he said. "You're perfect the way you are. Leave the Green Bone worries to me." He cupped her breasts, holding their pleasant weight in his hands, and craned in for another kiss.

She pulled her face back, refusing to be diverted. "How many Fists *do* you have—good ones you can count on? Kehn tells me some of them are soft; they're used to peace, to policing and taxing, not fighting. How many of them have won duels? How many of them carry more than a few pebbles?"

Hilo sighed. "We've got our most green, and we've some dead weight, same as them."

She turned to face him. Wen possessed features that were not conventionally beautiful, but that Hilo found endlessly interesting—wide feline eyes and dark slanted eyebrows, a slyly lascivious mouth and almost masculine jawline. When she was particularly serious, as she was now, he thought she ought to be the subject of an art photography portrait—her straight gaze so coolly intense and enigmatic it defied a viewer to guess if she was thinking about sex or murder or grocery shopping.

"Have you stopped in to the Academy lately?" she asked him. "You could go see your cousin, take a look at the year-eights. Get a feel for which ones you can use when they graduate next year."

Hilo brightened. "You're right—it's been a while since I've paid Anden a visit. I'll do that." He pinched her nipples gently, gave her a final kiss, then stood up and reached for his clothes. He hummed as he pulled on his pants and adjusted the sheath of his talon blade. "That boy is really going to be something," he declared, buttoning his shirt in front of the closet mirror. "Once he gets his jade, he'll be like a Green Bone out of a legend."

Wen smiled as she pinned up her hair. "Just like his Horn."

Hilo winked at her flattery.

• Chapter Six •
HOMECOMING

Kaul Shaelinsan arrived in Janloon International Airport with the vaguely hungover cotton-headed feeling symptomatic of all thirteen-hour flights. Crossing the ocean, staring out the window at the passing expanse of blue, she'd felt as if she were turning back time—leaving behind the person she'd become in a foreign land and returning to her childhood. She was confused by the combination of emotions this aroused in her: a poignant bittersweet mixture of elation and defeat.

Shae collected her baggage from the carousel; there wasn't much. Two years in Espenia, an unaccountably expensive university degree, and all her worldly possessions fit into a single red leather suitcase. She was too tired to smile at this pathetic irony.

She picked up the receiver of a pay phone and began to deposit a coin into the slot, then stopped, remembering the bargain she'd made with herself. Yes, she was returning to Janloon, but she would do so on her own terms. She would live as an ordinary citizen of the city, not like the grand-daughter of the Torch of Kekon. Which meant not calling her brother to send a chauffeured car to pick her up from the airport.

Shae replaced the phone receiver in its cradle, caught off guard by how easy it had been to slip into old behaviors within minutes of setting foot on Kekon. She sat down on a bench in the baggage claim area for a few minutes, suddenly reluctant to take the final steps through the revolving exit doors. Something told her that when they spun her around and pushed her out, the journey would be irrevocable.

Finally though, she could delay no longer. She stood up and followed the stream of other passengers out to the taxi line.

When she'd left two years ago, Shae had never intended to move back.

She'd been full of anger and optimism, determined to forge a new life and identity for herself in the great wide, modern world beyond Kekon, away from anachronistic clans and the outsized male egos of her family. Once in Espenia, she found it harder than she'd expected to escape the stigma of being from a small island country known mostly for one thing: jade. Indeed, Shae learned that the name Janloon often provoked blank looks. The foreigners called it something else: Jade City.

When people abroad learned she was Kekonese, their reactions were comically predictable. Initially, surprise. Kekon was an exotic, make-believe place in the minds of most Espenians. The postwar boom in global trade was reversing its centuries of isolation, but not yet entirely. She might as well have said she was from outer space.

The second response: eager jesting. "So can you fly? Can you punch through this wall? Show us something amazing. Here, break this table!"

She'd learned to take it with grace. At first, she tried to explain. She'd left all her jade back on Kekon. She was no different from them now. Whatever advantages in strength, speed, and reflexes she possessed were accounted for by the fact that she still woke early and trained on her apartment patio every morning. Lifelong habits persisted after all.

The first two weeks had been almost unbearable, the feeling of being in a deprivation chamber of her own making. Everything so much *less* than it used to be—less color, less sound, less feeling—a washed-out dreamscape. Her body slow, heavy, achy. A nagging suspicion of having lost something vital, like looking down and noticing you were missing a limb. The nighttime panic and the sensation of being adrift, of the world not being real.

It would all be bad enough even if she wasn't surrounded by boisterous young Espenians who had the attention span of monkeys and were always talking about clothes, cars, popular music and the vagaries of their shallow, convoluted relationships. She almost relented; she even booked a flight back to Kekon after the first semester. But pride overcame even the near-debilitating horror of jade withdrawal. Fortunately, the flight had been refundable.

It was far too complicated to explain to her few college friends what it meant to be jaded, to come from a Green Bone family, and why she'd given it up—so she just smiled innocently and waited until their curiosity waned. Jerald always teased her. "You walk around acting all normal, but one day you're going to bust out doing some crazy shit, aren't you?"

No, she'd already done that. He was the crazy shit.

The sky was that odd mixture of haze and waning light. The concrete was damp with Northern Sweat—the incessant drizzle and mist that pervaded the coastal plain around Janloon during monsoon season. It was late, past dinner time. Shae stood in line and waited for a taxi. The other people in line did not pay her any attention. She was dressed in a colorful, short summer dress that was fashionable in Espenia but felt too clingy and garish in her home country, but excepting that, she blended in, looked just like any other traveler. Jadeless. It was with relief and a twinge of self-pity that she realized there was little chance anyone would recognize her.

The next taxi arrived. The driver put her suitcase in the trunk as Shae climbed into the back seat and rolled down the window. "Where to, miss?" he asked.

Shae considered going to a hotel. She wanted to shower, to decompress from the long flight, to be by herself for a little while. She decided against showing such disrespect. "Home," she said. She gave the driver the address. He pulled away from the curb and into the streaming jostle of cars and buses.

As the taxi crossed the Way Away Bridge and the steel and concrete skyline of the city came into view, Shae was struck by a sense of nostalgia so profound she found it difficult to breathe. The humid air through the open window, the sound of her native language being spoken on the radio, even the terrible traffic… She swallowed, close to tears; she had only the vaguest idea of what she was going to do in Janloon now, but she was undeniably *home*.

When they entered the Palace Hill neighborhood, the taxi driver started glancing back at her in the rearview mirror, eyes flicking up every few seconds. When the taxi arrived in front of the tall iron gates of the Kaul estate, Shae rolled down the window and leaned out to speak to the waiting sentry.

"Welcome home, Shae-jen," said the guard, surprising her with the now-inaccurate suffix as well as the sense of familiarity in attaching it to her given name. The guard was one of Hilo's Fingers. Shae recognized his face but could not remember his name, so she merely nodded in greeting.

The taxi drove through the gates to the roundabout in front of the main house. Shae reached for her purse to pay the driver, but he said, "There's no fee, Kaul-jen. I'm so sorry I didn't recognize you at first in those foreign clothes." He turned around to smile at her with earnest hopefulness. "My father-in-law is a loyal Lantern Man. Lately, he's having a little business trouble. If there was a way you—"

Shae pressed the money into the driver's hands. "Take your fee," she insisted. "I'm only Miss Kaul now. I don't have any say in the clan. Tell your father-in-law to send word up the proper channels to the Weather Man." She suppressed her guilt at the man's disappointed expression, got out of the taxi, and hefted her suitcase up the steps to the entrance.

Kyanla, the Abukei housekeeper, met her at the door. "Oh, Shae-se, you look so different!" She hugged Shae and held her out at arm's length. "And you smell Espenian." She laughed gaily. "But I shouldn't be surprised, now that you're a big-shot Espenian businesswoman."

Shae smiled weakly. "Don't be silly, Kyanla."

Through sheer workaholic grit, she'd graduated in the top third of her class despite the fact that she'd been studying in her second language and, having been schooled at Kaul Du Academy, found the Espenian classroom environment utterly bewildering—so much sitting around in large rooms and talking, as if every student wanted to be the instructor. In the spring, she'd interviewed with some of the big companies that recruited on campus. She'd even received an offer for an entry position at one of them. But she'd seen how the interviewers looked at her.

When she walked into the room, the men around the table—they were always men—assumed she was Tun, or Shotarian, and the first glimmer of prejudice would come into their eyes. When they looked at her resume and saw she was from Kekon, that she'd been raised to be a Green Bone, their expressions would cloud with outright skepticism. The Espenians might be proud of their military might, but they had little regard for her martial education. What use would it be in a civilized, professional place like an Espenian corporation? This wasn't Kekon, where the name Kaul was golden; the right word from grandfather wouldn't get her anything. In those moments, her romantic notions of making it on her own felt foolish. Foolish and lonely. Now here she was: back in the house she hadn't been able to leave fast enough a couple of years ago.

Lan was standing at the bottom of the staircase. He smiled. "Welcome home."

Shae went to him and embraced him tightly. She hadn't seen her older brother in two years, and was overwhelmed by the rush of affection she felt for him. Lan was nine years older than her; they had never been playmates but he had always been kind to her. He'd defended her from Hilo, had not judged her when she'd left, and had been the only member of the family to write to her while she was studying in Espenia. Sometimes, his letters, in their precise, even handwriting had felt like the only link she had to Kekon, the only evidence that she had a family and a past.

Grandda is not doing so well, he'd ended simply at the end of his last letter. *The decline is more in his spirits than his health. I know he misses you. It would be good of you to come back to see him, and Ma as well, after you graduate.* With the sting of splitting with Jerald still as fresh as an oozing burn, she'd reread her brother's letter, turned down the lone job offer, and booked a flight back to Janloon.

Lan hugged her back and kissed the center of her forehead. Shae said, "How's Grandda?" at the same time he said, "Your hair." They both laughed, and Shae suddenly felt as if she'd let out a breath she'd been holding for two years.

Lan said, "He's waiting for you. Do you want to go up?"

Shae took a deep breath, then nodded. "I don't suppose it'll get any easier if I wait." They climbed the stairs together, his hand on her shoulder. So close to him, she could feel the tugging hum of his jade, a barely perceptible texture in the air that her body responded to with a yearning squeeze of the stomach as she leaned in closer to him. It had been such a long time since she'd been affected by jade that she felt light-headed. She forced herself to straighten away from Lan and face the double doors before her.

"He's gotten worse lately," Lan said. "Today's a good day, though."

Shae knocked. Kaul Sen's voice came back with surprising vigor through the door. "I could Perceive you, you know, even without your jade, coming through the door and dawdling your way up here. Come in then."

Shae opened the door and stood in front of her grandfather. She should have changed her clothes and showered first. Kaul Sen's piercing gaze took in her bright, foreign attire, and the corners of his eyes tightened in a mess of wrinkles. His nostrils pinched and he leaned back in his chair as if offended by the smell of her. "Gods," he muttered, "the last couple of years have been as unkind to you as they have been to me."

Shae reminded herself that despite his tyrannical faults, her grandfather had been one of the most heroic and respected men in the country, that he was now old and lonely and deteriorating, and that two years ago, she had broken his heart. "I came straight from the airport, Grandda." Shae touched her clasped hands to her forehead in the traditional sign of respect, then knelt in front of his chair, eyes downcast. "I've come home. Will you please accept me as your granddaughter again?"

When she looked up, she saw that the old man's eyes had softened. The stiffness of his mouth melted and his lips trembled slightly. "Ah Shae-se, of course I forgive you," he said, even though she hadn't actually asked for forgiveness. Kaul Sen held out his gnarled hands, and she took them as she stood. She felt his touch like an electrical jolt; even at his advanced age, his jade aura was intense, and the bones of her arms prickled in memory and longing.

"The family hasn't been right without you." Kaul Sen said. "You belong here."

"Yes, Grandda."

"It's all well and good to do business with foreigners. I said it so many times, the gods know it's true, I said it to *everyone*: we must open up Kekon and accept outside influence. I broke my brotherhood with Ayt Yugontin over it. *But*—" Kaul Sen stabbed a finger into the air, "—we'll never be like them. We're different. We're Kekonese. We're Green Bones. Never forget that."

Her grandfather turned her hands over in his own, shaking his head sadly and disapprovingly at the sight of her bare arms. "Even if you take off your jade, you won't be like them. They'll never accept you, because they'll sense you're different, the way dogs know they're less than wolves. Jade is our inheritance; our blood isn't meant to mix with others." He squeezed her hands in a papery gesture meant as comfort.

Shae bowed her head in silent acquiescence, concealing resentment of her grandfather's obvious pleasure that Jerald was now a fixture of the past. She'd met Jerald on Kekon. At the time he was stationed on Euman Island with fifteen months left in his deployment and plans to go to graduate school afterward. The instant Kaul Sen learned of Shae's relationship with a foreign sailor, he furiously proclaimed it doomed. Even though his reasons had been mostly racist—Jerald was Shotarian (even though he was born in Espenia), he was a water-blooded weakling who was beneath her, he was a shallow bastard—it galled Shae that the old man's prediction had proven true. Come to think about it, the shallow bastard part had been correct as well. "I'm glad to see you looking so healthy, Grandda," Shae said mildly, trying to derail his monologue.

He waved away her attempt at redirection. "I haven't touched a thing in your old room," he said. "I knew you'd come home once you'd gone through this phase. It's still yours."

Shae thought quickly. "Grandda, I've been such a disappointment to you. I couldn't presume I'd have a place in the house. So I rented an apartment not far from here and sent my things there already." It wasn't true; she'd made no living arrangements and had no things to send. But she certainly didn't relish the idea of moving back into her childhood bedroom in the Kaul house, as if nothing had been gained or changed by two years and an ocean of distance. Living here, she would have to endure the jade auras of Green Bones coming and going, and her grandfather's condescending forgiveness. She added, "Besides, I could use a little time by myself to get settled. To decide what to do next."

"What is there to decide? I will talk to Doru about which businesses will be yours."

"Grandda," Lan interrupted. He'd been standing at the entrance of the room, watching the exchange. "Shae's come off a long flight. Let her unpack and rest. There'll be time to talk business later."

"Huh," said Kaul Sen, but he let go of Shae's hands. "I suppose you're right."

"I'll come back to see you soon." She leaned in to kiss his forehead. "I love you, Grandda."

The old man grunted, but his face glowed with a fondness she realized she had desperately missed. Unlike Lan, she had never known their father; Kaul Sen had been everything to her when she was a little girl. He had doted on her, and she on him. As she left the room, he mumbled after her, "For the love of all the gods, put your jade on. It hurts me to look at you like that."

She walked outside with Lan. They were alone. The sun had set, leaving a smoggy afterglow that outlined the roofs of the buildings positioned around the central courtyard. Shae sank onto a stone bench next to the draping maple tree and heaved a deep sigh. Lan sat down next to her. For a second they didn't speak. Then they glanced at each other and both laughed weakly.

"That could have gone worse," she said.

"Like I said, he was in a good mood today. The doctor says he needs to start wearing less jade, but that's a battle I've been putting off." Lan looked away for a second but Shae caught the wince that flashed across his face.

"How's Ma?" Shae asked.

"She's doing well. She likes it out there. It's very peaceful."

Long ago, their mother had resigned herself to a life of single parenthood and catering to her demanding father-in-law in exchange for a secure and comfortable life as the respected widow of the No Peak clan's ruling family. As soon as Shae had turned eighteen, Kaul Wan Ria had retired to the family's coastal cottage home in Marenia, a three-hour drive south from Janloon. To Shae's knowledge, she'd not been back to the city since.

Lan said, "You should make the trip out to visit her. No rush—once you're settled."

"And you?" Shae asked. "How're you doing?"

Lan turned his face toward her, his left eye narrowed. Everyone said that he looked like their father, but Shae didn't see it. Her brother had a steadfast and soulful manner, not like the ferocious-looking guerrilla in the old photographs on her grandfather's wall. He seemed about to say something to her, then appeared to change his mind and said something else. "I'm fine, Shae. Clan business keeps me busy."

Guilt washed in. She hadn't been reliable about responding to Lan's letters when she'd been in Espenia; she could hardly expect him to confide in her now. She was not even sure she wanted his confidence, not if it meant hearing about territorial disputes, or misbehaving Lantern Men, or Fists that had been killed in duels—clan things she'd told herself she would keep out of from now on. Nevertheless, she thought about how her brother had been shouldering the position of Pillar while coping with Eyni leaving him and their grandfather's dramatic decline, with only Hilo and nasty old Doru to help him. "I haven't been here for you," she said. "I'm sorry."

"You have to live your own life, Shae."

There was no reprimand in his voice, and Shae gave thanks to the gods that Lan was the first member of the family she'd met upon returning. He didn't make her feel ashamed for leaving, nor ashamed for returning. That was more than she deserved—and more than she could say for the rest of her family.

The jet lag was catching up and she was exhausted now. The lights went on in the house and then dimmed; Kyanla's shape moved in the upper windows, drawing shut the blinds. In the dark, the motionless outlines of the benches and trees Shae had played around as a child seemed cooly re-monstrative, like aloof relatives. She realized that Kekon had a special smell, a certain indescribable, spicy, sweaty fragrance. Was that what she'd smelled like to all her Espenian classmates? She imagined the odor seeping back into her pores. She put a hand on Lan's arm. His jade aura coursed around her like a low bass vibration, and she leaned in closer, but not too close.

Shae checked into a hotel room in the city and spent the next three days searching for an apartment. Though she didn't want to be too near the Kaul home, it wasn't as if she could live wherever she wanted. She could take off her jade but not her face or her name; there were parts of the city it would be best for her to avoid. Even confining the search to districts firmly in No Peak control, she spent from dawn until past dusk taking the malodorously crowded subway from stop to stop, sweating ferociously in the summer heat, visiting one building after another.

This could be a whole lot easier, she griped to herself more than a few times. The right word from Lan to a Lantern Man landlord would've yield-ed her a well-appointed apartment in no time. The rent would be half what it really was, if that, and the landlord would rest assured that some building permit or construction contract he'd been waiting on would be approved right away. She held fast to her pledge to do without family help. She had lived frugally as a student, and when converted, the Espenian money she'd saved from her summer internship last year would be more than enough to cover six months of rent in Janloon if she was judicious. By the end of the third day of searching, she was sore-footed and weary but had signed for a modest though convenient one bedroom loft in North Sotto and was pleased with herself.

Hilo was waiting in the lobby of the hotel when she returned. He was slouched in one of the overstuffed leather armchairs, but when he saw Shae come in, he sat up, and the Fist that was with him—one of the Maik brothers, Shae couldn't remember which one—got up from the chair next to him and moved to the other side of the room to let them talk alone.

Her brother didn't look any different than the last time she'd seen him two years ago and Shae wondered, with unexpected self-consciousness, if she looked any different to him, if her hair or clothes made her look older, and foreign. Hilo was her senior by a mere eleven months; when she'd left, they'd been equals, of a sort. Now she was unemployed, single, and jadeless. He was one of the most powerful men in Janloon, with hundreds of Green Bones at his command.

She'd known she couldn't avoid this moment, but had told herself it could wait a little longer. Had Lan told him where to find her, or had the hotel staff tipped off his Fingers? As he rose to greet her, Shae braced herself. A hotel lobby was really not the place she'd pictured doing this. "Hilo," she said.

He embraced her with great affection. "What are you doing here in a hotel? Are you avoiding me?" He sounded genuinely hurt; Shae had forgotten how sensitive he could be sometimes. He put his hands on either side of her face and kissed both her cheeks and her forehead. "I've forgotten the past," he said. "Everything's forgiven, now that you're back. You're my little sister, how could I not forgive you?"

He sounded like Grandda, she thought, with his forgiveness. No forgiveness on his part, of course, for calling her a whore and a clan traitor, and volunteering, in front of her, Lan, and grandfather, to kill Jerald if given the word. If Jerald hadn't been an Espenian military officer, and Lan hadn't been in the room to talk everyone down, Kaul Sen might very well have given it, too.

Part of her was determined to stay angry at Hilo. It would've been easy if he was still furious at her. But Hilo's magnanimity was like his jade aura—fierce and unequivocal. She felt its warmth gathering her in, thawing the tension she was carrying like armor plating in her back and shoulders. "I wasn't avoiding you," she said. "I just got in and I needed some time to get settled, that's all."

He took a step back from her, still holding onto her elbows. "Where's your jade?"

"I'm not wearing it," she said.

A frown marred Hilo's face. He leaned in and lowered his voice. "We need you, Shae." He brought his eyes level with hers, fixing her with an insistent gaze. "The Mountain is going to come after us. All the signs point to it. They think we're weak. Grandda just sits there and never leaves the house. I don't trust Doru far enough to spit on him. With you back, though, things will be different. Grandda always liked you best, and with the two of us together behind Lan—"

"Hilo," she said. "I'm not getting involved. Just because I'm back in Janloon doesn't mean I'm in the clan business."

He tilted his head. "But we need you," he said simply.

A few cruel words at this moment would drive him away. She itched to do it—to hurt him, to reject him, to provoke him—but she was tired of their old rivalry. Fighting Hilo was a crutch, an addictive bad habit she'd had all her life, one she'd tried to leave behind along with her jade, and did not want to return to. They were both adults. She had to remind herself that he was now the Horn of No Peak. If she was going to live on Kekon for any length of time, it wouldn't do to be on his bad side.

Shae quelled her defensiveness. "I'm not ready," she said. "I need to fig- ure things out for myself for a while. You can *try* to respect that, can't you?"

A few expressions battled openly on Hilo's face; he appeared to be holding his disappointment in check as he attempted to judge her sincerity. He had come to her, all smiles and brotherly warmth, and when Hilo put himself forward freely, he expected the same of others. Meeting him less than halfway was risky. When he spoke again, his voice was more measured.

"All right. Take the time you need, like you said. But there's nothing to figure out, Shae. If you don't want to be a Kaul, you shouldn't have come back." He raised a finger before she could reply. "Don't argue; I don't want to forget that I've forgiven you. You want me to leave you alone for now, I will. But I'm not as patient as Lan."

He walked away, his jade aura rapidly receding from her like a strong wave sweeping back out to sea. "Hilo," she called after him. "Say hello to Anden for me."

Her brother half-turned his head to speak over his shoulder. "Go say hello to him yourself." His lieutenant slid her a remonstrative look as the two of them disappeared into the warm night beyond the doors of the hotel.

• Chapter Seven •
KAUL DU ACADEMY

Even in the shade, sweat trickled down the backs and faces of the year-eight students. Ten of them stood nervously, each behind a short tower of hot bricks. "One more," said the master, and the assistant year-threes hurried to the fire pit with tongs, carefully but quickly removing bricks from the flames and placing another on top of each of the ten smoldering stacks. One of the waiting year-eights, named Ton, muttered quietly, "Ah, what to choose, pain or failure?"

Ton had undoubtedly intended the question for his classmates and not meant for it to be overheard, but Master Sain's senses were sharp. "Considering that if you fail to pass the Trials at the end of the year, you'll never wear another pebble of jade again in your life, I would venture to say pain," he answered dryly. The schoolmaster glared down the row of hesitating pupils. "Well? Are you hoping for the bricks to cool?"

Emery Anden rubbed the training band around his left wrist, more out of habit than any real need for additional contact with the jade stones studded into the leather. He closed his eyes, trying to grasp and focus the uncommon energy only a small percentage of Kekonese ever learned to manipulate. A choice between pain or failure indeed, as Ton had put it. Unleashing proper Strength would break the bricks, but exerting Steel would prevent him from being burned by the blistering hot clay. Unless, as this exercise was meant to instruct, a person could do both: use Strength and Steel in conjunction. A truly skilled Green Bone, of the kind Anden and all his classmates desired to be, could call upon any of the six disciplines—Strength, Steel, Perception, Lightness, Deflection, and Channeling—at any time.

Next to Anden, there was a resounding crack and a muffled yelp of pain from Ton. *This isn't as hard as algebra,* Anden reassured himself, then slammed the heel of his hand into the center of the top brick. It crumpled into the one underneath it, and that one into the one beneath it, in a cascading wave of force that lasted only a second but that Anden felt clearly like a line of slowly-toppling playing cards, the impact shuddering back up the other direction as well, dispersing into his arm, shoulder, and body. He pulled his hand away at once, snapping eyes open and examining his hands.

"Hold them out," said Sain, sounding nearly bored. He paced down the row of students, rubbing the back of his pebbly-skinned neck with disappointment. "I see some of you will be spending your break time this afternoon visiting the infirmary," he said, wrinkling his nose at the blistered hands. He kicked an unbroken brick on the ground. "Others will be bruising yourselves in remedial Strength training." He came to the end of the row, looked down at Anden's six broken bricks and unburnt hands, and grunted—the closest thing to praise the deputy headmaster ever offered.

Anden kept his eyes humbly on the cracked bricks in front of him. Smiling or relishing personal success would be an uncouth thing to do, and even though Anden had been born on Kekon and never been off it, he was always on guard against giving the impression of being foreign in some way; it was an old and unconscious impulse he'd had all his life.

Sain clapped his hands together. "Put your bands away. I'll see you next week, when we'll do this again until you improve or are too crippled to graduate."

The trainees touched clasped hands to their foreheads, stifling groans and shuffling aside for the year-threes who came forward to clean up the rubble. Anden turned away, unbuckled the training band from his wrist, and stowed it in its case. Then he squatted down, steadied himself against a wall, and squeezed his eyes shut as the crash hit. Higher jade sensitivity meant worse jade withdrawal, even from short exposure. Sometimes it took Anden twice as long as other students to recover, but he was practiced now. He breathed and forced himself to relax through the disorienting sensation of the world being torn out from under his feet, everything going dim and fractured around the edges, before finally righting and settling into a duller normalcy. In under a minute he had it under control and stood back up, shouldering his bag.

"I heard a grunt from Sain over there," said Ton, submerging his hand in the basin of cool water a pair of the year-threes had dutifully brought over to their seniors. "Nicely done, Emery." The name came out sounding Kekonese: *Em-Ri*.

"My bricks were thinner," Anden replied politely. "How's your hand?"

Ton winced, wrapping his palm in a towel and holding his arm stiffly across his stomach. He was a scrawny boy, shorter than Anden, but his Strength was excellent. Jade was strange that way; sometimes it was a skinny woman who could bend a metal bar, or a big, heavy man with the Lightness to run up a wall or leap from a roof—more evidence if there needed to be any that the abilities jade unlocked were something other than physical. "I wish medical Channeling worked better on skin wounds," Ton said, glum. "Had to happen right before Boat Day, too." He paused, glancing up at Anden. "Hey, keke, a few of us are planning to hit up the bars in the Docks before the ship sinking next week. You want to come, if you don't have other plans?"

Anden had the distinct feeling he was being invited as an afterthought—that was often the case—but of course he did not have other plans, and he thought that perhaps Lott Jin would be part of the group going, so he said, "Sure, that sounds good."

"Great," said Ton, "see you then." He cradled his burn and started across the field toward the infirmary. Anden began to walk in the opposite direction, toward the dormitories, musing as he went. After more than seven years at the Academy, he'd grown accustomed to existing in a respectable but somewhat lonely social borderland that only he inhabited, one in which he was never actually excluded, but never actively included either. His classmates were all cordial to him (they had to be), and he could count Ton and a few others as real friends, but Anden knew he made many of his peers faintly uncomfortable in more ways than one, and didn't expect complete acceptance.

Pau Noni, one of the other year-eights, jogged up to him from across the field, her face flushed from the humid midday heat. "Anden! You have a visitor waiting for you out front." She pointed down the path toward the Academy's entry pavilion.

A visitor? Anden squinted toward the gates, nudging his glasses up the sweaty bridge of his nose. Near-sightedness made it even harder to come off of jade and lose one's sense of Perception. Who might be visiting him? Anden's school bag bounced across his shoulders as he loped across the training field.

The small east field was one of several on the sixty-acre campus. Kaul Du Academy was built on a hill in Widow's Park, near the center of Jan-loon. Although the bustling city and its suburbs extended on all sides, the Academy's high walls, and the old elm and camphor trees that shaded the long, single-level buildings, separated the grounds from the metropolis and preserved the feel of a traditional Green Bone training sanctuary. The Academy was Kaul Sen's legacy, a tribute to his son, but even more profoundly, it was one of the most visible pieces of evidence that Green Bone culture had cemented itself into a central position in Kekonese society. When he stopped to consider it, Anden could appreciate that the Academy was as much a symbol as it was a school.

As he came to the small rock garden behind the main entrance, Anden slowed. A man was sitting on one of the low retaining walls, slouched in a posture of boredom. He wore tailored beige pants and his shirt sleeves were rolled halfway up his forearms; his jacket was draped on the wall next to him. At Anden's approach, the man rose to his feet with languid grace and Anden saw that it was Kaul Hilo.

A nervous sensation crept around Anden's chest.

"You look surprised to see me, cousin," said Hilo. "You didn't think I'd forget to come wish you a happy birthday, did you?"

Anden had turned eighteen a few days prior. The day had gone unac-knowledged as personal celebrations were considered gauche and frowned upon by the Academy's instructors. Anden recovered and touched clasped hands to his forehead in respectful greeting. "No, Kaul-jen, it's just that I know you're busy these days. I'm honored you'd pay me a visit."

"I'm honored, Kaul-jen," Hilo mimicked, his voice exaggeratedly stiff. The left side of his mouth curled into a teasing smile. "What's with all the formality, Andy? This place isn't sanding you flat, is it?" Hilo spread his arms wide. "It didn't work on me."

You're a Kaul. The whole school is named after your father. There was priv-ilege even among jadeless initiates; anyone with a different lineage or less talent would have been expelled for the number of misdemeanors Hilo had accumulated as a trainee. Now he was the Horn of No Peak. Go figure.

Anden tried to relax in his cousin's presence. Hilo was nine years older, but appeared not to have aged at all since graduating, so passerbys might have guessed them to be of similar age. "How's grandfather?" Anden called Kaul Sen his grandfather, just as he called the younger Kauls his cousins. "How's Lan-jen?"

"Ah, they're their usual Pillar-like selves." Hilo sauntered toward him.

Anden slung the pack off his shoulders, hastily removed his glasses, and stuffed them into a side pocket. They were new frames and he didn't want—

He barely had time to toss the bag behind him; Hilo grabbed him quick as a monkey snatching fruit, hands closing and rotating like metal vises on Anden's wrist and elbow. In a single violent twisting movement, he wrenched the younger man toward the ground.

Anden went with the momentum, dropping and sinking his weight to slacken the arm lock; he pulled his cousin close as they staggered together. Hilo kneed him in the side, twice, energetically, and Anden wheezed, folding up, clutching at Hilo's arms with the limp-limbed sway of a religious supplicant. His forehead bounced off of the other man's shoulder.

The sharp taste of jade energy filled his mouth. Hilo's jade. Clinched this close, its resonance washed over Anden—humming, throbbing, pulsing with Hilo's every heartbeat, breath, movement. Blood pounded into Anden's brain; it wasn't a true jade rush, but it was something like it. He grasped for it urgently, trying to hang onto the rippling edges of his cousin's aura, like clinging to steam. When Hilo moved to knee him again, he used the second of imbalance and drove a straight palm strike into Hilo's sternum with enough Strength to make him let go and stumble back several paces.

Hilo's smile stayed in place; he danced a couple steps to the side, then came back at Anden with light-footed menace. Anden braced himself. He couldn't run from Hilo; that was not an option. No matter how badly he expected to be beaten. Hilo struck him in the body with blindingly fast, playful blows that left Anden reeling and biting back whimpers. Anden smacked the next punch out of the way, shuffled in on an angle, just inside Hilo's range, and sheared his arm across his cousin's bicep, driving past his guard and smacking him under the chin with the ridge of his open hand.

Hilo's head snapped back; he stumbled and coughed. Anden didn't hesitate—he punched his cousin in the mouth. Hilo said, "Wow." He spun and buried a solid kick in Anden's stomach with enough Strength that the younger man was thrown from his feet and landed on his back in the gravel.

Anden groaned. *Why are we doing this?* He was only a student, prohibited from wearing jade outside of supervised training sessions. Hilo was a powerful Green Bone. The odds were not even remotely even. Of course, that was hardly the point. He scrambled unsteadily back to his feet and kept fighting; he had no choice, not if he wanted to avoid being beaten to a smear.

They'd attracted spectators. A number of nearby younger initiates had migrated over to get a better view of the Academy's top senior student being knocked around by the Horn of No Peak. Hilo seemed to enjoy the audience, glancing at the students occasionally with tolerant amusement. Anden was suddenly, absurdly concerned that the bystanders who did not know Hilo might assume he was angry or cruel. They might not notice the way he moved with a relaxed air, a friendly attentiveness on his face, as if he and Anden were having a conversation over lunch instead of beating on each other.

Anden took Hilo's punishment and gave back all he had; he attacked the ribs and kidneys, he bloodied his cousin's face again, he even stooped to going for the knees and groin. Finally, though, Hilo swept him to the ground and pinned him with a knee between the shoulders, and Anden lay staring sideways at the world and breathing dirt, unable to move, wishing it had been anyone in the family besides Kaul Hilo that had shown up this afternoon.

Hilo rolled off of Anden and sat on the ground beside him, legs extended, leaning back on his arms. "Whew," he said. He lifted the front of his expensive-looking shirt and wiped his face, leaving sweat and blood stains. "Less than a year before you graduate Andy. I have to take advantage of this time while I can. Lan used to beat the shit out of me when he was jaded and I wasn't yet, did you know?"

Lan, Anden did not say out loud, *thought you were crazy.* Lan had told Anden before, that Hilo would attack his older brother, insist on fighting him even though Lan was eight years his senior, larger, and jaded. Lan had no choice but to beat him near senseless on more than one occasion.

"Once you have your jade, you'll get me back. Look at you now. I'm a Green Bone. I'm the fucking Horn of the clan. And you gave me this—" he pointed to his bloody lip, "and this—" he touched a swollen lump on his head, "and this." He lifted his shirt and showed Anden the dark bruise on his torso. He dropped the shirt back down and grinned so cheerfully it made Anden stare. "I always knew you were something special. You could feel the jade on me, couldn't you? Could *use* it, even. You know how rare that is? At your age? Just think what you'll be like when you get your own green."

Anden appreciated his cousin's praise but did not feel nearly so proud of his performance. He hurt. He felt like a mouse that had been batted around by a bored tiger for several hours. He wondered: was it because he was not full-blooded Kekonese that he didn't find this remotely as fun as his cousin did? The Kekonese, so the gross ethnic stereotype went, couldn't say no to any contest of prowess. One could not go to any sizable social gathering without some physical duel breaking out—anything from spitting seeds into cups, to a heated game of relayball, to actual fights. It was customary politeness after such matches (which were usually benign but sometimes deadly serious) for the victor to voice a self-deprecating comment ("The wind was in my favor," "I had more to eat today,") or to extend some praise that allowed his opponent to save face ("You would be unbeatable with better shoes," "Lucky for me your arms were sore"), no matter how minor or unlikely the explanation.

So it was possible Hilo was just being polite in his approval. Anden didn't think that was the case, though. No, this had been Hilo's way of relating to him, measuring what he was made of, whether he was the sort of person who, outmatched and with no hope of winning, gave in or fought until he was no longer able.

Hilo got to his feet and brushed off his pants. "Take a walk with me."

Anden wanted to explain that he really ought to go to the infirmary. Instead, he struggled to his feet, picked up his dusty schoolbag, and limped silently along beside his cousin as the man strolled down the rock garden path. Now, apparently, they could talk.

Hilo pulled out two cigarettes and offered one to Anden. He lit Anden's first, then his own. "You'll have to start out as a Finger like everyone else;

that's just the way we do it. But if all goes well, you'll be a Fist in six months. I'll give you your own territory, your own people." Their spectators had dispersed. Hilo looked across to the far end of the field where some older students were lining up for training exercises. "You have to pay attention this year and start thinking about which of your classmates you'll want as your Fingers. Skill is important, but not everything. You want the ones who are loyal and disciplined. Who won't start shit but won't take any either."

The combination of the adrenaline crash and Hilo's words made Anden's fingers shake. He took a drag on the cigarette. "Kaul-jen," he started.

"Godsdammit Andy. Do I have to beat you up some more? Stop talking to me like that." He threw his arm around Anden's shoulders. Anden flinched, but Hilo pulled him in and gave him a fierce kiss on the cheek. "You're as much my brother as Lan is. You know that."

Anden felt a rush of embarrassed warmth. He couldn't help glancing around to see if anyone had witnessed Hilo's outburst of affection.

Hilo noticed, and teased, "What, are you worried about them getting the wrong idea? 'Cause they know you like boys?" When Anden stared at him, stunned, Hilo laughed. "I'm not stupid, cousin. Some of the most powerful Green Bones in history were queers. You think it matters to me? Just don't forget: soon you'll have to be careful about who you're with, who might be eying you for your green."

Anden sat down heavily on the stone retaining wall. He fished the glasses from the pocket of his bag and tried to wipe some of the sweat-muddied dirt off his face before putting them back on. His cousin's advice seemed silly; he was not in any romantic relationship and there were times he was resignedly convinced he might never be. He wasn't inclined to share that sentiment with the Horn though, and besides, he had more pressing anxieties related to his final year before graduation. "Hilo," he said slowly, "What if I can't handle jade after all? What if it's not in me? I'm only half-Kekonese."

"The half you have is plenty," Hilo assured him. "Some foreign blood might even make you that much better."

Jade sensitivity was a tricky thing. Only the Kekonese had the right amount of it to be Green Bones. Anden's mixed blood made him a borderline case. More sensitive, no doubt, which with the proper training might mean exceptional ability—or might mean a lethal propensity to the Itches.

"You know my family history," Anden said quietly.

A group of children carrying buckets and shovels were being led across the field by an instructor. They staggered with fatigue under the hot sun but knew better than to complain. The first two years at the Academy consisted of constant studying and demanding physical labor mingled with consistent, gradual jade exposure; these children wouldn't even begin studying the six disciplines until they were year-threes. Jade tolerance was built up through rigorous mental and physical conditioning, just like a muscle in the body, but beyond that there was an element of luck and genetics. There was no telling why some Green Bones could naturally carry a heavier load of jade without ever suffering the terrible side effects, while others could not.

Hilo scratched an eyebrow with his thumb, his other hand still on Anden's shoulder. "Your family history? Your grandda was a war legend, your uncles were famous Fists. They say your mother could Perceive a bird flying overhead and Channel from such a distance that she'd stop its heart in midair."

Anden stared at the tip of his burning cigarette. That was not what he'd been thinking of. "They called her the Mad Witch."

One night when he was seven years old, Anden had found his mother sitting naked in the bathtub in the middle of the night. It had happened after a hot day in the middle of summer, he remembered that—one of those scorchers when people iced their bedsheets in the evening and hung wet towels in front of fans. He'd gotten up to pee. The light in the bathroom was on, and when he walked in, he saw her sitting there. Her hair was hanging in limp, wet strands over her face, and her shoulders and cheeks were shiny under the yellow glow. The only thing she was wearing was the three-layered jade choker she never took off. The bath was half full, the water pink with blood. Anden's ma looked up at him, her expression blank and confused, and he saw that she held a cheese grater in her hand. The skin of her forearms was shredded, the flesh exposed like ground beef.

After a moment that felt as if it would never end, she offered him a small, sheepish smile. "I couldn't sleep, I was too itchy. Go back to bed, my little."

Anden ran from the room and called the only person he could think to call: Kaul Lanshinwan, the young man who was often at their house, his uncle's classmate and best friend, before his uncle had thrown himself off of the Way Away Bridge early one morning the year before. Lan and his grandfather came and took Anden's mother to the hospital.

It was too late for her. Even after they sedated her and removed all the jade on and near her, she could not be saved. When she awoke, she thrashed in her restraints, screamed and cursed them, called them dogs and thieves, demanded they give her back her jade. Anden sat in the hallway outside of his mother's hospital room, his hands clapped to his ears, tears running down his face.

She died a few days later, screaming until the end.

Eleven years later, the memory still crept into Anden's nightmares. When he was anxious or doubtful, it resurfaced. Waking unsettled in his dorm room, he couldn't bring himself to get up and go to the bathroom. At such times, he would lie staring into the darkness with his bladder aching and his throat dry, his skin prickling with a psychosomatic, insidious fear that his blood carried a curse that meant he too was fated to die young and deranged. Power ran in his family; so did madness. It was why, even though the Kauls had encouraged him to, he had never changed his name, preferring to keep the foreign name of Emery, which meant nothing to anyone, over his maternal family name, Aun, which came loaded with expectations of greatness and insanity, neither of which Anden desired for himself.

After the death of Anden's mother, Lan had spoken to his grandfather. Without any ceremony, the Kauls took Anden in, made him part of the family, fed and housed him until he was ten years old and of age to be sent to Kaul Du Academy with Kaul Sen's money and blessing. So it came to be, remarkably, that the ruling family of No Peak was all the family Anden had. His mother's side had flamed out in tragedy. His father was nothing more than a distant memory: a uniformed blue-eyed man who had fled back to his faraway country, to pale-haired women and fast cars.

"Your ma, she had a bad life—it started bad and it ended bad," Hilo said. "You won't be like her. You're better trained. You have all of us watching out for you." He stubbed out his cigarette. "And if you really need it, there's SN1 now."

"Shine," Anden said, calling it by its street name. "Drugs."

Hilo wrinkled his nose in contempt. "I'm not talking about the stuff that jade-fevered wannabes brew up in dirty labs to sell to weaklings and foreigners on the streets. Military grade SN1, what the Espenians parse out to their own special ops guys. It'll take the edge off the sensitivity, give you a bit of a buffer, if you need it."

"They say it's poisonous and easy to overdose, that it'll take years off your life."

"If you're an untrained, water-blooded foreigner shooting it up all the time like a junkie," Hilo said sharply. "You're not that. Everyone's different, you don't know what wearing jade will be like for you yet. I'm not saying you'll need help, I'm just saying it's there, we can get it for you no problem, if you need it. You're a special case. There's no shame in that, Andy."

Only Hilo was partial to calling him by that foreign-sounding nickname. At first it had annoyed Anden, but he didn't mind it now; he'd grown to appreciate that Hilo thought of it as something special between the two of them. Anden noticed that his cigarette had burned down. He ground it out and put the stub in his pocket so as not to litter the rock garden and earn any reprimands. "I wonder if shine would've saved my ma."

Hilo shrugged. "Maybe, if it had been available back then. But your ma had a lot of other problems—your da leaving, your uncle offing himself— that might've pushed her over the edge anyways." He studied Anden with concern. "Hey—why are you so worried all of a sudden? You're going to be a Green Bone soon, don't look so fucking glum. I'd never let anything happen to my little cousin."

Anden hugged his bruised torso. "I know."

"And don't forget it," said Hilo, leaning against the wall. "By the way, Shae says hello."

"You talked to her?" Anden was surprised. "Is she back now?"

But Hilo was unsmiling now and gave no indication he'd heard the question. Instead of answering he muttered, "We're going to need you soon, Andy." He scanned the grounds, as if noting the number of students. Most of them were already affiliated in some way with the clan—the children of Green Bones and Lantern Men. The Academy was largely a feeder into No Peak the same way its rival, Wie Lon Temple, was into the Mountain.

"Soon, we're going to need every loyal initiate we can get," Hilo went on. "Lan wouldn't want me saying this to you, but you ought to know. The truth is Grandda's got more than one screw loose and a few toes in the grave. Ayt Yu is dead, and that tough bitch Mada is coming after us. There's trouble on the way with the Mountain."

Anden regarded his cousin with concern but didn't know what to say. All summer there'd been rumors around campus that tensions were growing between the clans. So-and-so's older brother was a Finger who'd been insulted by someone in the Mountain and a duel was sure to follow. Someone else's aunt had been evicted after her building was taken over by a real estate developer affiliated with the rival clan. And so on. But it wasn't anything that Anden hadn't heard before, off and on over the years. There were always minor clan disputes going on. Being closed off in the Academy, the impending trouble Hilo spoke of seemed distant to Anden, something that concerned his cousins but was not anything that would affect him personally until he graduated next spring.

He was wrong. It came for him the next week.

• Chapter Eight •
BOAT DAY ENCOUNTER

It came as a result of going to piss alone.

The beginning of Kekon's typhoon season was always marked by Boat Day, and the conclusion of it, three months later, with the Autumn Festival. Boat Day is a holiday centered on bribing the petulant typhoon god Yofo with enough destruction to satisfy him for the coming year and forestall any Earth Scourers—the fiercest types of storms, capable of ripping up trees, leveling villages, and triggering landslides. Children and adults build paper boats (as well as matchstick houses and model cars), and destroy them with much fanfare—lighting them on fire and blasting them with hoses being a common method, but throwing them from high places and crushing them with bucketfuls of rocks and mud also being practiced. On Boat Day evening, Janloon harbor was the site of a staged naval battle, complete with flames, booming cannons, and sailors leaping overboard, ending with the ceremonial sinking of one or two old ships.

Anden had seen the harbor spectacle enough times during childhood that he didn't feel the need to see it again, but he took up Ton's offer to go down to the waterfront with several classmates to take in the general revelry. In order to instill a spirit of austerity and discipline, the Academy served modest, bland meals, prohibited alcohol, and gave the students few days off, so on special holidays the year-sevens and year-eights, who were allowed to leave campus unsupervised, tended to overindulge, eating and drinking themselves sick before, in time honored tradition, being brow-beaten and punished by unsympathetic masters the next day. Anden, Ton, and three others, Lott, Heike, and Dudo, visited four bars in the Docks, ate half a dozen varieties of street food from the boardwalk vendors, and by mid afternoon were debating whether to stay put and watch the boat sinking or fight their way upstream against the current of arriving spectators.

Anden's bladder was full to bursting with no toilet facilities in sight. It was hot and humid, as usual, and over the last half hour he'd been consuming a great deal of soda while blaming his weak Espenian blood for the fact that it didn't take much hoji—Kekonese date liquor—to make him light-headed. "Let's go back up there. I need to piss," he said, before realizing that he was speaking to no one in particular. Dudo was vomiting into a public garbage bin. Ton was standing next to him, offering moral support. Heike and Lott were having a heated argument about relayball.

Anden waited and watched them for a minute. Heike was taller, had nicer arms, and was arguably the better-looking of the two, but there was something about Lott Jin that always drew Anden's attention. A sulky but sensual curve to his bow-shaped mouth, slightly wavy hair that hung over unsmiling eyes hooded with long lashes. A sort of animal idleness in the movements of his well-proportioned body that made it seem as if he held everything in faint disdain.

Since the relayball argument was not reaching a conclusion and none of the others appeared ready to move anytime soon, Anden decided he had better see to his own needs. Rather than fight the crowds jostling for the best harbor view, he went further down the boardwalk until it ended in the ferry dock that ran boats to the outlying islands of Euman and Little Button. One would think there ought to be a restroom at the dock, but such was not the case. Anden crossed the street and jogged three more blocks before spotting a fried bread joint on the corner. Mumbling apologies as he pushed past the queue of people at the counter, he rushed into the restroom and shut the door, sighing with relief as he mumbled a quick prayer to Tewan, god of commerce, to bless the owners of the Hot Hut fried bread eatery.

To exit the small establishment, he again jostled through a crowd of teenagers loitering by the door. A young man near Anden's own age jostled him back roughly and said, "You're not going to buy something?"

"Excuse me?"

The teen jerked his head toward the Hot Hut, his eyes not moving from Anden. "You take a piss in there and don't buy anything? You don't like fried bread? It's the best in town. You should be more respectful, keke."

"He's not really a keke," said another of the teens lazily, swallowing a bite of his own piping hot stick of fried bread and sizing Anden up with an outthrust jaw. "He's a mongrel, and he's in the wrong part of town."

Anden glanced at the window of the Hot Hut and understood his mistake at once. In his haste, he'd crossed from the Docks into the Summer Park district. There was a paper lantern hanging over the cashier's counter, but it was pale green, not white. He was in Mountain territory, and he was wearing a shirt in Kaul Du Academy colors.

He had almost no money left on him, and the last thing his over-stretched stomach wanted was fried bread. "You're right," Anden said. "I'll go in and buy some bread." He took a step back toward the queue of customers.

The first teen gave Anden's shoulder a shove and squared his body in challenge. "Not in that ugly shirt, you're not." A smirk crept over his acne-scarred face. "Give it over. We'll accept it as your tribute to Wie Lon Temple and hang it over the urinals."

"I'm not giving you my shirt," Anden said, but he was uneasy now. Although he was eighteen, he was still a student with no jade of his own, not yet a man by the custom of his kind. Green Bones, governed by the honor code of aisho, were forbidden from killing any family members of their enemies who did not wear jade. Unfortunately, the code did not constrain the jadeless members of rival clans and schools. *They* were free to do what they wanted to him. Anden had been taught from a young age to never leave No Peak territory alone. Silently, he cursed his drunken classmates, his fifth shot of hoji, and his own carelessness.

There were three of them: the acne-pocked leader, his skinny friend, and the third thus far silent teen who was younger, perhaps fifteen or sixteen, but already bigger and heavier than the others. They closed in on Anden together, falling into natural positions that made Anden certain they'd skirmished together before. The leader in the center hung slightly back, the skinny friend and the larger boy circled to either side. "Touch your head to the ground and give us your shirt, mongrel," said the leader. "And then say that Kaul Du Academy is a school of thin-blooded shit eaters and bastards."

The other boys giggled. Returning with a bloodied Academy shirt and a good story of a beating well-delivered would earn the boys considerable status among their peers at Wie Lon Temple. Anden did not back away, but others did—the entire line of waiting customers shifted to the right like a snake, wrapping around the Hot Hut and giving the four of them a great deal more space on the sidewalk. The woman taking orders at the front of the counter rose up on her tiptoes and shouted at them, "Shoo! Shoo! Not in front of the glass doors!" She waved her arms to gesture them away.

Anden used the momentary distraction to attack first. He feinted right, then stepped left and clocked the skinny one across the face in a three-beat—left fist, folded left elbow, back across the jaw with the right heel of the palm—dropping him quickly.

It was better this way. He couldn't run without shaming his school, shaming Hilo, and he couldn't win—not without jade against three opponents, two of them larger than him. They wouldn't do more than beat him though—not in public, not on Boat Day, not if he fought well enough to be respected.

Anden seized his falling opponent by the shoulders and pivoted, spinning him around like a shield into the path of the charging leader. The biggest boy came up fast from behind, grabbing Anden in a powerful bear hug, pinning his arms to his sides while the acne-faced one leapt over his fallen friend and began burying punches in Anden's sides and stomach. Anden grunted at the bursts of pain; he sank his weight down sharply, kicking back at the large boy's shin and stomping his heel down on the top of his canvas shoe. The teen let out a curse and lifted his foot out of the way just as Anden drew up his own legs and thrust both his feet hard into the leader's chest.

His opponent stumbled backward toward the door of the Hot Hut, tripping over his fallen friend's legs, but was caught and shoved back by the people he crashed into. The large boy toppled off balance and had to let go of Anden to break his fall. Anden landed on top of him and threw an elbow blindly; he heard it connect with a solid smack. He rolled away fast, but before he could scramble back onto his feet, the younger teen's meaty arms encircled his waist and dragged him to the ground like an anchor, while the recovered acne-faced leader fell upon Anden, raining blows.

He felt only two of the punches connect with his cheek and ear when the attack stopped and the weight of his assailants was abruptly lifted off him. "What do you think you're doing?" demanded a man's voice. Anden looked up to see a dark-complexioned Mountain Green Bone hauling all three Wie Lon boys to their feet. They winced, cowed, no match for his Strength as he dragged them together like misbehaving puppies. "You little shits," he said. "It's Boat Day. Look at that park over there full of people. There are *tourists* here, and Wie Lon Temple students are rolling on the ground scuffling like dogs. What the fuck."

"We were teaching him a lesson, Gam-jen," whined the leader. "He's a Kaul Du brat, and mixed-blood to boot. Besides, he hit us first."

A different voice, slow but deep, like a bear roused to displeasure, said, "Is that how future Fingers address Fists?" Anden looked up at the approach of a man he had never seen, but recognized at once from reputation alone.

The teenagers became contrite. "No, Gont-jen," they murmured, eyes downcast. The leader said, a little sulkily, "Forgive us if we've overstepped."

Gont Aschentu, Horn of the Mountain, dispersed the crowd with his sheer size and air of dangerous authority. He turned his square chin to look down at Anden, then turned it fractionally toward the Wie Lon teenagers. "Leave now."

The three young men hastily touched clasped hands to foreheads as they backed away and fled, glancing over their shoulders as they went. Anden got to his feet, trying to adjust his bent glasses frames to sit straight on his face. Faced with the Horn of the Mountain, he almost wished his three attackers would come back. Anden clasped his hands and raised them in a wary, deeply respectful salute. "Gont-jen."

"You're Anden Emery," said Gont, his use of the foreign naming convention making Anden wince inwardly. "The son of Aun Uremayada. Adopted by the Kauls."

Anden hesitated. "Yes, Gont-jen."

Gont Asch had a distinctive appearance. He was bald, with thick limbs and a thick neck, and thick jade-encrusted armguards. He possessed the appearance of a powerful thug, the kind of Horn who would bark orders and profanities, who would maim first and ask questions later. In truth, he was soft-spoken, and it was said that his brutish appearance concealed a keen and patient cunning. "I'm told you're one of the best students at the Academy," he rumbled, still looking at Anden. Turning to Gam, "A shame you stopped the fight. I would've liked to see the outcome."

"I didn't know he was a Kaul," said Gam.

"Not by blood, but they treat him like one," said Gont, his voice taking on a shrewd quality. He studied Anden like an undertaker taking precise measure for a coffin fit. "In fact, Kaul Hilo thinks of you as a younger brother, doesn't he?"

Anden's heart began hammering again. He knew Gont and Gam would be able to Perceive his fear and he breathed slowly and silently, trying to reassert calm. He'd done no wrong, committed no crimes…it would be an unthinkable breach of aisho for these men to hurt him, no matter how much they wished harm on his cousins. "I'm sorry to have caused a scene, jen," he said, backing away, "I got separated from my friends at the harbor and wandered a little too far. I'll be more—"

The Horn's heavy hand landed on Anden's shoulder before he could take another backward step. "Let's have a talk, Anden. Good luck has surely brought our paths together." Gont said to his Fist, "Bring my car around."

Gam departed at once. Anden stood frozen, his mind racing. He could try to run, but it was ridiculous to think he could move faster than a Green Bone like Gont Asch. "There's no need to be afraid," said the Horn with an undercurrent of amusement in his low voice. "I know you're not a man yet."

Heat rose into Anden's face and blotted out his mounting alarm. He turned his head slowly to stare at the arm Gont had placed on his shoulder. Each piece of jade on the man's armguard had been carefully placed to form the abstracted but recognizable design of a river. The river was sacred; it brought down water for life, and jade for power. It was mild and harmonious, but glutted with monsoon rain it was unstoppable and deadly. Anden could feel Gont's many gemstones tugging at his blood like a gravitational force. He raised his eyes to the man's face. "I'm not afraid. My cousins, however, might not trust your intentions."

Gont laughed, an oddly soft chuckle, as a gleaming ZT Valor pulled up to the curb. "Get in," said the Horn, opening the back door. Anden suddenly felt weak in the knees, but Gont's arm was steering him unerringly into the vehicle. "Don't worry about the Kaul brothers. We'll be sure to let them know you're in our company."

With a great deal of misgiving, Anden got into the back seat of the boxy black sedan. Gont got in after him and shut the door. They began moving.

The driver of the ZT Valor—a ferrety man with a thatch of white hair and flakes of dandruff on his dark silk shirt—pulled the car through a number of side roads out of Summer Park. The car turned onto Patriot Street and began speeding west. Despite his situation, Anden stared out the window with great curiosity. He'd been raised to think of certain parts of Janloon as enemy territory and was a little disappointed to see that they did not look any different from the rest of the city: bustling streets and shops, construction cranes, shiny new buildings and muddy old shacks, dogs sleeping in the shade, foreign cars gliding past people balancing packages on bicycles. The ordinary people, the ones who were not Green Bones, moved freely around Janloon, so why would he have expected it to look like a different country?

He edged surreptitiously down the seat, trying to put more space between himself and Gont Asch's bare shoulders, which were massive and densely criss-crossed with raised white scars. The lore of how Gont had received his scars was well known, and the man clearly found it in his interest to wear sleeveless shirts that reminded people of it frequently. In the chaos of the early postwar days, a number of criminal gangs arose in Janloon, causing trouble in the streets and competing with the surviving, war-weary Green Bones. A few of these gangs acquired jade, which was not as strictly controlled back then as it was currently, and thus grew reasonably powerful even as the Itches swept through their ranks like an epidemic. A young Gont Asch found himself on the wrong side of one such gang and was one night ambushed and dragged before its leader.

Gont demanded a clean-bladed duel but was refused. He raised his bare knuckles and insisted on a "death of consequence"—a Green Bone's right to go down fighting instead of submitting to execution. Gont had been disarmed and the gang members were carrying knives, machetes, and hatchets. The gang leader smiled at the young man's bravado, but stopped smiling once the fighting began. Gont's talent in Steeling was unparalleled. He resisted a storm of cuts and took an opponent's weapon, then went on to kill all eight of the gang leader's men. It was said that the gang leader fell to his knees, clasped his hands to his head in salute, and swore an oath of allegiance to Gont Asch and the Mountain clan. Gont remained, to anyone's knowledge, the only living man to have walked away from a death of consequence.

"Turn that off," the Horn said. From the front passenger seat, Gam reached over and switched off the opera song playing on the radio, causing silence to suddenly fill the interior of the car and settle uncomfortably into the summer heat that the open front windows did little to dispel. Gont shifted his bull-like frame and looked at Anden with steady interest. At last he said, "I met your grandfather once, and your mother. It was about twenty years ago. The Auns were exceptional warriors, so gifted I think the gods didn't approve of such power in mortals and later sent bad luck to stalk them. I was a boy at the time, younger than you, though already a Finger— we didn't have the luxury of much schooling back in those days."

Anden blinked and said nothing, taken aback by the turn of conversation. It was hard not to be drawn in by the Horn's even and articulate baritone voice, which was quite amicable and relaxed, like that of a very good radio drama narrator. A counterpoint to the unnerving scale of the man's physical presence.

Gont went on. "The country was disorderly in those days. Growing and rebuilding like mad, but a stinking mess. The Green Bones kept the peace, made sure criminals and the foreigners didn't take over, but in the middle of all that, Ayt Yu and Kaul Sen had a falling out and divided the great One Mountain Society. I remember the Auns were among the most vocal in wanting Ayt and Kaul to reconcile their differences and keep Green Bones united under one clan.

"In the end, your grandfather sided with the Kauls, but the Aun family was divided in its loyalty. Your uncle went to the Academy and became the closest friend of Kaul Lan, but your mother went to Wie Lon Temple. If she'd lived and had her say, you would be swearing oaths to the Mountain this year."

Anden kept his eyes forward; his jaw was firmly clenched. What was Gont playing at? "My mother didn't have a say," he replied stiffly. "Kaul Sen took me in after she died. I owe him for my education, for the jade I'll wear when I graduate."

Gont shrugged, a motion that rippled his shoulders. "The Torch of Kekon is an old man now. You ought to consider whether your debt to him constrains you to being an underling of Kaul Hilo." Up until now, Gont's even voice had given away very little but now it slipped, leaving no doubt of his disdain for the other Horn.

The car had turned onto a road that was winding its way up into the hills. Lush greenery rolled past on both sides, occasionally broken by road-side stands with weathered paint, and private lanes barred by rusty metal gates. Anden tried to keep his growing anxiety out of his voice. "Where are you taking me?"

Gont settled back, depressing the seat. "To the top of the Mountain."

• Chapter Nine •
SKIRTING AISHO

Lan was in a meeting with Doru and two prominent Lantern Men when Doru's secretary interrupted them, knocking apologetically and squeaking, "I'm so sorry, but Kaul-jen? There's a man on the phone asking for you. He says it's urgent."

The Pillar frowned; perhaps it was someone from the Espenian Ambassador's office again, expecting to sweet talk or bribe him into shifting his stance on the jade export quotas. He excused himself and stepped out of the door that Doru's secretary held open for him. She smiled shyly at him. Lan did not know her name. The Weather Man seemed to go through secretaries quickly. This one was especially girlish and wearing an almost transparent pink blouse through which Lan could see her black bra. She hurried ahead of him to her desk and transferred the waiting call to his office.

Lan did not really think of it as his office, though it was reserved for his use whenever he wished to conduct business out of it. It sat unoccupied the rest of the time. The top floor of the No Peak–owned office tower on Ship Street in Janloon's Financial District boasted an incomparable view but it was the Weather Man's domain. Lan preferred his study in the Kaul house.

He picked up the phone and took the call off hold. "Kaul-jen," said a deep and unhurried man's voice. "We have your young friend, Anden. We crossed paths with him at the Boat Day festivities. No rules have been broken. We're just having a talk with him, a very cordial and civilized talk. In three hours, he'll be released in the Temple District, near the traffic roundabout. You have no need to be concerned for his safety…so long as no one in No Peak overreacts. I am referring to your Horn."

Lan said, "I understand." He knew he was speaking to a member of the Mountain clan; no one else would dare this. He suspected the man on the line was Gont Asch, though he could not be certain. Lan steadied himself against the desk and made his voice iron in its calm. "Trust me on this: I will hold you to your assurances."

"Don't worry about Anden. He's been most respectful and polite. Worry about your brother turning this into a bad situation." The caller hung up.

Lan depressed the receiver cradle on the phone and looked at his jade-backed wristwatch, making a note of the exact time. Then he released the phone switch and immediately dialed his brother's house, knowing it was highly unlikely he would find Hilo there. As expected, he received no answer. He phoned the main house and told Kyanla to have Hilo call him at once in his Ship Street office if she heard from him. Lan hung up and permitted himself a few seconds to calm down.

The Mountain's sheer nerve astounded and angered him. If Ayt Madashi had a message for No Peak, she could have arranged a meeting with Lan through the clans' Weather Men. Or she could have shown respect by sending a member of her own clan to deliver a proposal. Either would have been proper. Abducting Anden, the only jadeless member of the immediate Kaul family, and using him as a go-between skirted disturbingly close to breaking aisho. It put the onus unfairly on Lan to prevent violence. The caller was right; now he had to worry about his Horn. If Hilo found out Anden had been taken by the Mountain, his rage would be unpredictable.

Lan took out his address book and found the number for Maik Wen's apartment. Receiving no answer there either, he phoned both of the Maik brothers without success until he remembered that it was Boat Day and Hilo's people were bound to be patrolling the waterfront and its establishments. He called the Twice Lucky and asked the owner, Mr. Une, to put him on the phone with the highest-ranked Green Bone he could find in or around his restaurant. A few minutes later, a man's voice came on the line. "Who is this?" Lan asked.

"Juen Nu." One of Maik Kehn's men.

"Juen-jen," said Lan, "this is the Pillar. I need to find the Horn immediately. Call either of the Maiks if you know where they are and send any Fingers you have with you out running. Have my brother phone me at the Weather Man's office as soon as he gets the message. Don't start a panic, but do it at once."

"Right away, Kaul-jen," said Juen, sounding worried, then hung up.

Lan walked back to Doru's office. He apologized to the two Lantern Men—real estate developers seeking clan approval, financial support, and help with expediting permits for a new condominium complex—and sat back down, no longer paying much attention to the meeting. He was worried about Anden. The young man was like a true nephew to him and Lan felt a great deal of responsibility for him. He still remembered holding Anden's hand, comforting the grieving boy, bringing him into the Kaul house and telling him that this was his home now. Lan believed Gont had been sincere about not harming Anden, but things might change. The Mountain might hold him hostage if something went wrong. Where the hell was Hilo?

Doru would have to be Perception-deaf to not notice the aggravation that had come into Lan's jade aura. Sure enough, the Weather Man wrapped up the meeting as quickly as possible without appearing openly rude. He promised the petitioners that the clan would take care of their business needs with, naturally, an expectation that the Lantern Men's tributes to No Peak in the future would reflect such patronage. The Lantern Men gathered their papers, saluted to Lan while gratefully reiterating their allegiance, and left the room.

"What has happened, Lan-se?" Doru asked.

"The Mountain has Anden," Lan said. When he explained the situation, Doru blinked and made a skeptical smacking noise with his lips. "They can't have planned this. The boy is always in the Academy, out of reach. This is an aggressive and opportunistic move on Gont's part, but if they meant insult or harm they wouldn't have phoned to alert you. They must be sincere in wanting you to hold back Hilo."

"Are they truly?" Lan said, remembering something else. Last year, business dealings between the Mountain and a minor clan called Three Run had gone sour and turned violent, resulting in the Mountain annexing the smaller clan. The story was that two Mountain men had picked up the fiancée of the Three Run Pillar's son, driven her two hours outside of Janloon and left her by the side of the road to walk back in the dark without shoes. The enraged heir of Three Run had led his clan in an attack against Gont. It had ended badly for him and his family.

Hilo often complained vociferously about things the Mountain was doing—skirmishes and territorial disputes that Lan left mostly to his brother's attention—but now Lan considered the possibility that Gont snatching Anden might be just like what the Mountain had done to Three Run. Not breaking aisho explicitly but baiting their rivals into violence, then sweeping down in retaliation while claiming grievance.

The phone rang and Lan picked it up at once. Hilo said, "It's me."

"Where are you?" Lan asked.

"I'm in a phone booth outside of Gont's nephew's apartment building in Little Hammer and I've got twenty guys with me." Hilo's voice was low but Lan could hear the barely contained fury. "Gont's got Andy. An informer in Summer Park saw a scuffle break out and said that dogfucking bastard drove off with my kid cousin in his car."

"Calm down," Lan said. "I know about it. Gont called me. They'll release Anden on the Temple District side of the traffic circle in about two hours." He was almost afraid to ask. "Have you done anything that might change that?"

A pause before Hilo said, "No. I have this godsdamned building surrounded though and it's going to stay fucking surrounded until I get Andy back without so much as one of his hairs out of place. Gont's gone too fucking far. My own little cousin!"

Lan breathed out in silent relief. "He's my cousin too, Hilo, and whatever game the Mountain's playing, we can't give them any excuse to break aisho. Keep our guys under control, and get over to the place they're supposed to drop him. The important thing now is that we get him back."

Hilo breathed into the receiver harshly. "I know that," he snapped, and hung up.

Doru laced his thin fingers around one bony knee, and said with a stiff-lipped smile, "I take it our Horn has not yet started a war, gods be thanked. If the Mountain is indeed trying to provoke us, Hilo would play directly into their intentions. You're quite right to keep a cool head."

The Pillar did not reply; although he agreed with Doru's words, he found the man's tone faintly condescending. Cold, careful judgment was the mark of a good Weather Man, but perhaps Doru's commitment to peace between the clans was blinding him. Hilo might be impetuous but at least Lan could trust that his first concern was also for Anden's safety. Doru on the other hand had never formed any meaningful relationship with the adopted boy and seemed to be treating today's events like a very interesting business negotiation, instead of what Lan knew it to be: flagrant intimidation. The Mountain showing that it could reach into the Kaul family.

Lan considered going over to the Temple District to join Hilo, but decided it was more important to stay put in case the Mountain attempted to make contact again. "Cancel the rest of the day's meetings. I'll be in my office," he told Doru, then left to wait alone for news from the Horn.

• Chapter Ten •
THE MOUNTAIN HOUSE

They took him to the Ayt mansion.

Ayt Yugontin, when he was Pillar of the Mountain, had fittingly chosen the highest point of elevation in the city to build his residence and had endeavored to recreate the feel of a Green Bone training sanctuary like Wie Lon Temple in his own residence. The approach into the property looked like the entrance to a forest fortress, but when Gont rolled down the car window and nodded to the two guards—his own Fingers, no doubt—the thick doors swung open on silent automatic controls.

Anden had never seen a house more impressive than the Kaul residence, but the Ayt mansion was just as splendid in an entirely different manner. While the Kaul home was grand and modern, with both Kekonese and foreign-influenced architectural touches, the Ayt residence was classically Kekonese—a sprawling single story structure with stone facade and dark wooden timbers, swooping rooflines, green tiles and wide walkways. It might have been the home of a Kekonese landlord hundreds of years ago, if it wasn't for the security cameras, motion sensors, and expensive imported cars in the driveway.

The ZT Valor pulled up to the front. Gont got out of the car. When the driver opened Anden's door, he stepped out nervously and followed Gont through the entrance. Two Fingers stood to the side. They saluted their Horn but gave Anden no more than a cursory glance; they could Perceive that he was not wearing jade.

Gont pointed to a padded bench standing against the wall near the front door. "Wait here and don't move until you're called," he ordered Anden. With no further explanation, he strode down the wood floored foyer and disappeared down a hallway.

Anden sat down as he'd been told. Gazing around, he found it hard not to admire the landscape artwork and the antique blades mounted on the walls, even as his palms kept sweating and his insides twisted themselves into knots.

Surely he had been brought here as a hostage, to be held against the Kauls because of something that was going on between No Peak and the Mountain—the trouble that Hilo had spoken of last week. Should he have resisted, or tried to get away? He doubted it would have made any difference. What would Lan do when he found out what had happened? What would Hilo do? The threat of the Mountain hurting Anden or keeping him prisoner might provoke violence between the clans. Was that what the Mountain wanted? He glanced around, wondering if he could escape this place, and noticed Gam standing by the door with the guards, keeping a close eye on him. He didn't know all the key people in the Mountain, but he knew Gam was Gont's Second Fist and had a reputation as a formidable fighter. Anden remained where he was.

A good deal of time passed, perhaps an hour. Long enough that Anden's anxiety turned to boredom and then to impatience. Finally, Gont returned. "Come with me," he said, again with no explanation, and led the way back down the hall. Anden hurried to keep up with his long, purposeful strides.

Along the way they passed two men in suits walking in the opposite direction. Glancing at them, Anden suspected one of them was Ree Turahuo, the Weather Man of the Mountain, as he'd heard that Ree was a short man. The other was probably one of his subordinates, or a highly-regarded Lantern Man. Gont and Ree did not acknowledge each other. Interesting. Apparently No Peak wasn't the only clan in which the Weather Man and the Horn maintained a frosty relationship.

Gont stopped outside a thick, closed door and paused, turning his broad shoulders toward Anden. "Don't look so nervous," he advised. "She doesn't like nervous men." He pushed open the door and motioned Anden through.

Ayt Yugontin had perished without an heir. His wife and infant son had died in the war, buried under merciless tons of mud and earth when

Shotarian bombs started a landslide that destroyed the small village that had been Ayt's birthplace.

During the war, the people called Ayt the Spear of Kekon. He was the daring, vengeful, ferocious Green Bone warrior that the Shotarians feared and hated, a man who spoke little but wrecked deadly havoc on the occupiers, only to always escape into the shadows and up into the mountains.

His closest comrade, Kaul Sen, was the elder, more seasoned rebel, a shrewd and masterful tactician who, along with his son Du, distributed secret pamphlets and broadcast subversive radio messages that inspired and organized the network of Lantern Men that became the key to the One Mountain Society's success.

The Spear and the Torch.

A year after the end of the war, Ayt Yugontin adopted three children, orphans from his former village. Advocating that Green Bone abilities and traditions needed to be preserved and passed on to future generations of Kekonese, he gave all three adoptees—a teenage girl and two younger boys—a martial education at Wie Lon Temple. The girl had undeniable natural talent, despite beginning training late. The elder of the boys, Ayt Im, had an ego greater than his skill and was killed in a duel of clean blades at the age of twenty-three. The younger, Ayt Eodo, had enough ability, but grew up to be vain, more interested in becoming a playboy and art collector than a clan warrior. His sister, Ayt Madashi, became the Weather Man of the Mountain.

An hour after her father's abrupt death, Mada killed the longtime Horn of the clan. This was followed immediately by the murder of three other rivals, all of them among the Spear's closest friends and advisors. The Green Bone community was stunned—not by the fact that she'd done it, but that she'd done it so quickly and publicly, before her own father's funeral. No one expected the Weather Man to best the Horn in battle. Her opponents within the clan clamored to Ayt Eodo, hoping he would return from his vacation home in the picturesque south of the island and stand up to his sister's rampage.

The Kekonese term "to whisper a man's name" originates from the occupation period when the identities of foreign officials targeted for assassination were passed secretly through the rebel network. Ayt Mada whispered the name of her adoptive brother and a day later, Eodo's mistress emerged from the shower to find him lying on the bed with his throat slit and his jade gone.

When the bloodshed was over, Ayt Mada sent a message to her father's estranged comrade, Kaul Sen, expressing her deepest respect, her condolences over the recent loss of his wife, her sadness over the unavoidably violent internal transition of power within the Mountain, and her utmost desire for the continuation of peace between the clans. Kaul Sen instructed Doru to send a generous delivery of white heart blossom and dancing star lilies, symbolizing sympathy and friendship, respectively, to the funeral of his old friend, addressed to his daughter, the Pillar.

In the two and a half years following, two minor clans threw in their lot with the Mountain. The Green Winds clan did so willingly; its patriarch retired to the south of Kekon and its remaining leaders took positions within the Mountain. The other was the Three Run clan, which was made to see reason when Gont Asch cut off the head of its Pillar.

The office of Ayt Mada was spacious, bright, and cluttered. Books and papers were piled on the wall shelves, the desk, and the floor. Sunlight flooded in from the large windows. The space was divided in two: the office proper, and a reception area with a sofa and brown leather armchairs. Ayt was sitting in one of the armchairs, a short stack of file folders balanced in her lap. She was a woman nearing forty years, in loose linen pants, a sleeveless green top, and sandals. She looked as if she had just come straight from a workout or brunch. She wore no makeup, and her long hair was pulled back into a single functional ponytail.

Anden wasn't sure what he'd been expecting. He'd imagined that perhaps the Pillar of the Mountain would be a glamorous and deadly femme fatale. Or perhaps a hard-bitten she-man who exuded toughness and iron authority. Instead, she appeared ordinary, except for the spectacular amount of jade running up both her arms. Mounted in coiling silver bracelets that twined up her forearms and biceps like snakes, there must have been at least a dozen stones on each arm. So much jade, worn so unpretentiously— Green Bones had no need for any other symbols of status.

Without looking up, the Pillar said, "You made the call?"

Gont made an affirmative noise. "He understood. A reasonable man, as you say. His brother has massed a small army in Little Hammer, but so far they're waiting."

Ayt closed the file she was perusing and tossed the stack onto the polished wooden coffee table. She motioned Anden to the sofa across from her without ceremony. Even with a short distance between them, Anden could feel the woman's jade aura—a steady, focused red intensity. In the center of the coffee table was a bowl of oranges and a cast iron tea pot. "Tea?" Ayt inquired.

Caught off guard, Anden didn't answer immediately. Only when Ayt raised a gaze as formidable as her aura did he manage to say, "Yes, thank you. Ayt-jen."

Ayt opened a cabinet under the coffee table and brought out two small clay cups. She set one in front of Anden and one in front of herself. "It's a fresh pot," she explained, as if it were important that hostages were served hot tea and not stale, oversteeped dregs. She poured for herself first, then for him. An honored guest, particularly a fellow Green Bone, would be served before the host, but Anden did not qualify as either. Anden glanced at Gont, who settled his large frame into an armchair near Ayt's. She did not offer to pour him a cup, nor did he help himself; apparently he was not a party in this conversation and remained present only as a silent, disquieting observer.

"I'm sure you're wondering why you've been brought here." Ayt did not waste additional time with pleasantries. "We've taken a large risk in seizing this opportunity to speak with you. After all, there's a chance your adopted family might attribute dishonorable motives to our actions, when in truth they are entirely to your benefit."

Anden sipped just enough tea to wet his dry mouth. He was more perplexed than ever but sensed with trepidation that what was happening now was different from what he'd initially suspected, a more complicated ploy than merely holding him prisoner to provoke violence or to gain a concession from No Peak over some dispute.

"I'm told you're the best student at Kaul Du Academy." Ayt went on. "When I was young, my father never allowed anyone with foreign blood to train at Wie Lon, but times are different now. I'm not like my father. I break from tradition when I see that there is cause to do so and when there is gain to be had. I believe differences can be overcome; disagreements in the past can be set aside. Your lineage is impressive, and even without the Kaul blood or name, you are a representative of the family.

"I'm making you an offer to join the Mountain."

Anden's heart began to pound. He knew both Ayt and Gont could Perceive his fear, though neither of their expressions changed. His reaction was a sign that he understood what was happening, what was truly being said. Betraying his patron and his adoptive family by crossing over to the Mountain would be suicide; he could never accept such an offer and they knew it. No, this was a thinly-veiled proposition not to him, but to the Kauls themselves, to the clan of No Peak. An opening position.

The realization that he'd been brought here to be a messenger at the highest level, that Ayt expected him to infer the import of her words and take them directly back to Lan, filled Anden with a certain amount of relief. He was not going to be harmed or imprisoned. Then, on the heels of that relief came a burst of bewilderment and anger at the excessiveness of it all. Why force him into a car instead of conversing somewhere neutral? Why provoke Lan and Hilo to the brink of attack? Why include him at all?

Anden imagined standing up, tossing his cup of tea into Ayt Mada's face, and saying in a voice cold with disgust, "The Pillar of No Peak would never kidnap a jadeless student from Wie Lon. Kaul Lan would have the decency not to play mind games like this."

Of course, Lan would not want him to do anything so stupid. He'd want him to stay composed, pay attention, and return safely. Anden remained still, keeping both his face and his voice calm as he responded, carefully, "I'm flattered, Ayt-jen."

Ayt smiled at his discomfort. "I'm glad you understand the significance of such an unprecedented offer. You would be a Fist with many Fingers, in a position of considerable status and responsibility. But not here in Kekon. In Ygutan."

Anden blinked. "Ygutan?"

"We've established vital new operations there. I need enterprising and talented Green Bones to be in charge of our expansion in that country. You would work under the Horn, but you would report directly to me."

Ygutan was cold and desolate, the food was awful, and there wasn't a pebble of jade in the whole vast country. Why on earth would the Mountain want to expand into Ygutan? Perhaps Perceiving his bafflement, Ayt lifted her lips in a thin smile. "The world is opening up. International trade is flourishing. Why should we Green Bones concern ourselves only with the bit of land that is Kekon when vast opportunity exists abroad?"

"But…what's in Ygutan?"

Ayt paused with the tea cup below her mouth. "SN1 production." She sipped and put the cup down. "We're going to sell shine to the Ygutanians."

Anden was speechless. Shine was both illegal and reviled on Kekon. It was a drug engineered by foreigners, a shortcut to allow jade to be worn by non-Kekonese, by people without the hard-won tolerance that Green Bones proudly possessed. An entire civilization and culture was built around the inviolable truth that jade destroyed any wearer except the most worthy Kekonese warriors.

The Espenians, arrogant and inventive beyond compare in the world, had circumvented that. As soon as they'd established military bases on Kekon, ostensibly to help their allies defend and rebuild after the Many Nations War, they'd gone to work in secret labs to determine how their own soldiers could acquire the same legendary jade ability as Green Bones. Ten years ago, they'd succeeded, albeit imperfectly, by creating SN1.

The formula of the experimental serum had leaked from Espenian military bases on Kekon, and the illegal shine trade ballooned. Apparently a lot of people, here and overseas, were willing to trade years of life for a dangerous drug that allowed them to wear jade without being Kekonese, without putting in the years of hard training, and without dying horrible deaths from the Itches. Less acknowledged, and universally scorned, was the fact that there were some Green Bones who secretly used it too, to artificially enhance their own natural jade tolerance.

SN1 was a contentious topic among Green Bones. Anden had heard more than one argument at school and even a debate in the Kaul house once, with some firmly of the opinion that the drug was an unmitigated social ill and others contending that limited use was acceptable so long as it was by sanctioned, highly-trained individuals such as Green Bones who might, due to illness or injury for example, benefit from medicinal use to temporarily bolster tolerance.

Anden wasn't sure which side of the issue he fell on, especially given the instability of his own bloodline. Nevertheless, in his experience, the one thing everyone agreed upon was that the illegal spread of shine was counter to Green Bone interests and values and had to be combated. The fact that Ayt Mada, the Pillar of the largest Green Bone clan in Kekon, was planning to *sell* shine was so astounding to Anden that when he was able to speak again, he forgot his role and his caution, and blurted, "You're going to give more foreigners the ability to wear jade? Isn't that exactly what we *don't* want?"

He realized his outburst had probably come across as disrespectful, but Ayt seemed amused. "What we don't want is to lose control. The Espenians already use SN1 on their own soldiers. Other countries will aspire to follow suit. Soon there were will be an expanding population of foreigners wearing jade." Ayt leaned forward. Anden didn't mean to, but he leaned away; the woman's jade aura and her straightforward gaze felt like solid surfaces pushing implacably outward. "This could be the greatest threat we've ever faced, or an unparalleled opportunity. The faster Kekon speeds toward modernization, the more vital it is that Green Bones take strict control of our own resources. We can be driven out of our rightful place, or we can stand to profit greatly.

"My father strived to keep the foreigners out, but let's accept reality: they're here to stay. Kekon is no longer a mysterious backwater of civilization. People around the world know about jade, and thanks to the invention of SN1, now they can have it. Rather than try to fight the inevitable, let's give them what they want. At a price we control, under conditions we control. The shine trade on Kekon has given us better knowledge of SN1 than anyone besides the Espenians, and we can ensure the security of the production facilities we establish. If *we* develop the SN1 supply, then *we* decide the extent to which jade can be used by outsiders."

Anden felt entirely out of his depth. He made himself sit forward, reach for his tea cup, and swallow down the now lukewarm liquid. In doing so, the proximity of Ayt's jade prickled his Perception for an instant. The Pillar's tone was pleasant but firm. She didn't sound threatening. But he sensed menace. A dogged avariciousness.

"Green Bones were once united against foreign threats. It's time we were that way again. Time that the clans came together in a new alliance. That's why I'm proposing that you join us. The rewards would be great for you." Ayt sat back, and her expression shifted, became flat and chilling. "If you spurn the hand we're holding out to you, well, that is your choice of course. Just remember that we're extending this offer in good faith and complete honesty. I strongly urge you to reciprocate that respect by not taking some position in the future that might place us at odds with each other."

Anden's pulse was racing and he shifted uneasily in his seat, his neck hot. Ayt was making the proposal as clear as if she was sitting here speaking directly to another Pillar. "Ayt-jen." He cleared his throat. The near certainty that he would be returned in one piece to deliver Ayt's pronouncements to No Peak gave him the courage to speak up with more force than he had before. "May I…ask a candid question?"

Ayt raised her eyebrows. "Please do."

"I'm only a student, so forgive me if I don't understand, but…why go to the trouble and risk of bringing me here and involving me this conversation? If you want to propose an alliance with No Peak, why don't you do so directly?"

Ayt smiled a satisfied, enigmatic smile that held no real warmth. "You sell yourself short. My offer to *you* personally, is quite real. You have an important future role to play in ensuring peace between our clans, if your Pillar recognizes so. As for conversing with your clan…" She opened her hands in a gesture of helpless disappointment. "I would welcome a discussion with Kaul Lan, but how is that possible when his Horn keeps giving offense against us? He never passes up an opportunity to harass us over territorial lines. His Fingers spy on us; his Fists pick battles over minor disputes. How are we supposed to expect a reasonable dialogue with No Peak?" For the first time during the entire conversation, Mada Ayt glanced at her Horn. She and Gont shared a brief, silent exchange before she turned back to Anden. "If the Pillar gave us some sign that he was serious about peace, then that would be a different matter."

Ayt stood up, smoothly and casually. Gont rose as well and Anden followed suit at once. Ayt was taller than he'd expected. Anden was taller than most Kekonese and her eyes were on a level with his. The sunlight struck the coils of jade on her arms and lit the steel settings with motes of light.

She said, "We're taken enough of your time this afternoon; let's get you home before anyone misses you...too much." A touch of the sardonic in both her voice and the movement of her mouth. "You have our offer. You know what to do next. I'll wait for an answer, but not for long."

Anden clasped his hands and touched them to his forehead. "Ayt-jen."

• Chapter Eleven •
WHERE THE PILLAR STANDS

The ZT Valor pulled over to the side of the curving boulevard and let Anden out in front of the wide green space between the Temple of Divine Return and the handicraft market plaza. As soon as Anden stepped out of the car, he saw his cousin Hilo waiting for him, a posse of men behind him. Hilo's face was flushed with relief and murderous intent, and for one ridiculous second, Anden was afraid for Gont's driver. He shut the back door of the vehicle quickly and the ZT Valor took off at once, losing itself in traffic as it sped back across territorial lines.

Hilo strode up, seized Anden by the back of the neck, and shook him roughly. "I ought to give you another beating. What the fuck were you doing in Summer Park? You're going to be green in less than a year; you have to pay attention *every fucking second* because I can't always be there if there's trouble, understand?" Anden nodded, shamefaced. Hilo grasped the younger man's chin in his hand, eyes narrowing dangerously at the swollen bruise on Anden's cheek that the trio of Wie Lon Temple boys had given him as a souvenir of his careless wandering. "They do this to you?" he asked. "Gont or his men knock you around at all?"

"No, no, it wasn't them," Anden said hastily. "That was just a stupid thing that happened with some Wie Lon guys earlier. Gont's people didn't touch me."

Hilo searched the teenager's face for sincerity, then, finally relaxing, embraced Anden with a warmth that melted the last of the tension. "Am I ever glad to see you, cousin." With one hand resting protectively between Anden's shoulder blades, he walked them over to the Duchesse, which was parked quite prominently in the plaza's loading zone along with two other No Peak vehicles. Maik Tar was leaning restlessly against the trunk, but straightened up to open the car door for them. "I need to talk to Lan," Anden said a bit weakly as they got in. Now that he was safe, the low level of adrenaline that had been flowing through him for the past few hours was draining out like gutter runoff after a heavy rain, leaving him shaky.

"Lan's in the Weather Man's office," Hilo said.

It took only fifteen minutes to get to Ship Street. When they arrived, Hilo gave some brief instructions to his men: "Go tell the guys in Little Hammer to clear off." Then he and Tar walked with Anden straight through the lobby without bothering to check in at the reception desk.

Anden had never been in the Weather Man's building before. This was a side of the clan he knew little about and he was intimidated by all the Luckbringers in pressed suits, carrying briefcases and file folders. Hilo and Tar, with their sleeves and collars loose and sweaty from waiting in the sun, moon blades still slung over their shoulders and talon knives sheathed at their waists, seemed out of place here. People paused and looked over as they passed, some saluting shallowly.

They took the elevator up to the top floor. Lan was waiting for them, his expression no less calm than Anden was accustomed to, but he too embraced Anden joyfully. "Come in here and sit down," he said, leading Anden to his own office.

"They brought me to meet with Ayt Mada," Anden said. "Lan-jen…she wanted me to talk to you right away." He placed slightly heavier emphasis on *you*.

Lan understood. When they got to his office, the Pillar turned to Hilo and said, "I want to talk to Anden alone first. Find Doru and wait out here for me." Hilo looked piqued but not surprised, and quirking his mouth at Anden to show that he was not really sour about it, he jerked his head at Tar and the two of them moved off as Lan shut his office door.

Anden sat down in the nearest chair, gratefully accepting the bottle of lemon soda water that the Pillar took from the mini-fridge and handed to him. "I won't lie; you had us all a little worried today," Lan said. Watching Anden gulp the soda, he said, "Take your time. Then tell me what the Mountain wants."

When his cousin was done, Lan was quiet at first. Then he said, "You did well, Anden. You kept your cool and did exactly what you were supposed to. I'm sorry it ruined your Boat Day, and you ought to be more careful in the future. I'm sure Hilo's already told you that. But you ended up doing a brave thing for the clan."

"I'm sorry to have caused trouble, Lan-jen."

Lan smiled. The boy—the *young man*, Lan reminded himself, was always like this—a little anxious, a bit overly formal. When he was in the Kaul home, he still acted like a guest, waiting for subtle permission to sit or eat or voice opinions, even through he'd lived in the house since he was a child and resided there still during the Academy's holiday breaks. "You're never any trouble, Anden," Lan told him. "I think the Mountain has been planning to give us a shake like this. You just happened to give Gont a way to do it." He stood up and Anden stood with him.

"What are you going to do?" Anden asked. "About Ayt's proposal?"

"I'll discuss it with the Horn and the Lantern Man," Lan said. "That's not something you need to worry about. You just focus on school and preparing for Trials this year. Are you still on track to graduate Rank One?"

"I think so. I'll try my best," Anden promised, and Lan felt a surge of pride. Anden was a good kid; he'd come from a tragic family situation, but he'd grown up well. Not a day went by that Lan didn't feel thankful he'd convinced his grandfather to take Anden in and make him a Kaul.

Lan took his cousin out to the chairs in the elevator lobby where Doru, Hilo, and Maik Tar were waiting. Tar took Anden back to the Academy while Lan returned to his office with the Horn and the Weather Man. He poured all three of them a generous splash of hoji over ice and said, "Take these, we're going to need them." He swallowed his own drink and regarded the two other men: Doru sitting in one of the chairs with his long legs crossed, patient curiosity on his face; Hilo leaning against the wall, his gaze sharp and expectant. Their jade auras hummed steadily in Lan's awareness: cool and murky on one side, smooth and hot on the other.

Lan said, "The Mountain has a plan to produce and sell SN1 in Ygutan. It could make them a lot of money, and Ayt proposes we join in with them on it."

After Lan had explained what he'd learned from Anden, Hilo

straightened up from the wall. "What does Ayt take us for?" His expression was angry, but his voice was more perplexed than anything else. "The Mountain's been digging at us for months and today Gont grabs Andy off the street. Just about starts the war right there. And they think we're going to get into bed with them after *that*? If Ayt really wanted to talk business, she would've come to you properly, with respect. This proposal isn't serious. It's an insult."

Hilo was right; the Mountain sending a message to No Peak in such a vaguely threatening way was a blatant slight, but at least Lan knew from Anden what Ayt's purported reason was. *I would welcome a discussion with Lan Kaul, but how is that possible, when his Horn keeps giving offense against us?* The other Pillar was letting it be known that she would not deign to negotiate directly with Kaul Lan until he reined in or removed his brother from his position as Horn.

It was an outrageous demand. Was it even possible to attempt any discussion under such flagrantly disrespectful terms as one Pillar stipulating the other's choice of his Horn? Lan had no doubt Hilo and his men made life difficult for the Mountain, but his brother maintained that it was all in response to the Mountain's escalating overreach. Was Hilo truly the aggressor standing in the way of peace, or was he simply too good at his job, someone Ayt wanted out of the way so she could more easily seize No Peak outright? Acceding the clan's military position was out of the question, but perhaps the Horn did need to be reminded that he was not blameless. Lan kept his eyes on his brother and said, "Ayt says she'll talk in person if we put an end to street skirmishing and show we're interested in getting in on the business side." He caught a glimpse of Doru nodding and suspected the old advisor had inferred the more specific demand precisely.

"So she'll talk if we lie down and let the Mountain walk all over us?" Hilo nostrils flared in a derisive snort. "I know you think I'm touchy about things sometimes, that I get angry and take things personal, but trust me Lan, I know what's going on out there. Gont looks like a meathead, but he's crafty. Every time I'm not looking, he takes a bit more from us. Little by little but never enough to provoke an outright war. I'll find out two of our Lantern Men are now paying tribute to his Fists. Or that somehow the lease on a building that housed our businesses went sour, and the landlord sold it to a cousin in the Mountain. They can't swallow us whole like they did to the Three Run clan, so they're picking and picking at us instead."

Lan turned to his Weather Man. "What do you think, Doru?"

Doru took his time responding. A little too much time, Lan thought, as if he was deliberately trying not to come off as being too ready with an answer. "I think Ayt-jen's proposal has merit. The Fists of both clans can only see as far as they can swing their blades; whatever petty disagreements they have over territory are not terribly important in the larger scheme of things and shouldn't influence our decision when it comes to big business." A criticism of the Horn's side of the clan, discernible in his gravelly voice. "Ayt-jen is right about how the foreigners all want SN1, how there's a great deal of money to be made in establishing a reliable supply that we Green Bones control. Since the operations would be offshore in Ygutan, there's no danger of it polluting our own country. Green Bones have always been strongest when united; instead of trying to divide Kekon between us, we could strike an alliance with the Mountain to increase the gain for us all."

Hilo's lips were drawn back. "There's no such thing as an alliance with the Mountain. Three Run found that out the hard way. At the end, we'll be two clans with two Pillars, or one clan with one Pillar." Hilo tipped back an ice cube from his glass and crunched it, his face set in a sure scowl. "If we show interest in this, if we agree to work with them, they'll only use the opportunity to control us. I don't believe for a second that Ayt is serious about sharing power. She's not the type. She hasn't even made it clear what she wants from us. Financing? Manpower?"

"For a start, it seems she wants our assurance that if nothing else, we won't stand against them," Doru said. "It makes perfect sense; why else make a play for Anden? When the boy graduates, we can send him to work for the Mountain in their new Ygutanian operations. It's a good job, like Ayt-jen said, full of responsibility. Through him, we would know everything about the Mountain's operations there, and for their part, they would be certain we were invested in keeping the peace, not undermining them or going to the Espenians. So there'd be trust on both sides."

"Send Andy over to the enemy?" Hilo's eyes bulged with disbelief; his aura was becoming uncomfortable to Perceive.

Doru said, "During the Three Crowns era, royal houses often exchanged children so both sides were motivated to maintain good relations."

"You mean offer Andy as a *hostage*." Hilo spun toward Lan with a snarl. "*Never*. Not a fucking chance!"

"Sometimes, the old ways are not without wisdom," Doru sniffed.

Lan held up a hand to forestall Doru saying anything more, and looking into Hilo's flushed face, he said quietly, "Calm down. Anden's not a pawn and we're not sending him anywhere he doesn't want to go." Lan had been swirling the melting ice cubes in his glass as he listened and pondered, and now he set his glass down on the table, having come to an inescapable conclusion about what his response to the Mountain had to be. Hilo had a tendency to react personally, while Doru evaluated options with cold-blooded, strategic pragmatism, but there was a third angle that neither of them had voiced, that was, for Lan, the deciding factor.

Lan turned to Doru. "I'm going to prepare a reply to the Mountain and I want you to send it through their Weather Man's office, the way it ought to be done in business matters like this. We don't have to act improperly just because they do. I'm going to decline any alliance or partnership with the Mountain when it comes to the production of shine. However, we won't stand in their way either. They're free to pursue their venture, so long as it doesn't threaten any of No Peak's businesses or territories." He paused, then added, "Make no mention of Anden; he's not part of this. If Ayt wants assurance of our neutrality, she'll have to take our word for it."

Doru inclined his head but it was easy to see from both his tight expression and the prickly change in his aura the disappointment he felt in the matter. "If I might ask, what is your rationale for deciding on this important matter so quickly?"

Lan didn't really want to hear whatever counterarguments he knew Doru was sure to provide but he owed his highest advisors an explanation. "It takes us down a dangerous path. If more foreigners have access to shine, demand for jade will rise as well. There'll be pressure on the Kekon Jade Alliance to increase mining and to reform export quotas to sell not just to the Espenians, but to the Ygutanians and others as well, or risk the black market filling that demand with smuggled jade."

Lan could not condone that; he had just voted against an increase in jade exports at the last KJA meeting. Jade was Kekon's most precious natural resource. It was the birthright of the Kekonese people and lay at the center of the Green Bone culture and way of life. Selling it as a militarily useful substance to foreigners, to people who had no jade warrior training or upbringing, who did not understand aisho and could not appreciate what it meant to be green…it sat uneasily with him. Yes, the export of jade maintained the alliance with the Espenians and enriched the national coffers, but it had to be strictly limited. That was why the Green Bone clans held authority over the Kekon Jade Alliance in the first place. Now one of the major clans was proposing something that was sure to undermine the power of the KJA in the long run, and that disturbed him greatly.

"Forgive me, Lan-se," Doru argued with more forcefulness than usual, "but surely the KJA is an example that our two clans *are* capable of existing in partnership. Any future mining and export decisions will have to be made jointly between us and the Mountain. It seems premature to worry about them now."

Lan glanced at the Weather Man in mild surprise. He would not personally have held up the Kekon Jade Allinace as a shining example of clan partnership. The tiers of accountability and stakeholder voting requirements seemed to ensure that no KJA decisions were ever made in less than six months. "You obviously have a more optimistic view of the KJA than I do," Lan replied. "But there are other reasons not to get involved."

"Such as the fact that Ayt's whole proposal is a set-up," Hilo insisted. "A way for the Mountain to appear reasonable while gaining an advantage over us."

Lan was inclined to agree with Hilo's suspicions but he did not voice this out loud. "Shine is a poison," he said firmly. "It erodes the natural order of society. It encourages people who shouldn't have anything to do with jade. Like those boys, the thieves that Hilo caught at the Twice Lucky last month." Lan set his jaw. "If we get involved in producing shine in any way, we'll be contributing to the trafficking and unsanctioned use of jade. I won't judge another Pillar's opinions, but to my thinking, doing this would be a violation of aisho."

"Is it not the highest level of aisho that Green Bones protect the country?" Doru asked. "Working together to control SN1 will make the clans stronger. That will make Kekon stronger, less vulnerable to foreigners."

"And what if the Espenians find out that Green Bone clans are selling drugs to the Ygutanians for military use? The Mountain is courting conflict and I don't want No Peak involved." Lan cut off Doru's attempt to say anything further. "Doru-jen, my decision on this is final. Are you going to fulfill your responsibilities as Weather Man and handle this the way I've asked?"

The old advisor's tapered chin dipped in unenthusiastic acknowledgement. In a final attempt to argue his position, he said with clever mildness, "Of course I will Lan-se, but perhaps we should talk to Kaul-jen before making a final decision."

Lan had had enough. "You're talking to Kaul-jen now," he said, so coldly that the startled Doru fell silent. Hilo smiled.

Despite having made what he thought was the right decision, Lan was disheartened. Gods in Heaven, it was difficult to be Pillar with his impetuous younger brother on one side and his grandfather's cagey old crony on the other. It wasn't hopeless, however. Hilo had kept his head this afternoon, and Doru was, however reluctantly, falling into line. Now that the hard talk was over, Lan spoke in a more conciliatory tone. "I think our nerves are a little frayed. You should know, both of you, that I value your opinions."

"So now what?" Hilo asked. "We wait to see how Ayt responds?"

"Not quite. I said we won't interfere with the Mountain, but knowing what they're up to, we need to be more careful. Doru, I want you to set up a meeting for me with Chancellor Son." Having been so strongly put in his place a minute earlier, the Weather Man nodded without complaint.

Lan turned to his brother. "Hilo, what I told you about the Armpit now applies to Sogen and all our border territories as well. Bolster defenses where you have to, but no bloodshed without family approval. No retaliation for them taking Anden either. Maybe they spat in our eye, but he's back with no harm done and we're denying them the alliance they want, so best not to create more hard feelings for a while."

Hilo crossed his arms, shrugged. "If you say so."

"One other thing," Lan said. "I want to make sure Shae is protected. Her apartment is in North Sotto, so there shouldn't be any trouble, but I'm talking about when she's going around in Janloon. Have one or two of your people keep an eye on her."

Now Hilo looked displeased; he made a face that Lan thought was childish, as if he were eight years old and being upbraided to be nice to his sister. He said petulantly, "Shae's plenty able to look after herself."

Lan said, exasperated, "You know she's not wearing jade. She's not part of the clan business, but maybe the Mountain doesn't know that. After what happened to Anden today, we should take precautions."

"*If* she wore her jade, she'd be plenty able to look after herself," Hilo amended, clearly still grumpy about it, but not disagreeing. Lan let it go. He was glad to have Shae back, with or without her jade, but saying so would only make Hilo sulk. Lan had concluded long ago that there was little he could say or do if his younger siblings were determined to be cruel to each other.

• Chapter Twelve •
A MAN NAMED MUDT

Bero's face healed crooked, and when he looked in the mirror he mused that he was ugly now. Also, he limped a little when he ran. These things did not matter so much to him, but when he noticed them, which was often, he remembered the disaster of the night at the Twice Lucky. He remembered the Maik brothers' heavy fists, the Horn's casual disdain, and even more cutting, the Pillar's look of undisguised pity, as if Bero were a three-legged dog, not even worth killing.

But most of all Bero remembered jade. What it had been like to have it, and what it had been like to lose it.

Sampa, that Abukei pussy, had gone straight as a rod. With the fear of anything green beaten into him, he'd taken a job as a bike courier. Bero saw him huffing and puffing down the streets of their poor dockworkers neighborhood at the edge of the Forge, his doughy body straining on the pedals as he hauled boxes and bundles on a squeaking rusted bike trailer. When Bero called out to him, Sampa ignored him. In retaliation, Bero slashed Sampa's tires and the boy missed his deliveries one day and lost his job.

Bero's aunt worked twelve hours a day as a seamstress in a garment factory and Bero slept on the floor of her apartment when she was not there. The aunt's boyfriend worked in a warehouse at the docks and knew how to skim a little for himself. Not enough to get caught and fired but more than enough to sustain his drinking habit. Though the bastard never did Bero any favors, it was through him that Bero caught wind of a man named Mudt, who fenced stolen goods out of the back of a discount goods store in Junko.

That in itself was not so interesting to Bero, but the other rumors he heard were. He found the man in the backroom of his store, counting boxes. Mudt was a tawny-looking man with crinkly hair and and small eyes; he might have had a bit of Abukei blood in him. "What do you want?" asked Mudt.

Bero said, "I heard you've got work, for people who want it."

"Maybe." The man coughed into his elbow and turned toward Bero with watery, pinprick bright eyes. Even in the muggy heat, he wore a gray shirt with sleeves down to his wrists; the armpits and collar were dark with sweat. "It's not work for pussies though. Can you drive? Can you handle a gun?"

"I can do both." Bero studied the man. "Is it true? That you're green?"

Mudt smirked. Then he stuck out his tongue, showing off the jade stud pierced through the center of it. "Oh, it's real," he assured Bero. "I don't mind telling you because I know you're cut, keke. You're *hungry*." He tapped the center of his own forehead with an index finger and grinned with crooked teeth. "Perception, you see."

If it was true that Mudt had jade, then the rest of what Bero had heard was probably true as well: that Mudt had false papers and a reliable source of shine, that as a small business owner in No Peak territory he paid nominal tribute to the clan, but made his real wealth as an informer for the Mountain. Mudt was a self-made man. Proof that you didn't need to be born into the right family or go to the right school to have what the Green Bones had, to take power when it wasn't given to you.

"I want to work for you," said Bero.

• Chapter Thirteen •
A FAVOR ASKED

Shae was beginning to quite like her new home in North Sotto. Tackling the tasks of settling into an apartment made her feel productive and, even if she wasn't sure what she was going to do next as far as work was concerned, it gave her confidence that she could do this—she could live in Janloon and be near her family but still maintain her independence. She purchased attractive but basic furniture, stocked the apartment with necessities, and got used to cooking for one person again. She began exploring the neighborhood around her building and was pleased to find it contained an assortment of shops selling everything from brand name handbags to malodorous herbal powders, and a range of eateries from oyster bars to nighttime noodle stands. More upscale than the crowded, unkempt Sotto Village, North Sotto was a gentrifying, trendy district populated by young professionals, artists, and a decent smattering of foreign expats. Shae could wear bold prints and bright skirts from her Espenian wardrobe and far from looking out of place, appear trendsetting and stylish. This was Janloon at its most cosmopolitan and worldly.

However, even though an innocent visitor to the city might not notice it, it was apparent to Shae that the clan ruled here as strongly as it did anywhere else. She saw white lanterns—real ones or cheap paper cutouts—hanging in windows wherever she went. More than once she passed one or two, occasionally three, of Hilo's people. Without her jade, she could not Perceive their auras but they were easy to spot: tough, hard-bodied young men and sometimes women, well-dressed, casually armed with knives or blades, jade almost always on prominent display. Most people hurried past them, not wanting to draw any undue attention. Shae did the same, though for different reasons.

Her neighbors consisted of a twenty-something couple who looked as if they worked in the Financial District (the woman owned a tiny dog with the size and charm of an overfed rat), a single middle-aged woman who was always having her other single middle-aged woman friends over to drink wine and play loud card games, and a college age young man who moved into the apartment down the hall from Shae's about two weeks after she arrived. He seemed to come and go frequently, and after they'd nodded to each other several times when passing in the hallways or on the stairs, Shae thought she ought to introduce herself. She was hesitant to do so. Once she said the name Kaul, her pleasant anonymity here would end.

She told herself it was ridiculous to let such a thing prevent her from ever meeting anyone new. When she next saw her neighbor, they happened to be leaving the building at the same time. "I keep seeing you but I don't know your name," she said to him, smiling.

"Ah," he said, looking slightly abashed. He tipped his shoulders forward and touched his forehead in informal greeting. "I'm Caun Yudenru."

Shae returned the gesture. "I'm Shae."

Caun Yu raised his eyebrows. Heat rushed into Shae's cheeks. She'd meant to give her full name but somehow only the diminutive personal had escaped her mouth. *Gods*. He must be thinking her a shameless flirt. Caun *was* attractive—though he was younger than her and always wore the same black skull cap hat that made him look like a delinquent—but that wasn't the point. She wasn't interested in a rebound relationship. "It's nice to meet you, Mr. Caun." Shae backpedaled into formality, secretly cringing at what an odd mess she was making out of a simple encounter. "I will…see you soon, then."

Somehow, she kept her poise, smiled benignly, and strode down the street without hurrying, as if she'd meant to make a fool of herself all along.

Determined to start making some headway on finding employment, she went to the city library and perused business directories of Janloon, jotting down the names and addresses of companies that interested her into a coil-bound notebook. After a couple of hours of this, she was struck again, as she had been with the apartment hunt, by how needlessly slow and ineffective the process was. No Peak controlled businesses in many sectors, some through direct ownership but far more through patronage relationships with tribute-paying Lantern Men. A few well-placed phone calls and she could bypass all this legwork. She wondered if adhering to her policy of no help from the family was truly a worthy principle, or if she was just being prideful to the point of idiocy.

She knew what Hilo's opinion on that would be. Stubbornly, she persisted for another half an hour before closing the books and leaving the library, still not sure if she'd wasted her time or spent it well. On the way home, she bought a typewriter, to update her resume. She'd been back in her apartment not more than twenty minutes when there was a knock on her door.

She opened it to find Lan standing in the hallway. "May I come in?" he asked pleasantly.

She was so nonplussed that she didn't say anything, merely held the door open for him to enter. He stepped into her apartment, leaving his two bodyguards waiting outside, and closed the door behind him. For a moment, he glanced curiously around the main room. Shae felt a pang of deep embarrassment. How meager this place must appear to him, how cheap and unworthy a residence for a member of the Kaul family. She crossed her arms and sat down on her stiff new sofa, feeling defensive even though he hadn't yet said a word. If Hilo were here instead of Lan, he would be walking around, touching things. "It's nice," Hilo would say, shrugging and smiling like someone amused by a child who has thrown a fit and is now insisting on sleeping outside. "You like this place, Shae? So long as you like it, I guess."

Lan said, "Do you have anything to drink? It's still hot outside." He started toward the small kitchen, but Shae jumped up and said, "I'm sorry, let me get it. I should've offered but you…surprised me." She hurried past him into the kitchen, which really only fit one person comfortably anyways, and took a pitcher of chilled spiced tea from the fridge. She poured him a full glass, hastily arranged some sesame crackers and roasted nuts onto a plate and brought them back out to the front room.

Lan took the glass from her with a smile that seemed almost apologetic, as if he had not meant to put her to any trouble, then motioned her back to the sofa and sat down next to her, shifting on the overly firm new cushions.

"Is…everything all right?" Shae asked. She could not understand why

Lan would come to her instead of summoning her to the Kaul house.

Lan said sternly, "Do I need an excuse to come see my little sister?" When she froze at the apparent rebuke, he winked at her to show he was teasing, and the gesture was both so much like Lan at his most relaxed, and also so at odds with the earnest air of command he possessed as Pillar that Shae laughed.

Lan drained half his glass, then turned to her with a more serious expression. "I *am* here for a reason, Shae." He chose his words before speaking. "I've been having doubts about whether Doru is telling me everything I need to know. You can't find a more seasoned Weather Man, and you know how close he is to Grandda. But there are things he's said, small things, that make me think that I can't count on him completely."

Shae made a face; she despised Doru. "You should replace him."

He turned his characteristicaly straight gaze on her. "I respect your decision not to be a part of the clan business. I don't like the idea of you walking around the city without jade, but I'm not going to stop you either. Whatever it is you decide to do, I'll support you. I've told you that before and it hasn't changed."

"But," Shae added. Her shoulders sagged. *It was only a matter of time…*

"I need someone I trust, someone who knows the business, to go up to the mines and take a look around. Go through their books, check to see that everything's in order, and make sure it matches official KJA records. As a favor to me."

Shae didn't answer right away. Now she understood why he'd come to her apartment on the pretense of a visit instead of having this conversation in the house where Doru might notice and wonder. "Is that all?" she asked.

He furrowed his brow, as if suspecting sarcasm. "It's weeks of work."

"I know, but this is all you're asking for, nothing else after that?"

"No," he said. "This is all. I won't pull you into the clan business by stealthy degrees, Shae, if that's what you're suspecting of me." There was a slight harshness in his voice that made Shae drop her eyes guiltily. Years ago, her work for the Espenians had begun with a few small, simple requests that had led to slightly larger requests, that had led to her having her own code name and file folder on the desk of an Espenian colonel. Shae had not forgotten that a single step in one direction might portend an irrevocable change in one's path. But this was her brother asking, not Jerald or any of his smiling superiors. By suspecting Lan's intentions, she'd affronted his pride after he'd already stooped to coming here and asking his younger sister for help.

As Pillar, Lan could demand her allegiance; he could ask her to kneel and reaffirm her oaths, and could cut her out of the family if she refused. He had not done that. She did not think he would consider it even if she said no to his request. She'd always taken Lan for granted and she was reminded of that now.

A sudden trip south into the interior of the island would delay her admittedly vague job hunting plans, but it wasn't as if she was under any deadline. "I'll go, Lan," she said. "As a favor to you."

• Chapter Fourteen •
GOLD AND JADE

As the Pillar, Lan had a handful of personal staff headed by his longtime Academy friend, Woon Papidonwa, who were part of neither the military nor business halves of No Peak, and did not answer to either the Horn or the Weather Man. They managed Lan's schedule in addition to administrative and household tasks such the maintenance and security of the Kaul estate and other clan properties such as the beachhouse in Marenia. Although they held little formal authority in the clan, these individuals were not to be disregarded; the lead Pillarman was often a confidante of the Pillar and oftentimes went on to hold more influential positions.

His grandfather's stubborn lack of cooperation notwithstanding, Lan was more intent than ever to transition Yun Doru into retirement and appoint his own Weather Man within the year. Given recent events and the tension between the clans, however, it would be unwise to lose the current Weather Man until Lan had a new one that he had complete confidence in, ready to take over. Woon was secretly one of his leading candidates to replace Doru but Lan had doubts as to whether his ever stalwart aide was clever enough to step into such an important role in the clan. He resolved to include Woon in more substantive tasks over the next few months to see how he handled them. In the meantime, perhaps Kaul Sen would soften his stance.

So he took Woon alone with him to Wisdom Hall to meet with Chancellor Son. A wide and imposing structure of dark brick and red tile, Wisdom Hall housed the legislative chambers of the Royal Council of Kekon, the official governing body of the nation. It sat a stone's throw away from the Triumphal palace, where Prince Ioan III and his family lived in state-funded ceremonial leisure. Both buildings were located in the Monuments district, which, despite being less than fifteen minutes away from the

Kaul estate, was the most clan neutral territory in Janloon aside from the Temple district. The driver pulled Lan's silver Roewolfe roadster right up to the long reflecting pool in front of the imposing tiers of marble steps. Lan and his Pillarman got out and crossed the stone pathway that bisected the still, glass-like water, both of them stopping, as was tradition when one reached the end of the walk, to salute the Warrior's Memorial.

The Warrior's Memorial was a pair of large bronze statues. The smaller one was of a boy holding up a lantern, presumably illuminating the face of the other statue, a nameless Green Bone warrior who knelt in front of the child. It looked as if the man had come across the child alone and was kneeling down to bring him to safety. Or it might have been that the child had come across the warrior, bereft in the darkness, and was holding out the lantern to light his way. Either interpretation would be suitably nationalistic. The inscription on the base of the monument read:

Out of Darkness
In memory of the Mountain Men who fought for Kekon's freedom
and the brave citizens who aided them

Lan tried to picture his irascible old grandfather as the young warrior captured in bronze, one of the patriotic freedom fighters who opposed fifty years of Shotarian rule and eventually forced a powerful empire, weakened by the Many Nations War but still possessing far superior numbers and weaponry, to relinquish Kekon to its people. It struck Lan as remarkable that it had been only a generation ago that Green Bones were persecuted as bandits and criminals, secretly abetted by a populace that celebrated their superhuman exploits. Now here he was, walking into Wisdom Hall to meet with one of the highest-ranking politicians in the country. In some ways, Lan thought, it must have been simpler—dangerous but more heroic—to be a Green Bone back in his grandfather's days, when the enemy had been a cruel foreign power.

The statue of the kneeling fighter was depicted with a moon blade carried at his waist and the armbands he wore had settings for many small gems. Walking past the memorial, Lan noticed that the settings were empty; vandals had stolen the memorialized warrior's jade, even though they were nothing more than inert decorative green rocks.

The foyer of Wisdom Hall was a splendidly wide space with pale marble tiling and thick green columns stretching up to the elaborately painted ceiling. Lan and Woon were met by a young aide, who saluted them respectfully and escorted them to the Chancellor's office. "Son is bound to ask for something," Lan said to Woon in a quiet aside as they walked. "Think on what that might be and what we ought to grant him."

They were shown through a set of double wooden doors. As they entered, the Chancellor came around his massive desk to salute and greet them. Son Tomarho was a powerfully-built man of about fifty with a dimpled chin and bushy eyebrows. He must have been a physically formidable man in his youth but years of good living in middle age had melted the cords of muscle into rolls of fat. The Chancellor beamed a broad politician's smile at Lan. "Kaul-jen, come in, come in, how are the gods favoring you?"

"Well enough, Chancellor," Lan replied, exchanging a few minutes of pleasantry before settling himself into the seat in front of Son's desk. Woon positioned the other chair properly behind and to the left of Lan's before seating himself.

The Chancellor sank into his high-backed leather chair, which gave a protesting sigh. Lacing his hands over the curve of his generous paunch, he regarded Lan with nodding attentiveness. "What troubles the Pillar of the clan, that I can help with?"

Lan gathered his thoughts. "Chancellor Son, I'm afraid I'm paying you this visit out of a sense of great concern."

Unlike his siblings, Lan remembered his father. In the last year of the Many Nations War, some months before Kaul Dushuron fell in one of the final battles against the beleaguered Shotarian army, Lan asked his father, "Who will be in charge of Kekon when the Shotties are gone? Will it be you?"

"No," said Kaul Du indulgently. "It won't be me."

"Will it be Grandda? Or Ayt-jen?"

"It won't be any of us. We're Green Bones." His father was copying a list of names, a train schedule, and a map onto three separate sets of paper and sealing them in unmarked envelopes. "Gold and jade, never together."

"Why do people say that?" Lan had often heard the phrase in casual conversation. "Gold and jade" was a Kekonese idiom that referred to greed and excess. An inappropriate level of overreach. A person hoping for too much good fortune might be warned, "Don't ask for gold and jade." A child who demanded a custard tart after already having had a sweet bun was, Lan knew from personal experience, likely to be scolded, *"You want gold and jade together!"*

Lan's father glanced up at him with a squint. For a moment, Lan was afraid that his persistent questions had annoyed his father and he would be sent out of the room so the man could finish his task in peace. Kaul Du was not a regular presence in the house; he and Lan's grandfather were gone for long periods of time on secretive missions, and when they were back, Lan's grandmother and mother treated the occasion like a personal visit from the gods—a great honor, an unnatural disruption, something to be celebrated but best gotten through quickly. Kaul Du kissed his children but did not know how to relate to them. He spoke to Lan as he would an adult. In the other room, Lan's infant brother Hilo wailed as their mother tried to comfort him.

"A long time ago, many hundreds of years before the Shotarians came, there were three kingdoms on Kekon." Kaul Du spoke while directing half of his attention back to his lists and maps. "The kingdom of Jan along the northern coast where we are now, Hunto in the central basin, and Tiedo on the southern peninsula. Hunto was the largest, but the Hunto king was thin-blooded and obsessed with jade. One night, he went horribly insane from the Itches and swept through the palace murdering his family, including his own children."

Lan's eyes shifted to the ample jade his father wore around his neck and wrists. Noticing this, Kaul Du grinned and snatched Lan by the arm, pulling him close with rough affection. "Does that worry you, son?" Kaul Du yanked his talon knife from the sheath on his belt and held it up between them. Lan could see how fine the edge was, how the hilt was weathered to his father's hand. "Are you worried about you da? What might happen to him?" Kaul Du asked.

"No," Lan said, his voice calm. At the age of eight, he knew that all the men of his family were Green Bones and this meant they wore jade and swore oaths to a secret clan that fought against the injustice of the foreigners.

"Good," said his father, his arm still tight around Lan's shoulders. "You needn't be. Some people are meant to carry jade, and some aren't. You are, and so is your little brother, same as your da and grandda. Here, hold the talon knife—don't you have one of your own yet? Gods, you should, I ought to have seen to that already. Go on, it's only a few stones, it won't hurt you."

Lan held the weapon and spun it in his grip the way he'd practiced with a toy knife. The jade pieces in the hilt were smooth to the touch and made his chest buzz in a warm and pleasant way, as if he'd taken a great gasp of air after holding his breath for a long time. His father looked on approvingly. Lan said, "So what happened, after the king killed his family?"

Kaul Du took his talon knife and returned it to its sheath. "With the Hunto royal family all dead, the kingdoms of Jan and Tiedo invaded and carved it up between them, then went to war with each other. Eventually, Kekon was united. From then on it was decreed for the safety of the country that those who govern would not wear jade, and those who wear jade would not govern."

In the other room, Hilo's colicky screams, which had blissfully abated, started up again with renewed vigor. "Curse that howler demon of a baby," Lan's father growled, but a smug smile crept over his exasperation. The oft-quoted Kekonese old wives' tale was that the more unmanageable the infant, the better of a fighter he was destined to become. In the distance, a new sound pierced the night: air raid sirens over Janloon, shrieking atop Hilo's bawling.

Lan's father ignored the noise and continued in a calm undertone. "A man who wears the crown of a king can't wear the jade of a warrior. Gold and jade, never together. We Green Bones live by aisho. We defend the country from its enemies and the weak from the strong." Kaul Du held his son out at arm's length. His left eye narrowed and his expression grew thoughtful. "After this war is over, after the Shotties are defeated, the clan will have to rebuild the country and protect the people from disorder. Ah, I don't think I'll be alive to see it, Lan-se, but you'll have to be a different kind of Green Bone than me."

"I want you to pass a law," Lan said to Chancellor Son. "One that prevents any one clan from gaining majority shareholder status of the Kekon Jade Alliance."

The Chancellor pursed his thick lips. "Interesting," he said slowly, "considering that ownership structure of the KJA has remained largely unchanged for the past fifteen years, with the two largest clans in the country each holding roughly equal ownership."

"Thirty-nine percent held by the Mountain, thirty-five percent by No Peak, with the rest divided among the minor clans," Lan clarified. "And if I might correct you, Chancellor, the most recent shift occurred last year, when the Mountain increased their ownership by two and half percent after annexing the Three Run clan. Which they accomplished by killing all the jaded members of the Run family." Chancellor Son grimaced and Lan suppressed a wry quirk of the mouth. It never hurt to remind politicians that Green Bones operated on a different standard of speed and violence.

"Is this law you're proposing a…defensive move, Kaul-jen?" Son's voice was coolly probing now. An indent formed between his thick grey eyebrows as they drew together. Lan could guess at what the man was thinking: did he have reason to fear that the Mountain might conquer the smaller clans, or gods forbid, take No Peak itself?

"It's a defensive move for the country," Lan said firmly. "The KJA was formed after the war under the reasonable assumption that Green Bones should be in charge of managing the country's jade supply. The thinking was that naturally all the clans would have a vested interest in cooperating to restrict and protect the supply of jade. But that was before the invention of SN1, before money from foreign exports started rolling in, and before… certain changes of leadership in the major clans."

Son was blunt. "Do you think the Mountain is seeking to control the KJA?"

"I think it's in the national interest to remove that temptation."

"The national interest, or No Peak's interest?"

Lan dropped a strong hint of reprove into his voice. "I'm not seeking an advantage for No Peak. Any law the Council passes regarding the KJA would apply equally to my clan as it would to Ayt Madashi's." He leaned forward so his elbows rested on Son's desk. The motion tugged up his shirt sleeves and for a second the Chancellor's eyes flicked down to the glimpse of the jade-studded cuffs on Lan's forearms. "Jade is our national resource; it should never be controlled by any one person or group. There needs to be a balance of power."

Chancellor Son scratched the side of his face and said thoughtfully, "It would be difficult to word such a law to prevent circumvention. A determined party could work through subsidiaries or intermediaries to gain a controlling interest."

"I'm sure the Council has clever people who could figure it out." Lan relaxed his tone, realizing with satisfaction that they were moving from the *if* into the *how*. "Trigger an automatic redistribution of ownership among the other shareholders if any one clan and its affiliates reaches a forty-five percent ownership threshold. Or create a provision that nationalizes the KJA if it falls under single-clan control. I don't think there would ever be need to take such an extreme measure," Lan added, upon seeing the Chancellor's incredulous expression, "but it would dissuade any clan from thinking it can control the country's jade by eliminating rivals."

Son breathed out heavily through his nose and drummed his sausage fingers on the desk. "A law isn't made and enacted by magic or by my will alone of course," he said with a smile. "It would need to pass the Council; for that, we would need the support of every No Peak-affiliated member and nearly all the independents."

"It's a good thing then," said Lan with an equally meaningful smile, "that I came directly to someone whose friendship to the clan is so old and strong. A man who has the influence to make these things happen."

The Chancellor grunted and gave a little wave of his hand but looked pleased. Before entering political life, Son Tomarho had been a reasonably wealthy Lantern Man in the No Peak clan. His daughters now ran the family textile business and still paid their clan tributes in the proper amounts and on time. Son was the highest No Peak man in government; everyone knew that. Nearly all the councilmen and their staff in Wisdom Hall were affiliated with one of the Green Bone clans; the Council Treasurer, in the office down the hall from Son, was a well-known Mountain loyalist.

Gold and jade, never together, Lan's father had told him more than twenty-five years ago. The axiom had not turned out to be as simple as that. After the war, the Green Bones, led by the examples of Kaul Sen and Ayt Yu, had indeed faithfully acted in accordance with aisho, eschewing political power and retiring to private life. But they were out of the shadows for good. They no longer hid and trained in the mountains, but lived openly in the cities they'd fought to liberate. In the years of postwar chaos and rapid growth, the common people continued to look to them for protection and favors just as they had under decades of oppressive foreign rule, and they provided it. Their secret network of affiliates—the Lantern Men—became a vehicle for business instead of war. They wielded influence and granted appointments and contracts to comrades and loyal allies from the occupation days. Those that the Shotarians had branded as criminals had become the ruling class of the island. And while not formally a part of the Kekonese government, the clans were so enmeshed in its workings that the two had become in many ways indistinguishable.

It was why, coming to this meeting, Lan had had no doubt of its eventual outcome—Son Tomarho would do as Lan had asked. It was only a matter of how quickly, how enthusiastically, and at what price. Now the Chancellor sat back and said, with the practiced friendliness of a senior statesmen, "Kaul-jen, you know me. I want what's best for the country, and I agree with you one hundred percent. We are in full accord on this issue. But I anticipate that it might be difficult to get all the votes we need. Loyal to the clan as they may be, some of the councilmen would be wary of publicly supporting something that appears to deliberately single out the Mountain's behavior. It would be much easier to garner support for your proposal if the clan gave some sign that it was eager to take other substantial steps in the public interest."

"Didn't we agree that creating this law is itself a large step in the public interest?" Of course, Lan had anticipated that Son would push for more, but secretly, he was annoyed all the same. The Chancellor ought to realize that protecting the KJA from one-clan rule was within his civic duty to pursue regardless of whether No Peak granted him other patronage requests. But Lantern Man habits died hard.

"We did, we did," Son conceded amiably, "but the common citizens also have more immediate, more tangible concerns. The smooth functioning of our city port, for example. As you surely know, there was a worker's strike in the Docks some months ago that dragged on to the city's detriment. My family and several others asked for assistance from the Horn of No Peak but were, unfortunately, not granted it."

"I leave the Horn's decisions to the Horn," Lan said, "and in this specific case, I agree with his judgment." The Son family and other Lantern Man petitioners had wanted Hilo to send his men to intimidate the union bosses and break up their gatherings, rough folks up if needed, force them back to work. Hilo had snorted. "What do they think we are? Hired thugs?" The workers in the Docks were No Peak constituents too. The union bosses paid tribute. Lan had been impressed by his brother that time. Hilo was never hesitant to show force, but at least he was calculating about it, and he knew not to let Lantern Men think they could get away with asking for too much.

Now though, Lan needed Son's cooperation, so he said, "I appreciate your concerns and understand the burden it must have been to take those business losses. I'm sure there's something we can do to ease the strain. The Weather Man is especially busy these days, so I'll ask Woon-jen to make sure this is prioritized."

In saying this, Lan communicated that he was giving Woon permission to speak. As was expected of any subordinate member of the clan in this situation, he had remained entirely silent as the Pillar alone did the talking, betraying no emotion but carefully observing the opposing party so he could later corroborate or dispel his boss's impressions. Now though, the Pillarman leaned forward and Lan waited, with some nervousness, to see how his test would go.

Woon said, "Chancellor, I understand that some industries, textile and garments for example, are facing stiff competition from foreign imports. Perhaps a clan-enforced tariff at point of entry would help level the playing field for our Kekonese producers?"

Lan was pleased. It was a good thing to offer: increasing dock taxes on imported foreign textiles would bring in revenue for the clan, would be fairly easy to implement and enforce, and would benefit the Son family's business handsomely without granting too much for nothing to other Lantern Men. The Chancellor was pretending to ponder Woon's words but Lan could see the satisfied smile he was holding in check. "Yes, that would indeed be beneficial."

Lan stood up, straightening his cuffs. "We're agreed, then."

The Chancellor heaved himself to his feet and walked them to the door of his office. "Your grandfather—may he live three hundred years—how is he these days, Kaul-jen?"

"Sadly, age steals from all of us eventually, even Green Bones," Lan said mildly, recognizing the seemingly considerate question for what it was: a prying into how much Kaul Sen still ran No Peak from behind his grandson. Son wanted to know if he could count on the agreements he'd made with Lan to be the final word from the clan. "My grandfather is not his old self, but he is still well, and enjoying his much deserved retirement."

Son touched his soft, meaty hands to his forehead in salute.

• Chapter Fifteen •
A BARGAIN WITH DEMONS

Outside the warehouse stood a dozen souped-up Torroyo motorcycles in the garish neon shades preferred by Janloon's northside bikers: violent red, lime green, electric blue. Hilo paused to admire a couple of them, patting the contoured leather seat of a particularly striking vehicle, bending to examine the gleaming engine and peering briefly over the dash before continuing on to the aluminium door of the repurposed building, which vibrated with the pounding bass of loud music.

With him was Maik Tar and two senior Fingers that Hilo hoped to soon promote to Fists: the clever but slightly pudgy and unassuming Obu had better Deflection than anyone Hilo had ever met, but needed to learn how to command if he was to advance; the other Finger, Iyn, had no especially superlative jade talent, but like many female Green Bones, particularly on the Horn's side of the clan, was accustomed to working harder than her male counterparts, which Hilo appreciated. Iyn Ro and Maik Tar had an on-again, off-again relationship which was currently off; they were too similar and as lovers, they fought like cats.

The four Green Bones strode into the motorcycle gang's headquarters. Roughly twenty bikers, almost all between the ages of sixteen and twenty-five, were sprawled on battered old sofas, drinking and smoking, some shooting pool, a few watching television. Three men were openly counting a pile of money in one corner. Hilo looked around with interest. As far as gangs in the Coinwash district went, the Chrome Demons maintained one of the better equipped and appointed abodes, with relatively less filth, vermin, and drugged indolence.

All eyes turned to the intruders. A second later, every member of the Chrome Demons was on his feet, hands going for guns and knives and whatever other weapons were on hand: bottles, pool cues. The trio of men in the corner jumped up and tried, amusingly, to hide the large stack of money behind them.

Tar shouted, "Listen up, curs!" Someone shut off the music.

"Who owns the beautiful fire red Torroyo RP550 out front?" Hilo asked.

"I do," came a reply from the back of the room. A surly man stepped forward. He was heavily built and wore, as was the style of his gang, a leather jacket with the sleeves sliced into tatters. His thick hair was styled into two stiff and vaguely phallic humps on his head. He appeared a few years older than most of the youths around him, and Hilo deduced from his superior vehicle and his authoritative swagger that he was the leader of this cell of Demons.

"What do you value more, your face or your bike?" Hilo asked him.

"What?" growled the man uncomprehendingly.

"Your face or your bike," Hilo repeated. "Which would you choose?"

The man's eyes flicked down to the jade studs visible across Hilo's collarbone, and then over at Maik, Obu, and Iyn. "My face," he said hesitantly.

Instantly, Hilo struck him, breaking his nose. The man fell back, eyes streaming, stunned with pain; he hadn't even had time to raise his hands in defense. A few of the younger Demons, who were less wise to the world, made sudden moves to unload their pistols but before a single shot could be fired, Obu flung a Deflection that hurled every member of the gang back against the walls and caused the sofas and heavy pool table to skid several feet.

As the Chrome Demons staggered back to their feet, Hilo said reasonably, "We've heard many complaints about the noise and disorderliness of street racing in this neighborhood. Also the number of robberies is getting out of hand. It's obvious from such fine rides parked outside that the Chrome Demons are not short on money. So it's only fair you criminals should pay tribute to the clan that takes care of the law-abiding people you so carelessly inconvenience."

As Hilo spoke, Iyn walked the warehouse floor with a large canvas bag, collecting the ample pile of cash from the back table and confiscating guns with businesslike efficiency. With Maik and Obu watching every move, no one dared to put up an additional fight. The Chrome Demons were a rough lot, with street-hardened, tattooed, glowering killers among them, but many of them rapidly handed over their weapons and money in resignation; they'd obviously been fined by Green Bones before and understood that they were guaranteed to get out alive if they cooperated and guaranteed not to if they didn't. Clan oversight over every aspect of society, including crime, was largely accepted as part of life in Janloon. One foolish man leered at Iyn but she turned such an eagerly murderous look on him that he stopped contritely and emptied his pockets before she could break any of his bones. Hilo was pleased with both of his Fingers; so far they had taken their cues from him and applied the proper amount of force. Neither had overreacted, yet no one in the room questioned they would shed blood without hesitation. It was a tricky balance that a Green Bone had to strike.

Iyn came back and set the bag of weapons and money on the ground at Hilo's feet. "Normally," he said, "I would take your ill-acquired gains and leave you with the warning that if I heard more complaints I would send you and your bikes to the bottom of the harbor. But that's something I could've sent any of my Fists to do. It's not why I'm here."

"Why the fuck *are* you here?" slurred the leader, holding his face.

"Good of you to ask," said Hilo. "You know of Three Fingered Gee?"

"Gee's dead," someone in the room called out.

"Feeding the worms," Hilo agreed. "The man who killed him works for the Mountain. I'm sure of it but I want to know *how*. I want to know what he's doing and who he's working with. A lot of this—" Hilo nudged the sack of money and guns with his foot, "—comes from the brewing and selling of street shine to jade thieves and smugglers. The sort of folks that buy and trade with black market carvers like Tem Ben. So here's my offer: follow your contacts. Your thieves and pickpockets, your shine dealers and pimps. Do it *quietly*. Find me Tem Ben and as many of those who work with him as you can, and I'll walk out, leaving this bag on the floor." Hilo turned his hands up and gestured magnanimously around the disordered warehouse. "Obu, Iyn, and Maik Tar will come back expecting news, but you won't see me again so long as you don't cause any more trouble in No Peak territory. What you do or take from across the border however—in Fishtown or the Stump—*that*, I'm willing to overlook."

There was a pregnant silence punctuated by murmuring shuffles. The

Horn of No Peak had, with certain caveats, essentially given the Chrome Demons a free pass. A reprieve from clan repression and taxation in exchange for information, and he'd all but encouraged them to wreck havoc in Mountain territory and steal back across to Coinwash without repercussion if they could get away with it. The men in the warehouse shifted with dubious excitement; the Horn must be angry indeed. Clan war might spell opportunity.

"We should agree, Okan," one of the younger bikers said in an eager whisper to the leader, who was staunching his bleeding nose with his shirt.

"*I'll* decide what we do," Okan snarled at the youth, evidently trying to reassert his severely diminished authority. He turned back around and frowned fearsomely at the intrusive Green Bones but did not quite meet their eyes, staring instead at the bag between the Horn's feet. The man had no jade aura, of course, but Hilo could still Perceive the tension in him clearly: humiliation and pain, warring with the growing sullen awareness that he was being offered something he would be deeply foolish to refuse. At last he said, "So do we get a cut when you take out Tem Ben and the Mountain's people?"

"Don't be ridiculous," Hilo said sharply, and the easy manner that he'd displayed thus far vanished so quickly that everyone in the warehouse, even Hilo's own people, flinched at the change. "That's *clan* business. You find me Tem and tell me about his activities and connections, but what happens after that is between Green Bones. I'm putting you in a better spot than the Reds or the Seven Ones or any of the other gangs. You abuse my generous nature on No Peak ground and I'll find out, and gods help you. Now tell me your answer."

Okan mumbled, "All right; we understand each other. We agree."

"That's 'Yes, Kaul-jen,' and kneel when you pledge your word to the Horn, you dog," said Maik Tar angrily. Hilo thought that last bit was unnecessary; the gang leader was already resentful and cowed enough, and as much as Hilo appreciated the younger Maik's fervent nature, Tar's excitable cruelty detracted rather than added to the impact of the Horn's words.

Hilo said nothing, making a mental note to himself to correct Tar later. Instead, he picked up the canvas bag at his feet and handed it back to Okan with an air of mild ceremony, symbolically restoring enough of the man's lost respect that he was reasonably confident the rest of the gang would abide by the agreement reached tonight.

The leader of the Chrome Demons, still seething, knelt in front of Hilo on the concrete floor of the warehouse and raised his hands in a salute.

• Chapter Sixteen •
THE JADE MINE

Shae paused to wipe the sweat from her forehead. The Espenian city of Windtown where she'd attended business school had been an arid, high-altitude place surrounded by prairie farmland and heavy manufacturing. She'd hated the bitterly cold, howling foreign winters, but now she found the oppressive humidity of Kekon's mountainous interior difficult to adjust to. Despite the brief downpour the night before, here on the southern side of the island, this was already considered dry season. At the height of the spring blossom rains, torrential downpours washed out the roads and shut down the area entirely.

The mine site office was a short but steep walk up a muddy path from where the driver had parked the coughing, rusted truck on a gravel lot next to two dirt-encrusted excavators. Each step in Shae's two day journey had been taken by progressively slower means: first, the city subway to Grand Island Station, then the long bus ride out of Janloon to the predominantly Abukei town of Pula, then the hired truck, and now the last bit covered on foot, each squelching step taking her a little closer to the source of jade itself.

The canopy of green overhead filtered the sunlight that cut through the high branches in bright shafts. The chittering of birds and the occasional hoot of a monkey reminded her of how vibrant and alive the forest was, and despite the fact that her shirt clung unpleasantly to her skin and beads of sweat ran down between her breasts and made her itch, Shae felt happy to have agreed to Lan's request after all. Janloon was a study in contradictions that could befuddle even someone born there; a bubbling, dirty stew and a modern, glamorous metropolis at the same time, a place overly conscious of trying to be a world-class city, despite being at its core a system of clan fiefdoms.

Outside the city though, Kekon was a lovely island. Shae could see why in ancient times foreign sailors had called it the "cursed beauty." Being up here on the mountain was just the thing she'd needed to remind herself viscerally why she'd returned. There was something special about her home, about being Kekonese, that ran deeper than the unavoidable difficulties of being a Kaul.

The mine supervisor's office was a small shack that looked as if it had survived a few landslides and still clung precariously to the mountain by dint of the logs roughly driven into the ground on its downslope side to prop up its tilting walls. Shae knocked on the door. She could hear the rumble of machinery and activity down in the mine pit, so someone must be on duty. She waited, but when no one answered, she opened the door and went straight in.

She found the supervisor engrossed in watching a relayball game on the small black and white television in the back room. He jumped when she walked in. "Who are you?" He shut the television off hastily and looked her up and down in surprise. She guessed he did not get young city women coming up here often, even ones in dirt-caked boots and trousers rolled halfway up their calves.

"I knocked but you must not have heard me," Shae said.

"Yes, yes, sorry. I'm half deaf," he said. "What do you want? Are you with anyone?" He squinted at her suspiciously. It wasn't unheard of for spectacularly unwise thieves to try and steal from the mine site itself. The supervisor glanced at his desk, where, Shae guessed, he kept his gun.

"I'm here to inspect the operations and your records," Shae explained.

"I wasn't told anything about an inspection. Under whose authority are you here?"

"Under the authority of my brother, Kaul Lanshinwan, the Pillar of No Peak." Shae pulled out an envelope and handed it over. The supervisor broke the seal and scanned the letter, frowning. It was written in Lan's hand, signed with his name and his title as a director on the board of the Kekon Jade Alliance, and stamped with the clan's circular insignia in red ink.

The supervisor folded the letter and looked up at Shae with grudging politeness. "Very well. What would you like to see, Kaul-jen? Miss Kaul?" He studied her uncomfortably again, clearly confused that she did not appear to be wearing any jade.

"Miss Kaul is fine," she said. "If you wouldn't mind taking me out to see the work site?"

The supervisor grumbled a little to himself, but ushered her out of the backroom into the office proper. He put on a brimmed straw hat and led the way out of the sagging building and down the path that followed the ridge. The noise of machinery grew louder, drowning out the sounds of the forest. As they walked, Shae felt a flutter of sensation that prickled her skin like a shift in the damp air. It grew stronger with each step she took, until it became an unmistakable tug in the gut, pulling her like a cord through the navel as they emerged from the trees onto a ledge that overlooked the entire stadium-sized pit. Shae let out a soft breath of awe.

In the old Abukei myths Shae remembered Kyanla telling her as a child, the First Mother goddess Nimuma fell into the ocean and perished from exertion after creating the world. Her body became the island of Kekon, and the veins of jade that ran under these mountains were her bones. Her green bones. If she imagined it like that, Shae thought, then the scene below was the largest grave digging operation imaginable. Here, the most valuable and coveted gemstone in the world was exposed to the air and pulled from the earth. From where Shae stood on the ledge, the huge rock-breaking machines and rickety aluminum roofed buildings were the size of toy models and the Abukei workers were small figures moving industriously around hills of debris. The air smelled of diesel exhaust and vibrated with the shrill whine of water-cooled diamond saws cutting into rock. Among the boulders on the ground, and in the beds of the enormous flat bed trucks where the muddy gray rocks had been cut apart, she saw the green gleam of raw jade.

"Careful, miss," called the supervisor as Shae started down the metal ramp that zig-zagged down the side of the pit to the activity below. She put a hand out to grip the railing as the soles of her muddy boots clanged down the latticed steel walk. The supervisor followed after her. "Stop at the sign, please!" he shouted over the rumbling noise of trucks and heavy equipment.

At the bottom of the second to last ramp was a small observation deck and a large mounted sign. *ATTENTION. Authorized personnel only beyond this point. This area is hazardous to those with jade sensitivity. Proceed at your own risk!*

Shae stopped. There was more raw jade here than was properly safe for anyone without immunity to be exposed to. Shae watched the Abukei workers walking on the ground below. They wore hard hats, thick gloves, and muddy canvas pants but worked bare-chested in the heat. Like their ancestors, only they could safely live deep in the interior of Kekon. In the modern world, the Abukei had carved out their second class place in society based on their immunity. The scrawny workers down there worked all day, every day, leaning up casually against the huge boulders and touching all that lustrous green without feeling what Shae felt now—the woozy craving in the bottom of her stomach, even deeper and more gnawing than hunger.

Deep-seated Kekonese prejudice maintained that the Abukei were an inferior race, but Shae had studied history and science at an Espenian university and knew that belief was erroneous. The Abukei had inhabited Kekon centuries before the first arrival of the Tun, so in truth *they* were the survivors. They lived unaffected by the substance that drove later explorers to murder each other or throw themselves into the sea. Ironic then, that now the more fortunate Abukei such as these ones worked for the Kekon Jade Alliance, performing back-breaking labor in order to drink and gamble and whore away their earnings during the idle three month height of the rainy season, while the less fortunate of their kin squatted in ramshackle huts by the river and dove for runoff.

Shae took a few more steps down the catwalk. If she'd been wearing any jade at all, the thrum of energy vibrating through her body would have been too much, overwhelming. The supervisor called, "Miss Kaul, did you read the sign?"

"I'm not going far," she shouted back. What would happen if she ignored him and went up to one of those boulders and placed the flat of her hand on the raw jade? She wondered if it would knock her unconscious or stop her heart. Would she, for an instant, experience a moment of unsurpassed power and clarity that would make her feel like a moth burning in ecstasy in a flame? Or would it have no immediate effect, but tomorrow, or a week or month from now, would she lose her mind in stages, and start cutting herself when the Itches came?

Pay attention. I'm here as a favor to Lan and no reason else. Shae pulled a pad of paper and a pen from her canvas rucksack and leaned over the railing, counting the trucks and workers. She made note of how many bulldozers and excavators were on site. Everything seemed to be in working order, nothing unusual or out of place. The men were dark and ropey from hard labor but they seemed to be healthy, efficient. She turned and made her way back up the ramps, the relieved supervisor tailing her. When they reached the tilting office again, Shae said, "I'd like to see the last two years' worth of financial records."

"The KJA has it all in their files," the supervisor said. "You could get copies from the Weather Man's staff in Janloon. All we have are original expense reports—"

"I'd like to see them please," Shae said.

Reluctantly, the man led her back into the room with the television. He opened a closet and turned on a single naked bulb. The closet was packed with cardboard filing boxes, stacked on top of each other and organized by date written on them in thick black marker. He cleared the television off the folding table and wiped the layer of dust off its surface with his bare forearm. It left damp streaks. "You can use this table," he offered, clearly resentful that she would make it impossible for him to sit back down in front of his relayball game for some time.

"Thank you," Shae said. "Would you please tell the driver of the truck I hired to wait. I may be a few hours. Do you have a copy machine?"

The man pointed it out to her, then left her alone. Shae could hear him clomping around, then turning on the radio in the other room. She found the most recently dated cardboard box, hefted it out of the closet and onto the small table and opened it. She pulled out the first thick file folder and sat down. Daily production reports. She flipped to an empty page on her pad of paper, then sat down and started to read. This was going to take a while.

It felt a little strange to examine the mining of jade with such analytical detachment. Scanning the dull files, jade mining came off like any other business, one with inputs and outputs, revenue and expenses. There were accounting statements, and invoices, and purchase orders. No different really than anything else that people manufactured and sold. Traditional Abukei folklore connected jade to the First Mother and the creation of the world. The Deitists believed it was a divine gift from the gods—the path to human salvation. Some foreign religions said it was an evil substance from the devil, a belief the Shotarians had forcibly espoused during their decades of rule. Jade was imbued with so much myth and emotion, so much mystery and power, and yet, here it was—boring. Something to be dug up, cut up, moved, carved, polished, sold for profit.

She made copies of the pages she thought were of importance, then moved on to the next folder. Personnel manifests. She flipped through them. She wondered what exactly she was looking for. Lan had told her to audit the operations, but he hadn't told her precisely what he thought might be out of place. The personnel lists corroborated the rising salary costs. There had been little turnover, but a couple of injuries and a number of new hires. It all seemed very ordinary. Some of the reports used technical terms, acronyms, and abbreviations she wasn't familiar with, but she possessed a solid enough grasp of the Kekonese mining sector to understand most of it. During her last two years at the Academy, she'd been tutored by old Doru, back when the clan had aspirations for her to hold a high post on the business side of No Peak—perhaps, even, to one day succeed Doru as Weather Man.

Unlike her brothers, Shae had not had a lot of friends at Kaul Du Academy. Of the other female students, the one she was closest to was Wan Payadeshan, the talented but shy daughter of a middling Lantern Man. Paya's mother had died from illness some years ago and Shae often brought her friend over to the Kaul house. One day Shae was searching for something, she could not even remember what, when she stumbled upon a manila envelope full of photographs in Doru's desk. Pretty Paya, in her underwear, Paya on her hands and knees, wearing a dog collar, Paya naked, legs spread, pale and awkward looking, eyes moist.

Her friend had cried in shame and abject relief when Shae told her never to come back to the house. She begged Shae to understand: she wasn't that kind of girl, she'd never wanted to do it, but Doru-jen was being so good to her father's business, what could she have said or done?

Shae told her grandfather that she would not be tutored by Doru anymore. She'd learn whatever else she needed to about the clan business from the senior Luckbringers such as Hami Tumashon, but she would not have anything more to do with the Weather Man. Be reasonable, Shae-se, Kaul Sen had said. Every man has weaknesses; you don't know what they did to

Doru-jen during the war; he has never treated *you* with any disrespect.

Years away had not dimmed Shae's loathing of Yun Dorupon. He'd cost her not just a friend, but the once matchless admiration she'd had for her grandfather.

Shae rummaged in her sack for a lunch tin—onion buns, shredded vegetables, and a marinated egg from the kitchen of last night's inn—along with a bottle of water. She ate as she continued to peruse documents. The mine supervisor poked his head into the room to ask how she was doing; Shae said she was fine. She'd figured out the filing system now and was efficiently pulling and copying the monthly financial summaries so she could read them in greater detail later and compare them with annual KJA statements. Her plan was to rent a room in Pula; that way she could come back up the mountain if she needed to. Even if she didn't find anything particularly interesting to report back to Lan, she would treat it as a working holiday of sorts, doing something useful while taking the time to relax in the countryside before having to begin her job hunt in earnest. At the very least, she would familiarize herself with the mining operations and if she could give Lan some advice on how to make improvements, she'd be putting her business degree to some immediate use. She lifted the lid on a new box and opened the next file. Equipment purchase orders.

The mine had made several significant capital investments in the past year—diamond-tipped core drills, heavy hydraulic spreaders, larger capacity trucks—most of it going to new and expanded mine sites. It struck Shae as poor planning to absorb all the cost in a single year; she wondered if the Weather Man's office applied any pressure on the KJA to do proper investment appraisals. She wrote: *Capital budgeting?!* in her notebook, then pulled another folder she'd marked and checked the financial statements; first year depreciation on new equipment was indeed driving most of the rise in operating expenses. Mine production was up fifteen percent over last year, though the increase hadn't been realized as revenue yet; perhaps the KJA was holding all that extra jade in inventory? The cartel kept strict control over how much jade was allotted to Green Bone schools, Deitist temples, and other licensed users in the military or health care fields, and how much was sold—primarily to the Espenian government. The rest was kept locked away in a massive national vault underneath the Kekon Treasury building.

Shae's eyes skipped over the equipment purchase order pages one more time. Her gaze landed on the signature at the bottom. It was not one that she had seen anywhere else in the files. She studied it for second before she realized whose name it was: Gont Aschentu. The Horn of the Mountain.

Why would the leader of the military arm of the Ayt clan be signing mining equipment purchase orders? Although the Green Bone clans were controlling stakeholders of the KJA, the mines themselves were state-operated, not managed by the clans directly. The annual budget for the mine's operations was approved by the KJA board, so any signature on this form ought to be from a representative that sat on or answered to the board—either Doru, or Ree Tura, the Weather Man of the Mountain, or one of their direct subordinates. What could it mean that Gont's signature was on this page, and several others?

Shae copied all the pages and tucked them carefully into her bag. She replaced the files, put the box back into the closet, and left the room. She wouldn't be staying in Pula tonight after all. She had a long trip back to the city and needed to get on the road as quickly as possible.

• Chapter Seventeen •
NIGHT AT THE LILAC DIVINE

The charm girl's voice was exquisite, by turns operatically high and pure, then sultry and suggestive. She played the Tun harp and sang with eyes closed, her dainty head and waves of dark hair swaying to the melody. Resting on the plush cushions, Lan let the tension drop out of his shoulders, and his mind fall quietly into the music. He was the only one in the opulent room; this was a private performance. The song was about a lost traveler missing his island home. No one here would have the poor tact to sing him lyrics about love or heartbreak.

Lan was accustomed to traveling with one or two bodyguards, but he came to the Lilac Divine Gentleman's Club alone. He wanted to enjoy himself without being tailed by anyone else in the clan. While he was here, he didn't want to think about being the Pillar. Mrs. Sugo, the Lantern Man owner of the Lilac Divine, was appreciative of that fact, and could be counted on for her discretion as well as her excellent taste. There was never any trouble at this place either; everyone knew it was a No Peak-frequented establishment and a person would have to be suicidal to cause problems, even if the gambling downstairs got out of hand.

Green Bones could take credit for certain things, Lan figured. On the whole, Janloon was one of the safest cities in the world. The clans kept out foreign criminals and gangsters, stamped down street crime, and taxed and controlled vice at a level acceptable to the politicians and the public. If some of Mrs. Sugo's late-night offerings were not entirely legal, she had the good sense to make her clan tribute payments timely and generous, and to spare no effort in making Lan's visits enjoyable.

Yunni, the charm girl, stretched out the last melancholy note of the song, her throat vibrating as her fingers danced lightly across the harp strings. Lan set down his wine glass and applauded. Yunni ducked her chin with false shyness, looking up at him through dusted eyelashes. "Did you enjoy that one, Lan-jen?"

"Very much so. It was beautiful."

She started to stand and let the silk scarf fall from her shoulders, but Lan said, "Do you have another song?"

She sat back down gracefully. "Something a little more cheerful, perhaps?" She plucked at the strings and launched into a light-hearted ballad.

Lan rested his eyes on the curve of her neck and the plump red gloss of her moving lips. He admired the way her gauzy dress hung off the slopes of her breasts and pale thighs. It was getting easier to work himself up to being with her. As Pillar, he could have any of the girls here, more than one at a time if he wanted, but the first few times he'd come, after he'd accepted that Eyni was gone for good, all he'd asked for was to sit and listen to Yunni sing. He'd told himself he didn't want sex—just an escape, just company. He shuddered at the sorts of places Doru had attempted to suggest to him on a few occasions. But Yunni was easy to talk to, and beautiful in both voice and body. She was neither overly deferential nor too eager to please; she conversed with him about music and foreign films but never asked him to say anything about the clan or its affairs. When he did finally take her to bed, he found her pleasing and energetic.

Tonight, though, he found it harder than usual to forget his worries. There had been no further communication between the clans for over two months, but Lan knew that Ayt could read his actions clearly enough. He'd declined the Mountain's proposal to join forces in producing shine, he'd set Chancellor Son to proposing KJA reforms, and instead of removing Hilo, he'd allowed his brother to bolster clan presence along all territorial borders. He believed he'd acted correctly in each case, but Lan knew he was walking a perilous line, particularly with the latter decision.

Just last week, there'd been a minor spate of motorcycle gang violence between Coinwash and Fishtown—enough to garner a short mention in the news, which was saying something as both neighborhoods were such crowded, destitute slums that a few killings there would normally never merit attention. Green Bones were not directly involved, so neither clan could claim offense, but everyone knew the Horns on both sides of the border not only kept the criminal class in line but manipulated it as well. Lan worried that it would only take one Green Bone or Lantern Man being caught or implicated in a violent incident for it to escalate to something that openly involved the clans themselves.

Lan knew his brother well. Subtlety was not in Hilo's nature. He respected clan hierarchy too much to ever disobey the Pillar on important matters, but he had complete day-to-day authority over the clan's activities on the streets, and his personal code was to leave no doubt that he would go further than his enemies if wronged. A look would be returned with a word, a word with a blow, a blow with a beating, a beating with an execution. Perhaps it *would* be better to have a Horn that was more prudent and restrained, who wouldn't raise overflowing tensions even further.

However, alienating his brother might be the worst possible move. There was no one who could, or would, step in to fill Hilo's role. The Fists of No Peak, and by extension the Fingers, weren't just loyal to the clan, or to the office of the Horn—they were loyal to Kaul Hilo. It disturbed Lan far more than he cared to admit that, if forced to choose between him and Hilo, many of the Green Bone warriors in the clan might side with his younger brother. By asking that he replace his Horn as a condition for future negotiation, Ayt was demanding that he knowingly weaken and sow dissent within his own clan. She was placing him in a dilemma that held all the makings of a trap.

"You look as if you could use a massage." Yunni had finished playing her song and come to sit beside him. Lan had barely noticed.

"I'm sorry," he said. "I know I seem distracted."

"You have a lot on your mind," she said kindly. He appreciated her patient acceptance; it was something Eyni had not been willing to give. He ran a hand down her long sleek hair and brought some of it to his face, enjoying the feel and smell of it as she unbuttoned his shirt and drew it over his shoulders.

"Wait," he said. He stood up and went to the dresser in the corner of the room. In the mirror, under the dim red lighting, he saw himself, bare-chested, and wondered if he really could live up to being the person he appeared to be—a strong, assured man, a hard-bodied Green Bone warrior, a leader adorned in jade. A man like his father.

Lan took off his jade-studded belt and the cuffs on his forearms, leaving on only the beads he wore on a chain around his neck. He shut his belt and cuffs in the safe below the dresser and turned the combination lock. Yunni claimed she was half-Abukei, nearly a stone-eye, but he removed most of his jade out of consideration for her anyways, just to be safe.

In truth, after the initial disorienting few minutes of withdrawal, he found it strangely relaxing to be without all his jade. His surroundings became a little foggy and soft around the edges. With his senses dimmed he felt as if he was making love in a dark room, in a pleasant dream perhaps, and could just let himself act without seeing too clearly, without thinking too much. He felt more detached, more serene. He wondered if this made him unusual among Green Bones. Hilo, after all, studded jade into his body so it could never be removed. Shae had gone too far in the other direction. Lan wondered how she could stand it, being jadeless.

That was another thing troubling him tonight. Last month, Shae had gone to the mines as he'd asked and phoned from Pula to tell him that Gont Asch was ordering equipment purchases at the mines. Neither of them knew what to make of it; did it mean Gont was usurping Ree Tura's authority? Three weeks had passed before she'd phoned him again. It was as Lan had feared. "I've gone through the numbers over and over, and it looks as though the equipment purchases Gont approved aren't being reflected in the KJA's financial statements," Shae told him. "The Mountain has been getting involved in the mines directly without consulting the board of the KJA." Shae said she was going to the Kekon Treasury to examine its records. She'd get back to him soon.

He'd been highly reluctant to pull Shae into the clan business, but now he knew it had been worthwhile. Shae had verified his mounting suspicions that Ayt Mada had been a step ahead of his meeting with Chancellor Son and had already begun to try to wrest greater control over the country's jade supply. In addition, Lan was now convinced he could not rely on Doru. There was no excuse for the Weather Man to not be aware of such information, or to keep it from him. If he confronted the old advisor, he was sure Doru would deny any subterfuge or negligence, give him some reasonable explanation, and go to Kaul Sen for support. No, he needed solid evidence to justify not just removing the man from his post but from the inner circle.

Woon would have to be ready to take over immediately and completely, with no transition.

That was another reason he couldn't demote Hilo—the clan couldn't be without a veteran Weather Man and a Horn at the same time. So many problems.

Yunni led him to the bed, undressed him completely, and guided him down onto his stomach. He closed his eyes as she rubbed his back with scented oil. "You're tense," she said soothingly, working her thumbs into the muscles of his neck. "Perhaps from carrying so much jade." Lan let the pillow under his face hide the twist of his lips. The charm girls here knew a few things about Green Bones and how to flatter them. Even the ones that wore the most jade were insecure about their power.

Everyone's tolerance was different, though. Lan carried a considerable amount of jade by the standards of any respectable Green Bone, but he felt no desire to press his limits. There was a point beyond which more jade him feel off-kilter, wired, moody. The problem was, although there was much more to being Pillar than how much jade a man wore, people were superficial. According to the older generation, the great Kaul Du had carried more jade than any other warrior in his day. When his son's rival, a woman Pillar, carried conspicuously more jade, it was talked about. It was whispered as if it was a personal failing.

Yunni massaged down to his waist. She spread warm oil on her hands and forearms and slid them up and down his body. She reached and stroked between his legs. He wasn't sure at what point her dress came off, but he felt her bare breasts rubbing against his back, her long hair trailing against his skin as she glided herself up and down slowly and sensually against him.

When she turned him over and straddled him upside down, her bare stomach and crotch over his face, every troubled thought finally exited Lan's mind. He lifted his head to drink in her odor as she worked her elegant harpist's hands over his chest, stomach, pelvis, and inner thighs. He was truly impressed by how many skills she possessed. For a few seconds, he thought of Eyni and missed her bitterly, but the emotion was fleeting, made dull by familiarity. His arousal flagged only briefly, returning once Yunni's hands and mouth began their masterful and exciting ministrations, and when he felt close to climax, he asked her to lie down. Yunni moaned and sighed, and whispered, "Ah yes, this is what I want," grabbing his hips as he took her. He came faster than he'd expected, then sagged, everything leaving him as he rolled off her and sank into the soft mattress.

Yunni brought a warm, moist towel and rubbed his face and neck and chest. "You can stay as long as you like," she cooed. He knew that was not true, but out of all the lies he had to deal with, Yunni's were the most innocuous and easy to swallow. He was pleased that she seemed to enjoy their time together. Even if it was a skillful artifice, he appreciated it. Out of habit, he closed one hand over his jade beads as the room dissolved and he began to drift off.

There was a knock at the door. Lan wasn't sure he'd heard correctly; no one ever interrupted him here. Yunni frowned in disapproval and sat up, reaching for a robe to cover herself. She started to get up and go to the door, but Lan stopped her.

"Who is it?" he called.

"Kaul-jen," came Mrs. Sugo's voice, sounding high and apprehensive through the door. "Please forgive me for disturbing you. I would normally never... but there is someone from the clan here for you. It's very urgent."

Lan pushed off the bed and put on his pants. "Stay here," he said to Yunni, then went to the safe and tried the combination twice before the lock popped open. He put on his belt and jade cuffs, then clutched the edge of the dresser with both hands as the energy surge hit him, flooding into his system. Everything swam, then sharpened; noise and vision and feeling blasted into his skull. He breathed deeply through the adjustment, then straightened. He glanced at himself in the mirror again—shirtless, but with every pebble of jade in place. He walked to the door and opened it.

Mrs. Sugo backed out of his way, white-faced. Behind her stood Maik Kehn, breathing hard, enraged, his tan jacket splattered with blood that was not his own. "The Mountain did it," he gasped. "They whispered Hilo's name."

• First Interlude •
HEAVEN AND EARTH

Long ago in Heaven, according to Deitist teachings, the great extended family of gods lived in dazzling palaces of jade. Like any large family, the gods had their share of quarrels but for the most part they went about their immortal lives happily, although once they had children and those children had children, residential space in Heaven grew too tight for comfort. So the gods constructed a second home, which they modeled after the first, and called Earth.

Earth was, at first, in every way as beautiful as Heaven, with vast seas, high mountains, lush forests, and countless wondrous plants and animals. Unfortunately, the numerous children of the gods, having grown up spoiled, fell to squabbling over Earth even before it was completed. Several wanted the same ocean, others bickered over who would take the highest mountain range or the biggest continent.

At last, the fighting grew so constant and unbearable that the god parents grew enraged. "We built a perfect home for you and this is how you repay us—by spoiling it with pettiness, greed, and jealousy, turning brother against brother, sister against sister. Have Earth then, but suffer for it, as you'll have nothing else from us." And the parents stripped their children of their divine powers, made them small and weak and naked, and exiled them from Heaven.

Yatto the Father of All, blasted to shards the first and only half-constructed jade palace on Earth, and buried under it a mountainous island.

The gods though, being parents, could not resist keeping an eye on their struggling, estranged children. Some, like Thana the Moon, or Poya the goddess of agriculture, took pity on their descendants and hovered close, helping to light their way at night, or ensuring they had food to eat. Others, like Yofo the typhoon god, or Sagi the Pestilence, refused to give up their grudges, and unless placated, would descend on occasion to remind humanity of its longstanding offenses.

All earthly conflict, so the Dietist philosophers say, stems from the original offense of the children against their parents and of siblings against each other. All human progress and virtuous striving is likewise an attempt to achieve familial forgiveness and a return to the spiritually and physically divine state, which lies latent but distantly remembered.

• Chapter Eighteen •
THE WHISPERED NAME

A frantic call had come earlier in the evening from Mr. Pak, who, along with his wife, had run a grocery in the Armpit for twelve years.

"I have to go," Hilo said to Wen after he hung up the phone.

He was frustrated because she refused to move out of her cramped apartment in Paw-Paw and live with him in the Horn's residence on the Kaul estate unless they were married. "I have to ask Lan properly, and then we'll plan the wedding, and it'll take months," he'd argued. "Things are getting worse between the clans. I visit here too often; it's not safe for you. If you won't be reasonable, I'll have to post Fingers to watch over you, which means Fingers that I won't have elsewhere. The house is secure. Bigger, too. You could fix it up, you're good at that. You'd like it."

Wen folded her arms and gazed at him with immovability. "I'm not going to give your family any additional reasons to look down on me. We'll live together when we're married, and not before. In the meantime, I have a gun, and I know how to use it. I won't be a burden. I can take care of myself."

"A gun." Hilo gave an ugly laugh. "Is that supposed to reassure me? My enemies are Green Bones. You're a stone-eye."

"Thank you for the reminder," she said coolly.

On the street outside, Kehn honked the horn of the Duchesse and Hilo growled. "We'll talk about this later."

When he arrived at the grocer's with the Maiks, he found Mr. Pak sitting on the sidewalk with his head in his hands and Mrs. Pak crying as she swept up broken glass inside. Two young men with jade studs in their eyebrows had smashed the windows, broken the neon sign over the door, and knocked over several shelves of merchandise as punishment for the couple's failure to pay tribute to the Mountain clan. Hilo scowled as he surveyed the wreckage, his mood worsening. Nothing was stolen, but incidents like these were costing No Peak dearly, not just in money to take care of the damages, but in goodwill from the Lantern Men in the district.

"I can't pay tribute to two clans," Mr. Pak moaned.

"We'll take care of it," said Hilo. "It won't happen again."

Later, there was some question as to whether the Paks had been turned by the Mountain and were in on the plot. When Mr. Pak learned of what happened, he cut off his own ear to proclaim his innocence and threw himself on the mercy of Kaul Lan. The couple's home and store were searched and they were cleared of suspicion, but two months later, the Paks shut down their store and moved out of the Armpit for good.

On that night, however, Hilo had his Fingers ask questions until he learned that the two men who'd vandalized the grocery were Yen Io and Chon Daal and they could be found at an all-night arcade on a busy commercial strip of the Armpit. For smaller transgressions, Hilo would have sent one of his Fists and a couple of Fingers, but he was sick and tired of Lan's restraint and the bullshit situation in the Armpit. People needed to know No Peak was strong here and would not be trifled with. Vibrant, noisy, colorful, and seedy, the Armpit was one of Janloon's most valuable districts. By day it attracted tourists and shoppers; after dark, both stockbrokers and dockworkers mingled in its streets, entertaining themselves with the myriad of restaurants, gambling dens, bars, strip clubs, and theaters. No Peak could not afford to lose ground here. Hilo decided it was necessary that he handle this offense personally. The Pillar had ordered him not to take lives, but that didn't mean he couldn't make a public statement.

They parked in a pay lot down the street from the Super Joy arcade. Kehn was suffering from a sinus headache and was blowing his nose into a soggy handkerchief. The elder Maik brother had had his cheekbone fractured in his teens and ever since then had a difficult time on days when the pollution and humidity in Janloon were high.

"Stay in the car," Hilo told him. "Tar and I won't be long."

Kehn agreed readily, turning on the radio and lighting a smoke as Hilo and Tar got out and walked down the sidewalk toward the Super Joy. Kehn being left behind in the car was what saved the Horn's life. As Hilo and Tar crossed the street, two men raced up on motorcycles. As they roared past the

Duchesse, Kehn understood in an instant what was happening. He shouted out in warning and laid hard on the Duchesse's horn. It was not the blare of noise however, but the surge of Kehn's visceral alarm that reached Hilo first, a fraction of a second before he Perceived the murderous intent of the assassins as they opened fire with handguns.

One bullet tore the shoulder of Hilo's jacket and another whined past his ear as he fell to a crouch and threw up a wall of Deflection that veered the shots to either side around him. They punched into car doors and the walls of nearby buildings. Screams erupted as people ran from the scene, pushing and shoving each other to get away. The salvo of gunfire was just an opening, meant to stun. Both the attackers leapt, Light, from the backs of their motorcycles, as Yen Io and Chon Daal appeared from the parked car where they had been lying in ambush.

Hilo rose, talon knife in a fighting grip. Jade energy surged alongside adrenaline. The two men flew straight for him, moon blades cutting down in a vicious arc. Hilo slid aside and slammed his crossed wrists into one man's elbow, cleaving into the joint with his talon knife. Directing the momentum of the moon blade into the attacker's thigh, he jerked the talon knife through, severing tendons. The second man's blade slashed across his midsection. Hilo barely had time to focus his Steel; as he curved his torso away from the cut, the moon blade flexed from the enormous tension, opening a bloody gash across Hilo's stomach with grisly slowness as the attacker's Strength met and strained against his defenses. Hilo's eyes met the assassin's and he recognized him: Gam Oben. Gont Asch's Second Fist.

Only narrowly did Hilo escape disembowelment. With a snarl of effort, he leapt Light, backwards onto the top of a parked car. Gam released a powerful wave of Deflection and Hilo's feet were knocked out from under him as he landed; he slammed chest first onto the roof. His chin smacked metal and his vision wavered. He heard Maik Tar let loose a howl of pain and rage.

The Duchesse Priza, with Kehn at the wheel, barreled onto the street like a rhino. It clipped one of the motorcycles, sending it spinning, then plowed into Chon Daal. Gam barely leapt out of the way as the boy flipped over the silver grille and bounced off the hood of the car. Chon's Steeled body shattered the windshield, then flew through the air onto the sidewalk as Kehn slammed on the brakes. The elder Maik burst from the driver's side, bellowing.

Hilo rolled, hit the ground and was up again. He lunged at Gam but before he could reach him, the Mountain fighter whose elbow he'd torn with the knife careened into Hilo with a determined roar and dragged him down. As they both crashed to the asphalt, Hilo managed to wrap his arms around the man's torso. The other Green Bone's aura spiked wild as he twisted in Hilo's grip, and Hilo took all of it, all the jade power he could gather, and with a sharp thrust of his palm, Channeled it into his opponent's heart. The assassin's Steel buckled like balsa wood and his heart spasmed and burst.

The blowback of energy from the Green Bone's death rocked Hilo hard. With explosive force, the man's life lit out of the confines of his body. The resulting jade-amplified rush was worse than a physical battering against Hilo's skull. He reeled; for a second he could barely breath and his mouth filled with a bitterly sharp metallic taste. Only because he knew what was happening was he able to keep his wits intact. He tore himself off of the body before he could become addled. Talon knife still firmly clutched, he clambered to his feet and looked for the next man to kill. Instead, he saw that Yen Io lay dead on the road by Kehn and Tar's hand. Gam, and Chon, who'd somehow survived being thrown from the hood of the Duchesse, had fled.

Less than two minutes had passed from the start of the attack.

Tar was leaning against the twisted grille of the car, bent over with a hand to his side. He'd taken bullets from the diverted gunshots meant for Hilo. His shirt was soaked with blood. Kehn pulled his younger brother into the back seat of the car. Hilo could see him pressing on the wound with both hands, Channeling his own energy into Tar, but he was no doctor, and could only slow the bleeding, not stop it.

Icy fury rose and spread like a white mist across Hilo's vision. It steadied his body and his voice as he pointed into the throng of frightened bystanders that pressed like packed fish into doorways and behind cars. "You," he said, picking out a newsstand owner, "You. And you." He pointed at two others, a woman clutching a briefcase to her chest, and the doorman of a club. "Come here!" They turned pale and looked as if they wanted to run, but did not dare disobey the command in Hilo's voice. The doorman took several steps forward nervously, and the other two had no choice but to follow. Hilo looked at each of them in turn, making sure they knew who he was, knew that he had seen and remembered them, that he speaking directly to them.

"Spread the word up and down this street and tell everyone you speak to, to tell others." Hilo raised his voice so others would hear. "Anyone who gives me the whereabouts of the two men who fled here tonight is a friend of No Peak and a friend of mine. Anyone who helps them or hides them is an enemy of mine and my clan." He pointed to one of the dead men in the street, then the other. "*This* is what happens to my enemies."

He set to work quickly. They needed to get Tar to a hospital right away, but a Green Bone was entitled to the jade of slain foes and never left it behind for thieves. From the body of one man, he pulled three jade rings, a bracelet, and circular pendant. From the other, he collected a belt, two eyebrow studs and a jade-backed watch. He had to hack at flesh inelegantly to get the rings and studs. He gathered up the jade-hilted weapons that had fallen: two moon blades and a talon knife. Hilo ran back to the Duchesse. He threw open the door and tossed the talon knives and moon blades onto the floor of the passenger side seat. "Keys," he demanded.

Kehn fumbled in his pocket and passed them over. Hilo wiped the bloody fingerprints off of the metal teeth with the sleeve of his shirt and started the engine. In the back, Tar gave a low moan. The car lurched forward, sending broken windshield glass across the dash; Hilo spun the wheel around and slammed on the gas.

• Chapter Nineteen •
COUNCIL OF WAR

It was past midnight and there was no one left in the Kekon Treasury except for a couple of night security guards in the lobby and two women janitors who moved from cubicle to cubicle in the records department, emptying trash bins and vacuuming the floors, chatting to each other in the lilting, long-voweled Abukei dialect, though they kept their voices down around Shae and did not disturb her at her work. The building had closed hours ago and it was only because of her identity as a Kaul and the letter in Shae's pocket—the one written in Lan's hand and bearing the clan's insignia—that she'd been allowed to remain at this spare desk for as long as she needed, which, for the last several days, had been late into the night.

Shae put down her pen and calculator and leaned back, rubbing her eyes, which were sore from hours studying numbers underneath the unfriendly florescent lights. It occurred to her that she was nearly alone with the largest amount of jade stored in one place in the world. Several floors below her, under immense layers of concrete, were lead-lined vaults of processed jade, cut into various sizes from single gram gems to one tonne slabs. Considering that it housed in its bowels a stockpile that comprised a considerable portion of the nation's fortune, the Kekon Treasury was less heavily guarded than one might expect, not only because anyone who attempted to steal from it would be marked for certain death by every Green Bone clan, but because state-of-the-art security systems ensured that if any vault was breached, the intruder would be sealed inside. Unless the thieves possessed complete immunity, being locked in a vault full of jade meant a slow, agonizing descent into insanity before death.

And yet, someone *was* indeed stealing from the Kekon Treasury. Shae had gone through the calculations multiple times, cross-referencing records from the mines, from the Kekon Jade Alliance's official financial statements, and now, from the Treasury itself. She'd forgotten that she was good at this—doggedly following hunches and crumbs of information until they arranged themselves into a clear picture. Staring at the figures that covered pages of her notebook, even fatigue at this late hour did not blunt the astonishment and anger Shae felt as she saw with finality her suspicions borne out in cold, hard math. The mines were producing jade that was neither being officially accounted for by the Kekon Jade Alliance, nor being taken in and stored in Treasury vaults. There was jade missing from the national reserves.

Despite the fact that she had never intended to get involved in the clan's affairs, Shae was shaky with triumph and outrage as she packed up her findings and left the building. Her steps echoed down the empty halls as she took the stairs down to the ground floor and asked one of the security guards to let her out of the locked doors. The guard was a bored, middle-aged Green Bone wearing the ceremonial flat green cap and distinctive sash that marked him as a member of Haedo Shield, a minor clan dedicated to the sole purpose of providing security for Prince Ioan III and the royal family, as well as government buildings including Wisdom Hall and the Kekon Treasury. Knowing that she would not be returning the following evening, Shae thanked the night guard as she left. She was not worried about the man tipping off anyone about her activities. The members of Haedo Shield swore ironclad oaths of neutrality with respect to the other clans; they did not even hold votes in the Kekon Jade Alliance.

It was a short subway ride from the Monuments District to North Sotto, but as the trains ran less frequently this late, it was forty minutes later by the time Shae was walking the few blocks from the subway station to her apartment building. She was so engrossed in her thoughts, in what she would say to Lan in the morning, that she was only a few hundred feet from home before she realized she was being followed.

She was so stunned and mortified with herself that she simply stopped in her tracks and turned around. If she'd been wearing jade, she would've Perceived the man behind her long ago. Even jadeless, if she'd been paying attention, she ought to have sensed his footsteps trailing hers.

Shae dropped her bag unceremoniously to the sidewalk and drew the talon knife from the sheath strapped to the small of her back. It was not a jade-hilted knife like the one she'd carried for years but had stored away. This was just a plain, everyday sort of street weapon, but of good quality and certainly lethal enough in trained hands. She'd been raised in a culture that deemed it unthinkable not to respond to a challenge; it did not occur to Shae that she could run less than thirty seconds to the safety of her apartment building.

The man coming up behind her did not stop, nor did he rush at her. He kept pace but took his hands out of his pockets and opened them to show that he meant no harm. In another instant, Shae saw it was Caun Yu, her neighbor. He nodded toward her respectfully, amiably, his eyes dropping to her weapon and noting that she held it in a steady, practiced grip, her stance instinctive, coiled and evenly weighted across the soles of her feet. "You look like a Green Bone," he said with a crooked smile.

"You were following me," Shae said, defensive.

"I live in the same building."

"What are doing coming back so late?"

Caun looked incredulous. "I work in the evenings. What about *you*?"

Shae's toes curled inside her shoes. Of course, it was none of her business what hours Caun kept. She'd been disappointed in herself and was taking it out on someone who didn't deserve her ire. She stowed her talon knife and picked up her fallen bag. "I apologize, that was rude of me. You caught me off guard. Shall we walk back, then?"

He nodded and walked alongside her, keeping some distance between them. "You seem very much on guard to me, Miss Shae. If I'd actually been a man with bad intentions, I wouldn't have wanted to face you with that talon knife."

Shae wanted to change the subject. "So what do you do for work, Mr. Caun?"

"I'm a security guard," he said. "It's nothing very dangerous. Rather boring, to be honest. I'm hoping I'll get a new job soon, something more interesting." He opened the door for her, and they climbed the stairs to their apartments on the third floor. He did not ask her a question in return, but when they reached Shae's apartment door, Caun paused and said, with a flash of teasing in his eyes, "Good night. From now on, I'll be sure to call out hello to you when I'm still well out of knife range." As Caun continued down the hall to his own apartment, Shae sorely missed having the sense of Perception that might have given her a hint as to what the man might be thinking.

Shae put Caun out of her mind, went to sleep, and called the Kaul house as soon as she awoke the next morning, before the sun was up. Doru answered the phone. "Shae-se," he said, with false, mincing surprise, "Why haven't I seen you? I thought you would be at home more often."

Shae grimaced. "I've been busy, Doru-jen. Getting settled. Lots of little things to take care of, you know."

"You should have come to me," he said. "Why are you living in that place, anyways? I could have gotten you somewhere nicer, much nicer."

"I didn't want to trouble you." The fact that he knew where she lived made her grimace stretch further. Hastily, "Is Lan home?"

"Ah," said Doru. A long pause that began to ring alarm bells in her head. "There's been trouble, I'm afraid. Perhaps you ought to come over."

Shae hailed a taxi to take her straight to the Kaul home. It crawled infuriatingly slowly through morning traffic, fighting the crush of honking cars, motorcycles, and parcel-laden bicycles, all of which employed a survival-of-the-fittest approach to intersections and road sign compliance. The whole way there, Shae stared unseeing out the window. She felt sick at heart. Not because men had tried to kill her brother Hilo. That was hardly shocking to her; if anything she was surprised it didn't happen more often. Yet no one had phoned to tell her. Not even Lan. Had she not called the house this morning, she would still be oblivious. Perhaps in all the commotion last night it simply hadn't occurred to them to call her. She'd been out of the country and out of touch for years. Perhaps she shouldn't be so upset that she hadn't been informed right away.

She arrived to find her brothers in a council of war. Armed and severe-looking Fists were everywhere, guarding the gate and the entrance to the house, prowling the property and standing in the hallways. In the Pillar's study, Lan and Hilo were smoking grimly and plotting. Doru was with them. When Shae walked in, their postures told her everything: Lan leaned against his desk, tapping ashes into a tray, his face stiff and drawn. Hilo was sitting forward on the edge of one armchair, elbows on knees, staring at nothing, cigarette dangling from the fingers of one hand. Doru rested back in the other chair, legs crossed, subtly apart, watching. The tension in the room was such that Shae's indignation failed her, driven out by an implacable sense of apprehension.

Hilo raised his eyes when she came into the study. There were lines on his face that made him look like a different person, not his usual insouciant self. Shae noticed dried blood under his nails and beneath a white shirt that she suspected was actually Lan's, gauze bandages encircled his midsection. "Tar is in the hospital," he said, as if she'd been standing there the whole time.

Shae was not even sure which one Tar was, whether he was the man she'd seen with Hilo in the hotel. "Will he be all right?" she asked, because that seemed to be the appropriate thing to say.

"He'll live. Wen is over there with him." Hilo got up and circled restlessly, like a dog unable to lie down. The door opened and Maik Kehn thrust his head into the room. He wasn't the one she'd seen at the hotel; that must've been Tar, the one now in the hospital. "Everyone's here," Kehn said. "We're ready to go."

"Lan-se," Doru spoke up. "I'll ask you again to reconsider. This could go badly for us. We can still negotiate a truce in the Armpit."

"No, Doru," Lan said, stubbing out his cigarette in the ashtray and walking to the door with Hilo. "Not anymore." From the angle of the men's bodies, Shae understood: Doru was being nudged out. Lan no longer trusted him. The attempted murder of Hilo had pushed the Pillar too far, sided him with his brother. Doru must have known it as well because there was a deceptive impassiveness to his face and he did not move from his spot in the chair as the other two men left.

Shae followed her brothers. The foyer of the house was filled with Hilo's men, armed to the teeth with moon blades, talon knives, and pistols. As Hilo walked into their midst, they coalesced around him. He did not speak, but seemed, somehow, to acknowledge each of them, with a held glance, a nod, a touch on the shoulder or arm.

Shae went to Lan. "Where are you going?"

"To the Factory." He shrugged on a leather vest and tightened it.

Someone brought him his best moon blade—a thirty-four inch Da Tanori with a twenty-two inch tempered white carbon steel blade and five jade stones in the hilt. He strapped it to his waist. It had been some time since Shae had seen him look so military, so much like their father, that the effect was disorienting. Lan said, "That's where they are, the men who tried to kill Hilo. Gont is there as well, and Ayt too, perhaps."

The realization hit her squarely: they were leaving to do battle. Shae gripped her brother by the arm. "What can I do to help?"

Lan looked at her and she realized how ridiculous her question was. She couldn't help, not in this, not now, not jadeless as she was. "Nothing," Lan said. "Don't let Doru take over the clan." *If he was killed.*

"I found out more," she said, almost desperate to delay his departure. "At the Treasury. I didn't want to say anything in the room with Doru there, but I need to talk to you."

"When I get back." He gave her a quick kiss on the forehead.

"Why didn't you phone me last night?"

"There was no need. You don't have to be part of this," he said. "I promised not to pull you in any further beyond what I've asked of you so far, which I know is already more than you wanted." He looked over her shoulder and his face tightened.

Shae turned. Kaul Sen stood on the stairs like a baleful mummy, wearing a white robe that hung off his scrawny frame. His fierce gaze roamed the assembled fighters and alighted with blistering disdain on Hilo. He pointed at his youngest grandson, leaning into the gesture as if his bony finger were a weapon. "Your fault," the old man snapped. "What've you done now? You were always nothing but an impulsive hooligan. You're going to ruin this family!"

"Grandda," Lan said warningly.

Hilo stepped forward through his pack of warriors. "They tried to kill me, Grandda." His voice was soft, but Shae knew that Hilo spoke softly when he was most angry. "They nearly killed one of my Fists. It's war now."

"Ayt would not go to war with me!" Kaul Sen's arms shook as he gripped the banister. "We were like brothers. We had our differences, but *war*, war between Green Bones! No, *never*. If anyone tried to kill you, you deserved it!"

Hilo's eyes flashed fire and hurt. Then he turned away, scorn flowing from him like a cape. "Let's go." His fighters flanked him as he stalked through the door and out of the house. They piled into the line of cars parked in the roundabout.

Kaul Sen sagged and sat down on the stairs, his limbs folding like a rickety chair frame, his robe draping over his bony shoulders and knees like a sheet.

"Kyanla," Lan called. "Help grandfather back to his room." He put a hand on Shae's back. In a low voice, "Stay with him."

Shae nodded, trying to think of something more to say, such as, "Be careful," or "Good luck," or "Please come back," but none of them seemed to be right, and Lan was already leaving, going down the steps of the front walk, climbing into an open car door that one of the clan's Fists held open for him.

• Chapter Twenty •
CLEAN BLADES AT THE FACTORY

The Factory was an old manufacturing facility just across the territorial border, in the Mountain-controlled Spearpoint district. The building still read Kekon Special Textile Co. in large faded paint on the outside wall, but it had been converted years ago into a gathering place and training hall for Mountain Green Bones. According to the No Peak Fingers and Lantern Men who'd called in overnight and early this morning, the two surviving assassins, Gam Oben and Chon Daal, had been seen fleeing the Armpit on foot and coming here.

They arrived in a convoy just before noon, six cars packed with No Peak fighters. They parked in front of the Factory and piled out in a storm of slamming doors and glinting weapons. Lan and Hilo stood together at the front, conferring. The brick building was tall and the windows were covered; it was impossible to tell how many Mountain Green Bones were waiting inside. Hilo pointed out the sentries watching them from the roof. So far, no one had come out of the building.

"Send in a message," Lan said.

Hilo motioned forward one of the Fingers, a young man with hair hanging longer on one side, and two jade piercings in his lower lip. The fighter dropped to his knees and touched his head to the ground. "I am ready to die for the clan, Kaul-jens."

Hilo gave him his instructions, and the Finger was sent, unarmed, up to the front door of the Factory. The demand was simple: hand over the heads of the two men responsible for the attack on Hilo, and cede control of the Armpit district, or No Peak would come down from the forest. 'Coming down from the forest' was an old Green Bone phrase that meant open war; all of the Mountain's territory, people, and businesses would be fair game.

The Kauls watched as the messenger was met by two guards. Words were exchanged, and the man was admitted into the building.

Hilo sat down on the hood of the Duchesse to wait. Lan leaned against the door of his Roewolfe roadster and watched the front of the building with taut nerves and a parched feeling in his mouth. It was one of those days when sun and cloud grappled with each other in the sky, and the waiting men were bathed in alternating patches of heat and shadow, as if the weather itself was unsure of how the day would proceed. Since the moment Mrs. Sugo had interrupted him in the Lilac Divine the night before, it was as if he'd been swept along by a tsunami. He felt as if he had little control over its direction and was battling merely to ride near the surface of it.

Lan did not want a clan war. It would be bad for everyone—for Green Bones, for business, for the people, for the country itself. All this time, he'd believed that so long as he treaded carefully, he could avoid outright conflict with the Mountain. He'd ignored Ayt's disrespect, politely rejected her forceful overtures to form an alliance, and taken reasonable steps to secure the KJA and safeguard his own clan's position. Now he saw that his actions were the defensive maneuverings of a dumb bull being set upon by a leopard. They had only emboldened the enemy, sent the impression that the Pillar of No Peak was soft, not someone to be feared.

He'd been a fool. He'd known that the Mountain wanted Hilo out of the way but he hadn't anticipated that the enemy Pillar would act so quickly and with such violence. Was it because his rival was a woman that he'd assumed she would hesitate to shed blood first? If so, it had been a near fatal oversight on his part. Now Ayt had whispered the name of the second son of No Peak and no matter any other business or territorial considerations between the clans, that was not something that could be negotiated away. The Kaul family name could not command any authority or respect unless it answered such an offense unequivocally. They would not leave the Factory today without bloodshed; Lan was certain of this.

A mile-long freight train passed a short distance away, blaring its approach and rumbling on and on over the rails, hauling goods from across the island into the port stations in Summer Park and the Docks. A breeze skimmed westward off the water. Half an hour passed. The Factory remained silent and inscrutable. The No Peak men grumbled and paced and smoked.

Maik Kehn came up. "They're not answering. They've probably killed him by now." Maik's face was creased with impatience and murderous drive. "What are we going to do if they don't answer?"

Hilo said, "We're going to storm the fucking place and drag Gont Asch out by his tiny balls." This satisfied his lieutenant, who grunted in agreement, but it worked Hilo up further. He jumped off the hood of the Duchesse and prowled halfway to the entrance of the Factory. "You see this, Gont?" he shouted. He spread his arms wide and turned in an arrogant circle. "I'm still alive! Don't send your puppies to kill me. Come out and do it yourself, you dogfucking coward!"

Behind him, the Fists roared their assent and pounded on the cars.

At that moment, an understanding struck Lan clearly and heavily: the Mountain had sent men to kill Hilo, not *him*—not Lan, the firstborn, the Pillar. It was Hilo that the enemy viewed as a threat, Hilo who was ferocious and violent and could lead Fists in war. Now he'd survived an assassination attempt and gained for it.

Lan knew what that said about him in turn: he was Pillar on account of birth, and Kaul Sen's decree, and a face that reminded people of his father. He strived at all times to be a strong and prudent leader, to maintain peace, to respect the legacy of his grandfather, and while those things gave him respect and credibility within the clan, they did not intimidate or dissuade rivals. The enemy had struck first, not at the clan's political head but at its top warrior, and in so doing, dispelled any doubt that the Mountain intended to move in on No Peak and conquer it by force.

He was, by nature, a man slow to anger, but Kaul Lan's hands curled into fists and a churning pool of shame and rage rose in him like a cloudy tide.

The door of the Factory opened and three men emerged. Lan and Maik Kehn walked up together to join Hilo, who stood his ground and faced the approaching men. First came the young No Peak messenger. He hurried forward and dropped to his knees once again, looking almost apologetic to still be very much alive. "Kaul-jens, I regret the dogs didn't give me a chance to die for No Peak. But they sent me back out with these two."

Behind him came two Mountain Green Bones. "That's them," Hilo said to Lan. "The limping one is Chon. The dark one's Gam."

The two sides regarded each other with hesitant mutual hatred. Chon, a

mid-rank Finger, was both injured and scared. Sweat slicked his bruised face
and he could only glance at the No Peak fighters for a few seconds before
shifting his eyes. Gam was far greener in both body and spirit; jade hung
around his neck, studded his nose, encircled his wrists. He looked directly
at Lan and spoke first.

"My Pillar agrees to your demands," Gam said. "She approved the attack
on your Horn out of a sense of great insult for his many transgressions against
our clan, but realizes she may have acted in anger and haste. So, to show her
willingness to negotiate, we will withdraw from the Armpit except for the
small section south of Patriot Street that we have always controlled."

"How generous," Hilo scoffed, "but that's not all we demanded."

Gam's cheek twitched but he kept looking at Lan. "My Horn offers you
our lives as punishment for our failure. This one here," he jerked his head at
Chon, "isn't worthy of a warrior's end, but my clan and my honor demand
that I die befitting my rank, like a proper Fist of the Mountain. Kaul Lanshinwan, Pillar of No Peak, I offer you a clean blade."

Lan was honestly stunned. Then his eyes narrowed. "I accept."

The No Peak men had gathered around to hear the conversation, and
now all of them stepped back at once, clearing a large circle of space. All
except Hilo. He angled his body in front of Lan and lowered his voice.
"Gam deserves an execution, not a duel," the Horn said. "This is some kind
of trick."

"You'll be here watching to see if it is," Lan said. "But I don't think
so." He didn't elaborate on how he was certain this was Ayt's belated way
of measuring him. She already knew something of Hilo. She'd tried to
have him killed, and failed. Now she wanted to know if Lan was as weak
as she'd taken him for. The knowledge would determine her next move; it
was apparently worth surrendering most of the Armpit. If the Pillar of No
Peak backed down, he would lose face in front of the enemy and his own
Green Bones.

"A death of consequence, then," Hilo suggested. "Kehn and I would
do it."

Lan answered him with a scalding look and the Horn fell silent. Hilo
was injured and had already survived an attempt on his life; what sort of
Green Bone would Lan be, to send his younger brother to fight Gam again

instead of answering a direct challenge himself? Ayt was surely watching to see if he would do precisely that. By endeavoring to preserve peace between the clans, he'd lowered himself in her estimation. Now he saw that force was the only language Ayt understood; only an unmistakeable show of strength on his part might cause her to rethink her ambitions of conquest. So it had to be this way. He had no doubt that, like it or not, he was to be a wartime Pillar now, and the most unwise thing he could do was to continue elevating Hilo's battle prowess over his own in front of the clan's Fists and the enemy's eyes.

Gam retreated several paces. "Knife or blade?" It was the prerogative of the one who'd been challenged to choose the weapon. Hilo favored the talon knife—compact, vicious, always within reach—but Lan was not a street fighter and the formality and elegance of the moon blade seemed more appropriate. "Blade," he said.

Hilo was still skeptical. "You expect me to honor this?"

The offer of a clean blade was an ironclad pledge. The victor took the loser's life and jade without consequence—no relative or ally would seek retribution. Hilo's question was rhetorical, and Lan looked at him askance. "You're worried I might lose?"

Hilo turned his chin slightly to glance at Gam. Among the Janloon clans, Gont's Second Fist was well respected as a warrior, perhaps on a level with the Maik brothers when it came to skill, although Lan clearly held a size and weight advantage over the slender man. Hilo brought his eyes back and lowered his voice. "He's not trivial."

"Neither am I." Lan said it more sharply than he'd intended.

"You're the Pillar, your life is worth more than his," Hilo said. "I have a dozen Fists here who'd fight Gam in your name."

Lan's reply was low and cold, intended only for Hilo. "If I can't defeat Gam, then I can't be Pillar." Finally; he had acknowledged out loud what others surely said behind his back: that the son of the fearsome Kaul Du needed to prove himself worthy of his inheritance.

Lan drew his Da Tanori moon blade from its sheath and held it out to his brother, who spat on the white metal for good luck, though he didn't smile.

"He has good offensive Deflection," Hilo said. "Better to fight him from close in." He squeezed Lan between his shoulder and neck, then retreated to stand beside Kehn. A nameless pang touched Lan in the chest; he ought to say something else to Hilo, just in case, but doing so seemed as if it would be bad luck.

Lan was not devoutly religious, but he sent up a silent prayer to Jenshu the Monk, the One Who Returned, the patron of jade warriors. *Old uncle in Heaven, judge me the greener of your kin today, if it be so.* Then he turned and faced Gam and touched the flat of his blade to his forehead in salute. The other man returned the gesture. They circled each other. The sky had abruptly cleared and the sunlight beat stark on the pavement. The embedded stones seemed to pulse under Lan's palm, layering jade energy into him, stretching his clarity, changing the way space and time moved. Seconds lengthened, distances shortened. Gam's heartbeat throbbed in the center of his Perception. He sensed the man's jade aura shifting, testing, expanding and contracting, subtly judging when and how to attack.

For a terrible second, doubt rushed in. Lan had once been at the top of the Academy and won his fair share of violent contests, but it had been years since he had dueled. Gam Oben had been groomed by Gont Asch and had greater and more recent experience as a fighter. Perhaps Ayt was gambling intelligently. He might lose to this man, might doom his clan.

Perceiving Lan's instant of uncertainty, Gam chose that moment to attack. He stepped into a classic opening high sweep cut, then changed his direction deftly and sliced low. Lan caught the misdirection in time and deflected the blade; he circled his own weapon around in an upward piercing strike. Gam twisted away, throwing his arm up against the side of his head; Lan's blade sheared against his Steeled arm.

Lan launched into an offensive flurry of quick cuts. Their blades sang together in a lethal duet. Blocking and deflecting, Gam gave ground, then pivoted sharply and slammed a kick into the Pillar's side. Lan felt his ribs compress and heave under the man's Strength. He pulled himself Light and flew back, landing on his feet. The watching men hurried backward to make more space.

Out of range now to reach his opponent with the blade, Lan remembered Hilo's warning just as Gam flung his left arm forward with a shout and a heaving burst of jade energy, ripping a wave of Deflection through the air strong enough to hurl a grown man to the ground. Lan rooted into a forward stance and threw up his own Deflection in a vertical shield that parted the other Green Bone's attack like the prow of a boat. He felt the clash of energy reverberate through his frame, clattering his clenched teeth as he skidded backward into his planted heel.

Like the suck of a receding tide, he felt Gam pull his aura in, readying another spear of Deflection. Lan rushed his opponent, Lightness and Strength turning him in a blur of speed. His moon blade carved a deadly path toward the side of Gam's neck. The other Green Bone whirled under the slice and slammed a palm strike to Lan's sternum.

All the energy the Fist had gathered for the Deflection, he Channeled into the blow. Lan gave every fiber of his being into Steel, knowing in that instant he would live or die based on whether the other man's force could break him.

Everything dimmed; he felt Gam's energy batter and buckle him. It pierced his ribcage and seized his heart. Lan felt death tickle the edge of his mind. His Steel splintered, but it did not break. It held in a moment of stalemate, and then it roared outward, scattering the force of the killing blow. He was after all, a Kaul.

Gam had given all of himself to the attempt. He swayed on his feet for an instant, his jade aura wafting pale and flimsy. Lan sunk his blade into the man's side like it was a block of soft bean curd. He had almost nothing left either, but he pulled across, parting tissue and arteries. His Perception clamored white as if drowning in psychic noise—the final spike of pain and fear from Gam, the backwash of energy as the man's life fled him, the multitudinous rush of triumph and elation from the watching warriors of No Peak—and then the Second Fist of the Mountain slumped to the ground.

Lan fell to his knees, gasping. "Thank you, old uncle Jenshu, for your favor," he whispered. Then, raising his voice so all could hear, he spoke to his opponent's body. "You carried your jade well, and you died a Fist's death. You were a worthy opponent, Gam, a loss to your Horn." He wiped both sides of his moon blade down the inside sleeve of his left arm and raising it high, rose to his feet. "My blade is clean."

From the sidelines, Kaul Hilo gave a curt nod to Kehn Maik. The Fist stepped around Chon Daal, who knelt in resignation of his fate. Maik pulled the man's head back and opened his throat from ear to ear with a deep, swift stroke of a talon knife, then pushed him face forward onto the asphalt.

"No Peak! No Peak!" the Green Bones erupted in chorus. "Kaul Lan-jen! Our blood for the Pillar!" They dropped to their knees and beat their fists on the ground in a drumbeat of applause, their exuberant, pent-up Strength denting the pavement. Lan cut off his enemy's jade chokers and bracelets and tore the studs from his face. So much jade in his hand made his throat feel dry with heat and his scalp tingle as if the roots of his hair were charged with electricity. He was moving as if in a dream, dizzy with relief.

He stood. "We're leaving," he shouted. "But let our enemies know this: No Peak defends and avenges our own. You wrong any one of us, you wrong us all. You seek to war with us, and we will return it a hundredfold. No one will take from us what is ours!" Lan thrust the fistful of jade he'd won above his head and the din increased. He saw Hilo cross his arms and rock back on his heels, smiling.

The Green Bones piled back into the cars. The bloodthirst they'd arrived with, if not fully quenched, had been sated by the outcome of the duel. Lan allowed himself the grim satisfaction of seeing the clan's warriors hailing him, as he knew they hailed Hilo. To anyone watching, the fight had seemed quick and decisive. The Mountain would not retaliate over the kills. No Peak had not lost any lives and the Armpit was now almost entirely theirs. It was a victory. Wasn't it?

Lan walked past his own silver roadster and pulled open the back door of the Duchesse instead. Sitting alone in the wide back seat, he let the jade he'd taken drop next to him. He unstrapped his bloody moon blade and rested it on the floor across his feet. He throbbed and ached. The jade around his arms and waist seemed unusually heavy, and he felt injured, somewhere deep inside. He wondered if anyone else had noticed how close the fight had been.

Hilo got into the front passenger seat. Once Maik Kehn had pulled the car onto the General's Ride and they were speeding back through the city, Hilo twisted around and offered his brother a cigarette, then lit it for him. He turned back around to face the front and rolled the window down halfway. "Must hurt like a bitch," he said quietly. "Lie down, Lan. No one here to see but us."

• Chapter Twenty-One •
FAMILY TALK

Shae sat next to her grandfather, her hand over his knobby one. After the commotion of her brothers' departure, the house had fallen incongruously quiet. She wondered where Doru had gone, whether he was still in the house or if he'd departed to make phone calls or do whatever else it was that he did. She thought about going to check, but didn't want to leave her grandfather. He seemed shrunken and frail in a way she had never seen. Underneath his liver-spotted skin, she still felt the thrum of his powerful presence, a weighty jade aura anchored by an iron will, but the way he sat now, there was deep resignation in his slack posture, a bitter understanding that he was no longer the beating heart of the clan. No longer the Torch of Kekon.

Kyanla brought Kaul Sen a bowl of cut-up fruit on a tray and fussed over his blanket and cushions, making him more comfortable in his chair by the window. He swatted her away and turned clear but weary eyes on Shae. "Why don't you come live at home? What have you been doing all this time?" Shae tensed, but her grandfather's questions were less angry than perplexed. Sad. "You want to live in Janloon but not be with your family? Are you seeing another man? Another foreigner you don't want to bring home?"

"No, Grandda," Shae said, irked now.

"Your brother needs you," he insisted. "You should help him."

"They don't need my help," Shae told him.

"What is wrong with you? You don't know who you are anymore," Kaul Sen declared. "I used to say *you* were my best grandson. You remember that?"

Shae did not answer him.

She tried not to keep watching the front drive the way one might watch a pot of water on the stove. She realized with dull despair that she'd become what she'd sworn she'd never be—a woman like her mother, sitting at home worrying while the men went off to meet danger and mete violence. Her younger self would be disgusted. She was a daughter of Kaul Du, a grandchild of Kaul Sen, indeed his *favorite*. Growing up, the idea of being any less than her brothers had been anathema.

Somewhere at the bottom of a drawer in her childhood bedroom, there was a journal she'd kept as a teenager at the Academy. If she were to set it on its spine, it would fall open to a page with a vertical line drawn down the center, dividing it into two columns. On the top of one column was her name; on the other was Hilo's. For years she'd recorded every score and rank she received as an initiate. Without his knowledge, she did the same for Hilo. He was more talented in some areas, but she practiced more consistently, studied harder, wanted it more. She graduated at the top of their class, despite being the youngest in their cohort. Hilo came in sixth.

She'd been a more highly-ranked Green Bone than her brother, and proud of it. It had taken her a few more years to realize how little it meant. The demerits that had pulled down Hilo's scores—reprimands for skipping class, sneaking off campus, instigating street fights—had won him the admiration and following of peers. The countless hours Shae had spent alone, obsessively studying or practicing, had isolated her from the other students, especially the other women. Hilo had spent that time idling with the wide posse of friends who would become his most loyal Fingers and Fists. Looking back on it now, Shae could almost laugh at her teenage naïveté, her hopeless earnestness, her inevitable disappointment.

One day, Hilo had discovered her journal and the two-column page meticulously comparing their ranks. He'd laughed so hard tears came to his eyes. He'd told his friends, and they'd teased her about it mercilessly. Shae had been furious and humiliated by how amused he was, how utterly nonchalant he felt about her mission to best him. Her anger only baffled and entertained him further.

"What're you saving this for?" He'd waved it in front of her. "So you're better than me at school, sure. Are you planning to lord it over me ten years from now?" He tossed it back to her, smiling, and this infuriated her further—how he didn't even bother to take it away or rip it up. "What do you need to try so *hard* for all the time, Shae? Lan will be Pillar someday; I'll be the Horn, and you'll be Weather Man. Who's going to care about our grades then?"

It had almost turned out that way. Lan was Pillar now, Hilo was the Horn. She was the one who'd ruined the triumvirate. She was the broken piece. Hilo had been so furious when she'd left, not because he hated Espenians, or Jerald, or even the things she'd done and the secrets she'd kept. It was her refusal to fall into proper place in his vision of the world that had enraged him. In the hotel, he claimed he'd forgiven her, but she found that difficult to believe.

She tried to interest her grandfather in the bowl of fruit, but he wouldn't have it, so she ate it herself. "The war was an easier time," Kaul Sen muttered all of a sudden. "The Shotarians were cruel, but we could resist them. These days? Espenians buy everything—our jade, our grandchildren. Green Bones fight each other in the streets like dogs!" His face twisted as if in pain. "I don't want to live in this world anymore."

Shae squeezed her grandfather's hand. He might be an old tyrant, but it disturbed her to hear him talk like this. She tugged on her right earlobe, remembering that Jerald had always teased her for the superstitious Kekonese habit. "Don't say that, Grandda." She glanced back out the window and stood up so quickly she nearly knocked over her grandfather's tray. The gates were opening. Cars were driving through and parking in the roundabout.

Shae called for Kyanla and hurried down the stairs. Her brothers were walking through the front door together. Relief swept over her, weakened her knees; she put a hand on the banister to steady herself. Lan gave her a smile that looked thin around the edges. "Don't look like that. I told you we'd be back, didn't I?"

Hilo said, "You missed all the fun, Shae." He threw a proud arm over Lan's shoulders and called back to his First Fist. "Kehn, get these guys sorted. I need some time for family talk. Don't let anyone else in."

They went back into Lan's study and shut the door. "What about Grandda?" Shae asked. "And Doru?"

"They can wait," Lan said.

Shae was astounded; to her recollection, Lan had always included Kaul Sen and Doru in the clan decisions. Shutting out the patriarch and the Weather Man was an affront. It sent the unmistakeable message that the winds in the clan had shifted dramatically.

More disturbing: *she* was in here. Her brothers had included her, even though she wasn't wearing jade. People might begin to think she was replacing Doru. She didn't want that at all, but she couldn't leave now. Even as she told herself she ought not to be in here, she sat down in one of the leather armchairs. Lan lowered himself gingerly into the one across from her, and she realized he was hurt. He wasn't bleeding, but he looked pale and drained, fragile in a way she'd never imagined her older brother could appear.

"Lan," she said, "you need a doctor."

"Later," he said. Shae noticed his left hand moving, rolling beads of jade in his palm—new jade, she realized. Jade he'd won.

"What happened?" she asked.

"We sent two of theirs to the grave." Hilo remained standing. He was still armed to the teeth, and hadn't relaxed. "Lan took one of their best Fists with a clean blade, and we executed the other. The Armpit's ours."

Shae said, "You're not smiling." Walking through the door ahead of his men, Hilo had been grinning and triumphant. Alone with Lan and Shae, he wore a scowl.

"This is just the opening move," Lan said. "They'll try again."

Hilo paced a short line in front of Lan's neatly-ordered bookshelves. "Ayt had men ambush me last night. Gont sent out his Fist to challenge Lan today. The Mountain's shown they can hit us hard at the top and not even show their faces. We might look like we're ahead for now, but they came too close. They hurt us. People will talk and it'll be bad for us."

Shae said, "You killed four of their men."

"Ten Fists don't matter next to the Pillar," Hilo said.

Lan shifted his attention to Shae. He seemed to be trying to move as little as necessary. "Tell us what you found out. From the Treasury."

Involuntarily, Shae glanced around the room, almost expecting to see Doru hovering in the corner. "I told you about the new equipment, the ones Gont Asch signed for. Well, it's being put to use. Production at the mines is up fifteen percent this year, the biggest increase in a decade," she said. "So I wondered, where is the extra jade going? I examined both KJA financial statements and there's no accounting for the increase. Foreign sales haven't increased; you told me yourself the vote to raise the export quota didn't pass. Allocation to the martial schools, temples, and licensed users is only up six percent. That leaves an awful lot of jade that's been mined but not distributed."

"So it's sitting in the vault," Hilo said.

"No, it's not," Shae said. "I went to the Kekon Treasury and checked the last three years of records. There's no increase in jade inventory that matches the growth in production. Somewhere between the mines and the vault, jade is going missing."

"How's that possible?" Lan asked. "The Weather Man's office audits—" He stopped himself. His back teeth came together, flexing his jaw line.

"Doru." Hilo spat the Weather Man's name. His head swung toward the closed door. "He's in on it. The Mountain is producing extra jade and smuggling it away under our noses, hoodwinking all the other clans in the KJA and the Royal Council too. That ball-less old ferret has been covering for Ayt and keeping us in the dark."

A shadow fell heavily across Lan's face. "Doru has always been loyal to the family. He's been like an uncle to us since we were children. I can't believe he would betray us to the Mountain."

"It's possible he doesn't know about the discrepancies," Shae suggested. "Someone under him could be tampering with the reports that he sees."

"You believe that?" Hilo asked.

Shae hesitated to answer. As repulsive as she found Doru, she had to agree with Lan that it was difficult to imagine the veteran Weather Man ever undermining the clan. When it came to war and business, her grandfather had trusted him absolutely for decades. How could the Torch himself have been such a poor judge of character? "I don't know," Shae said. "But he has to go. If he's not a traitor, then he's a negligent Weather Man."

Lan exchanged a glance with Hilo. "We'll find out which it is. We keep this to ourselves for now." Turning back to Shae, "You're certain you have proof of everything you've said?"

"Yes," Shae said.

"Document all of it and send three copies of your findings to Woon Papidonwa by tomorrow. Woon and no one else." Lan paused. "Thank you Shae. I appreciate what you've done, finding this out for us. I hope it didn't inconvenience you too much. I'm sorry if it did."

That was it. As quickly as they'd brought her in, she was being shown out. "It wasn't a burden," she managed to reply. Weeks of traveling, sitting in the Treasury's records room, combing through files, studying ledgers and reports until her eyes ached and it was dark outside. She could feel the weight of Hilo's stare following her as she stood up and went to the door.

"Shae," Lan said. She paused with a hand on the door, and he said in a gentler voice, "Come for dinner at the house sometimes. Whenever you want. No need to call ahead."

Shae nodded without turning, then let herself out. The heavy door clicked shut behind her. Shae leaned against it and shut her eyes for a moment, fighting down the same bewildering mixture of emotions she'd sat with in the taxi this morning. Why was she upset at being dismissed, when a few minutes ago she hadn't wanted to be in the room in the first place? She felt like slapping herself hard across both sides of the face. *You can't have it both ways!*

It was well that Lan had made her go. With shame, she admitted her grandfather was right after all; she didn't know who she was anymore.

• Chapter Twenty-Two •
HONOR, LIFE, AND JADE

Once the door closed behind Shae, Lan said to Hilo, "Have someone you trust watch Doru. Someone with little enough jade that he won't notice. You have a nose in the Weather Man's office?" When Hilo nodded, Lan said, "I want to know if he's had any contact with the Mountain. If he's really a traitor."

"Seems we could bring him in here and find out pretty quick right now."

Lan shook his head. "What if we're wrong? Then again, what if we're right? Doru is like a brother to Grandda. He's the only one Grandda has left from his glory days. You haven't seen them together every morning, those two. I have; they still drink their tea and play circle chess under the cherry tree in the courtyard, like an old married couple. It would kill the old man to see Doru accused of treason." Lan closed his eyes for a moment, then opened them again. "No," he said. "We have to know for sure, and if it's true, we have to handle it quietly, so Grandda never knows."

"Doru will suspect we're on to him," Hilo said, "and everyone else will ask questions. How are you going to explain the fact that we kept him out just now?"

"I'll smooth it over," Lan said. "I'll say we were talking privately with Shae, brother to sister, trying to convince her to come back into the clan."

Hilo sat down finally, in the seat Shae had vacated. Lan had to edge back in his own chair slightly. With new jade in his hand and in his pocket, Hilo's aura seemed too bright in his mind.

"What about Shae?" Hilo asked.

"What about her?"

"You told me not to push her. You said we're to leave her alone and let her walk around embarrassing herself with no jade on, if that's what she wants to do."

"That's right," said Lan.

"Then you send her to dig into clan business. You didn't even tell me. If I'd known she was working for you, I would've been nicer to her." Hilo tilted his head. "Don't get me wrong, I'm not disagreeing. But which is it? You want her in or out?"

Lan exhaled slowly through his nose. "I wouldn't have asked her to do anything for the clan, but I needed someone with a brain for numbers, someone not in Doru's control, to follow my suspicions. Considering what she found, I don't regret it, but it doesn't mean I've changed my mind."

"You're going to need a new Weather Man soon," Hilo pointed out.

"No," said Lan, sharply now. "If she decides she wants in, that's one thing. I'm not going to guilt, order, or threaten her back into the clan. She especially doesn't need any pressure from *you*. She gets enough from Grandda as it is. Shae has an Espenian education now—something neither of us has—so she has other options in life that we don't. Janloon's not just for Green Bones. You can choose to live without jade, an ordinary citizen with an ordinary life, like millions of other people."

Hilo held his hands up. "All right."

"You're not kids anymore. The two of you can make your own choices. I don't need to wipe bloody noses and tell you to show some respect to each other."

"I said all right." A moment of silence passed before Hilo said, "Lan. I didn't notice until I was sitting closer to you, but your aura doesn't seem right. It's..." He squeezed his eyes shut and turned his face aside, concentrating his Perception. "It's flaring, pulsing, kind of. It feels off. Not like you."

"It's all the new jade," Lan said. "It's taking a little getting used to. You know how it is." He was sitting still, but his heart was beating fast.

Hilo opened his eyes. "I don't think you should wear it."

"I won this jade." Lan was startled by his sudden defensiveness. "It's mine by right. You wear all the jade you've won, don't you?"

His brother shrugged. "Sure."

"What did you take last night?"

Hilo leaned back and shifted his hip off the chair so he could reach into his pockets and pull out his spoils. "The rings, bracelet, and pendant. I'll get them reset, obviously." He held them out for Lan's inspection. "The watch and these studs belong to the Maiks. There's a belt in my car that's their's by right too." He returned them to his pockets and sat back. "It's not as much as Gam's."

"You still have more overall." Lan blinked; had he just said that?

Hilo's eyes widened, surprised as well. "Is that what this is about?" He ran his tongue over his lips. "I'm the Horn, brother. People don't expect me to be smart. They do expect me to carry a shitload of jade. Everyone's different."

"Some people are better. Thicker-blooded." Lan wondered what was wrong with him, that he was sounding so bitter and testy. The fatigue from staying up for more than thirty-six hours straight, the fight in front of the Factory, and now the jade—it was all getting to him. Too much, too quickly. "It's been years since I've dueled, Hilo," he said. "Ayt killed her father's own Horn, and two of his Fists. Today I had to fight in front of our men, and I had to win. Tomorrow people will be paying attention, to see if I'm wearing the proof that I'm thick-blooded enough for No Peak to stand up to the Mountain in a war. You know better than anyone that it's true."

Hilo's gaze was straight. "You're right. It's true." He glanced down at the carpet, lips pursed, then back up again. "You don't have to do it right now, though. After what Gam hit you with? You're hurt. Put it down, Lan. Give yourself a break." He got up and held his hand out, offering to take it.

In a surge of possessiveness, Lan's fist tightened around the jade. *His* jade; how dare his little brother think to take it from him? Hilo's aura was too harsh and close, mentally blinding. He kept standing there though, hand extended, and Lan Perceived no greed, only concern.

In a burst of clarity he knew the jade was doing this: setting him on edge, skewing his emotions. He'd been taught the early warning signs of jade overexposure since he was a child; every Green Bone had. Severe mood swings, sensory distortion, shaking, sweating, fever, a racing heart, paranoia and anxiety. The appearance of symptoms could be sudden or gradual. They might come and go for months or years, but were exacerbated by stress, poor health, or injury. If left unaddressed, they could progress into the Itches, which were almost always fatal.

Hilo was looking at him intently now. Lan forced himself to open his hand and set the jade studs on the side table. He removed the chokers from his breast pocket and pushed all of Gam's jade away from himself.

A few seconds passed before the change kicked in, and then it was dramatic, as if a high fever had suddenly broken. His heart rate came down, the painful sharpness of the room receded. Hilo's aura returned to its usual smooth hum. Lan took a slow, deep breath and let it out again, trying not to let his relief appear too palpable. "Better?"

Hilo nodded and sat back down, but there was an uncertainty in his eyes that Lan did not like. So even Hilo doubted his ability. Kaul Sen was a decrepit old man, Doru might be a traitor, and Shae refused to even wear jade. It was only him and Hilo now. What was happening to the great Kaul family?

"You should go, Hilo," he said. "We both have things we need to do."

His brother did not move from the chair. "I have something else to ask you," he said. Lan had almost never seen his brother look nervous, but now Hilo rubbed his hands together and cleared his throat. "I want to marry Wen."

Lan tried not to sigh out loud. "Do we have to talk about this right now?"

"Yes." Hilo's voice took on sudden urgency. "After last night, I don't want to waste time, Lan. I don't want to be lying on the pavement bleeding out the last seconds of my life thinking I didn't do everything I meant to. That I didn't give her this one thing when I had the chance."

Lan's head ached and he felt dehydrated. The dramatic addition and then withdrawal of jade made him feel as if his skull had been pulled out too far and then squeezed back down too tightly. He rubbed his brow. "You really love her."

To his surprise, Hilo looked insulted. "Why would I be asking otherwise?"

Lan felt like telling him that love wasn't enough, not when it came to marriage. There was a time when he'd thought it would be enough. Eyni had thought so too. She'd known he would one day be Pillar. She'd assured him she understood what that meant, that everything would work out fine in the end because they loved each other. He'd convinced her, and maybe himself, that stepping into his grandfather's role wouldn't change him, wouldn't change things between him and Eyni. They'd been wrong of course. Looking back, Lan could see now that there'd been cracks before-hand, but him becoming the Pillar had shaken those cracks into impassable fissures.

Warnings about the impermanence of love would not work on Hilo, though. He was not the sort of person who would ever view something so important to him in such an abstracted fashion. "You know how I feel about Wen," Lan said. "She's a lovely girl. She's always been respectful to the clan and I'd gladly treat her like my sister. But her family is beneath you. Everyone knows the Maiks were disgraced. A lot of people in No Peak still think they can't be trusted, and even if they don't say it out loud, they assume Wen is illegitimate."

Hilo's neck flushed and his face grew stiff. "All that happened years ago. You shouldn't blame the Maiks for their parents. I made Kehn and Tar my First and Second Fists—I wouldn't have done that if I didn't trust them with my life. And I don't care who Wen's father really is. She's of the No Peak clan as far as anyone is concerned, and she's a good person—caring and loyal."

"I'm sure she is," Lan said. "She's also a stone-eye. There are always go-ing to be people who see her as bad luck, or whisper she was born that way because she's a bastard and a punishment to her parents. Don't look so angry at me. I'm only telling you that the clan can have long and superstitious memories. You're the Horn; you have to think about that."

"I don't care what anyone else in the clan thinks, it's *you* I'm asking." Hilo sounded almost desperate. "You're willing to forgive Shae completely and welcome her back, but you balk at accepting the Maiks?"

"That's different," Lan said. "Shae is a Kaul no matter what. You're mak-ing the decision to bind our family to a disreputable name, and to father children with a stone-eye wife."

Hilo's aura roiled with tension. Tautly, "What can I say to convince you?" His eyes fastened to Lan's. "I swear I'll never ask you for anything else."

Sometimes it astounded Lan that his younger brother could be so dif-ferent from him. Short-sighted, yes, but fully committed. Passionate in a way that left so little room for doubt. Lan said, "You've already made up your mind. I've said my concerns, but it's your decision, Hilo. You don't need my permission."

"Don't say that," Hilo snapped. "That's a bullshit excuse." He leaned so far forward in his chair that he half-rose from it. "You're my older brother. You're the Pillar! When Grandda was Pillar, he didn't let a leaf drop in the courtyard without his permission. People came to him to approve their marriages, their new businesses, the names of their kids and dogs, the color of their fucking wallpaper for all I know. Give me your blessing, or condemn me, but don't wash your hands of me. It wouldn't mean anything for me to marry Wen without the approval of the Pillar. No one would take it seriously."

On the other hand, if Lan endorsed the union, he would be publicly forgiving the Maik family. He would be sending the message that their past betrayal had been wiped clean. The Maiks would be elevated to the right hand of the Kauls. Other families would be jealous and angry. If he did not give his permission, however, he would hurt Hilo—and Hilo could be dramatically hurt. He would damage the relationship with his brother and his Horn at a time when the clan could not afford any further weakness in the family.

Lan's arms and legs felt heavy enough to sink him straight through the cushioned chair. It seemed everything in the clan required a decision from him that would invariably hurt or offend others and cause further problems.

Looking at Hilo's face, though, he realized he couldn't find it in himself to refuse his brother's request. Even if he'd known how things would turn out with Eyni, would he never have taken a gamble on overcoming the odds? He didn't think he could say so. As for Hilo and Wen, all the objections Lan had voiced—past sins, clan politics, superstition—they didn't touch those few seconds last night in the Lilac Divine when Maik Kehn had answered the Pillar's unspoken panic with, "He's alive. He's fine," and Lan had understood, as he gripped the door frame, that he wasn't ready to be a wartime Pillar. He wasn't equipped to handle that kind of violent loss in his own family.

"You're right, Hilo. It's better to think about today when tomorrow might not happen. I give you my blessing to marry Maik Wen," Lan said. He did his best to sound as sincere and positive as such a statement warranted. "Set a date. As soon as you want."

Hilo left the chair and knelt on the carpet. He raised clasped hands to his forehead. "The clan is my blood, and the Pillar is its master," Hilo said, reciting the ceremonial Green Bone clan oaths they'd both taken years ago. "Should I ever be disloyal to my brother, may I die by the blade. Should I ever fail to come to the aid of my brother, may I die by the blade. Should I ever seek personal gain at the expense of my brother, may I die by the blade." He bowed low, touching his forehead to the carpet. "On my honor, my life, and my jade."

Lan wanted to protest the overly dramatic display of gratitude, but when Hilo straightened up, he was smiling his open, easy smile—the one that suggested he was not worried, and no else need be either, and all was as it should be. He didn't look like someone who'd been through the same day as Lan had.

Hilo got off the floor, gathered his weapons off the desk, and rested a hand on Lan's shoulder as he left the room. He pointed at the pile of Gam's jade. "Get some sleep before you try putting it back on."

• Chapter Twenty-Three •
AUTUMN FESTIVAL GIFTS

The wind howled and needles of rain hit the back of Bero's neck as he hefted the last of the boxes into the van and clambered in after it. The other boy, who they called Cheeky, yanked the back doors shut. "Go! GO!" Bero shouted at the driver.

The van squealed into motion, throwing Bero against the wall of the vehicle. He crawled up and around the containers packed with cartons of expensive brand-name wallets, shoes, handbags, and belts—and squeezed through the middle of the van into the passenger side seat. He stuck his head out the window to look behind them—the truck driver was still lying on his stomach under his semi-trailer with his hands over his head. There was no sign of pursuit.

Pulling his head back into the van, Bero rolled up the window and relaxed a little, then more so once the van hit the KI-1 freeway, speeding southward away from the Docks. The rain picked up, splattering the wind-shield as fast as the noisy wipers could handle. Through the shimmery glare of water, the lights of the other cars on the road were bright red splotches, like Autumn Festival lamps. Bero shoved the pistol more securely into the waistband of his pants and whooped as he punched the van's ceiling. "That was *cut*, kekes."

The entire operation had taken less than five minutes. Speed and plan-ning were the key to a successful lift. Security was tight, and mistakes were deadly; armed guards protected the ships, and Green Bones patrolled the Docks. The best approach was to hijack trailer trucks once they had been loaded but before they entered the motorway. Bero was new at this game but he was a quick study and hungry for work. This was his third successful lift in as many weeks. That pleased Mudt, which in turn, pleased the people behind Mudt, people Bero very much wanted to meet.

The driver of the van, an untalkative man named Tas, who had bad skin and only ever wore black tee shirts, pulled the van off the freeway into the south part of Junko. He drove into the alley behind the Goody Too discount store and backed up to the open garage door. Mudt came out to inspect the goods. He grunted in satisfaction and counted out payment on the top of a secondhand pool table while Cheeky and Mudt's son unloaded the merchandise. "You have to be more careful now," he said, throwing in an extra bit of cash for each of them. "The clans are going at each other."

Clan war was both opportunity and danger. Green Bones busy fighting each other were less vigilant against thieves and smugglers, but they made up for the lapse by being more merciless to those they caught, especially any with possible ties to enemy clans. "You got more tips for us?" Bero asked, zipping the money into the inside pocket of his jacket. A gust of strong wind rattled the half open garage door.

Mudt pulled a folded manila envelope from his back pocket and held it out to Tas. The man shook his head. "I'm out."

"You're out?" Bero exclaimed. "After that kind of a lift?"

Tas grumbled, "Not ready to die yet. Gonna quit while I'm ahead." He jerked his chin at Bero. "Give it to him." Tas walked back to the van.

Mudt didn't even watch Tas go. He passed the envelope to Bero, who opened it and glanced inside quickly. Several sheets of paper stapled together: a list of JK Trucking company's schedule in and out of Summer Harbor for the next sixty days. He smiled, impressed at Mudt's access to such useful information. He stowed it inside his jacket next to the cash.

A blast of rain blew into the garage, drenching the concrete floor, shaking box flaps and loose items. "Hey!" Mudt shouted at his son. "Close that door before we drown here. Then go back out front and start taping up the windows. Yofo's in a fucking mood. Typhoon's coming, tomorrow or the day after, for sure." He ran a hand through his damp, wiry hair. His sleeve fell a few inches down his forearm and Bero glimpsed needle track marks on the inside of the man's wrists. Mudt motioned Cheeky over, then said to both him and Bero, in a conspiratorial voice, "You boys have been doing good. So good that someone wants to meet you. Maybe move you up, give you some more work. You cut with that?"

"Yeah, I'm cut," Bero said. Cheeky gave a nervous sniff but nodded.

"I thought so." Mudt turned toward the store. "Let's go then."

"He's here right now?" Bero asked.

"Right here, right now," Mudt sang out, jovial, gesturing for them to follow him. "Today's your lucky night, kekes."

They walked through the inside garage door into the front of the store. It was long past closing time and the place was locked up. One strip of florescent lighting was turned on near the back, illuminating racks of sunglasses and bins of plastic sandals near the entrance to the restrooms. Shadowy aisles stretched away into the rest of the building. The only other two people inside were Mudt's teenage son, who was unrolling blue masking tape in large Xs across the windows, and a man, sitting in the dark on the cash register counter, a duffel bag on the ground below his feet.

Mudt walked Bero and Cheeky over to the man and brought his hands up to his forehead in salute. "These are the guys I told you about," Mudt said. "One of them wasn't hungry enough and bailed out, so it's just the two of them now."

The man hopped off the table. He was a Green Bone, with a short goatee, jade bolts through his ears, and a jade ring in his nose. He wore a long forest green rain slicker over dark clothes and boots. He looked Bero and Cheeky over with mild interest, the hollows of his eyes shadowed. "What're your names?"

Bero told him, then raised clasped hands. "And what do you call you, jen?"

"You don't call me anything," said the Green Bone. "I don't know you and you don't know me. This is No Peak territory. So if you're caught by any of Kaul's men, and they torture the shit out of you, you won't be screaming my name." At the boys' silence, a smile curved the man's mouth. "Does that frighten you? If it does, you might want to consider stepping back out that door the way you came."

"We're not frightened," said Cheeky, not entirely convincingly.

"I want what Mudt has," Bero said. "Just tell me how to get it."

The Green Bone gave a knowing nod. "Jade fever's a bitch, isn't it? If you got your hands on a piece of green right now, without any training or some quality shine, you'd give off an aura like a fucking fire alarm. The first

Green Bone to come anywhere near you would know you for a thief and kill you in three seconds flat." The man paused, tugging lightly on his goatee. "Now Mudt here is a special case. See, he's a friend of the clan: he tells us things we need to know, he does work for us in places we can't be. We appreciate that, so we take care of him. He has, let's call it…associate status. You could have that too, if you prove yourself to the clan."

The boys nodded.

"Good. Green Bones take jade from the bodies of their enemies. So if you're going to be a warrior, you'll need weapons." The goateed Green Bone knelt and unzipped the duffel bag at his feet. He withdrew a Fullerton C55 submachine gun. He handed it to Bero, then pulled out a second one and gave it to Cheeky. Bero felt the weight of the thing in his hands and sucked in a breath. He'd never owned anything bigger than a pocket-sized pistol and couldn't believe his luck. He felt as if he were holding a baby; he didn't know where to put his hands, how to properly cradle such a valuable object. "Shit. This is for real? You're giving these to us?"

"Happy Autumn Festival," said the man. "You better practice a whole lot before I send you to use them. Mudt will show you how." The Green Bone rose deadly fast and wrapped a hand around each of the boys' throats. With no time to move or gasp, they froze. With his Strength he could tear out both their windpipes. "If I hear that you held up a gas station or shot any bystanders, I'll break all your bones, and then your necks. You work for me now, you understand?"

The boys nodded and he released them, giving them each a reassuring pat. "For the time being, learn to use those things. Keep pulling the lifts at the Docks that Mudt's been setting you up with. Keep your eyes and ears open, and *don't get caught*. When I need you, I'll let you know, and I'll expect you to be ready. You cut?"

"We're cut, jen," Bero said.

Outside, the wind had picked up. The silhouettes of trees whipped back and forth under the swaying streetlights. The roof of the building shook and creaked. Mudt's son had finished taping the windows and disappeared into the backroom.

The goateed Green Bone slung his duffel bag over his shoulder. "Best be going. The neighborhood and the weather aren't so friendly. Mudt, good doing business with you, as usual." He extended to Mudt the final item he'd brought out from the bag, an unmarked white cardboard container the size of a small shoebox, sealed with packing tape. Mudt reached for it eagerly but the Green Bone pulled it back at the last second, holding it just out of reach. His voice lowered, treading a line between friendly concern and unmistakeable threat. "Are you following the rules, Mudt? Same dose every day, no hoarding or reselling?" When Mudt nodded vehemently, the Green Bone handed him the box and smiled. "Always important to have safety reminders."

"Sure. Thank you, jen," Mudt murmured, his relief palpable.

The Green Bone lifted the hood of his rain slicker over his head. His boots clomped down the dark center aisle of the Goody Too. He turned the lock, opened the door, and walked out into the approaching typhoon.

• **Chapter Twenty-Four** •
AFTER THE TYPHOON

Typhoon Lokko hit Kekon two days before the Autumn Festival, as if Yofo the Unforgiving had awoken in time to meet the end of season deadline. In Janloon, businesses and schools closed as residents hunkered inside, wadding towels around their windows and doors as savage winds and torrential rain pounded the east coast of the island. Red lamps, woven grass streamers, and other Autumn Festival decorations honoring the fertile marriage of Thana the Moon and Guyin the Mountain King were ripped from eaves and sent hurtling through flooded streets.

At Kaul Du Academy, classes were canceled but work was not. The main Gathering Hall was filled with pallets of dried and canned food, bottles of purified water, and stacks of plastic tents and blankets. No Peak had paid for all the supplies. Academy students divided and packed them into smaller boxes for distribution to people who would need them in the typhoon's aftermath. Green Bones protected and came to the aid of the common people in times of need; it had been that way for as long as there had been Green Bones.

Anden cut the plastic wrapping off flats of canned vegetables as the lights shook and water sluiced the dark windows like the inside of a car wash. The campus had a backup generator in case of power outage, but if that failed, they would have to work with headlamps and flashlights. Despite the raging of the elements outside, the conversation inside the hall was animated.

"My folks have two shops in Sogen," said Heike heatedly, "which will be a godsdamned war zone. If the Mountain can't have the Armpit, they'll go after Sogen. I already told them, if things get any worse, it's not worth the risk; you either close up those locations or you eat the cost of double tribute until things sort themselves out."

"Going to war with the Mountain," muttered Lott, breaking apart jumbo blister packs of batteries. "The Kauls are out of their minds." His hands stilled in mid-motion and he glanced over at Anden, so quickly no one else noticed it. Quick defiance flashed across Lott's features. He shifted his gaze away and pushed the hair from his eyes. "Green Bones are always bloodthirsty, though. How would we prove who's greener if we didn't look for excuses to fight each other? That's what we're here for after all, isn't it? To become *warriors*."

There was a moment of uncomfortable silence from the others. If Lott had spoken in a casual or self-deprecating manner, they might've brushed it off or grumbled some mildly cynical agreement, but his delivery had been too resentful and acidic. Anden dropped his own eyes, his face warming.

"That's a narrow way of looking at it," replied Pau Noni, with some heat of her own. Pau came from a family wealthy and modern enough to have sent not just sons but daughters to the Academy—a more common occurrence on Kekon these days than back in the time when Ayt Yu had sent his adopted daughter to be trained in the same manner as her brothers. "Being educated as a Green Bone opens up opportunities," Pau pointed out. "We're part of an honorable tradition. Even if you never fight in a duel, once you're a graduate of the Academy, you've proven something. No one can take that away from you."

"Unless they kill you," Lott replied. "If there's a clan war, we'll be expected to fight. We'll be fresh meat for the Mountain as soon as we get our jade."

With a touch of challenge in her voice, Pau said, "You could also say there're bound to be more chances to move up in the clan. If you're the right sort."

Lott countered coldly. "And what if you don't want to be the '*right*' sort?"

Dudo threw up his hands. "What are you going to do, Lott? Become a Year Eight Yomo?" That made everyone chuckle uncomfortably and diffused some of the tension that had been building. A few students dropped out of the Academy each year—much to the everlasting shame of their families—but typically such occurrances happened early in training. Only one person, over a decade ago, had left the Academy in his final year and not graduated as a Green Bone. His name was still invoked by the instructors, with near mythological overtones, in harsh cautionary reference to the possibility of spectacular failure and disgrace at the eleventh hour.

A touch of color crept into Lott's face and he dropped his eyes back down to his work. "Of course not," he muttered, though scorn remained in his voice.

Ton shifted the conversation back to the situation in general. "I think it's the Horn that wants war. Kaul Lan isn't the type."

"*That* sort of talk is exactly why the Pillar had to take a stand," Dudo exclaimed. "About fucking time, too. The Mountain came after his brother; what did they expect? Good for him, showing everyone that he's as thick-blooded as the old Kaul." Dudo was a typical Academy student. The second son of a prominent Lantern Man family, his elder brother would inherit the family business while Dudo would wear jade and swear oaths to serve the clan, thus ensuring the family's continued favor and prominence within No Peak. This seemed to suit Dudo fine, as he had no interest in component manufacturing, or tact. "Ever since the Torch got old and retired, the other clans assume No Peak's in decline. They won't pay us respect unless some blood gets spilled once in a while."

The assassination attempt on Kaul Hilo and the ensuing showdown in front of the Factory had been the subject of constant conversation at the Academy for the past two weeks. Everyone, it seemed, had a relative, or friend, or relative of a friend, who was a Finger in No Peak and had been there and seen Kaul Lan kill Gam Oben. It gave Anden a strange feeling to know that Gam—the dark, athletic-looking Second Fist who'd saved him from the Wie Lon boys outside the Hot Hut, a man with no small amount of jade—was now dead by Lan's hand.

Anden stacked cans of wax beans in boxes and stayed out of the discussion. Perhaps because he was unlucky enough to have inherited his father's light coloring and foreign eyes, when he remained quiet about clan issues, the other students tended to speak freely around him, forgetting who he was. He was already a mixed-blood bastard, the prodigious son of an infamous mother, and, they all suspected, queer (though how that had, mortifyingly, gotten back to Hilo, Anden still had no idea). At any rate, he wasn't keen to openly advertise the Kaul family's patronage and give his classmates more reason to keep him at a wary distance.

Listening now, however, he had to bite back frustration. For once, he wanted to flaunt his status in the clan and speak up, to tell his classmates that they didn't really know the Kauls. Lan and Hilo were human beings with worries and flaws like everyone else, and they were doing the best they could for the clan—no jadeless student had a right to judge them. Certainly not Lott Jin—what did he know?

Anden clamped his jaw and moved away from the group to unload another box. Why hadn't he said something to rebuke Lott before Pau and Dudo had? It was *his* family involved in the war, his cousins—more like his brothers—that Lott had openly disparaged. If Anden had been a Kaul in blood and name, those might've been fighting words. He ought to have demanded an apology, but now it was too late. His lifelong habit of being unassuming, and his feelings for Lott Jin, had stuck his tongue and now the moment had passed.

The wind outside of the Gathering Hall roared like an animal in pain. Anden tried to tell himself it was better that he'd kept quiet. There was no call to take any of the talk personally. To most people in Janloon, clan war was like the typhoon outside: a force of nature, something to hide from, endure, bemoan, and remark upon, the deadly toll inevitable and later to be tallied. Out of all the students in the room discussing the war, to Anden alone was it so personal.

He'd heard the news of what happened no sooner than anyone else, passed initially as rumors in the dining hall at breakfast: "Did you hear? The Horn's been shot dead." Anden had nearly dropped the bowl he'd been carrying. A horrible icy shock and disbelief had flooded him from head to toe. Before he could even turn around to locate the speaker, someone else spoke up: "That's not true. They tried to kill him, but it was one of his Fists that was shot. The Horn's still alive, but some of the assassins escaped and now the Kauls are going to go after the Mountain."

"Where did you hear this?" Anden demanded, his hands shaking.

The table of year-sixes looked up at him with startled expressions. "My brother's a Finger who patrols the Armpit," said the boy who'd just spoken. "I talked to him an hour ago. He said they've been up all night and have just been called to the Kaul house."

The news continued to build into wild speculation and conflicting reports by midday. The Pillar and the Horn had gone to the Factory. Blood had been shed. The residents of the Academy had no personal phones in their rooms; it was evening by the time Anden, in a frenzy that everyone seemed to know more about what was going on than he did, managed to get onto the phone in the dormitory hallway and call the Kaul house. Kyan-la gave him the number to reach Hilo at his girlfriend's apartment.

"Don't worry, Andy." Hilo sounded to be in remarkably good spirits.

"Is there anything I can do?" he asked.

"Can you graduate by tomorrow? No? Then like I said, don't worry."

"How about Lan-jen?" Anden was still having a hard time imagining Lan killing a man in a duel to the death. Not that the Pillar wasn't one of the most powerful Green Bones he knew, but he'd never seemed in need of violence. Lan rarely even raised his voice. "Kyanla said he was out of the house seeing a doctor. Is he all right?"

There was a brief pause on the line before Hilo said, "He's the Pillar, Andy. He can handle whatever the Mountain throws at us, like he did today. Didn't I say to you there'd be trouble like this? So don't be surprised. Pass your Trials, is all."

"I will," Anden promised. "Six more months, and I'll be able to help."

"I know, Andy, relax. I'm counting on it."

When he hung up, he was still edgy and troubled and had a hard time falling asleep that night. All his life, Anden had thought of the Kauls as near invincible. He could muster nothing but resentment and contempt for his foreign father (Espenians were all the same: vapid, arrogant, and faithless) and his mother had been a tragedy of poor judgment and insanity that in-spired in him a combination of grief, disdain, and horror. The Kauls were the family he wished he'd been born into.

Now, as Anden busied himself in a corner of the Gathering Hall, stack-ing finished boxes and not returning to the conversation with Lott and the others, he thought about what had happened to him on Boat Day. When he'd been taken into Gont's car and driven to meet with Ayt, he'd been viewed as a Kaul, had been anxiously aware of being a Kaul—and yet also treated like a child and powerless to help in any meaningful way. He felt the same way now.

When the typhoon was over, Janloon looked as if it had been power washed by a horde of clumsy giants. Trees and electrical poles were knocked down, cars overturned, some parts of Fishtown, The Forge, and the Temple district were flooded. Anden and his Academy classmates spent several days manning relief centers, distributing supplies to people without electricity, running water, or enough food. At times like this, there was peace on the streets. The clans tended to the people of their own territories and helped their Lantern Men to clean up and rebuild. In disputed or neutral areas the clans worked alongside each other in unspoken temporary truce.

On the afternoon of Autumn Festival itself, Anden found himself clearing debris from the roads in the Temple district. The typhoon had broken the last of the summer heat and cleared the skies into startling, smog free blue. "Happy Autumn Festival!" people shouted to each other, with some sarcasm, as they threw rubble into industrial garbage bins and swept sidewalks. The crowds milling in and out of the district's many houses of worship were smaller than usual, but there were still plenty of chanting and firecrackers to be heard echoing up and down the neighborhood.

"Let's wheel that bin over there to the curb," Lott said, pointing to a dense tangle of fallen tree branches in the street. Anden followed Lott, hauling the trash bin behind him. They set it down and worked together, gathering and breaking the splintered wood, filling the container. They did not speak at first; Anden was trying to decide whether to still be angry at Lott for his comments in the Gathering Hall two days ago. If Lott noticed Anden's frequent, involuntary glances at him, he did not acknowledge or return them. He seemed absorbed in the current task and distant in his thoughts, his sulky mouth set in a slight frown as his ropey arms tensed, snapping branch after branch.

Anden turned away, exasperated with himself, and bent to pick up scattered roof shingles. Anden did not personally know anyone else who was queer besides Master Teoh, the senior Perception instructor. Lott, he was not sure about. They were in the same circle of friends, but Anden could not call Lott a friend in a personal sense—they were always together with other people, and Lott had closer companions such as Dudo and Heike, with whom he spent his free time. Anden had never tried to interject himself into their close circle or to be so presumptuous as to seek his classmate out alone. He'd heard Lott express interest in women in the typical casual way, although as far as Anden knew, those had never turned into anything particularly serious. Serious relationships were not easy for anyone to accomplish at the Academy, which maintained a traditionally monastic attitude regarding romantic relationships between students—which was to say, it was officially forbidden.

Still, there were times when Anden thought he caught *something* from the other young man—a gaze held overlong, a quickness to be on the same side in a game of pick-up relayball, an interest glimpsed in an act as mundane as sharing the task of breaking up and clearing debris from a street.

The Kekonese viewed queerness as a natural occurrence in the population, much like stone-eyes, and did not blame the person in question any more than one would blame a child for being born deaf. Like stone-eyes though, they were considered unfortunate and unlucky, a sign that a family had fallen into disfavor with the gods, who saw fit to prune the offending lineage as punishment. Anden was not surprised or particularly troubled by this view. He already knew his family was cursed. In general, however, people were uncomfortable around misfortune, and reluctant to admit to their own. He was certain that some people at the Academy tugged their right earlobes behind his back—but glancing at Lott again, watching him pause to draw a forearm over his sweaty brow and stretch his long spine before reaching for another branch, he felt a hurtful pang in his chest to imagine that Lott might be one of them.

Abruptly, Lott said, "I heard about what happened to you on Boat Day."

Anden was startled. He paused before tossing a chunk of rubble into the bin and wiping his dusty hands on his pants. He hadn't told anyone at the Academy about what had happened on Boat Day, not because he meant to keep it a secret, but because it was not in his nature to draw attention to himself. The conversations he'd had with Gont and Ayt seemed like clan business that Lan and Hilo might not want spread around, so he'd told his classmates he'd gotten lost in the crowd and made his way back to the Academy alone.

Lott said, "I heard it from my da."

Anden nodded slowly. It had slipped his mind that Lott's father was a high-ranking Fist. It was strange to think he probably answered directly to Hilo. "He was there?" Anden couldn't remember all the men who'd been flanking the Horn that day.

"He was disappointed the Mountain let you go." Lott's sulky mouth twisted with black amusement. "The Horn would've gone to war for you, he said. He would've gotten to storm Little Hammer, win more jade for himself, my da. Had a building surrounded already and everything."

Anden looked away, pulling off his glasses and wiping specks of grit from the lenses to hide his confusion. Whenever he felt he and Lott shared some moment of possible friendship, some connection, no matter how minor, there would be, not long after, something to suggest the complete opposite. This seemed to be one of those instances. Why would Lott tell him such a thing?

"Then I guess your da is happy now, with the war looking so likely," Anden said, his voice a monotone that did not hide the fact he thought Lott's comment had been in poor taste. "I didn't even have to die to start it."

Lott smirked. "Don't take it personal, keke. I don't care what my da thinks." He tossed another branch into the trash bin, then leaned against it, his dark eyes climbing over Anden with interest. Anden's pulse gave a skip.

Lott said, "You've got a lot more going on than you let show, don't you? You're more clan than the rest of us, but you stay quiet about it. I can't quite figure out if that's who you really are." His tone was idly curious, but there was a perplexed intensity to his gaze, perhaps even a touch of anger.

Uncomfortably, Anden tried to think of how to answer.

From the other side of the intersection, Ton called out, "Look at that." Anden turned around and his stomach lurched in a jolt of recognition. A shiny black ZT Valor was driving slowly down the street, towing a flatbed trailer with two Mountain Green Bones, a man and a woman, sitting perched on the end of it. The car stopped on a street corner and honked. The two Green Bones hopped off and began handing out yellow cakes from long aluminum trays crammed with the traditional festive treat. A crowd quickly formed, pressing eagerly but respectfully up to the vehicle. "Happy Autumn Festival," the Green Bones said, "One each, please. Happy Autumn Festival."

The door of the Valor opened and Gont Asch stepped out. Even dressed for the holiday in a white shirt and dark suit, with most of his jade out of sight, his physical presence was such that the throng made room for him at once. "Thank you, Gont-jen," they called, saluting him. "May the gods shine favor on the Mountain." The Horn of the Mountain nodded amiably, spoke to some of the crowd, remarked upon the cleanup efforts, handed out yellow cakes. Anden went back to his work, studiously ignoring the scene, but his jaw was clenched as he broke discarded tree branches over his knee with greater and greater force.

"You four. Academy boys," Gont's deep voice called. "Come here."

They hesitated, looking at each other, but it would be blatantly impolite not to obey. Ton and Dudo approached, and after another moment of hesitation, Lott and Anden followed. Gont handed each of them a yellow cake—warm and soft, freshly baked, smelling of butter and fruit paste. "For your hard work," said the Horn.

Ton, Dudo, and Lott looked down at the cakes in their hands with nervous surprise. "Thank you, Gont-jen," Ton murmured, and the other two echoed him, saluting one-handed as they retreated judiciously. Before Anden could do the same, Gont wrapped an arm around his shoulders with the slow weight of a python's coils. He spoke in a low rumble, too near Anden's ear for the others to overhear. "I'm disappointed you didn't accept our offer."

The first time he'd met Gont in front of the Hot Hut in Summer Park, Anden had been intimidated, impressed by the man's powerful and eloquent presence. Now he thought: *Gont Asch tried to kill my cousins. He wants to see everyone in the Kaul family dead.* He could feel all the jade on the man's arm, the weight of its dense energy resting across the back of his neck. Anden forced himself to raise his eyes to meet the Horn's. "I may look Espenian on the outside, Gont-jen," he said. "But that doesn't mean I can be bribed like a dog."

With no surprise or hint of affront in his voice, Gont said, "Today is the Autumn Festival and the gods expect us to show generosity. So I will give you some advice, Anden Emery. Don't insult the Pillar's regard for you by offending us in the future. It would be a shame for us to be enemies." Gont released Anden and returned to the Valor and its towed cargo of cakes.

Anden rejoined his classmates, who were standing on the other side of the street, wiping cake crumbs from their mouths. "What did he say to you?" Lott asked, looking at Anden with even more curious uncertainty than before.

"He wished me a Happy Autumn Festival." Anden stared down at the warm pastry in his hand but did not feel like eating it. He watched Gont's car move down the street. "And he wanted to make it clear that if I become a Fist in No Peak, the Mountain will make a point of killing me."

• Chapter Twenty-Five •
LINES DRAWN

Although the Mountain stopped terrorizing No Peak's properties in the Armpit, Kaul Hilo was well aware that his clan had otherwise gained little from the agreement. Their rivals had surrendered the parts of the district that were rightfully No Peak's to begin with and shrewdly kept control of their strongholds south of Patriot Street which included some of Janloon's most profitable betting houses.

He could spare neither the time nor the manpower to further bolster their position in the Armpit, on account of being diverted by trouble in the Docks. *The Docks!* Of all places. Undisputed No Peak turf, home to longstanding businesses like the Twice Lucky and the Lilac Divine. A crime spree had erupted—thieves were raiding transport trailers carrying imported luxury goods, and reselling them on the black market. The culprits, as far as anyone could tell, were common street gangs, but the scale and timing of the outbreak were cause for suspicion. Hilo's intuition was confirmed when Kehn and his Fingers caught three of the thieves who, under persuasion, admitted that a man whose name they didn't know—a man with *jade*—had provided them with trucking schedules and cargo manifests out of Summer Harbor.

"What do we do with them, Hilo-jen?" Kehn asked over the phone.

Hilo pulled the metal phone cord as far as it would go, stepping around the corner and turning his back to the nurse wheeling an empty bed down the hospital corridor. He put a hand over the other ear to block out the clatter of wheels on linoleum. In the background of wherever Kehn was calling from, he heard cursing, sobbing, and incoherent muffled noises. Thieves were the most despised kind of criminal on Kekon. Lifting shipments of watches and handbags normally merited a beating and a branding, but this was different. This had Gont Asch's fingerprints on it. The Mountain was not above recruiting jadeless criminals to harass No Peak on their behalf.

"Kill two of them, let the most talkative one go," Hilo said.

He hung up and went in to see Tar. "Good news," he said. "They're telling me you'll be out of here in a couple of days."

Tar was sitting up in bed. Bullets had lacerated his spleen and perforated his bowel; he'd been through surgeries and transfusions. Some of his jade had been removed before he'd gone into the operating room and he was only now strong enough to be wearing it again, but his aura was as thin and prickly as his mood. "About time. The doctors here don't know shit, and the food is terrible."

"I'll have someone bring you something you like. What do you want? You want some takeout noodles? Something spicy?"

"Anything. I feel a lot better. That green doctor you sent did a good job."

"Prized family resource," Hilo said. Green Bone physicians, technically beholden to no clan but skilled at Channeling therapeutically, were rare and in high demand. Hilo had had Dr. Truw, the staff physician at Kaul Du Academy, pay a few visits to Tar. Technically, that wasn't allowed by the hospital, but no one was going to argue.

"I'm going to marry your little sister," Hilo told him. "Lan agreed, so it's official in the clan. I'll take good care of her, I promise."

Tar said, "You know I'd follow you anywhere, whether you married Wen or not, right? Just get me out of this hospital already."

"I know," Hilo said. "Relax while you can. I'll be needing you plenty, as soon as you're out." It was plain that Tar was bitter about being wounded and away from the action, but Hilo didn't feel like assuaging his Fist's ego, or talking business. "You have a good suit?" he asked. "You'll need to look good for the wedding."

Hilo was, at least, pleased and relieved that after the attempt on his life, Wen had quickly acquiesced to living on the Kaul estate. "I'll move into the main house," he'd reassured her, though the thought of rooming down the hall from his grandfather made him grimace. "You'll be in the Horn's house. You can do whatever you like to it. New carpet, new paint, whatever. Spend what you like, the money doesn't matter."

"Yes," she said, her lips pale and firm, her face weary from nights spent at the hospital by Tar's bedside. She glanced around her small, but tidy and well-decorated apartment with detachment, as if she was ready to leave at once. "You're right. Now I know how badly our enemies want you dead. My pride isn't worth the risk of them using me to hurt you."

Having gotten his way, he felt grateful and affectionate. He gathered Wen into his arms and kissed her face many times. "There's nothing for you to be ashamed of," he said. "We're engaged now. I asked Lan. He gave us his blessing. Kaul Maik Wen—don't you like the sound of that? We can plan a wedding, a big one. Pick a date. I was thinking soon—springtime, what do you think?"

Wen wrapped her arms around his ribcage and held onto him so tightly that the new jade studs dug into the still tender flesh of his chest and he laughed at the discomfort. She said, with little expression, "Lan is a good peacetime Pillar but he's not a commander of Fists. There's no one else with enough jade and respect in the clan to be a strong wartime Horn in your place. The Mountain knows that without you, Lan will have no choice but to give in to them. That's why they're clever to want to kill you first, and why they'll try again."

Hilo frowned. This wasn't the discussion he'd hoped to elicit after sharing the news that they were to be married. "Let the fuckers try." He cupped Wen's chin to look into her eyes. "Are you worried about being a young widow, like my ma? Is that why you're not excited about the wedding? *I'm* excited. I thought you'd be excited."

"Should I be? Womanishly thrilled about dress shopping and banquet planning, while others plan the murder of my fiancé and my brothers?"

"You don't have to talk down to me like that," Hilo said, irritated. "I'll always have enemies, but that doesn't mean you shouldn't be happy. You have to trust me, Wen. If anything happens to me, or to Kehn and Tar, you'll be taken care of, I promise you that. I'll make sure everything I leave is in your name. You won't even be tied to the clan like my ma was, if you don't want to be."

Wen was silent for a moment. "Now that I'm going to be part of the family, there's no reason why I shouldn't work in the clan. Kehn and Tar are your First and Second Fists. You could use me too, put me somewhere in No Peak where I'll be of help in the war when it comes."

Hilo shook his head. "This war's not for you to worry about."

"Because I'm a woman?"

"Because you're a stone-eye," he said. "This is between Green Bones."

Wen let her arms fall to her sides and stepped back, opening space between them. "I come from a Green Bone family. You said yourself I have the heart and mind of a jade warrior."

"That doesn't make you one." Hilo was disturbed by the direction this conversation had taken. "You know I don't believe the bullshit about jade bringing people closer to the gods, or stone-eyes being bad luck, none of that. But if you're not a Green Bone, then there's a different life for you. Not better or worse, but not a Green Bone's life. You can do anything else you want, but not this."

"Other clans have made use of their stone-eyes. Stone-eyes can move freely through the city, we can handle jade without giving off an aura. You told me that Tem Ben the Carver is a stone-eye from the Mountain and does their bidding still."

A sense of terror and rage rose and coated the inside of Hilo's nose and mouth. "You're not anything like Tem Ben," he said in a low voice. "Tem Ben is a puppet; I'm going to follow every one of his strings back to the Mountain and cut them off. He's a dead man. You will *never* be like him." He seized Wen by the arms, so quickly that she didn't even have time to flinch. He was aware at all times of how slow and soft she was, how vulnerable, how easily he could hurt or break her—and the thought of her in peril from his enemies, other Green Bones, filled him with a fear he did not have for his own life. "The Mountain will do *anything*. They'll recruit common thieves, they'll send a stone-eye to smuggle inside No Peak territory, I suppose next they'll send children against us. I won't do that. I won't send a stone-eye into a Green Bone war. I won't *ever* use you like that. Nothing will change my mind on this. Understand?" He shook her.

"Yes," she said meekly.

He softened and enfolded her again with a sigh. "I think maybe you're bored at your job." Wen worked as a secretary at a legal office. "You're too smart for that kind of work. After we're married, you can quit and do what you want. You want to go back to school? You could do that. Or you want to start your own business, doing interior design type of stuff? You're good at that for sure. We can think about it."

"Yes," Wen said. "We can think about it more. Later."

Surely a talk with the Weather Man's office would provide Wen with a number of good options. The clan had Lantern Men with connections in almost any field one could think of. He was not about to approach Doru though. He would wait until Lan had the old pervert ousted, then he'd speak to someone like Hami Tumashon.

He needed to speak to Shae again as well. He hadn't seen or spoken to her in weeks. As someone who was open and expressive with his emotions, Hilo had long harbored the vaguely resentful suspicion that he loved his family more than they loved him back, and with no one was this feeling more pronounced than with his sister. How could Shae be so cold? It bothered Hilo more than he let on. Had she come back to Kekon merely to make the rest of them feel sorry for her? To punish them with rejection? Clearly, she was suffering self-esteem issues, what with the way she continued to inflict jade deprivation on herself as some abnormal form of penance. He thought that perhaps he'd been too hard on her, said hurtful things at one time (as if she hadn't done the same), and that was one reason she'd run off to Espenia. But he was ready to forget all that. They were both adults now. They were Kauls; they had responsibilities. The three of them had to stand together if they were going to keep No Peak strong. Sometimes he felt as if he was the only one who could see that clearly. If he talked to Shae again, and if Lan would stop handling their sister with kid gloves and back him up, he thought he might convince her of his sincerity and get her to ease off her aloof and intransigent position.

Not that he had seen much of Lan lately either. Their conversations on the phone were frequent, but brief and tactical—what was happening, what needed to be done. Hilo instructed his Fists to kill any other gangsters caught thieving in the Docks. Elsewhere, he shored up his clan's defenses. He promoted Iyn, Obu, and a few other senior Fingers to Fists and reassigned territories to more effectively protect No Peak's most valuable areas and holdings. He went around the city, personally visiting and reassuring all the Lantern Men. "Keep your moon blades sharp," he told his warriors. Mountain jade was theirs for the taking if they came across the opportunity. His spies compiled as accurate a report as they could of Gont's organization: how many Fists and Fingers he commanded, where they could be found, which ones carried the most jade and were most formidable.

Studying the list, it was apparent to Hilo that while strength of numbers was roughly comparable between the two clans, No Peak was at a disadvantage. The core swath of the clan's territories bordered enemy-controlled districts to both the north and south. The Mountain had eliminated two smaller rivals in the past couple of years and their Green Bones were on average more experienced fighters. Hilo needed more warriors. Next spring, an especially large cohort of new Green Bones, including his cousin Anden, would graduate from Kaul Du Academy, but until then, Hilo mused unhappily, he would have to make do.

Theoretically, the clean bladed duel at the Factory between Lan and Gam Oben had preserved the peace, but in truth, it had merely given both sides an opportunity to regroup and consider their next moves. Even though the clans were not officially at war, Hilo was certain it would not be long before the current skirmishing and harassing escalated into outright bloodshed. Hilo also had no doubt that the Mountain would not be discouraged after only one failed attempt on his life. As he was rarely at home anymore, he had to remain constantly on guard. Sometimes after a long night, he parked in a shady spot he felt was safe, and stretched out in the backseat of the Duchesse and napped while Kehn sat watch.

Being the Horn had become entirely too much work and stress.

• Chapter Twenty-Six •
WAR MANEUVERS

Every seat in the long boardroom of the Ship Street office was taken. A dozen Lantern Men of No Peak—the presidents and executives of some of the country's largest companies—had come to hear directly from the Pillar and to question him about defensive measures and security for their operations. While disputes over territory and business were not uncommon, the prospect of outright war between the two largest clans in the country was unprecedented, and it had the crowd of businessmen in a state of considerable consternation.

"Will projects that have already been granted the clan's patronage be allowed to continue on schedule and as planned?" asked a real estate developer Lan recognized as one of the Lantern Men he'd met on Boat Day.

Doru bobbed his elongated head. "Currently, all initiatives that have been approved and funded by the clan will continue to be supported."

"Will greater security measures be taken to protect our business properties?" asked a Lantern Man who had several retail locations in the Armpit.

Lan said, "The Horn had been taking steps to ensure that clan territory is defended. Priority will be given to districts where the threat is greatest."

"What about the possibility of the Mountain disrupting commerce? They control much of the trucking sector. Might they not attempt to lock us out and make it difficult for us to deliver goods?" asked a man with a furniture import business.

"And what of sectors that will be hurt by the drop in tourism?" interrupted a hotel owner. "Does the clan plan to do anything to support the hospitality industry?"

Lan stood up; the murmurs running around the table ceased. "I cannot guarantee there will not be any impact on your businesses," he said. "We are being threatened by another clan and have to be prepared for difficult times. What I can promise is that we will defend ourselves—every part of the clan, every sector, every business."

This seemed to make an impression on those gathered. The Pillar noticed their gazes lingering on all the new jade he was wearing, the irrefutable proof that he'd recently been victorious, that he could back up words with force. Lan cast an assessing look down the table. "I'm afraid we can't address every question at this time. If you have additional specific concerns, make an appointment to discuss them with the Weather Man and myself. Enjoy your afternoon, gentlemen."

"May the gods shine favor on No Peak," some of the Lantern Men murmured, saluting as they exited. When they were all gone, Lan turned to Doru.

"I would like you to go to Ygutan," he said.

Doru adeptly masked any surprise he felt. "Is that necessary, Lan-se? Surely, it's important that I remain in Janloon at this time to help you deal with the Lantern Men."

"We can put off additional meetings with the Lantern Men for a few weeks. I want you to find out what you can about the Mountain's shine-producing operations in Ygutan. Where are their facilities, who are their suppliers and distributors, how much business they're already doing. Pull every string we have in that country and do it quietly. We need to know where our enemy is investing. It might be information that we can use against them in the future if we need to."

Doru pursed his thin lips. Perhaps he sensed an ulterior motive; ever since the duel at the Factory, Lan had been guarded around the Weather Man and Doru surely understood that he was out of favor, but Lan did not want him to suspect anything beyond that. Allowing some of his true anger to show, the Pillar said harshly, "I need someone I trust to do this, Doru-jen. I wouldn't send anyone less capable or discrete. We've had our differences lately, but we can't afford to have any doubts come between us right now. Will you do as I say from now on or not? If not, I'll accept your resignation as Weather Man. You can keep the house; I wouldn't make you move."

He saw that he'd gambled correctly; the old advisor relaxed a little. Surely if the Pillar suspected Doru of treachery or meant to harm him, he wouldn't show his emotions like this. He would be careful to pretend to reconcile and keep him close. Doru was reassured; he said quickly, "You wound me, Lan-se. I've disagreed with you only out of concern for the clan and for your safety. You're right of course, we must find out more about the Mountain's operations in Ygutan. I'll leave tomorrow."

Lan nodded and said, sounding mollified, "I appreciate your concerns, uncle Doru. I need you now more than ever. I'm sending two of the Horn's men with you to Ygutan. It's not a very safe country, and gods forbid anything should happen."

The faint smile that had begun to crawl over Doru's mouth dissolved at this news. He guessed at the truth: Lan did indeed want information about the Mountain's operations in Ygutan, but more importantly, he wanted Doru out of the way, watched constantly by Hilo's men, something he could not accomplish here where Doru held sway on Ship Street, surrounded by his own people. He wasn't worried about Doru's activities in Ygutan. Hilo's men would report back regularly and would corroborate everything Doru discovered. There was nothing the man could do against the clan.

Lan's outburst of pique had disguised any other negative intent Doru might have Perceived, and having already agreed to go, the Weather Man could not disagree with the Pillar's security measures. "Whatever you think necessary, Lan-se," he said.

As soon as Doru was on a plane, Lan asked Woon to arrange an urgent meeting on short notice with Chancellor Son Tomarho and twenty-five other members of the Royal Council of Kekon over an invited lunch at the Grand Island Grill & Lounge.

The Grand Island was on the penthouse floor of the twenty-eight story Eight Skies Hotel in upscale North Sotto. The Lantern Man who owned the Eight Skies shut it to other customers at Lan's request. The Pillar arrived early with Woon and greeted each of the councilmen as they arrived. News of the duel at the Factory had been all over Janloon and everyone Lan met these days noticed and remarked on the new jade he'd added to his belt, the cuffs on his wrists, the cord of beads around his neck. If it weren't for the immense importance of public perception right now, Lan would've resisted wearing all the acquired jade. The injury he'd sustained from absorbing and repulsing Gam's Channeling attack lingered and made it hard to bear the heavy load. He'd been to Dr. Truw for healing sessions and wasn't feeling as ill as he'd been immediately after the duel, but he wasn't feeling well either. Sometimes his heart would begin to race or he would break into a dizzy sweat. Anxiety flared without warning. His sleeplessness worsened and he was often edgy, off-kilter.

"Far do your enemies flee, Kaul-jen," the councilmen said as they arrived, voicing the traditional expression of congratulations given to a recently victorious Green Bone.

"By the luck of Jenshu's favor," Lan replied, thanking them before inquiring, "How's your wife's health, Mr. Loyi?" or "Mrs. Nurh, did your house fare all right in the typhoon?" These twenty-one men and four women were the most senior politicians loyal to No Peak. They came from longtime Lantern Men or Green Bone families and they owed their political and financial success to the clan. Together, they held significant sway over the three hundred member Royal Council of Kekon.

After a two hour-long, no-expenses-spared lunch of mango coleslaw, fire breathing soup, and grilled octopus, during which no business was discussed, Lan motioned for the table to be cleared. He began by commending Chancellor Son at length for his far-sightedness in proposing the recent bill to reform KJA ownership laws. "The No Peak clan completely supports the government's wish to ensure that the stewardship of Kekon's jade is balanced and transparent. I'm grateful to be able to count on the clan's friends in the Council to do what is right for the country." Chancellor Son beamed and waved a fat hand modestly as the other council members tapped the table in applause. It was all in politeness, as everyone in the room was surely aware it had been Lan himself who'd instructed Son to take such steps.

Lan let the applause fade, then said, somberly, "Unfortunately, I must make you aware that these efforts come too late to rectify wrongs that have already occurred." He explained that he had brought them here so they would hear it from him first and directly: he would be exercising his co-directorship powers to suspend the activities of the Kekon Jade Alliance, bringing all mining operations to an immediate and indefinite halt. The clan had discovered significant financial discrepancies between mine production and Treasury records, he said, and given the importance of jade to the nation's economy, security, and identity, mining could not be allowed to continue until an independent audit was conducted. He strongly urged the Royal Council to call for and administer one as soon as possible. Operations would not recommence until the problems had been identified and the KJA reform bills passed to ensure future oversight.

Son Tomarho was the first to break the stunned hush that followed the Pillar's statement. The Chancellor leaned his heavy elbows on the table and cleared his throat loudly, in a way that Lan could tell was meant to express the man's disappointment that he had not been personally consulted before such a drastic decision. "With all respect, Kaul-jen, why is this the first time we are hearing about these accounting discrepancies? And why then is the Weather Man not here to explain them?"

"The Weather Man is away on other important clan business," Lan said, answering the second question and ignoring the first. Lan could not have discussed his intentions with Son earlier without risking Doru getting wind of them—unless he'd revealed to the Chancellor his unproven suspicions of treachery within the leadership of the clan, something he would absolutely not do with any Lantern Man, no matter how senior. If Doru was indeed a Mountain collaborator and complicit or responsible for the discrepancies Shae had discovered, by the time he returned from Ygutan, it would be too late for him to halt an official investigation into the KJA's books.

The long-faced councilwoman Nurh Uma asked the question on everyone's minds. "Are we correct to assume you believe the Mountain clan is behind this?"

Lan gestured for the servers to refill the guests' teacups. He didn't drink from his own steaming cup; he'd been running a slight fever last night and hot liquids made him sweat too profusely in public. "Yes," he said, "that's exactly what I believe."

"I find it difficult to believe that the Mountain is unilaterally manipulating the jade supply so egregiously behind the backs of the Council and the other clans," said white-haired councilman Loyi Tuchada with obvious skepticism in his voice.

"I would believe it," said Nurh, who had family members on both the business and military sides of the clan. "But Ayt Mada's representatives will surely deny any wrongdoing. What do you hope to accomplish with this audit, Kaul-jen?"

"The clans depend on the support of the people as much as the people depend on the protection of the clans; it has always been this way," Lan said. "The nation will not want one clan to become too powerful, to control more jade than all the others. If it comes to light that the Mountain has acted against the good of the country, public and political opinion will turn against them. The results of the audit will lend urgency and credence to the Council's goals of passing stricter oversight over KJA activities."

Lan stopped to take a surreptitious, focusing breath. He'd abstained from eating much lunch, but nevertheless he felt tired and mildly woozy. It was an effort to keep his attention entirely on controlling this important conversation. Fortunately, it was relatively easy to fool jadeless councilmen. They mistook his moments of weakness for authoritative pauses. "For years, Kekon has been fortunate to enjoy stability and economic growth," Lan continued. "We have foreign investment, people drive nice cars, our cities are booming—all things that my grandfather's generation couldn't have imagined. At the heart of this wealth and security is jade. Which means that the clans who control jade must be held accountable."

The councilmen nodded; this was a point on which they could all agree. One of them, Vang Hajuda, began to say something, but Lan's Perception began playing tricks on him—it turned abruptly white with background noise. The individual energies of the people in the room, combined with hundreds more on all the floors beneath them, all the way down to the thousands more walking on the busy street and driving past in the cars outside, all crowded into Lan's mind unfiltered, interfering with each other in a sudden cacophony of nonsense, like a bad television signal blaring static.

Lan's head throbbed with pain. He felt, for a second, as if he were dangling high in the air atop a column of nothing but meaningless energy babble. Under the table, he gripped one of his chair's armrests, hanging onto its reassuring solidity. Lan turned away and brought a hand up to shield his lips as he leaned over to Woon, sitting directly on his left. "Pretend to be telling me something," he whispered.

His Pillarman bent next to his ear worriedly. "Is it really bad this time, Lan-jen? Do we need to make an excuse to leave?"

"No," said Lan. Sweat had broken out on his brow but the moment was already passing. The feverish confusion of his jade senses receded. His Perception settled and grew focused again. "Just tell me what he said."

"He wants assurances there won't be more bloodshed."

Lan straightened to face the table just as Vang finished asking a question. "I apologize for the interruption," Lan said.

There was a minor ripple of consternation down the table; they were watching him closely. Vang repeated himself with a touch of pique, "If we bring these issues you've placed before us to the Royal Council, can we count on you Kaul-jen, to try to reestablish the peace between the clans? No one wants violence on the streets, frightening people and driving away foreign business."

"We all want peace," Lan said. He let his words hang as he wetted his mouth with a bit of tea. "Unless our families are attacked. Then we do what we must."

A number of the councilmen murmured in agreement. They were a strange breed, these politicians. As representatives of their districts, they pressured the Pillar for peace, but as clan loyalists and true Kekonese, they would never respect a leader unskilled or hesitant in dispensing violence. Lan killing Gam and wearing his jade gave them confidence in him as a leader and confidence in No Peak's assertions. They would return to Wisdom Hall and work towards the purpose he'd set them.

"We understand perfectly where you're coming from, Kaul-jen," Vang persisted. He represented an area of Janloon that included the contested territory of Sogen. "You've always come across as a reasonable man. But what about your Horn? Does he also want peace? Can we count on him to also be reasonable?"

Lan laid a flat stare on Vang. "The Horn answers to me."

Admonished, Vang fell silent. The Pillar drew his gaze slowly up and down the long table of faces. When no one questioned him further, he rose from his seat. "Stay as long as you like, my friends. Enjoy the tea, and the view." He nodded toward the expansive windows looking out over the downtown skyline, then turned back to the table. "Chancellor. Councilmen. Your friendship to the clan, and your service to the country are, as always, deeply appreciated."

Once in the elevator, Lan mopped his brow and leaned against the wall, exhausted. He'd kept it together, but just barely. Dr. Truw had told him that his kie—the essential aura-producing energy of each individual that could be amplified and manipulated by contact with jade—was damaged, like an overstrained muscle. It might be weeks, even months until it fully recovered.

Lan did not have the luxury of months. He couldn't afford to continue like this, with his jade tolerance and abilities handicapped, not with so much at stake. "Woon," he said, putting a hand on the Pillarman's arm. "I've always been grateful I can trust you. I have to ask something of you now which you must keep to yourself. You can't let it slip even within the family."

Woon regarded him with concern. "Lan-jen, I'll do whatever you require of me."

Lan nodded. "I need you to make a phone call."

• Chapter Twenty-Seven •
MISTAKES REVEALED

Shae sat quietly in the back row of the slow bus to Marenia, staring out the window and avoiding conversation while the tourists chatted and took photos out the open windows all along the scenic coastal highway. When she arrived in town, she found her mother walking on the beach behind the family's cottage. Her mother seemed neither surprised nor especially excited to see her. Perhaps Lan had called her already to tell her to expect Shae's visit. Kaul Wan Ria embraced her daughter warmly but briefly, as if she'd last seen Shae a month ago, instead of more than two years ago.

"We can stroll the beach and then have some tea," Shae's mother suggested. "If we walk an hour that way, there is a very nice teahouse. The owners are very nice." These days, she told Shae, she took long walks, gardened, watched television, and attended a class in watercolor landscape painting at the community recreation center. Shae ought to try it sometime. It was very restful.

The seaside town of Marenia held ten thousand inhabitants and was a far cry from the ceaseless activity of the city. Shae found that it was just what she needed to set herself at ease again, to escape the confusion she'd felt after being around her brothers, who were, she knew, now engaged in a clan war without her.

In the evenings, Shae practiced alone with the moon blade behind the cottage, the long expanse of wet sand a spongey black sheet under her bare feet, the roar of the ocean replacing the hum of traffic from her balcony in Janloon. In the morning, fresh fish stands sold the dawn's catch, surfers rode the warm swells, and people said hello to each other in the streets. No one was a Green Bone.

It was like when she'd been in Espenia. What a disquieting revelation it had been to live in a place that functioned perfectly fine without jade and without clans. The two things that all the men in Shae's family worshipped, that she'd been taught her whole life to hold above all else—other places did without them. Clan patronage and settling disputes through duels were seen as backward things. Green Bones were thought of as something exotic and magical, but ultimately archaic and savage. It was Jerald, really, who'd opened her eyes to the wider world; sometimes Shae was not sure whether to thank or blame him for it. Two years abroad had given her a perspective on her home country that she doubted most Green Bones possessed. Her college friends in Espenia could never understand Kekon; they would be bewildered by its apparent contradictions, by the seamless blend of modernity and casual brutality.

Shae found Marenia charming, but her mother's company depressing. Kaul Wan Ria was like a piece of artwork or furniture that blended into the rest of a house and went unnoticed. Before she'd been married off, she'd received a basic education and enough martial training to be able to tolerate jade contact but not enough to actually wear or use it. After her husband's death, she deferred to her father-in-law, and later to her eldest son. If she begrudged her place, it never showed. If she found her life now to be dull or lonely, that didn't show either. Shae watched her stirring a pot of soup on the stove; her mother had put on some weight and her hair was greying.

"The boys are always very busy," Ria said over her shoulder. "Lan comes to visit me sometimes. Hilo—only once. To show me his girlfriend. A very nice, polite girl, but a stone-eye." Shae's mother tugged on her right earlobe. "Still it's his choice, so long as he's happy and his brother agrees." She turned the stove off and moved the pot to the table. "They've been in fights, did you know that? Both of them! Hilo of course—always fighting—but Lan said he had to duel as well because of the disrespect to the family. So unfortunate." She clucked her tongue, as if the Pillar and the Horn of No Peak were small boys who'd been implicated in a schoolyard brawl. No doubt Lan sanitized the things he told her, but still, Shae wondered if her mother preferred to be willfully ignorant about what was going on in the clan, or if, growing up during war time, she'd long ago accepted such violence as the casual norm for all men.

"I made it extra spicy, the way you like it," said her mother, ladling out the soup. "I've heard the food in Espenia is not very good. What did you eat there?"

Her mother listened as Shae told her about Espenia. They discussed superficial things like the food, weather, and clothes. Kaul Wan Ria didn't ask about Jerald. She didn't inquire as to why Shae had returned, or what she was doing now. She did not even remark on Shae not wearing her jade, other than to sigh, "Ah, you worked so hard for it before. As hard as the boys! I'm glad you've learned to take it easier now. It's better for your health, not to always be working so hard. As long as your brother doesn't think it'll look bad for the family." As a general rule, she avoided asking prying questions or expressing strong opinions. As a child, Shae had gone to her mother for comfort, but never for advice. Indeed, she could think of little she had in common with her mother besides their eyes and somewhat mannish hands.

"Do you like it here, ma?" Shae asked. "Are you happy?"

"Oh yes," said Kaul Ria. "You and your brothers are grown up. There's no need for me to be around Green Bone troubles any more. Men cannot escape it of course, it's in their nature, but you took off your jade and went to live far away, so you understand."

She was not sure she did; even now, she couldn't say if she'd run toward Jerald and the enticing modern world beyond Janloon mostly to escape the sting of her grandfather's displeasure, the humiliation of seeing him, for the first time, openly side with Hilo against her.

On top of his extreme ire over Jerald, Kaul Sen had been furious to learn of her involvement with the Espenians. "At least whores only sell what belongs to them!" he'd raged. He'd never spoken to her in such a way, had always been kind and approving toward her even when he was stern. Only a few years out of the Academy, she'd been young, arrogant and disaffected, and not thought her actions to be harmful. Jerald, when he came to understand her family's position, had introduced her to some other Espenian military personnel who were eager to ask her questions. At first, they were simple questions that Shae knew the answers to or could discover easily through the clan's connections. The Espenians were keen to expand their political and economic influence, but they were uninformed about how things worked on Kekon. They wanted to know: Which clan leaders comprised the board of the KJA? When did they meet and who held sway over the jade export decisions? Who on the Royal Council was responsible for military spending? How could they secure a meeting with this person and what sort of gift would be appropriate to send?

What they were most interested in however, were their enemies. Ygutan was the only country the Espenians seemed to fear. Even here, on a small island so far away, they were always on the watch. They wanted to know what investments Ygutanian companies were making on Kekon. How much jade the clans believed was being smuggled to Ygutan through the black market. Could Shae ask around and find out why a certain supposed Ygutanian businessman was on Kekon? Where was he staying and who was he meeting with?

The Espenians were constantly appreciative. She did not need the money they gave her, but Espenians always paid for favors so they were not indebted; that was their way. Shae was more impressed by the student visa they agreed to arrange for her so that she might study abroad. An Espenian education was something few people on Kekon had—it would surely be even more impressive than graduating at the top of the Academy, would set her above and apart from her brothers. In the meantime, she was helping ignorant foreigners do business in Kekon, and in truth, she took a secret pride in it. It was something outside of the clan that was hers entirely. Information and relationships that belonged to her, not her grandfather, or her brothers, or Doru.

"How can you call yourself a Kaul, you selfish idiot girl?" her grandfather had demanded. "*Anything* you tell the foreigners might be used against the clan." The Torch had wielded all his considerable influence, had made angry phone calls to the Espenian Ambassador, who gave apologetic assurances to Kaul Sen that his granddaughter would not be approached by anyone from the Republic of Espenia's military or intelligence services again. Jerald was shipped back to Espenia, and Shae, burning with the indignity of Grandda swooping in to set her right, had followed him. She'd been a fool, but sadly, even fools were entitled to their pride.

Shae returned to Janloon feeling calmer and more rested, but also determined to rededicate herself to the job search and find meaningful work as soon as possible. There was really nothing, she mused, that motivated her quite so much as the abiding fear of becoming like her mother. If she had her own work to occupy her, she wouldn't spend time the way she spent it on the bus ride back to the city, speculating on what Lan and Woon would do with the damning financial information she had furnished them, or wondering when the Mountain would try to kill Hilo again.

She got back to her apartment and groaned aloud to discover that she'd left her keys on the kitchen counter at her mother's cottage. She was locked out of her place.

Shae left her bag sitting in the hallway by her door and went over to her neighbor Caun Yu's, hoping to use his phone to call the landlord. No one answered when she knocked. There was a pile of flyers in front of the door that suggested Caun had been absent for several days. She went back outside and climbed the metal fire escape stairs, intending to force a way back into her own apartment, but upon passing her neighbor's window, she stopped and stared.

Caun's apartment was almost empty. It was clear that no one lived in it. There was a small television on the floor and a telephone sitting on top of the television. Aside from a couple of cushions on the floor, there was nothing else—no furniture, no clothes, nothing on the walls, no sign of Caun himself. Shae began to tremble with suspicion and outrage. She pushed open the window and clambered into her neighbor's apartment. It was laid out almost exactly like hers. She walked into the kitchen and found that the cupboards were empty except for a bag of peanuts and a sleeve of crackers. The fridge contained only a few bottles of soda. Caun had supposedly been living here for as long as she had—nearly four months—but he had never moved in.

Shae went into the bare living room and sat down on one of the cushions to wait. She suspected it would not be long before Caun made an appearance, and sure enough, perhaps an hour later, the front door opened and the young man walked in, his accumulated junk mail gathered under one arm. He stopped in astonishment when he saw Shae sitting inside his apartment.

Before Caun could recover his wits, Shae got up and moved past him, shutting and locking the door. Turning around, she drew her talon knife and advanced. The young man backed up, licking his lips nervously, his eyes on the knife. His back touched the wall. Shae reached up with her free hand and pulled off the black skull cap Caun always wore. The man's short hair was messy and flattened, and the tops of both ears were pierced through with jade studs. Not much jade, not enough for her to notice an aura unless she was touching him.

Shae took a step back and pointed to the phone on top of the television. "Call him," she said. "Tell him to come over here right now."

Caun picked up the receiver and dialed, his eyes darting fearfully. Shae doubted it was her or her knife that made him anxious; it was his boss's reaction he was worried about. "Hilo-jen," Caun said after some minutes of being passed around on the other end of the line, "it's Caun Yu. Your sister... she, er, told me to phone you. She's holding a talon knife on me and wants you to come over here."

There was a moment of silence, and then Shae caught a snatch of her brother's laughter coming from the other end of the phone line. More words were exchanged, and then Caun hung up. "He says he's finishing up something but he'll come soon."

"Security, was it, Caun-jen?" Shae said. "You work in security. In a rather boring job, if I recall. One you've been hoping to get out of soon."

"I didn't mean it in that way," Caun explained, reddening. "It's not that I think *you're* boring. It's just that keeping watch over you isn't all that exciting, you know."

"No, I don't suppose it would be." Her sudden odd sense of hurt and amusement came out as a cold smirk. "And here I was, starting to think all our meetings were because you were working up to hitting on me."

"Touch the Horn's little sister?" Caun let out a nervous bark of laughter. "Come on, put the talon knife away. Don't you think you've pulled it on me enough lately? It doesn't seem very charitable, considering that I'm supposed to be protecting you." Caun seemed to be in a surprisingly good mood. He was smiling broadly now, the hair freed from his skull cap falling into his eyes in an irritatingly handsome way. Shae suspected that Hilo's reaction on the phone had reassured Caun that he was not in as much trouble as he'd feared, and now he was looking forward to the end of this undesirable assignment.

Shae sheathed her knife. "So you've been camped here, following me around."

"Only when you're out and about. Once you get back to your place every night, I slip out the window. I have to be back in the morning before you leave though." Caun backed into the kitchen and came back out with the sleeve of crackers and two bottles of mango soda. "Do you want some? It's all I have, I'm afraid. Or we could go wait in your place instead."

Shae gave him a dirty look and Caun shrugged, opening his soda.

Hilo arrived perhaps twenty minutes later. He knocked on the door and called, cheerily, "Shae, you haven't hurt poor Caun Yu, have you? I told him there were risks involved with this job." When Shae flung open the door, her brother stepped inside, smiling, and made to give her a hug. She shoved him back violently. "You've had me watched and followed all this time," she hissed.

Instead of answering, the Horn straightened the shirt Shae had rumpled, and turned to Caun, shaking his head. His voice turned harsh. "Gods in Heaven, this was the easiest job a Finger could get, Caun. Where and how did you fuck up?"

Caun's smile vanished at once. "I…I don't know, Hilo-jen," he stammered. "The doorman called to say she'd returned from Marenia. I came straight here but she got into the apartment and was waiting for me when I arrived. I'm sorry I failed you." The young man bent into an apologetic salute.

Hilo sighed deeply, looking around the bare apartment. "It's hard to fool my sister for long, but you should've done a better job of it. Go report to Maik Kehn—I'm sure he could use you in the Docks. You might even get a chance to earn some green over there, if you concentrate harder on not fucking up from now on." He opened the door in dismissal and Caun exited quickly with his eyes lowered. Hilo did not lose his stern expression but he gave the Finger a single pat on the back as he passed, and the young man glanced up with a nervously grateful expression. In one unfortunate instant, Shae's perception of Caun transformed. Her friendly, attractive next door neighbor was just another one of her brother's many underlings. She was bothered by how much it aggravated her that Caun did not even spare her a parting glance as he left the room.

Shae wheeled back on Hilo. "*Stay out of my life.*"

"You're flattering yourself, Shae. I need every Finger I have right now. You think I wanted to waste one of them on guard duty over you? I told Lan it was your choice to live here without jade and you could godsdamned take care of yourself, but after what happened to Anden, he insisted that you be protected. Don't blame me."

"Lan told you to set a guard over me?" Shae was taken aback. Hilo having her watched made her nearly speechless with ire, but she had never known Lan to be anything but prudent and well-intentioned. Some of her anger diffused into uncertainty. "What happened to Anden?"

"Gont Asch snatched Andy out of Summer Park on Boat Day, took him to Ayt and made a show of trying to turn him while offering us a sham alliance to make and sell shine in Ygutan with them. They gave Andy back but they made their point. They shook us up, and they insulted Lan. He turned them down flat. So they tried to take me out of the picture and here we are."

Shae shook her head. She didn't want to admit to being unfair to either of her brothers, particularly Hilo. "I didn't know about Anden. No one told me."

Hilo gave an incredulous and condescending snort. "What do you expect, Shae? You came back to Janloon but you're living out here jadeless like you want nothing to do with us. You made me search you out in a hotel and then treated me like a stranger. You haven't gone to visit Andy, you haven't seen any friends from the Academy. You didn't even go out of your way to come over and pay a bit of respect to Tar when he was in the hospital. You've never once invited me into your place, not even now when we're standing in the apartment next door. What's that supposed to mean, huh?" There was true bewilderment and hurt in his voice. "What are you even doing these days, anyhow?"

Shae felt her temper rising anew. "I spent weeks doing that work for Lan, remember? And I've been applying for jobs. I have interviews coming up."

"Interviews," Hilo repeated with dripping disdain. "For *what*? You're going to work as a suit in a bank? *Why*? I don't understand you, Shae."

Shae's face burned. "I don't need your advice, Hilo. Or your protection."

"No, you *didn't*, never before. But now we're at war with the Mountain and you're still acting like you've nothing to do with any of it. You're ignoring that you're a Kaul." Hilo advanced, his face tight, his voice edged with a vexed desperation. "I've got news for my tough little sister who thinks she's too good for her family. Lan won't come out and say it, but I will: you can't be an ordinary person, Shae. Not in this city. Not in this country. You don't like being kept in the dark, secretly guarded and treated like some helpless woman? Well, you put yourself there."

There had been a day some ten years ago, Shae remembered, when she and Hilo had squared off, spitting fire as they'd done many times before, and realized at the same moment that they were both wearing jade now and could fatally harm each other. They had stayed themselves on that day, and it was perhaps only this memory, and the knowledge that Hilo was wearing a great deal of jade and she carried none, that kept Shae from launching herself at her brother now.

"Say whatever you want to Lan," she said, her voice cold to hide all emotion, "but I don't want to see any of your men around my apartment or following me, ever again. Risk your own life how you like, Hilo—but leave me alone to live mine."

She caught a glimpse of her brother's stricken expression as she pushed past him out the door. She remembered, only at the last minute, that she was still locked outside of her apartment, but too proud to be seen struggling to get inside, she left the building and sat in misery at a tea shop down the street until it was dark.

When she returned, Hilo was gone, but the landlord was waiting for her, holding her bag and a spare key. "Kaul-jen said to make sure you returned home safely, miss," he said, saluting her solicitously. "I must apologize profusely for not realizing who you are. Please, from now on, if there is anything you need, you should call me directly." As he unlocked Shae's door, he turned over his shoulder and inquired, "Are you sure you're quite comfortable here? I have another property, a new one, only ten minutes away, run by my son-in-law, where the units are much larger. The rent would be the same for you, of course. No? Well, don't hesitate to let me know if you change your mind. My family and I have always been friends of the clan."

• **Chapter Twenty-Eight** •
DELIVERIES AND SECRETS

Anden had a bad feeling about the errand the Pillar had sent him on. It was simple enough; Lan had phoned him to inquire when his next free afternoon from the Academy would be. He wanted Anden to come see him. Could he please stop by a certain address on the way over and pick up a package and bring it to his cousin?

Anden agreed of course, but this was the second time Lan had asked him for the same favor, and that seemed odd. The Pillar had any number of subordinates he could send to pick up parcels. For him to ask Anden once might have been random convenience. Twice made Anden suspect he'd been singled out for the task.

The address was for a walk-up apartment just down the hill from the Academy at the edge of the Crossyards district. When Anden rang the doorbell, a man in baggy camouflage pants and a yellowed muscle shirt opened the door. "You again?" He had green eyes and might have been Espenian, though he spoke Kekonese without an accent. Anden couldn't decipher either the graffiti-style tattoos on his arms or the jangling music coming from the interior of the apartment. It was not particularly uncommon to see foreigners in Janloon, and becoming less so all the time, but encountering them always caused Anden some discomfort; he knew that must be how he looked to those around him. So he did not greet this man with anything beyond a polite nod.

"Wait here." The stranger closed the door, leaving Anden standing awkwardly on the landing. A few minutes later, the door reopened and the man handed Anden an unmarked white padded envelope. Anden took it and zipped it up inside his school bag. Lan had told him keep it out of sight, not to open it, and not to tell anyone about it.

He rode his bike to the transit station where he caught the bus to the Kaul home. That was another thing—there were faster methods of delivery than a student with no car. Anden could only conclude that the Pillar was trusting him with a confidential task he didn't want anyone else in the clan to know about. He would've been flattered, but instead was worried. Lan had never asked him for anything before, other than to do well at the Academy. He didn't think the Pillar would involve him in a secret errand for the clan unless he had no one else he could trust to do it.

On the bus, he reached into his school bag and felt the envelope, trying to guess at what was in it. It was well cushioned, but when he pushed on the bubble wrap, he could tell there were small, hard objects inside.

He got off the bus and walked ten minutes to the gates of the Kaul estate. The guard waved to him as he went straight through and into the house. "Hello?" he called in the foyer. Kyanla called back from the kitchen, clattering dishes. "Anden-se, is that you? Lan-jen is in the training hall."

Anden wandered past the Pillar's study, through the tidy courtyard, and rapped on the door to the training hall. Lan slid the door open. He was in a loose black tunic shirt, trousers, and bare feet. It was strange to see him looking so casual. It made him seem younger, the way Anden remembered him from before he'd become the Pillar. "Anden." Lan stepped aside, smiling. "Come in." Anden slipped off his shoes and entered the long, wood-floored room. Lan slid the door closed. "Do you have what I asked you to pick up?"

Anden swung his school bag off his shoulder and took out the padded envelope. As he handed it over, his fingers passed close to Lan's and he flinched. He still wasn't used to the difference in his cousin's aura. He knew he was more sensitive than the average person—most people could not sense jade auras unless they were trained Green Bones wearing jade themselves. To Anden, the new jade Lan had won in the duel made his aura seem incongruously sharp and shrill, as if it had been taken up several psychic octaves. It didn't suit him.

"I appreciate you going out of your way," Lan said.

"It wasn't any trouble." Anden wanted to ask what was inside, but from the way Lan quickly slid the envelope into a drawer and closed it, he was sure it wasn't a question the Pillar would answer. Lan took a towel

from a hook on the wall and wiped the sheen of sweat from his face.
"How's school?"

"Fine. Only a few months left."

"Do you feel ready for the Trials?"

"I think so."

Lan turned away and tossed the towel into a bin by the door. "What's
your strongest discipline?"

"Channeling, probably."

Lan nodded. "Your weakest?"

"Um. Deflection, I suppose."

"How are your academics? Math, and languages, and so on?"

"I'm passing all of them." Anden skirted barely above average in the
book study aspects of a Green Bone education. "Don't worry, Lan-jen, they
won't pull my final rank down much."

Lan said, a touch sternly, "I'm not worried about your rank, Anden. I'm
asking about school because I'm sure there's a lot of talk on campus these
days about the clans. You're bound to hear a lot of rumors and opinions, if
you haven't already. I don't want you to feel upset or distracted by it; just
focus on your own studies."

"I will," Anden promised.

Lan gave Anden an approving pat on the shoulder and gestured at the
empty training hall. "Well, since we're in here, how about some Deflection
practice?"

Anden tried to think of a good excuse to decline. He didn't relish the
idea of being put on the spot with the Pillar of No Peak watching him, but
Lan was already crossing to the other side of the room and taking a set of
darts from the shelf.

"You have your training band with you?" Lan asked.

Anden laid his schoolbag next to the wall. *It's just Lan. He wants to be
helpful; he's not going to make me feel bad.* Hilo and Shae were like true cousins
to him, but Lan was much older and had always been more like an uncle.
Anden dug around in the front compartment of his bag and pulled out the
plastic case containing his training band. As a year-eight, he was allowed to
carry it at all times and to use it under the supervision of an adult Green
Bone. It was a simple leather band with a snap closure and three jade stones.

If he kept his scores up, he could expect to get four in the spring.

Anden fastened it around his left wrist, closed his eyes, and took a deep breath. Every time he put on jade, he felt, just for a second, the moment of resistance that one feels before jumping off a high diving board or ripping off a sticky bandage. An instant of *ah, this is going to hurt*—and then it was done. He rode out the initial rush of adjustment, opened his eyes, and went to stand across the room, facing Lan.

Lan finished loading the darts into a dart gun. "Easy warm up," he said.

He fired the darts at Anden, one at a time. Anden Deflected each one, and they sunk into the cork board-covered wall behind him. Darts were light and moved slowly. Deflection became exponentially more difficult with faster speeds, heavier items, and multiple objects. Lan moved on to the pellet gun, which Anden didn't find too hard—throwing up faster, wider Deflections was not a problem for him—but he labored with throwing knives, especially two or more from different directions.

"Maintain control of them," Lan said. "Slingshot them around and make them *your* weapons."

Anden nodded, though he'd heard the same advice from his Deflection instructor a hundred times and was still not anywhere near as capable as he wished he was. When he Deflected the knives, they lost momentum and sailed into the ground behind him. Ideally, he could whip them accurately anywhere into the wall, or even, as Lan said, around his own body like a boomerang and back out with even greater speed. Anden rocked on the balls of his feet, shaking out his limbs, trying to stay relaxed and focused and not think about how he was disappointing his cousin.

"Ready?" Lan whipped another knife at him—nice and straight—and Anden swept his arm out in a tight, arcing Deflection. He felt it catch the knife and veer the weapon off course. Straining, he kept the momentum of the Deflection going as he pivoted tightly, and with a surge of effort, he circled it around himself and flung the knife back out toward Lan.

It didn't go far before it curved toward the ground, but Lan raised a Deflection of his own and straightened it out. He lunged and caught the knife out of the air. "Nicely done!" His face lit with a pride that made Anden warm. "Most new Green Bones aren't able to do that. Keep practicing and you'll ace the Trials."

"I hope so," Anden said weakly. He put his hands on his knees and bent over to catch his breath. Lan filled a paper cup with water from the cooler in the corner and brought it to him. Anden took it gratefully, but was struck again by the harsh texture of the Pillar's aura. The jade fastened around his wrist made it worse, much *louder*. He nearly pulled away.

Thankfully, his cousin crossed the room again and opened a storage cabinet. He rolled out half a dozen large plastic pop bottles filled with sand, the lids sealed with silver duct tape. Lan set them up like an array of bowling pins. "We shouldn't neglect offense," he said. Anden's stomach sank a little. Offensive Deflection was his weakest area, and Lan was watching him from the side of the room with an expression that seemed usually expectant. He'd always taken an interest in Anden's progress, but he'd never been pushy or demanding. Now though, he said, "Go on, what are you waiting for?"

Anden drew in slow breath. He focused on the heavy bottles, gathered his energy, and ripped a low wave of Deflection across the room. The first bottle tottered and fell over, knocking over the one next to it, but the others didn't move.

"Not bad," Lan said. He reset the bottles. "Try again."

The bottles were heavy, the training hall was long, and Anden was losing steam. His second try toppled three bottles in a row, but that took the rest of the wind out of him. His third Deflection barely tipped over one bottle, and his fourth merely nudged it out of place.

Lan said, "Come on, Anden, you're not really trying now."

"I'm sorry," Anden said. "I'm just tired." He'd already been to advanced Strength training in the morning, which was always exhausting. He hadn't known his visit to the Kaul house would result in an impromptu exam.

Lan snapped, "Do you expect to use that excuse in a life or death situation? Do it again."

Anden tried to muster the energy. He rooted more firmly into his stance and raised both hands, feeling them tingle and quiver with tension, then thrust them down and forward with as powerful an expulsion of breath and energy as he could summon. His Deflection tore across the room but went wide, rattling the cabinet doors as if they were in an earthquake. The bottles did not budge.

Lan rubbed a hand over his eyes. "If you can't knock over a bottle full of sand, how are you going to throw a man off his feet? Or defend yourself if someone tries to do it to you?"

"I'm not a Green Bone yet," Anden protested, slumping apologetically. "I'll practice harder; I've still got some time."

"You'll only be a student for a few more months." Lan's face hardened and his voice rose abruptly. "The Mountain's already shown that they're paying attention to you, Anden. They've tried to kill both Hilo and me, and when you're no longer protected by the code of aisho, your life will be up for the taking as well, by enemies with far more jade and experience. You can't be too tired or weak to defend yourself, *ever!*"

With one arm, he hurled a funnel of Deflection across the room, throwing the bottles into the air. They crashed into the back wall and thudded to the ground, rolling on the floor. Lan didn't even look at them. He strode over and seized Anden by the arm, hauling him up straight. The Pillar's voice was a low growl. "You're graduating into a war, Anden. You have to be ready for what it means to be a Kaul, or you won't survive. Understand?"

Anden gasped. The Pillar's fingers dug into his bicep, but the pain came from elsewhere, right through the center of Anden's skull. So much jade behind Lan's unfamiliar anger—it startled the breath from Anden's chest. "Kaul-jen," he pleaded. He stared into eyes he barely recognized. The irises were bright and glassy as polished marbles, swirling with tempestuous energy. The web of thin red blood vessels surrounding them stood out. Anden swallowed. "Lan?"

The Pillar let go, abruptly, almost shoving Anden back. Lan stared for a second, then shook his head as if to clear it. His jade aura churned, and Anden, without even trying, Perceived the Pillar's stark anger crash into a muddy jumble of indecipherable emotions. Lan pressed the heel of his hand to his eyes, then lowered it and said, more calmly, "I'm sorry, Anden. You didn't deserve that."

"It's okay." Anden's voice was a dull, stunned whisper.

"I've been short-tempered lately." Lan turned away. "There's been a lot to deal with, and so much teetering on the edge. We need to keep the Council and the Lantern Men on our side, and we have to consider the possibility that the Espenians might get involved…" He glanced, inexplicably, at Anden for understanding. He still seemed not quite himself, though he was trying hard to be. "No matter. I was too hard on you just now."

"No." Anden was confused, still reeling. "What you said is true."

"I *am* proud of you, Anden, I haven't said it enough." Lan came back toward him. "Hilo has you pegged for a Fist. With your talent, you'd be an asset to him. But I want you to know it's your choice. With things as they are now, you might consider other roles in No Peak, or even choosing a path outside of the clan."

Anden had no response at first. Then his bewilderment flared into defensiveness and his face turned hot. "I'm not a coward." He knew he didn't have the book smarts to be a Luckbringer. There were Green Bones who were outside of the clan: teachers, doctors, penitents; but how could he consider a profession like that in a time like this? "Hilo-jen told me you need as many Green Bones coming out of the Academy as you can get. I owe everything to the clan, to you and Grandda. What kind of person would I be if I didn't take my oaths?"

Before Lan could answer, there was a sharp knock at the training room door. Woon's voice came through. "Lan-jen, it's the Espenian ambassador on the phone."

Lan glanced toward his Pillarman's voice, then back at Anden. He stepped away, his expression unreadable. For a second, Anden's mind prickled uncomfortably with the Perception of some urgent desperation. "I'm sorry, Anden, we'll talk about this more later." He began to turn toward the door. "If you wait in the courtyard for a few minutes, I'll have someone drive you back to the Academy."

"No, it's fine," Anden said. "I can see myself out. I have to go back to the transit station for my bike, and I don't mind the bus ride."

Lan paused with his hand on the door and spoke somberly over his shoulder. "I would never suggest you're a coward, Anden. I only wanted to make it clear that you do have a choice. And no matter what you chose, you'd always be a Kaul, same as Shae." The Pillar slid the door open and followed Woon back toward the main house, his overly sharp aura receding along with the shape of his stiff back.

Anden let out shaky breath he hadn't realized he'd been holding. *What had happened?* He had never seen Lan's mood swing in such a way before, from warmth to anger to doubt and remorse. Was it the recent stress and new jade that was making him so volatile? Did Lan really think Anden wasn't ready to join the clan? Simply because of his poor performance in Deflection today, or because of something else? It was one thing for Anden to doubt himself privately, or to speculate idly on what he might do if he wasn't already pegged to become a Fist; it was quite another to have the Pillar of the clan suggest such unhelpful thoughts to his face.

Turning aside, Anden took off his training band and leaned his forehead against the wall. The jade crash made his anxious stomach flip worse than usual. He sucked in a steadying breath and forced down the sensation as he shut the band back in its plastic case and pushed it into his bag.

Before leaving the training room, Anden collected the scattered bottles full of sand and stored them back in the cabinet. He gathered the throwing knives and pulled the darts out of the wall and returned them to their proper place as well. The Academy was military in its insistence on orderliness. The Deflections he and Lan had thrown had shaken cabinet doors ajar; Anden shut them carefully and was about to push a loose drawer back into place when he paused, his fingers hovering over the slim crack that showed him the white padded envelope he'd brought with him, the one Lan had taken and shut away without explanation.

Anden opened the drawer and took out the package. As he stared at it, an awful temptation ballooned into an even more awful suspicion. Anden's heart began to pound. He glanced around the empty, tidy training room. If he opened the package, Lan would know he'd done so. There was a small space, however, between the envelope seal and the corner of the flap. Anden pulled it open a little larger. He turned the envelope upside-down and shook it, working two fingers under the flap under he touched something smooth and hard, like glass. His hands trembling now, he wriggled out a tiny cylindrical vial.

He knew what it was. What else could it be? Eleven years ago, he'd seen this slightly cloudy serum seeping into his mother's IV tube in the days before her death. Anden's heart dropped into his feet. He tore open the hole in the envelope, recklessly pulling out vial after vial of the stuff.

His mind spun. It was as he'd feared, and still he couldn't believe it.

The door of the room opened. Lan stood in the doorway. Anden's hands fell open; he dropped the envelope and its contents into the open drawer but his guilt was clear. So was Lan's; angry shame flooded the Pillar's face. Anden was sure that if he'd still been wearing his training band, he wouldn't have been able to stand the furious blaze of his cousin's aura.

Lan stepped inside and closed the door behind him. It scraped shut with a noise like a blade on a whetstone. "What are you doing, Anden?" Lan's voice was deceptively monotone.

"You had me pick this up for you. It's SN1." Anden words sounded choked. He felt the need to hold onto something to steady himself. "How…how could *you* need shine?"

Lan advanced and Anden, without meaning to, backed away until his shoulders touched the wall. "You had no right to open that package." Lan had never beaten him before, had never so much as struck him, but now he looked murderous and Anden felt, for the first time in his life, a flash of fear in his cousin's presence. He would rather be smacked around a dozen times by Hilo than know he'd infuriated Lan enough to hit him once. Of course, he deserved to be beaten now, and not even thinking to say anything in his own defense, Anden could only blurt, "You're not sick, are you? With… with the Itches?"

The despair on his face must have been so plain—for in that moment, he imagined Lan dying the sort of death his mother had died, cutting his own flesh and screaming with insanity—that it dispelled the Pillar's rage. Lan's face changed, twisted with internal strain. He raised a hand and keep it there, as if to say, *Hold on now.* "Keep your voice down," he said, harshly but more calmly than Anden expected, the undercurrent of anger kept in check this time. "No, I don't have the Itches. By the time a person has a full-blown case of the Itches, it's usually too late for SN1 to save them." Sympathy rose in his eyes as he realized what Anden had been thinking, but his voice remained hard. "I ought to throw you out of the house for what you just did. I wouldn't have believed it of you, Anden. But I don't want you to get the wrong idea, so I'll explain. This isn't something you can breathe to *anyone*, not even in the family, do you understand?" Anden was still too distressed to reply, but Lan smacked a hand hard to the wall next to his face. "Do you?" Anden nodded.

Lan said quietly, "Shine is a plague on society. It's used by people with no natural jade tolerance or training whatsoever—foreigners, criminals, jade-fevered addicts. That's why the illegal shine trade has to be stamped out. But SN1 isn't all bad. As a drug that blunts the detrimental side effects of jade exposure, it can be useful. There are times when a Green Bone's natural tolerance needs a boost." He paused. "You can understand that, can't you?"

Anden's mind flashed back to the conversation he'd had with Hilo on the grounds of the Academy, then unwittingly again to the memory of his mother in the bathtub. Yes, he understood what Lan was saying. But the Kauls were different—the epitome of impeccable Green Bone blood and schooling. If Kaul Lan, the Pillar of the No Peak clan, needed SN1, what did that mean? Especially for someone like Anden, with a family history of madness—what hope did he have? His thoughts churned in denial. "It's all that new jade you're wearing, isn't it?" Anden's voice was an agitated whisper. "Is there something wrong with it? It it dangerous because it used to belong to Gam?"

Lan managed a humorless smile. "No. Jade is an amplifier; it doesn't retain energy from its previous owners, no matter what old superstitions you've heard." He turned his face away slightly and his voice fell. "I didn't get out of the duel unscathed, Anden." He tapped his chest above his heart. "Gam disrupted something when he Channeled into me. I haven't been feeling quite right since then. It's made carrying new jade harder than it should be."

Worry crowded in. "Have you seen a doctor? The one at the Academy is—"

"I've seen Dr. Truw. The healing sessions help, but there's nothing else to be done for it besides time and rest." He grimaced, acknowledging that he was in short supply of both those things. Anden understood now why his cousin was so edgy, volatile. He'd been carrying a secret injury along with new green and the pressures of being a wartime Pillar. And now the shame of needing SN1 to be able to bear the jade he'd won in a public duel.

"Don't wear it, then," Anden insisted. "Not until you're better. It's too much."

Lan shook his head. "I can't disappear from sight right now. Every day, I meet with people—councilmen, Lantern Men, Luckbringers, Fists and Fingers—all of them looking for assurances and evidence that No Peak can stand up to the Mountain. Meanwhile, our enemies are searching for any sign of weakness on our part, waiting for another chance to strike. I can't give that to them." His expression was weary as he backed off from Anden. "This isn't your concern. When you leave this room, I want you to forget about it."

"But the shine, isn't it bad for you? It's addictive, right? And—"

"It's *temporary*," Lan snapped, eyes lighting up again in a way that made Anden shrink back and shut his mouth. "I'm not going to get addicted. And I can't have anyone else in the clan even thinking that might happen. I had Woon arrange for a private supply of SN1 because it would be suspicious for me to be visiting Dr. Truw too often. It's even too much of a risk to have my Pillarman seen picking up unusual packages. People are watching closely. I'm trusting you, Anden, despite what you just did. Your uncle was one of my best friends, and I've always thought of you as my littlest brother. You're more like me than Hilo ever was. I've never asked you for anything, but I'm asking you now, to keep this secret."

Anden swallowed, then nodded. As soon as he did so, he thought, *I should break this promise. I should tell Hilo.* He wasn't even sure how to reach Hilo these days; the Horn was out patrolling No Peak territory with his Fists at all hours. And what would Hilo say?

Hilo would say Lan was the Pillar and that it wasn't Anden's place to second guess him. That there were special cases when using shine was acceptable; Hilo had suggested Anden himself might be one of those cases. No Peak depended on the Pillar staying strong and in control of the clan. Taking minor doses of SN1 to help him adjust to the new jade load was far better than risking madness and the Itches. That was true for certain.

Lan's watching eyes were narrowed. "Can I still count on you, Anden?"

The censure in the Pillar's voice was like a slap. Before today, Anden had never given Lan reason to distrust him, and seeing the disappointment in his cousin's face now was enough to make Anden gulp with remorse. "I know what I did was wrong. I'm sorry, Lan-jen. I won't break your trust again; I swear it on all the jade I'll ever wear, but please..." Anden's fists clenched at his sides and he blurted, "There has to be a better solution than taking that stuff!"

The margins of the Pillar's grim stare softened. He seemed like himself again—steady, collected—but his expression was uncertain, almost forlorn, as if he'd expected something else, something Anden thought it was his fault he couldn't give. "It's my place to deal with this Anden, not yours." He looked at Anden sadly for another long moment, then went to the door and slid it open again. "You ought to get back to the Academy before it gets late."

For a second, Anden didn't move. Then he touched his hands to his forehead in a salute that hid his face. "I know. You're right, Kaul-jen." He walked quickly out of the training room. Once he was across the courtyard, he wanted to turn around to see if his cousin was still standing where he'd left him. Instead he set his gaze in front of his feet and hurried through the house. "Anden-se?" Kyanla queried from the entrance of the kitchen as he rounded the staircase in the foyer and rushed for the door. "Everything all right?"

"Fine. I've got to go. I'll see you later, Kyanla." Anden burst from the front doors and down the steps of the walk. He slowed down enough to avoid any curious looks as he passed the Fingers posted at the gates, but once he was off of the Kaul property and out of sight, he broke into a run. His school satchel bounced on his shoulders as his feet pounded the asphalt all the way to the bus stop. When the bus came a few minutes later, Anden got on in a daze. He fell into a seat at the back and leaned his head against the window. The tightness in his chest hadn't gone away even after he'd stopped running. He wished he could make himself cry to release some of the pressure, like lifting the top off a boiling kettle.

• Chapter Twenty-Nine •
YOU'LL PROBABLY DIE

Stealing from The Docks had become an even more dangerous proposition ever since Maik Kehn had picked up that one crew and No Peak had gotten wise to the scheme. Bero did not want to end up like those other poor bastards—the two with broken necks, or even the one who got off easy with just the broken arms. He still shuddered when he thought of the Maik brothers. So he was relieved and excited when Mudt asked him if he'd been practicing with the Fullerton and could shoot straight yet. He assured Mudt that he and Cheeky had been going out to the empty fields by the reservoir and firing off rounds three times a week.

"Come over to the store tomorrow night then," said Mudt.

The Green Bone with the goatee was shooting pool on Mudt's old pool table in the garage of the Goody Too when they arrived. Instead of a rain slicker, he was wearing a gray trench coat and the same combat boots as before. He was friendlier this time. "It's been more than a month and you boys are still alive and doing good work for us, so that means you're either smart or godsdamn lucky, I don't care which."

"I can do more than lift boxes of fancy purses and shit," said Bero.

"That's what I figured. Now you'll have a chance to prove it," said the goateed man. He put a hand on each boy's shoulder. "Mudt tells me you can handle the Fully guns I gave you. That's good. So now I've got a job for you. This job's not coming from me, it's coming from above the people who are above me, so listen carefully and don't fuck it up. If you do, you'll probably die, but if you don't, you'll be cut with the clan, as cut as can be, which means—" He looked significantly at Bero and winked, giving the jade bolt in his left ear a little tug.

"What do you want us to do?" asked Bero.

"The Lilac Divine Gentleman's Club, you know it?" The Green Bone smirked. Every teenage boy who lived on this side of town knew *of* the Lilac Divine, but it was a high-class establishment; Mrs. Sugo's muscled bouncers glared with contempt and cracked their knuckles threateningly if anyone the likes of Bero and Cheeky loitered nearby in futile curiosity. The Green Bone did not wait for them to answer his rhetorical question; he said, "One of these nights, either a Secondday or a Fifthday, you're going to get a call. A driver will pick you up and take you to the Lilac Divine; Mudt will arrange that. When you get there, I want you to put those Fullys to good use. Shoot up the place, break the windows, send every customer in there diving under the bed with his limp dick in his hands. You see some nice cars, especially a real nice silver Roewolfe, you fill it with lead. Spray and pray, kekes, got it?"

"The—the Lilac Divine's a No Peak place." Cheeky stammered a little. "There'll be big shot Lantern Men and Green Bones inside. They say even the Pillar of the clan goes there."

"Oh you figured it out just now, did you, genius?" The Green Bone smirked even more broadly. "You'll have to be quicker than that if you're going to get out of No Peak territory alive afterward. That part's not my problem. But you do this and come back and no one's going to question that you're cut, that you've got what it takes."

"We'll do it, if you promise this'll get us in." The words left Bero's mouth before Cheeky could do more than twitch. Mudt and his son were sorting boxes of stolen vinyl records, pretending not to be part of the discussion, but they paused and looked up at Bero's sudden vehemence. He didn't care what the Green Bone sent him to do, but he was getting impatient and he didn't want to be jerked around. "There's not going to be some other test after this, right?"

"I don't promise you a thing," the Green Bone snapped. "You do a good job, you make a big impression, show just how valuable you can be to the clan—*that's* when we talk for real."

Cheeky swallowed and nodded. Bero shoved his hands into his pockets and kept his crooked face stiff. Years ago, there had been an older boy in the Docks called Fishhook, who used to terrorize the smaller boys, who would chase and beat Bero every chance he got. One day, Fishhook looked the wrong way and said the wrong things to a pretty girl whose father was a union boss and No Peak Lantern Man, and shortly afterward, a couple of Green Bone Fingers arrived in their corner of the Docks and calmly broke Fishhook's shins. Fishhook was never able to catch Bero after that. All Green Bones reminded Bero of those Fingers, who walked into his world carelessly to break one person's bones and deliver another to a better life. They stirred in Bero not merely a boyhood awe and fear, but a deeply consuming resentment and envy.

The goateed Green Bone was no different. He smiled as if amused, but his eyes remained cold and knowing. "Wait for the call," he said over his shoulder as he left the garage. "It'll come soon."

• Chapter Thirty •
THE TEMPLE OF DIVINE RETURN

The odor of cut grass and sweet roasted figs permeated the thuds and grunts of the relayball game and the occasional gasped exclamation or murmur of appreciation from the crowd. Shae picked her way into a section of the low bleachers populated by Kaul Du Academy fans and settled into an empty seat. Glancing over at the scoreboard, she saw that the game was close. The Academy was a martial school where physical prowess was revered, but the wearing of jade was not permitted in professional sports. The opposing team was from a large city school that regularly turned out national league players; they were surely eager to show up future Green Bones.

Shae searched for her cousin and barely recognized him at first. He was no longer the awkward kid she remembered. Anden had filled out with an adult Green Bone's physique. He was wearing dark shorts and playing First Guard, sticking tight to his opponent as the ball sailed into their zone. The other player leapt to kick it to a teammate but Anden, both taller and faster, smacked it out of the air. The two teens collided and went down in a tangle as the ball bounced into the net. The whistle blew for the ball to be re-thrown.

A relayball field consists of seven zones separated by waist-high nets—five rectangular pass zones and two triangular end zones. Each zone is occupied by two players, one from each side, who are not permitted to leave their enclosed space as they attempt to throw, hit, kick, or bounce the ball off their body to their teammates down the field, zone to zone over the nets to the opposing team's end zone where it is the job of the Finisher to put the ball between the Guardian's point posts. As the game is essentially a series of violent one-on-one skirmishes, ample opportunity exists for personal as well as team enmity. As Anden got to his feet, the opponent in his zone glared at him and spat some insult at his back. Anden did not deign to turn around and react. He bent his knees, ready, squinting into the horizontal orange light of the setting sun.

The ball flew straight up from the referee's hands. Anden jumped to shoulder check the other player, reaching with one arm to seize the ball and hurl it over the net to his teammate in the instant before he was tackled to the ground. Shae stomped her feet appreciatively along with the crowd. She was impressed by her cousin's grace and aggression on the field, his workmanlike athleticism. He seemed to approach relayball as a duty, not a game—he took little outward satisfaction in a good play and grimaced only faintly after bad ones. Already, she could picture him as a Green Bone, one of No Peak's Fists.

She was not alone in this. In the row behind her, someone said, "The Academy First Guard there—that's the Mad Witch's boy, the one the Kauls took in. You can bet the Horn is counting down the days until that one gets his jade."

"Him and the whole crop of year-eights," someone else added.

A point was scored by the Academy Finisher and the spectators stomped their feet on the bleachers in approval. The applause was brief and faded quickly back to silence. Sporting events on Kekon were different from how they were in Espenia. Shae had been astounded by how rowdy and jovial the crowds were over there. The Espenians sang and chanted constantly, they cheered and booed, waved flags and shouted nonsensical instructions at the players and coaches. The Kekonese were no less passionate in their team loyalties, but no one would think to yell at the field or distract the participants. The Espenians, Shae had concluded, believed the athletes were there to entertain the audience; the energy of the crowd was part of the game. The Kekonese considered themselves separate from the conflict, mere witnesses to a feud waged on their behalf.

Kaul Du Academy won the game narrowly by a single point. Afterward, the players saluted their opponents, then milled by the bench, gathering their equipment. Shae went down and stood at the edge of the small field until Anden noticed her. He squinted in her direction. Breaking into a broad smile of recognition, he slung his bag over his shoulder and loped toward her.

"Shae-jen," he said, then flushed, embarrassed at the understandable but awkward mistake. He gave her a brief hug, warm but respectful, then took his glasses out of their case and pushed them onto the sweaty bridge of his nose. "Sorry. It'll take me a while to get used to just calling you Shae."

"You were fantastic out there tonight," she told him. "They would've tied it up if it hadn't been for that intercept of yours in the last quarter."

"The sun was in the other fellow's eyes," he said, polite as always.

"Do you want to get something to eat? We can do it another time if you'd rather go out with your friends tonight." The other Academy players were departing. She'd noticed that, even as a member of the team, Anden seemed slightly apart from his classmates. It had been that way for her as well at the Academy, and she didn't want to deprive him of the chance to be part of the group tonight.

"No, I'd rather talk to you," said Anden quickly, glancing back at his teammates for only a second. "If you have the time, that is. Do you?"

She assured him that she did, and they walked together from the field. The evenings were cool now, by Janloon standards, and Shae drew a sweater around herself as they wandered Old Town to a somewhat sleepy night market where hawkers sold colorful kites and wooden spinning tops alongside fake gold watches and music tapes, and the smell of spicy fried nuts and sugared beets rose up from the food stalls. They talked about the game, and when they'd exhausted that topic, Shae asked her cousin about school, and he asked her about studying abroad and how she liked her new apartment in North Sotto. Anden was not reticent, but he was not a particularly talkative sort, no more than Shae, so their conversation remained just shy of awkward, both of them trying to think of questions to draw out the other person, both hesitating to fill in the lapses.

A white paper lantern hung over the door of the barbecue restaurant on the street corner, but they waited in line with everyone else. Once seated at a small, yellow, vinyl-covered table on a lamplit patio covered by a sagging tarp, they ate sweet glazed pork and vinegary cabbage from greasy paper baskets. Anden dug in eagerly, but couldn't finish the hefty portions of roasted meat; too much rich restaurant fare didn't sit well with a stomach accustomed to the modest portions and simple food of the Academy.

"Anden, I'm sorry it took me so long to come see you," Shae said at last.

"I don't have a good excuse; I intended to do it sooner but couldn't get over how awkward it would be to visit the Academy. I've been busy job hunting, and before that I was traveling and doing something for Lan. It took me longer than I expected to get settled into a routine." She stopped offering further rationalizations. The things Hilo had said to her, accusing her of neglecting to show kindness to her family since her return to Janloon—they were true, and some had cut deep.

Anden stared at his hands, fastidiously wiping the sauce from under his nails with one of the moist square towelettes torn from a tiny paper packet. His brow was drawn down and creased. "Have you seen Lan lately?"

He appeared not to have heard anything she'd just said. "A few weeks ago. He's busy, I'm sure." She'd made no recent effort to go to the house.

"When are you going to see him next?"

Shae was surprised. She'd always known her cousin to be courteous, but the tone of Anden's voice now was almost demanding. "I'm going to the house for dinner in a few days. I'll likely see him then," she said. "Why?"

Anden was tearing the remains of his paper towelette into shreds and not looking directly at her. "I thought maybe you could talk to him. See how he's doing, whether he needs help with anything. Ever since the duel at the Factory, he seems…different. Stressed. You might…I don't know. Get him to relax a little, maybe."

Shae raised her eyebrows. She remembered that Anden had always idolized Lan, had always enjoyed a special attention from him. "Lan is the Pillar; it's not his job to relax," she said. "If he seems troubled or distant to you, it's because there are a lot of problems that he has to deal with right now." Anden was listening but still shredding the towelette, so she said in what she hoped was a more reassuring voice, "Don't worry too much."

Anden crumpled the torn towelette and dropped it onto the remaining scraps of his dinner. He spoke hesitantly, "Shae, I think…I think Lan might not be making the right decisions about some things. I know I'm not a Green Bone yet and it's not my place to say that. But I'll be getting my jade soon, and I want to help." His words sped into a low torrent. "I was thinking I ought to talk to Hilo, but he's got a lot to worry about too, and he'll just tell me to sit back and focus on school and not second guess the Pillar. I thought maybe you could—"

Shae broke in. "As much as I hate to admit it, Hilo's right." It was a little painful, to see Anden already so emotionally invested in the clan and its troubles. Her cousin was just as she had once been. "When I was a year-eight, I couldn't wait to graduate and get my jade and be a proper member of the clan. I shouldn't have been in such a rush. You're only a student for four more months—so just be a student. Don't get sucked into clan business so early on when you don't have to be. In fact, you don't ever have to be, if you don't want to. Being a Green Bone is only one way of life. You don't *have* to choose it."

"What else would I choose?" the teen asked, with a surprising amount of sullenness and heat. "I'm not naive. Why would Grandda have brought me into the family, why would he have sent me to the Academy, if it wasn't so I would be part of the clan someday? And that someday is now."

"Grandda doesn't always know best." Once, she would never have admitted this out loud to anyone. "Lan's the one who brought you in, and he did it because it was the right thing to do, not because he thought you'd become a useful Fist." She sighed. "I can tell you're worried about the war but—"

"Aren't *you* worried?" Anden exclaimed. He flushed at his outburst but seemed beyond caring if he was being rude.

Shae reminded herself that the Mountain had snatched Anden off the street on Boat Day. No wonder he was still furious and scared. She forced the defensiveness out of her voice. "Of course I'm worried. But I'm not involved. I'm not a Green Bone anymore. I made the choice not to be."

"Why?" A quiet question. It was the first time he'd ever asked her.

Shae realized she didn't know Anden very well. When she spoke to her grandfather or her brothers she fell into old cadences that sometimes made her feel as if she'd never left the island. She didn't have that familiarity with Anden. They'd gotten along well enough when they were young, but she'd missed out entirely on the last few years of his life, when he'd grown from a solemn, somewhat haunted-looking boy to this young man, the protégé of her brothers.

"The clan is all or nothing, Anden. I did some things on my own that didn't fit expectations. And I learned pretty quick that wasn't allowed." A humorless smile crept over her lips. "It was a bit more complicated, but you get the gist."

Anden was quiet. His eyes followed the night flies buzzing around one of the dim lamps, then returned to her. "So what do you plan to do now?"

"I have a job offer I'm thinking of taking." Shae straightened in her seat, glad to share her recent news with someone, though she doubted anyone in the family would appreciate what it meant to her. "It's a regional business development position at an Espenian electronics company. I'll be going back to Espenia for company training for a few months, and afterward working part of the time there and part of the time here, and traveling to other places in the world too. I think it'll be interesting."

Dismay rose on Anden's face. Only with a visible effort did he force it back into a barely neutral expression. "You're leaving again?"

Shae was nonplussed. "Only temporarily. Like I said, the training is only for a few months. After that, I'll be in Kekon at least half of the time. I wouldn't want to live in Espenia year-round, so I think this job will…" She trailed off, guilt and resentment stopping her throat. Anden had just asked her if she would prevail upon Lan on his behalf. He'd hoped that even if she held no official role in the clan and was no longer a Green Bone, that she would still be present and influential, a member of the family war effort that perhaps he could count on.

Hadn't she just told him that the clan was all or nothing?

"I'm sorry, that was rude of me." Anden seemed to suddenly rouse himself, to realize that his response had been selfish and inappropriate. Quickly, "It's only that I was glad you'd come back and thought I'd get to see you more before you jetted off again. I'm happy for you though. The job sounds like a really good one, an international businesswoman's kind of job. Congratulations, Shae. I mean it." And even though his disappointment was still palpable, he smiled with such an earnest desire to put things right between them that Shae could not help but soften and wish that she could recover as gracefully.

"It's fine, Anden," she assured him. "And I do think we'll get to spend some more time together. It's my fault we didn't do this earlier; I didn't even know until just recently about what happened to you on Boat Day. If I'd known, I would've—"

Anden shook his head sharply, almost angrily. "That was nothing," he said. "They didn't threaten or hurt me. I'm not a Green Bone yet."

Shae was silent for a minute. Behind them, the counter staff shouted out orders to the cramped kitchen, people chatted and laughed as they stood in line, moths fluttered, trapped, under the green canvas tarp over the patio. Outside, it was fully dark but a swollen moon hung over smeared clouds.

Anden said, "I guess we should go."

"What did you want me to talk to Lan about?" Shae asked. "If something's really bothering you, I'll mention it to him next time I see him. Is it something you've been hearing around the Academy?"

"It's fine," Anden said, shaking his head again. "You're right; it's not something he needs my opinion on. Don't worry about it." With deliberate joviality, he pushed back his chair and said, "This place was really good; the best meal I've had in months. You remember Academy food, don't you?"

"Unfortunately, yes." Whatever was gnawing at him, whatever he'd wanted to say, Shae could no longer press him for it. She let him lead their conversation back to lighter topics as they stood up and gathered their things. They walked to the nearest subway station with meager talk; Anden had gone a little quiet. When they got to the platform and the westbound train arrived, he gave her a brief embrace. "It was good to see you, Shae. Another time soon?" And then the doors were closing behind him and the long screeching cars were carrying him away. Shae watched the lights disappear down the yawning tunnel with the unshakeable suspicion that she'd let her cousin down, missed some vital opportunity between them.

Instead of going home, she took the eastbound line a few stops and got off at the station that let out almost directly in front of the Janloon Temple of Divine Return. The street she ascended onto had recently been widened; she certainly couldn't recall ever seeing so many lanes of traffic in front of the entrance. An office building now butted up against the nearby handicraft market plaza; the side of its new parking structure displayed a billboard for Ygutanian ale. The Temple itself, however, looked exactly the same as Shae remembered, even more ancient and solemn at night than during the day, the carved stone pillars and massive clay roof flickering with deep shadows in the headlights of passing cars. Shae hadn't been inside the Temple since she was a teenager, but tonight, feeling unsettled, she felt compelled to walk through its peaked green doors.

The Temple district contained not only the Temple of Divine Return, the oldest Deitist temple in the city, but also, two blocks away, the folk Shrine of Nimuma, and three blocks in the other direction, the Janloon First Church of One Truth. It was heartening to think of Kekonese, Abukei, and foreigners all worshipping within sight of each other, praying on common footing. The charter of the KJA allocated jade to the Dietist temples before any other group, and while the clans gave charitably to the upkeep of religious buildings, the penitent oaths eschewed worldy allegiances and gave sanctuary to all worshippers. Like Monument Park and the area around Wisdom Hall and the palace, the Temple District was neutral ground. Here the clans did not rule.

Shae passed through the quiet courtyard with its rows of devotion trees limned with the soft glow of moonlight, and into the dimly-lit inner sanctum where the resident penitents sat in continuous three-hour shifts of meditative prayer. When she saw the circle of green robed, motionless figures on the low platform at the front of the room, Shae's step slowed. She wondered how deeply the penitents could Perceive her. Was it possible, with enough jade power, to go beyond sensing a person's presence and the subtleties of their physical state, but to see into their thoughts, into their very souls?

Shae chose one of the kneeling cushions and lowered herself onto it. She touched her head to the ground three times as was custom, then straightened up with her hands resting on her knees, her eyes drawn again to the three men and three women penitents, their heads and eyebrows shaved, their eyes closed. Each sat cross-legged with hands resting on the top of a mounted jade orb the size of a small bowling ball. To be in contact with so much jade… Shae was reminded of the boulders she'd seen at the mine pit, the mad temptation to put her hand on one of them. The penitents must possess exceptional training and control. They could probably hear a fly landing on a cushion in the back of the room, or Perceive the people on the street outside, yet they were motionless, breathing slowly and steadily, their faces relaxed. At the end of the three hours, they would lift their hands from their stations, then stand up and glide away as another took their place. Each time, they were battered by jade rush and withdrawal. Shae knew what withdrawal was like and it made her cringe to imagine going through it in shifts, day and night, over and over again. The penitents believed it would bring them, and humanity, closer to godliness.

Shae let her eyes roam. Above the meditating circle hung the famous mural of Banishment and Return. The original had been painted hundreds of years ago but destroyed during the Shotarian occupation; what worshippers saw now was a skillful reconstruction based on memory and old photographs. Along the stone walls of the sanctum, fragrant incense candles burned in alcoves devoted to each of the major deities. The gentle trickle of water from the two wall fountains wound into the ambient road noise that intruded through the high open windows. At this late hour, the sanctum was nearly empty; there were only three other visitors kneeling on the green congregational cushions—an elderly man in the back corner, and three rows in front of Shae, a middle-aged woman with her grown daughter, both of them weeping and leaning on each other for support. Shae dropped her gaze to the floor in front of her own cushion, embarrassed to be witnessing their private family anguish. She felt awkward and hypocritical to have come to this holy place at all. She had not practiced the faith in years. She wasn't even sure she could call herself a Deitist anymore.

The Kauls were nominally religious of course. There was a sparsely-used prayer room in the house, and on the major holidays during Shae's childhood, the family had dressed in their best clothes and gone to the Temple. Members of their vast and powerful clan would mill about outside until the family car pulled up in front. Then there would be a flurry of saluting and respect-paying. At such times, Kaul Sen was at his best, greeting everyone with the same consideration and magnanimity whether they were the most prosperous Lantern Man or the most junior Finger. After an appropriate time, Shae's grandfather would lead Shae's mother, her brothers, her, (and later, Anden) inside, and the crowd of people would follow them in, and the whole sanctum would hum with their hushed voices and the throb of jade energy.

Kaul Sen was always front and center in the first row. His wife knelt on his left. To his right was Lan, then Hilo, then Shae, (then Anden, once he was a Kaul), then their mother. The service would drone on for hours. Learned Ones, the most senior lifelong penitents, would lead the assembled worshippers in the recitations of exaltation for the deities, and then guide the meditation prayers concerning the attainment of the Divine Virtues. During the chanting, Hilo would fidget and make faces, and Kaul Sen would glower at him. Shae's legs would go numb. She concentrated on ignoring Hilo.

When she was older, she grew to find the services tolerable. Eventually, she realized the recitations were hopeful and calming. Deitism was a deeply Kekonese faith. There were different sects, from the nationalistic to the pacifistic, but one thing they all agreed upon was that jade was a link to Heaven, a divine but dangerous gift meant to be used piously and for good. Green Bones had to strive to be worthy people. Virtuous people. People, Shae believed, like her grandfather.

As a child however, she didn't ponder spirituality; she thought about how much longer the ordeal would go on. When she slumped or leaned or groaned, her mother prodded her upright. "Sit straight and be quiet," she admonished. "Everyone is watching you."

That had been her mother's entire philosophy of life: *Sit straight and be quiet. Everyone is watching you.* Well, no one was watching Shae now. Without a jade aura, she might pass any of her old Academy classmates in the street and not even be recognized. When she'd gotten the phone call from the regional director of Standard & Croft Appliance, it had pleased her to know the job offer had been made in ignorance about her family. Yet she'd felt only a vaguely satisfied relief. Not happiness, not enthusiasm. She had a graduate degree, her own apartment, and a job offer from an international company, one that any of her business school classmates in Espenia wou've congratulated her on. She was at last the independent, worldly, educated woman who'd risen above the savagery and insular nature of her jade- and testosterone-fueled family. She was supposed to feel free and unencumbered, not lonely and uncertain.

Shae bent her head. She wasn't sure if she believed in the ancestor gods, or in the Banishment and Return, or even in the idea that jade came from Heaven. But every Green Bone knew that invisible energy could be felt, tapped, and harnessed. The world worked at a deeper level, and maybe if she concentrated hard enough, even without jade, she could communicate with it.

Guide me, she prayed. *Give me a sign.*

• Chapter Thirty-One •
NOT ACCORDING TO PLAN

Lan was in his study when the phone call came in from Hilo. It was on a line that was separate from the others. Only Hilo was aware of the number and he knew to use it only for urgent matters that required an absolutely secure connection.

"I found the proof you wanted," the Horn said, without preamble. "Doru's been in regular contact with the Mountain. He's been taking payment from them through secret accounts."

Lan felt a heaviness descend. "You're sure?"

"I'm sure."

Reluctance kept the Pillar silent for a second. "We'll handle this tonight, then." He looked at the clock. The work day was almost over; Doru would soon be leaving his office on Ship Street. There was no point in delaying—that would only spook the traitor and make the whole affair more painful for everyone.

He made the necessary arrangements with Hilo, then hung up and sat quietly and gloomily for a few minutes. The Weather Man had recently returned from Ygutan with information on the Mountain's activities in that country, including details on its shine-producing facilities and business dealings. The Fist and the Finger that had been sent as Doru's bodyguards had watched him closely and reported no suspicious behavior on the part the Weather Man during the trip.

Doru was not stupid; he knew he was on weak footing in the clan, and with Kaul Sen's lucidity growing more unreliable by the day, it appeared he'd decided to hunker down and behave. He'd even gamely swallowed the insult of Lan suspending the KJA in his absence and without consulting him. Even though Lan had mentally prepared himself for Hilo's call, the pleasant change in Doru's behavior had made him think, for a short while, that perhaps he'd been wrong about the man's compromised loyalties.

He called Woon into his office. When the Pillarman arrived, Lan stood up to greet him. "You've been a friend to me for many years, and a good Pillarman for the last three," Lan said. "Starting tomorrow morning, you'll be Weather Man of No Peak."

Woon could not have been entirely shocked by the appointment, but he was still overcome with gratitude. "The clan is my blood, and the Pillar is its master," he said, saluting deeply. "Thank you for this honor, Lan-jen. I won't fail you."

Lan embraced him and said, "I've given you more responsibility for the past several months and you've done well. You're ready." In truth, he was not entirely confident in his statement; he still felt Woon was not quite up to the caliber of a superior Weather Man, but he was capable enough and Lan held no doubt of the man's loyalty. In any case, there was no choice now; Woon had to step up to the task. "Not a word of this news to anyone, until after I give you permission tomorrow."

"I understand, Lan-jen," Woon said, with a proper somberness that showed he was perfectly aware he was coming into the role on account of another's misfortune.

"These are difficult times for the clan and you'll have to be prepared to take control of the Weather Man's office quickly. Go home early tonight and get a good night's rest, but let's have a drink together first." Lan took a bottle from his cabinet and poured them each a glass of hoji, which they enjoyed in muted celebration.

After Woon had reiterated his thanks and departed, Lan went through papers at his desk without truly paying attention them. These days, he never felt as if he were at his best, either physically or mentally. The lingering weakness in his body heightened his constant anxiety over the threats to the clan, and now knowing that the next twenty-four hours would be particularly difficult made it hard to concentrate.

An envelope sitting in an untouched stack of mail caught Lan's attention and when he extracted it, he saw that the return address was a postal box in Stepenland. A letter from Eyni. Lan fingered the edges of the seal, eager and deeply reluctant to break it open. Since the divorce, they'd exchanged only a

few letters—cordial and business-like, settling affairs, her telling him where
to mail belongings, that sort of thing. But seeing her handwriting, hearing
her voice in his head—it never failed to bring down his mood. With what
he already had to deal with today, he sighed aloud.

She'd confessed the affair to him. One of Hilo's men had seen her entering an apartment building with her lover and knowing her secret was
lost, Eyni had gone straight back to the house before the news could make
its way through the Horn back to Lan. "Please don't kill him," she'd begged
in a whisper, sitting on the edge of their bed with her hands squeezed between her knees. "He's not Kekonese, he doesn't understand our ways. I'll
stop seeing him and stay with you here, or I'll leave and you'll never have
to see me again—whatever you tell me to do. But please don't kill him. And
don't let Hilo kill him. That's all I ask." And it was this heartfelt plea, driven
by her obviously genuine fear, that saddened Lan the most, because even
after five years of marriage she obviously didn't really know him at all.

"Is he really such a better person than I am?" Lan asked dully.

Eyni looked up, eyebrows raised in surprise. Even distraught, her heart-
shaped face had a genuine and unpretentious prettiness. "Of course not. But
he's not the Pillar of the great No Peak clan. He doesn't cancel dinner plans,
he doesn't travel with bodyguards, no one recognizes him or salutes him
in public or stops him to ask for favors for their relatives. He can act silly,
and sleep late, and go away on vacation at a moment's notice, and do all the
things we once did together."

"You always knew I would be Pillar someday," Lan reminded her accusingly. "You understood it would be this way. There are plenty of women
who'd be thankful, *grateful,* to be the wife of the Pillar. You promised me
that you were one of them."

Eyni's eyes filled with tears of remorse. "I was once."

I should make her stay, Lan had thought with classic Kekonese vindictiveness. *In exchange for this foreigner's life, she has to stay and give me an heir,
for the clan.*

In the end, he couldn't bring himself to be so cruel to either her or
himself.

The envelope in Lan's hand now was square and stiff, like a greeting card. It looked thicker, like it contained a longer and more substantial

message than previous mailings. He imagined opening it to find a letter in which Eyni repented and begged him to take her back. Far more likely, in her well-meaning cruelty, she'd written to reassure him that she was fine, to wish him well, and to tell him about her new home overseas and all the things she was seeing and doing with her boyfriend.

Lan shut the letter in his desk drawer. In either case, this was not the right time to be distracted by melancholy thoughts of his ex-wife. He would open it later. And because it still taunted from inside the closed drawer, Lan got up and left the house. It was a Fifthday evening and there would still be plenty of time to get back and await Hilo's phone call.

Hours later, Lan did not, even after a meal and a lay at the Lilac Divine, feel considerably better. He sat on the end of the bed, finishing a cigarette and wringing a final few minutes of peace from the evening before he had to leave.

"Is something wrong?" Yunni crawled up behind him and looped her bare arms around his neck, but he disentangled himself and stood up. He pulled on his pants, then walked into the bathroom with its scented candles and red lighting. He splashed his face with cold water, then took a hand towel from the rack and wiped down his neck and bare chest. From the bed, Yunni coaxed, "Must you leave so soon? Come back to bed. Stay the night."

She'd like that. She'd make more money if he stayed; it would make up for the fact he'd been coming here less. "I'd like to be alone for a while now," he said, and because he couldn't bring himself to be cruel to her, "Please."

The charm girl's artfully polished facade faltered for a second. She crossed her arms across her breasts. He could sense her indignation at the dismissal: *Who did he think she was? A street whore?* Where was the sophisticated client she used to have, the one who enjoyed singing and harp music, conversation and wine?

She recomposed herself admirably and stood up with unhurried grace. "As you like, Kaul-jen." Yunni gathered her robe around herself, slid her feet into slippers, and padded out the door, shutting it behind her firmly to announce her irritation. Lan didn't watch her go. He put on his watch and looked at the time. Right now, three Fists were waiting to seize Yun Doru-pon from the door of his favorite brothel in the sleazy Coinwash district. The irony of how he and Doru were both spending the evening before their reckoning was not lost on Lan.

After the Fists picked up Doru, they would drive him to an undisclosed location. When they arrived, Hilo would call Lan at home. The Fists were under orders not to hurt or kill Doru, not yet, not until Lan arrived. He'd been clear about this. He wanted to face the man he considered an uncle, and ask him why, after so many years of faithful service, he'd betrayed the clan. Then Lan would have to decide how to handle the Weather Man's fate so Kaul Sen was never the wiser.

As the inevitable hour drew closer, he felt unsure of his ability to do the right thing. Even now, knowing Doru was a traitor, he did not want to have the old man killed. He could still remember Doru returning from business trips with sweets for the Kaul grandchildren. He was guilted by the image of Doru and Kaul Sen playing chess in the courtyard. But betrayal so close, and at such a high level of the clan—it could not forgiven. Was it possible, Lan wondered, to be both a strong leader and a compassionate person, or were those two things opposing forces, pushing each other away?

With the door closed and Yunni gone, Lan opened the combination safe and took out the rest of his jade. Another reason he'd stopped coming here as often: taking off and putting on so much jade was painful now—like being dunked in ice and then coals, or physically shaken as if he were a bug in a jar. Lan fingered the beads around his neck, touching each one as if accounting for them, then put on the belt and cuffs, heavy and further encrusted with the jade he had won from Gam. He braced himself.

There was a few seconds of delay, then the rush hit him hard, much harder than usual. The world tilted and folded. Lan's body screamed in pro-test, his chest seizing. He fell to the floor and clutched the carpet with curled fingers. *Breathe, breathe. Get yourself under control.* He fought back a moan. This was supposed to get better. The doctor had said that the damage Gam had inflicted was not permanent. But he still hadn't healed and on-and-off symptoms of jade overexposure plagued him. The lingering injury from the duel, the increased jade load, general stress and sleep deprivation—they were aggravating each other in a vicious cycle. Lan crawled onto the bed, reaching for his jacket hanging from the post of the headboard. He felt around until he found the rubber strip, vial and syringe he'd tucked into the inside pocket and drew them out.

The room seemed to be attacking him, the walls pressing in too close. His senses were wild, snapping in and out of focus. He caught a snippet of some angry conversation on the street outside as clear as if it was next to him. The next second it was gone but the texture of the bedsheets was so prickly it stung his skin. Lan pressed the heels of his hands to his eyes and grasped for the control techniques he'd first learned in the Academy, ones he hadn't needed since he was a teenager. He tensed then relaxed every muscle in his body, slowly counting out the rhythm of his breaths, until he'd pushed every feeling back to a tolerable distance and his hands no longer shook. Sitting on the pillow with his back against the headboard, he tied off his arm, uncapped the needle, drew the contents of the vial into the syringe, and hesitated.

The shock and disbelief he'd seen on Anden's face filled his memory. So did the shame Lan had felt that day, knowing he'd profoundly damaged the young man's admiration and trust in him. Lan shared his cousin's disgust; he hated needles, and he despised SN1. He loathed resorting to it for the jade tolerance he'd always taken for granted. He was doing all he could to combat the manufacture and spread of the poison, and yet here he was, carrying a vial of it around with him, nestled against his chest like a tiny explosive. The agony of having to justify himself to Anden had caused Lan to go without an injection for days. He knew that wasn't how you were supposed to use the drug, but each time he waited as long as he could, thinking that finally he was getting better and no longer needed to resort to its use—and then the edginess, the perceptual distortions, the sweats and racing heart would start up once more.

Tomorrow he'd go back to Dr. Truw, get checked over again, see if there wasn't something else he could do to hasten natural healing and build his tolerance back up to where he could carry his jade without chemical help. Perhaps he ought to take the risk of leaving Hilo in charge for a little while—a worrisome idea, but one that would allow him to get away to Marenia for a week, where he could wear a little less jade and recover his health. Tonight though, he couldn't be weak. He needed to be at his most clear-headed and decisive. There was no room to be mentally addled or emotionally volatile when you were sending a man to his death.

Lan slid the needle into his vein and emptied the contents of the syringe into his arm. He untied the rubber tourniquet and closed his eyes. The drug circulated up into his brain and in minutes cleared it like a television antenna finally finding a signal and resolving flickering static into a clear image. Copious jade energy hummed through him, but it was steady and under control, waiting to be manipulated by his will. His senses were sharp as glass but consistent and coordinated, no longer blasting in and out of focus. He felt good. Powerful. He could leap to a second story balcony or raise a Deflection that would move a car. Lan allowed himself a moment of amazement. Despite his moral objections to SN1 and all it stood for, it truly was a remarkable drug. No wonder the foreigners wanted it so badly. No wonder Ayt Mada wanted the fortune that could be made from selling it to them.

Lan stowed the items back into his pocket, then finished dressing and let himself out of the room. In the lobby downstairs, he waved aside Mrs. Sugo's sugary inquiries as to whether he was satisfied with his visit, reassuring her that he was, but unfortunately could not stay to enjoy himself further. He had to get back to the house before Hilo called and someone else picked up the phone.

Having sent Woon home and knowing the Horn was occupied following his instructions, Lan had not bothered telling anyone he was going out for a few hours. He'd opted to take a cab and leave his car in the garage to avoid any attention. The drive to and from the Lilac Divine passed only through undisputed No Peak territories so there was little danger. Outside, he flagged down another taxi and asked the driver to take him back to the house.

Bero's heart was hammering in his chest, but his hands were steady as he brought the Fullerton gun from the passenger side car floor onto his lap and readied himself to fling open the door. The call had come from Mudt half an hour ago, and the driver and car had appeared in front of his aunt's apartment building fifteen minutes after that. "It has to be tonight," Mudt had said.

Everything was happening very quickly, but Bero was fine with that. The sooner the better. There were two bouncers and several expensive cars parked in front of the elegant, dusky red façade of the Lilac Divine but no silver Roewolfe. Bero spoke over his shoulder. "You ready, keke?" From the seat behind him, Cheeky made a nervous noise of assent.

A man emerged from the Lilac Divine, a man Bero would recognize anywhere. As he watched in astonishment, one hand on the door handle, Kaul Lan, the Pillar of the No Peak clan, got into the back of a taxi. It pulled into the street almost directly in front of them.

Bero was frozen for only a second. Then everything fell into place for him and he spun forward in his seat to yell at the driver. "Follow that cab. Come on, go, drive!"

"What are you doing?" Cheeky shouted, pulling his partly open door shut as the vehicle began moving. "We're supposed to be shooting up the club! That's what they told us to do!"

"Forget the fucking club," Bero shouted back at him. "Why do you think they sent us to shoot it up *tonight*? Because the fucking Pillar of No Peak was there, that's why! And now he's in that taxi. He's who the Mountain wants. There's no point hitting the Lilac Divine if he's not there!" Bero was not only certain of this, he was certain that fate was shining on him at this instant, offering him the opportunity he'd been waiting for, something better than what he'd been promised. "This is it, keke," he said, half to himself, half to Cheeky. "Our big chance."

Do a good job, make a big impression, show just how valuable you can be to the clan—those had been the goateed Green Bone's words. What could possibly make a bigger impression, what could be of greater value, than taking out Kaul Lan himself?

Bero grinned, a little madly. It was not hard for him to call to mind the memory of the Pillar's dismissive, compassionate disdain. Soon Kaul Lan would realize how badly he'd underestimated Bero. Fate worked in mysterious and beautiful ways.

"Okay," Bero hissed. "At the next stoplight, pull up beside the cab."

The driver was a lumpy-faced, heavyset fellow who hadn't said a word all night. Either he was too dumb to be nervous, or considered drive-by machine gun shootings to be unremarkable in his line of work. Who knew where Mudt had found him. He didn't even respond now, merely shrugged at Bero's direction and sped up to close the gap to the taxi.

"You're out of your mind. The fucking Pillar of the No Peak clan," Cheeky's voice wavered on panic. He muttered, "We're worm food, keke," but still he cranked down his window. They readied themselves to thrust the barrels of the Fullertons out the right hand side of the car and open fire. It would be fast, and very loud, and very messy.

Lan noticed the black car following him. It wasn't the car itself he noticed first; from the distance of a city block, his heightened Perception sensed the unmistakeable hostility and fear directed squarely at him. Lan glanced over his shoulder and watched the vehicle take a turn after them, maintaining a two car-length distance behind the taxi. He turned back around to face forward, then stretched out and focused his Perception.

Three men. The driver's energy was cool and dull, the other two were burning flares of excitable aggression and fear. No jade auras. Not Green Bones, then. Common criminals, or hired grunts. Lan's mouth twisted. He removed cash from his wallet—enough to cover the cab bill and then some—and leaned forward, handing it to the driver. "This is far enough," he said. "Take a U-turn at the next light and drop me off at the corner. Then keep your head down and get out of here."

The taxi suddenly shot ahead and spun into a U-turn.

"Shit, what's he doing?" Bero exclaimed.

From the backseat, Cheeky said, "He's on to us. He's getting out of the cab."

"Turn around!" Bero yelled at the driver. "Turn around before he gets away." There was already traffic blocking line of sight between the two cars. The driver lost several seconds before taking a sharp turn up to the curb where Kaul had gotten out, and by then, the taxi was already driving down the street and the Green Bone was nowhere in sight. *Fuck!* Bero opened the door and jumped out onto the sidewalk, swinging his head back and forth, trying to see where their target had gone.

"What do you think you're doing now?" Cheeky hissed at him from the open car window. "Kaul's gone. We're not going to chase after him on foot. Get back in, before someone sees you standing there holding a fucking Fully gun. We can still go back to the club, do the job they told us to do."

He couldn't see Kaul in either direction on the sidewalk. The street bordered a steeply descending embankment. Bero ran to the railing and looked over, remembering, in despair, how fast Green Bones could move. The clumpy grass and dirt sloped down into darkness, all the way to the unlit pier where the silhouettes of small moored sailboats lined the edge of the harbor. Frustration welled behind Bero's straining eyes. This was going all wrong, not according to plan at all.

Then, miraculously, as if destiny had turned his face and made his eyes land on just the right spot, he saw a figure walking along the boardwalk by the water. It was too dark to tell for sure that it was Kaul, but Bero knew it was him. The set of his body, the way he walked—Bero was sure. He shouted in triumph. "I see him!"

Cheeky cursed and scrambled from the car. He leaned over the railing and stared at where Bero was pointing. "Forget it, keke. He's too far away now, and he already knows we're on to him. We'll get him another time."

"There won't *be* another time!" Kaul would get wise. He'd travel with his bodyguards or change his routine. In any case, after this failure, the goateed Green Bone brush Bero aside as unworthy, just another disappointing wannabe—and take away his chance at jade.

Bero slung the strap of the Fully gun over his shoulder and clambered over the railing. "Stay here if you like," he said. "When I come back with Kaul's head, I'll tell them what a thin-blooded coward you were. You better get out of town."

Cheeky was a pussy, just like Sampa, but the difference was that he couldn't stand to be called out on it; Bero had figured that out early on. Bero dropped to the other side of the railing and started sliding and scrambling down the hill as fast as he was able to with a heavy weapon weighing him down. He didn't look back once. He was sure Cheeky would swear a bit and follow him, and even if he didn't, Bero didn't care—he wasn't going to give up and let his one best chance slip away.

The goateed Green Bone had promised him a pebble of jade for gunning the Lilac Divine, but if instead he killed Kaul Lan—*the Pillar of the No Peak clan!*—hell, Kaul's jade was his by right. Green Bones took jade from the bodies of their enemies, everyone knew that.

Lan had vaulted the railing and leapt Lightly down the steep embankment to the empty wooden walkway that ran along the harbor. He straightened his jacket and walked, leaving his pursuers behind. He wasn't worried about them following. His Perception was incredible, the strongest and clearest it had ever been. He could sense the confusion and disarray he'd left behind and he was sure the goons were not even professionals. They'd been hired to take a run at him. Lan was almost insulted.

He was also aggravated by the idea that he and his family might not be as safe inside No Peak territory as he'd assumed. During foreign occupation a generation ago, Kekonese rebels had been masters of guerrilla fighting, sneak attacks, and constant low-level harassment. Hilo had told him about the organized thieving in the Docks; the Mountain clan was almost certainly behind it, and Lan was sure this was part of the same thing—an ongoing effort to wear No Peak down, to distract and overwhelm its leaders. Their enemies were feigning peaceableness, refusing to show themselves while hiding behind the activities of common criminals who were reckless and stupid enough to do their bidding. It had the makings of a patient war based on tactics that Ayt Yu and Kaul Sen would have approved of against Shotarians, but it was entirely counter to the tradition of open duel between Green Bones in dispute with each other. It was offensive and disrespectful. It angered Lan and he could see why it infuriated Hilo.

Perhaps he ought to go back and kill these men. He didn't have time for that though, and he didn't want to create a scene that would slow him down right now. There were bigger problems to deal with tonight and he was supposed to be in his study awaiting Hilo's call. Lan walked faster. The boardwalk stretched all the way down near where the General's Ride passed under the KI-1 freeway. There, he could climb back up to street level and hail another taxi to take him home unmolested.

He was nearly there when his chest began to hurt. It was a sudden, constricting pain, as if his diaphragm had been seized in a huge fist. Lan slowed, alarmed, as he put a hand to his sternum. Nothing moved in the near darkness. The streetlight from the road above illuminated only the flat shapes of sampans and the masts of junks bobbing ever so slightly, the water slapping gently against their hulls.

Lan felt abruptly confused, as if he'd stepped from one place into an entirely different one through a door in a dream. He shook his head, trying to get his bearings back. What was going on? What was he doing here? His breaths were growing short and shallow, and he wondered why his heart was pattering irregularly.

He was at the docks. Trying to get home. He'd left the Lilac Divine, gotten in the taxi, been followed…that's why he'd left the cab and was down here. Why had it all escaped him so completely for a second back there? He took several more steps forward and staggered, unsteady on his feet. Something was wrong. A fog was descending over him, siphoning the clarity from his mind, the strength from his body. He felt warm and flushed, but when he put a hand to his brow he found he was not sweating; his skin was fever hot and dry.

These weren't jade-related symptoms; they weren't anything he'd experienced before. It occurred to him that perhaps he was having a stroke or a heart attack. Then the more obvious explanation struck him: the injection of SN1 he'd taken a few minutes ago. How many days had it been since his previous injection? Eight? Nine? After that long an abstention, he should've taken a half dose. He must've been distracted and rushed and taken a full dose instead.

Lan tried to focus. He had to get to the street and find a phone right away. He'd taken the precaution of keeping SN1 counteractant in the house; he simply needed to get back there. He put one foot in front of the other, misjudging the distance to the ground and stumbling. His fists clenched. He could do this; he *willed* himself to. The street was not far, and he was a *Kaul*—his father had once spent three days crawling through the jungle with a bullet in his back. Lan fixed his eyes ahead. He forced steadiness into his breath and took another step, then another. His mind cleared, his gait steadied.

A noise behind him made him turn. Lan was astounded, not just by the fact that the two men—no, *teenagers*—from the black car had followed him, but that, in his state, they'd been able to sneak up to within fifty meters without him noticing. When he turned, the boys stopped and a second of silent immobility passed. The taller youth on the right fumbled with the bolt of his Fullerton machine gun, but it was the sallow, dark haired teen on the left that made Lan stare in incredulity. *"You?"*

They opened fire.

A detonation of bewilderment and rage burst in Lan's skull. *Enough.* Enough with this. He brought his arms up—unleashing Steel and Deflection together in a massive expulsion of jade energy. The teenagers were not very good shots; adrenaline and fear made them worse. Bullets tore up the wooden planks around Lan's feet, zinged into the air above, chopped into the hulls of boats, and even sent up rows of tiny splashes in the water. The ones that would have hit the Pillar were caught up like flies in a blast of gale wind. Just as he'd taught Anden, Lan gathered them into the sucking wake of his Deflection, whipped them around and hurled them back out like a fistful of thrown marbles.

They did not have the deadly speed and accuracy of bullets fired from a gun, but they were still dangerous. One of his attackers dropped the Fully gun, clutching his arm, the other took lead to the knees and went down with a cry, his weapon clattering to the boardwalk. Lan was already moving, faster than shadow. Blazing with Strength, he stuck one gunman in the throat, crushing his windpipe before he hit the ground. He turned to the other youth, the one whose life he'd spared six months ago. The wounded teenager was trying to bring his weapon back up with his left arm. Lan tore the gun away, bent the barrel in his hands, and flung it aside. The boy scrambled backward, his face a crooked white oval as fear finally overtook reckless greed.

"You want this, do you?" Lan held up the jade beads around his neck. "You think it's worth dying for. You think it'll make you someone you're not." He reached to grab the fool by his hair, pull him forward and break his neck like a duck's, as Hilo had intended before. "You're stupid, then. Too stupid to live."

His hand closed on air as his legs suddenly buckled beneath him. Lan collapsed, his body engulfed in an agony of heat raging under the surface of his skin. The pain in his chest returned, redoubled, emptied his mind of thought.

The teenager backpedaled, staring with wide, confused eyes. Then he turned and ran. His footsteps reverberated like cymbal crashes in Lan's hollow chamber of a skull. Lan didn't notice. He couldn't breathe. His mouth was dry; his throat was burning up. He needed to make it stop. Put out the fire. Fire was like jade, and greed, and war, and unfulfilled expectations—consuming what it touched. Water. Get to the water.

The world was dulling. He was crashing out rapidly now, as if his jade was being ripped away from him all at once. He felt frantically for the beads around his neck, the cuffs around his arms—he still had every stone. *Get up,* he urged himself. *Keep going.* He heaved himself back up and took a few more steps. Lan had once run lightly on thin beams across the Academy's training grounds, but now he lost his balance and put a foot down too close to the edge of the pier. He pitched over, and when he hit the water, it was such an instant cold and silent relief that he didn't struggle when the silence closed over his head.

• Second Interlude •
THE ONE WHO RETURNED

The most well-known scripture of the Deitist religion, the *Pact of the Return*, is the story of a pious man named Jenshu, who, a very long time ago, spoke out against the evils of a despotic king and was forced to leave his land. He packed his large family, including his younger brothers and sisters and their families, on a great ship and went in search of the fabled ruins of the original jade palace on Earth.

After forty years of sailing the earth, stopping but never settling, aided by some gods and hampered by others, surviving adventures that would form the basis for many myths in Kekonese culture, Jenshu and his clan arrived on a lush and unspoiled island. Impressed by his dedication and piousness, Yatto the Father of All spoke to Jenshu, who was by now an old man, and led him into the mountains where he found stones of jade: the remains of the divine home once meant for humankind. A gift from the gods.

While his family constructed a village by the shore, Jenshu retired to a hermit's life of meditation in the mountains. Surrounded of jade, Jenshu developed and mastered godlike wisdom and abilities, growing ever closer to a state of divine virtue. His grandchildren and great grandchildren would seek him out to ask for his help and he would emerge briefly from his isolation to settle disputes, quell earthquakes, beat back storms, and repel barbarian invaders. When he was three hundred years old, the gods agreed that Jenshu alone, of all their human descendants, deserved to be brought home to Heaven.

Devout Kekonese Deitists consider themselves the descendants of Jenshu and closest in favor to the gods. Green Bones who practice the religion today trace their way of life to Jenshu's favorite nephew, Baijen, who went into the mountains to learn from his uncle and, after Jenshu's departure from the earth, became the protector of the island's people, the first and fiercest jade warrior in island legend. While all Kekonese revere Jenshu as the One Who Returned, only Green Bones consider themselves close enough to his legacy to refer to him simply as "old Uncle."

Upon Jenshu's ascendance, the gods further proclaimed that when the rest of humankind followed Jenshu's example and achieved the four Divine Virtues of humility, compassion, courage, and goodness, then they too would be welcomed back to godliness. All Deitists believe in this final promised occurrence, which they call the Return.

• Chapter Thirty-Two •
THE OTHER ONE WHO RETURNED

The phone call came before dawn, waking Shae on the morning of the day she'd expected to go to the family house for dinner with her grandfather and brothers. When she picked up the phone, she was astounded to hear Hilo's voice.

"Stay where you are," he said. "I'm sending a car to pick you up."

"Hilo?" For a second, she was not sure it was him.

"You have to come to the house, Shae."

"Why? What's wrong?" The grogginess of sleep fled at once. She'd never heard Hilo sound near panic. "Is it Grandda?" There was silence on the other end, so deep she might have heard her own voice echoing down a well. She squeezed the phone receiver. "Hilo? If you won't talk to me, hand the phone to Lan."

Something in the pause that followed filled her with the truth a split second before she heard the words. "Lan's dead."

Shae sat down. The phone cord pulled taut and Hilo's words stretched thin as thread, barely reaching her from the other side of a vast gulf.

"They got him last night at the Docks. Workers found his body in the water. Drowned."

She was staggered by the depth of her grief, the suddenness with which it arrived. "Send the car. I'll be ready," she said. She hung up and waited. When Hilo's large white Duchesse Priza pulled up in front of the apartment building, she walked out without locking the door or turning out the light. She got into the back seat.

Maik Kehn turned over his shoulder, sliding her a look of compassion so sincere she would have wept, if it had not been too early for that yet.

"I need to stop by the bank," she said.

Maik said, "I'm supposed to take you straight home."

"It's important. Hilo will understand."

Maik nodded and pulled the car away from the curb. She gave him directions to the bank and when they arrived, he parked and got out of the car with her. He was loaded with weaponry—moon blade, talon knife, two handguns. "You can't come into the bank like that," she said.

"I'll wait outside the door."

The bank had just opened. Shae went in and requested access to her safe deposit box. The manager said, "Of course Miss Kaul, come with me," and showed Shae into the back room with its wall of small steel doors, then left her alone.

Shae had not opened her safe in two and a half years. When she turned the key in the lock and opened the box, irrational fear gripped her for an instant. What if it was not there? But it was—her jade. All of it. Even before she reached inside, she felt the tug of its power setting off a tide in her blood like the moon's gravity pulling on the ocean. She counted every stone as she put on the earrings, the bracelets up both her forearms, anklets, choker. Then she closed the safe deposit box door and sat down on the ground, her back to the wall, and hugged her knees to her chest.

It had been so long since she'd worn jade that she felt the rush coming like the wave of a tsunami looming before it engulfs the beach. She did not tense or cringe from it. She raced alongside and let it sweep her up in its inexorable path. She rode it high, let it carry her simultaneously above her own body and more deeply inside it. She was inside the storm; she *was* the storm. Her mind spun in elated disorientation—the kind that comes from returning to an old house and opening the drawers, touching the walls, sitting in the furniture—remembering what was once forgotten. Guilt and doubt rose in opposition, then fell, carried swiftly away by the flood.

Shae got up. She walked out of the bank and back to the Duchesse with Maik Kehn. She got into the passenger side front seat, and Maik asked, "You want me to take you to the house now, Kaul-jen?" Shae nodded.

They did not speak during the drive. Shae's mind was being torn asunder so that her face and body did not know how to react. Someone observing her, such as Maik Kehn, who occasionally slid a glance in her direction, would think that she was frozen, that she felt nothing at all.

Lan being dead opened a chasm of desolation in Shae so vast she could not see the other side. Her eldest brother was the rock in the family, the one she felt she could always count on no matter what. He had never been unkind or judging toward her, had always given his attention to her and respected her even though she was much younger than he was. She wanted to be alone with the pain of her loss but also could not help reveling in the rediscovery of her jade senses. The sense of euphoria in her own reclaimed power was inescapable—and it suffused her with terrible remorse. And all the while, another part of was thinking clearly, if feverishly, toward vengeance.

When they arrived at the house, she walked past the sentries and found Hilo standing in the kitchen, his hands leaning heavily on the table so his shoulder blades jutted up and his head seemed to hang between them. Like Maik, he dripped with weaponry. He appeared in control of himself, almost thoughtful, but his jade aura heaved and roiled with the fiery consistency of explosive lava. Fists flanked him left and right, so the family kitchen was crowded with ferocious waiting men, the collective aura clamor of their jade-adorned bodies assaulting Shae's reawakened sense of Perception so much so that she paused to brace herself before entering.

Elsewhere in the house, she heard Kyanla quietly sobbing.

Hilo raised his head to look at her but didn't move.

"I'm going with you," she said. "I know where we should go."

Hilo straightened and came around the table toward her. She tried to see into his eyes but they were as black and distant as she felt. The Horn placed his hands on her shoulders, and pulled her close, and laid his cheek against hers. "Heaven help me, Shae," he whispered into her ear. "I'm going to kill them all."

• Chapter Thirty-Three •
DOWN FROM THE FOREST

Gont Asch spent most Sixthdays at the Silver Spur Cockfight Pit & Bar, which was owned by his cousin, a Lantern Man in the Mountain clan. A long-time aficionado of the sport, Gont owned and played a dozen prize gamecocks that his nephew bred and trained for him. Right now one of them was finishing off his opponent in a feathery melee of flapping, pecking, and flashing steel spurs. Excited shouts and disappointed groans rose from the bettors ringing the arena. Money exchanged hands as the referee lifted both birds, depositing the twitching loser in a blue plastic bucket and handing the victor back to his smiling trainer.

The arena and seating took up the main level of the Silver Spur. The open second floor contained the restaurant and bar where half the tables overlooked the action on the floor below and those without a direct view could see the fights on the hanging closed circuit televisions. In between watching the matches, Gont was having a late lunch and talking business with three of his Fists when a messenger barged through the door and ran straight up the stairs to his table with the news: Kaul Lan was dead, and Kaul Hilo was coming here now to kill Gont himself.

The Horn was taken aback but it didn't show on his face. Gont was an expert at keeping his thoughts and emotions to himself. Only his First Fist, Waun Balu, noticed the small shift in his expression—a flaring of the nostrils, the tightening of his mouth into a skeptical scowl. Gont looked around himself. He was in a building in the south Wallows, deep inside Mountain territory, in broad daylight, surrounded by several of his Green Bone warriors. Was Kaul really so insane as to try and attack him here?

Gont decided he was.

"Call every Finger you have nearby," he demanded of his Fists. "Clear the people out of here. Send lookouts to either end of the street and guard the doors." His men scrambled to obey. Gont found his nephew and told him to take their valuable birds out the back door and far away. The owner of the Silver Spur refused to flee with the customers, so Gont made him and his staff lock themselves in the kitchen with a pair of shotguns pointed at the door.

The battle to come would be bloody. The second Kaul son was a heavily-jaded and ferocious fighter, and for all the Mountain's internal assertions that No Peak was in decline, Gont knew that it was still a formidable clan with committed young warriors. After the failed assassination attempt and the duel at the Factory, Ayt-jen had instructed everyone to be more careful, more focused on the Mountain's eventual goal. So Gont had not expected a violent showdown so soon. As much as he looked forward to separating Kaul Hilo's head from his body, he wondered what had gone wrong, why their plans had failed. No time for speculation now.

Green Bones filled the Silver Spur and its surrounding streets. In a few minutes, Gont had a total of fourteen men in and around the building—three Fists and eleven Fingers. They took up positions near the door and in the upstairs windows. Half a dozen more jade warriors were gathering down the street in the Mountain-owned Brass Arms hotel, where they would close in behind the No Peak fighters and attack from the rear. Gont expected No Peak would outnumber them, but this was Mountain turf and he held the advantage of ground.

Gont considered phoning his Pillar but decided against it. Reinforcements would not arrive in time and besides, he intended to meet and kill Kaul Hilo himself.

The ruse was Shae's idea.

Before she'd arrived at the house, Hilo had been ready to head straight into the heart of Mountain territory to kill Gont himself. He'd already drunk a shot of hoji and cut his tongue on a knife with his Fists—the traditional Green Bone ritual before undertaking a mission one expected not to return from.

She faced him down from across the kitchen table the way she used to when they were children. "We have to be smarter than that. If we die today, the Mountain wins." They had to think ahead, even in this terrible time. "Gont will be ready and waiting for us. Even if we kill him, we won't defeat the Mountain. Won't *destroy* it."

Perhaps this unfettered outburst of emotion, surging Shae's jade aura with a vehemence that Hilo could not ignore, forced the Horn back into thinking clearly. He looked at his most trusted senior Fists and saw some of them nodding at what Shae had said. He turned to her. "I wish to the gods it hadn't taken this to bring you back," he said. "But you're green, and one of us again, so tell me what you have in mind."

Once she explained her idea, he smiled with a cold, satisfied determination and seized upon it with as much conviction as if it had been his own. He gave quick orders to his men, who sprang to carry them out. While the Maik brothers organized the attack parties, Shae went to the armory room behind the training hall to find herself some weapons. When she returned, Hilo was sitting on the stairs with Wen, saying goodbye. Their heads were bent close together, and they were speaking quietly. Wen's eyes were dry but her fingers trembled as she smoothed Hilo's hair behind one of his ears with a tenderness that made Shae turn away, feeling like an intruder witnessing a private moment. She went to stand outside and watch as the Duchesse and five other cars departed the estate.

The convoy of vehicles would be sighted entering the Lo Low Street tunnel and word would reach Gont Asch that Kaul Hilo was on his way to seek a showdown at the Silver Spur. The Mountain would rush to mount a defense while the Duchesse-led convoy took its time circling the Wallows district before returning to No Peak territory.

Seconds after the decoy cars exited the roundabout of the Kaul house, the Maiks and three other Fists pulled up in nondescript vehicles hastily borrowed from a nearby Lantern Man's car dealership. Hilo came out; gone was the gentleness Shae had glimpsed earlier—he strode down the front steps, then turned to face the house. There he fell to his knees and touched his head to the concrete. The Horn rocked back and raised his face to the sky. "Can you hear me?" he bellowed, and Shae was not sure who he was screaming at: his troops, the window of their grandfather's room, the departed spirit of their slain brother, or the gods themselves. "*Can you hear me? I'm* ready to die. The clan is my blood, and the Pillar is its master."

Shae had always strongly disliked Hilo's penchant for dramatic gestures, but she bowed her head and swallowed thickly at the sight of the assembled Green Bones falling to their knees and crying out in a fervor, "Our blood for the Horn!"

The three largest and most profitable betting houses in the city were the Palace of Fortune, the Cong Lady, and the Double Double. They were located side by side on the same strip of Poor Man's Road in the south part of the Armpit still belonging to the Mountain. Ranking among the Mountain's most well-known holdings, they were where high-rolling Lantern Men conducted after hours deals and where the clan's business and poltical associates where rewarded or bribed with luxury and entertainment. A fitting place for an unprecedented retribution.

Hilo had nodded in admiration of Shae's choice: "Lan fought for the Armpit and it's ours by right—*all* of it." They crossed Patriot Street with a dozen of No Peak's strongest Fists. Shae took the Cong Lady with the four other fighters Hilo sent with her, while the Maiks stormed the Double Double with another crew and Hilo went with his team to destroy the Palace of Fortune.

The whole thing felt like a violent fever dream to Shae. The car pulled up right in front of the casino; Shae got out and strode past the shocked valet attendant who shrank aside at the sight of them, past the lighted fountain with the statue of the dancing lady in the center, up the marble steps to the revolving glass doors. No hiding in the crowd now; the waning sunlight flashed on her jade bracelets and fearfully expectant eyes followed her every move. She felt sick with eagerness, and powerful in a way she hadn't felt for years. The foreigners were right: the Kekonese were savages. Lan had not been savage, not at heart, but he was dead now.

The senior Fist next to her, a grey-eyed man named Eiten, seemed unsure of how to deal with her presence. He was one of Hilo's higher-ranked lieutenants but she was a Kaul; he couldn't decide whether to order her around or defer to her. "What's the plan, Kaul-jen?" he asked just before they reached the doors.

She drew her moon blade and held it out to him; he spat on it for luck. "Kill anyone wearing jade," she said.

That was simple enough to agree upon. Screams erupted when they came through the doors. Shae picked out the four other jade auras in the room like a cobra sensing body heat. They stood out like beacons amid the rest of the irrelevant motion and noise. A couple of them had already Perceived the murderous approach and were ready; they leapt upon the intruders at once with drawn moon blades.

It had been years since Shae had last fought to kill. For a few minutes on the drive over here, she'd wondered if she still had the skills, the reflexes, the instinct for it, or if two and a half years of jadelessness and peaceable Espenian life had ruined her.

So she was almost surprised when she cut the first man down in a few seconds. She deflected his first attack, white metal singing against white metal, then made an obvious swing for his abdomen. The man Steeled and curved his spine away from her attack. His head tilted forward with the motion and Shae's left hand whipped up to thrust her talon knife into his unprotected throat. She bounded Light over his body, yanking out the knife and already moving onto the next target.

It felt like an exercise at the Academy, another timed trial. Training and experience took over. She became focused and efficient, and the jade energy playing through her blood was like a song she hadn't heard for a while but still knew by heart. She fought another man on the first floor until Eiten cut his throat from behind. Shae leapt Lightly onto the balcony of the second floor.

A woman Fist guarded the room where the staff had taken refuge. She greeted Shae with a battery of hurled Deflections that overturned chairs, sent cards and betting chips into the air like confetti, and rattled the walls. Shae weaved through the barrage, scattering the attacks with her own Deflections, until she closed in and they matched talon knives in the narrow hallway. The woman's Steel could not be broken by the knife. In the end Shae landed a crushing stomp kick to the woman's kneecap. As her opponent buckled forward in agony, Shae dropped her elbow down on the back of the Fist's head with all the Strength she could summon, caving in the skull.

When every Green Bone in the building was dead—six in all—they tore the door to the back room off by its hinges, and Shae addressed the huddled, cowering staff members of the Cong Lady. "All the businesses on Poor Man's Road are now the property of the No Peak clan," she said. "You can leave now with your lives. Or you can swear allegiance and tribute and keep your jobs with equal terms and pay under new management. Make your choice quickly."

A quarter of the employees left—the ones too senior or too well connected in the Mountain clan, who were truly loyal, or too frightened of the repercussions if they turned. The rest stayed and recovered from the disruption remarkably quickly; the Kekonese are accustomed to local changes of administration and treat them like natural disasters—incidents of sudden and unpreventable violence, the damage calmly dealt with afterward so business can return to normal. Soon the remaining casino staff were busy righting furniture, sweeping up broken glass and blotting bloodstains before they set into the expensive carpet or upholstery.

Shae gathered the jade from the enemy fighters she'd killed, then walked outside, leaving Eiten and the rest of Hilo's men in charge. She found her brother on the street, shouting orders, pointing here and there with the tip of his bloody talon knife, his face and aura bright with battle mania. The Double Double was on fire—whether it had been set accidentally or deliberately, by the Mountain as it fled or by an overzealous No Peak fighter, no one seemed able to tell. The smoke curled out of the upper story windows, mingling with the washed-out hues of the sky.

Hilo glanced at her as she approached, at the handful of jade she clutched, and his mouth moved in something that was not quite a smile. He turned his face back toward the melee—the fire, the running people, the intermittent sounds of continued fighting. Not just from Green Bones; people from the No Peak side of the Armpit were pouring across Patriot Street. There was shouting and clashing in the streets between civilians rallying in support of one clan or another.

"It's not enough," Hilo muttered. Shae was not sure what he was referring to—the amount of jade in her hands, the betting houses themselves, or the number of Mountain Green Bones killed that evening. She was too rattled to respond.

It took another thirty minutes for the fire in the Double Double to be put out and for the chaos to fade into the silence of an eerie aftermath. At some point, when the sun sank out of the smoky sky, Hilo organized his people to carry on through the night, and Shae ended up in the rear seat of a car headed back to the Kaul house. It was all a blur to her by that point, a surreal art house film of revenge and brutality.

Gont Asch took the phone call in silence, but every one of his men with any skill in Perception shifted away from him. Gont felt cold with astonishment. Then his neck flushed red with rage.

Twenty-one members of the Mountain clan were dead in the surprise attack, Fingers and junior Fists who'd hastened to defend the trio of betting houses on Poor Man's Road but were no match for the killers Kaul Hilo had assembled from No Peak. A couple of foolish Lantern Men who had fired on the attackers were in the hospital. Every square inch of the Armpit was under No Peak control. It was an outbreak of clan-on-clan violence such as Janloon had never seen.

Gont hung up. For several seconds he was motionless. Then he tore the phone and its casing off the wall and hurled it across the room with such force that it embedded into the far wall on the other side of the Silver Spur. His men froze, shocked by the uncharacteristic outburst.

"Kaul Lan is dead," Gont said. "His family has come down from the forest. We are now at open war with No Peak. Their lives and livelihoods are for the taking, and jade goes to the victor."

• Chapter Thirty-Four •
YOU OWE THE DEAD

Shae was confused when she woke up. It was the middle of the night and she was in her childhood bedroom. She hadn't been in this room lately other than to pick up old clothes and belongings. When she opened her eyes, the moonlight dimly illuminating her room revealed a pile of blood-stained clothing and weapons on the floor next to her old globe lamp and a stack of paperback novels. She realized she'd crawled under the covers in nothing but her underwear—and her jade.

Everything came back to her then. Lan's death, putting on her jade and weapons, going with Hilo to wreck brutal vengeance on Poor Man's Road. From deep inside a pressure built and expanded like a balloon inside a box, until a great sob ripped itself from her chest. She curled tightly onto her side, squeezing the pillow to her face, and wept, long and hard, until she ran out of tears and energy. Then she lay still, breathing raggedly, and took stock of her new and terrible reality.

She'd been possessed. It was the only explanation—or perhaps merely an excuse. A dam that had been straining under hairline fractures had burst inside her yesterday, and instead of feeling appalled, she'd welcomed the final destruction, had reveled in it, in the sweet power of jade and the frenzy of violent retribution.

In the cold clarity of the aftermath, however, she felt numb. She'd done something irreversible last night, equally cowardly and brave, and she wondered if this mixture of sadness, strange elation, and calm acceptance was what one would feel in the moments of free fall after jumping off a high bridge. One could not change fate after such a decision, only own the choice and anticipate its inevitable outcome. This thought, somehow, calmed her, and slowly her body unclenched.

Perception told her she was not the only one awake. Now that she could once again sense jade auras as automatically as she discerned color, it seemed unthinkable that she would never again feel the cool, heavy texture of Lan's presence. Yet there it was—a truth more immutable and unforgiving than gravity on a falling body.

Shae got out of bed and turned on a lamp. In her closet, she found an old tee shirt and a pair of sweat pants—clothes she hadn't bothered to move out. Slowly, she dressed herself. Her body and mind were sore. Regular training was still not the same as carrying and fighting with jade. She had dark bruises and shallow cuts she hadn't noticed at all last night, and she suspected it would be more than a week before she could move or extend any jade abilities without pain. In the mirror over the dresser, she saw that she looked battered and weary, more like a victim of domestic abuse than a Green Bone warrior, except for the jade on her arms, her ears, her neck.

She walked out of the room and down the unlit hall toward the glow of a single light emanating from downstairs. It was still dark out. The only sounds in the eerily quiet house were the ticking of the clock, and the clinking of a spoon against ceramic. They seemed deafening. She descended the steps, walked into the kitchen and saw Hilo sitting alone at the table, eating a bowl of hot cereal. He was still in his clothes from the previous day. His sheathed moon blade was propped against one of the other chairs, and his stained talon knife lay on the granite kitchen counter. He had not shaved, nor slept by the looks of it, but he was eating breakfast so calmly one might have been fooled into thinking nothing at all was out of the ordinary.

Shae sat down silently in the seat opposite him.

"There's a pot on the stove if you want some," he said after some time. "Kyanla made it yesterday but no one ate it. It's still good, just add a little water."

"Where is everyone?" Shae's voice sounded dry. "Where's Grandda?"

Hilo pointed the handle of his spoon up to the ceiling. "In his room. Probably still sedated. Kyanla had to call the doctor yesterday while we were gone. Sounds like he gave the old man some strong stuff to calm him down."

Shae croaked, "What's wrong with him?"

"He's old and crazy." Hilo turned darkened eyes on her. "He had a breakdown when he heard about Lan. He thought he was back in the war, and it was Du that had been killed—he's been ranting and raving about the Shotarians. Doesn't recognize me. When he does, he blames me—says I'm the reason Lan's dead."

Hilo said it with a flat affect to his voice, but Shae was not fooled. She wanted to rush up to see her grandfather, but if she got up now, Hilo would be hurt and it seemed dangerous to hurt him right now. Their grandfather had always been kinder to Shae than to her brothers, and he had always been the least kind to Hilo.

Hilo went back to eating, and she wondered: how can he even eat right now? She hadn't eaten in over a day but she had no appetite at all; she wasn't sure she ever would again. "What about everyone else?"

"They're busy, Shae," he said. "We're stretched thin. I left Kehn in charge of the mess. I sent Tar running around the city to make sure we're defended elsewhere."

Shae sat up as something else occurred to her. "Where's Doru?"

Hilo's lips went crooked. "The traitor? We picked him up that night, you know; Lan was supposed to meet us, to handle it himself. I called but couldn't reach him; no one knew where he was. That's when I knew something was wrong."

"Did you kill Doru?"

Hilo shook his head. "That was going to be Lan's call. So what was I supposed to do with the old ferret? Anyway, I stripped him of his jade and locked him in his house under guard. He's been there ever since. No phones, no visitors."

Stripped of jade. What abject humiliation for an elderly Green Bone who'd once been the trusted confidante of the Torch of Kekon. Despite her hatred for the man, Shae imagined him in the advanced throes of jade withdrawal, watched over by Hilo's unsympathetic men in his own house, and she felt pity for him, traitor or not.

"I can't execute him now," Hilo said. "I wouldn't taint Lan's funeral with bad luck like that. But he's no longer Weather Man; I've made that clear to the clan."

Only then did the realization truly strike her. Hilo was the Pillar.

She stared at her brother. There had never been a Pillar under the age of thirty. Hilo was barely older than her; he'd been the youngest Horn in memory. There he sat, blood-spattered and reeking of fire smoke, eating a bowl of cereal after having led a massacre. His aura had the sharp edge of new jade he'd taken. Shae reeled. *This will be the end,* she thought. *This will be the end of the No Peak clan.*

Hilo's spoon clattered into his empty bowl. The chair scraped back loudly as he got up from the table. He probably didn't even need to Perceive her emotional reaction—it was on her face—but he said nothing. The new Pillar placed his dishes in the kitchen sink, then washed and dried his hands. He grabbed a chair and pulled it up in front of Shae's, then sat back down and took her by the elbows, their knees touching.

"They'll come after us now," he said. "With everything they have."

"Yes," she agreed. Mada Ayt might have bargained with Lan. After last night, after what Shae and Hilo had done, there would be no mercy. The Mountain would come down from the forest and would not rest until the remaining Kauls were dead. Their closest allies would be executed, this house would be burned to the ground. The remnants of the clan would be absorbed into the Mountain.

"I need you, Shae." The strain on Hilo was showing at last; every line of his face looked sharper than before. "I know we haven't always agreed. I know I've said things, gone too far at times—only ever because you're my sister, and I love you. Even if you're still angry with me, I know you care about the clan. Grandda built it, and Lan died for it, and now I need your help. I can't do this without you." His grip on her tightened; he bent forward and tilted his head to look up into her downcast face, his unwavering gaze a solemn plea. "Shae. I need you to be my Weather Man."

Only a few days ago, she'd insisted to Anden that she'd put clan issues and the life of a Green Bone behind her. *Don't get involved, don't worry, Lan doesn't need help, these problems aren't your problems.* Selfishness. Hubris. Dispassion. The opposite of the Divine Virtues she'd contemplated when she'd knelt in the Temple of Divine Return and prayed for a sign. An unequivocal message. She'd gotten what she'd asked for.

The gods were often cruel, everyone knew that.

If No Peak held any hope of surviving, the Pillar needed a Weather Man he could trust. Who else in the clan could stand up to Hilo? Who else could moderate him, could keep him from getting himself killed and taking the clan down with him? Lan's spirit would never be at peace if that happened. *It's not true that the dead don't care,* Shae thought. *You owe the dead.*

Shae slid slowly from the chair and knelt on the cold kitchen tile. She raised clasped hands to her forehead. "The clan is my blood, and the Pillar is its master. On my honor, my life, and my jade."

• Chapter Thirty-Five •
AN UNEXPECTED RECEPTION

The one thing Bero was not short on was cash. There was an all-night clinic in the Forge, one of a few in the city where doctors of questionable training patched up wounds with no questions asked so long as one could pay for the service. In the early morning after the events at the pier, at roughly the same time that Kaul Lan's body was being found, Bero was sitting on a steel table under a buzzing strip of florescent light while a wrinkled man with watery eyes and strings of hair like dirty floss pulled two shallowly embedded bullets from his arm and bandaged him up, unrolling the gauze with such slow deliberation Bero wanted to smack him. He'd spent hours huddled in the bushes under a freeway overpass and felt quite mad by now.

By the time he got out of the clinic, the news was raging through the city. Bero overheard it while standing in line to buy a meat bun and soda from the first convenience store he found. Kaul Lan, Pillar of No Peak, was dead—suspected to have been assassinated by the Mountain. Bero's pulse pounded wildly; he was confused, but a grin rapidly began to spread across his face and he had to force it down. It was only luck—the sweet, merciful luck of the gods—that he was alive at all while that dumb turd Cheeky was dead, but now Bero was certain that even more luck was showering down on him. It had been dark and he'd run in a panic. He hadn't noticed it, but Kaul must have been hit by the barrage of gunfire after all, he'd just taken a little longer than usual to die, was all. Which meant *he*—Bero—had killed the Pillar of No Peak! He began to grin again. No one else, not a single Green Bone in the city, could say that. He kicked himself for running, for not returning to the pier to check.

It took him the better part of the day to get all the way back to the

Goody Too at the far south end of Junko. He bought new clothes and a hat and threw the old ones in a dumpster; then he walked, not trusting anyone including cab or bus drivers, in case any witnesses had seen him last night and the clan was searching for him. This was loyal No Peak territory and many people were upset. Bero saw a lot of somber faces, crowds of people huddled at the windows of electronics shops to watch the local news on television, even weeping in public. The sight warmed Bero more, put a spring into his weary steps. These people on the street, they'd lynch him if they knew what he'd done. They'd string him up, cut him to pieces, light his remains on fire.

On his third attempt at knocking, Mudt opened the back door of the Goody Too. He stared aghast at Bero as if he were a ghost, then yanked him inside by the arm and shut the door. "Go out front and keep watch; shout if you see anyone coming," Mudt yelled over his shoulder at his son, who put down the box he was carrying and hurried to do as he was told. Mudt turned back to Bero. "What the fuck happened?"

"I did it," Bero said. "I killed Kaul."

To his surprise, Mudt looked horrified. "Where's Cheeky?"

"Cheeky's dead."

Mudt's mouth moved like an airless carp's. Finally, he said, "Fuck the gods. *Fuck.*" He paced back and forth a few times, shaky fingers pulling at his wiry mop of hair. He spun on Bero with suddenness. "You have to get out of here now."

Bero grew angry. This was not the reception he'd expected. "What for? I spent the whole godsdamned day walking here. You don't know what kind of night I've had. I did it; I killed Kaul. So pick up the phone and call *him*—that Green Bone. I did what he asked and I want in now. I want my jade, I deserve it, no question now."

"You dumb fuck," Mudt spat. "No one told you to kill Kaul. You were supposed to shoot up the Lilac Divine and drive away. Give Kaul a scare in his own territory, ruin his car and one of his favorite businesses, piss him off, not *kill* him. The idea that you two halfwits could kill a Green Bone like Kaul Lan…" Mudt gave a derisive snorting laugh. Soberly, "We're fucked."

"The Mountain wants Kaul dead, don't it?" Bero demanded, refusing to believe what he was hearing. "Make a big statement, that's what the Green

Bone said we were supposed to do. You telling me you never thought we could do it?"

"A man with as much jade as the Pillar? You're not going to take him out with a Fully gun spray from two kids who can barely shoot straight! We figured you'd cause a panic, maybe hit a few bystanders, and be lucky to get away alive. I don't even know how it's *possible* that you did it, how you're even here…" Mudt trailed off in disbelief, then seized Bero by the upper arm and began pulling him across the backroom cluttered with boxes, papers, and cleaning supplies.

Bero yanked his arm away. "What're you doing?"

Mudt opened a closet door. He pushed aside a wheeled filing cabinet and rolled aside a flap of carpet to reveal a trap door in the floor. "*He* already phoned once, asking if you'd come back here," Mudt said, tugging on a big brass ring to pull the door open. "He'll come back around here today, any minute now. If he finds you, you're a dead man, keke. If you're lucky, they'll just kill you for screwing things up. If you're not, they'll hand you over to No Peak as an offering. Though it's probably too late for any of that; they say No Peak's Horn is already on the warpath…"

"So you're saying I should run?"

"Gods, you really are missing some lights upstairs, aren't you?" Mudt muttered. He pointed down into the opening in the floor. "I don't think anyone saw you come in, and better not to take any chances on them seeing you leave. The tunnel goes all the way down under Summer Park and lets out near the water. Dead useful for smuggling, and it'll be dry this time of year. If you're lucky enough to have lived this long, maybe you'll be lucky enough to get the hell out of Janloon."

"Out of Janloon?" Bero exclaimed. "How?"

"I'm not helping you there, keke," Mudt said. "This is as much as I'm doing. If the Mountain finds out I'm even doing *this*, they'd cut my tongue out for starters." He paled. "Goodbye jade, goodbye shine, goodbye eating solid food."

Bero squinted at Mudt. "Then why're you doing it?"

The man paused and looked at Bero as if he was seriously asking himself the same question. Then he grimaced as if he didn't like his own answer. "You made me a shitload of money and never got caught even though most of the others got caught, and then *somehow*, by some *dumb kind of miracle* I can't even fathom, you killed Kaul Lan and show up with nothing but a bandage on your arm. I don't know what it is with you, keke, but you got some strange luck of the gods on you, and I'm not messing with that. No way." He pointed at the set of stairs leading underground. "Don't touch a thing down there. Now *get*—before I change my mind."

Bero couldn't believe this was happening. He'd done everything right, taken every opportunity presented to him, been daring where others had been meek—and this was what he got for it? Earlier, he'd felt near invincible, convinced his rewards were finally coming to him. Now he saw that it was nothing more than a nasty joke. He thought about refusing to leave. He'd wait right here in the back of the Goody Too until that goateed Green Bone bastard showed up and then he'd *demand* his due.

Mudt was right though. There was some strange luck on him and it was best not to question it. Just as it had told him to chase after Kaul last night, it told him now that if he stayed, he wouldn't live long enough for his fortune to turn again.

He started down the tunnel. "It's dark down there," he protested. Mudt handed him a flashlight and he switched it on. When he got to the last of the steps, Mudt slammed the trap door shut and Bero jumped. He heard Mudt rolling the filing cabinet back into place overhead and a sudden sick panic gripped him by the throat. What if this wasn't an escape route after all, but a trick? What if Mudt had trapped him down here, to hand over to either one of the clans later, or simply to die?

Bero swung the flashlight around. The beam shook with his fear, dancing over unlabeled crates and boxes. This must be where Mudt kept his most valuable contraband. Under other circumstances, Bero would've been eager to open them up and take a look, but when the yellow circle of his flashlight passed over the nearby items and disappeared down a long, beckoning tunnel, relief opened into Bero's veins and he hurried toward it, away from the hated sting of being wronged yet again.

• Chapter Thirty-Six •
LET THE GODS RECOGNIZE HIM

At least, Hilo thought, it was not raining.

Lan's funeral procession wound its long, slow way through the streets to the family's ancestral burial grounds on a hillside cemetery in Widow's Park, not far from Kaul Du Academy. There was no threat of violence—it would be unthinkable bad luck to interrupt a Green Bone's final death parade— but the tension was palpable, hanging as low over the ceremony as the thick late autumn clouds. Four days of illusory calm had descended over Janloon while the clans buried their dead. No Peak had returned the bodies of the Green Bones slain in the betting houses so the Mountain could hold rites for them. In the No Peak parts of the city, ceremonial spirit guiding lamps had gone up in the windows of homes and businesses to honor Kaul Lan, grandson of the Torch, Pillar of the clan—let the gods recognize him.

Hilo had been walking directly behind the hearse for hours. Shae and Maik Kehn, the newly-appointed Horn, walked side by side behind him. After them came the heads of the other prominent families in the clan—all of them Fists, Luckbringers or Lantern Men—and behind them, a long trailing crowd of other clan loyalists who'd joined the march to pay their respects. Wen was back there somewhere with Tar. Hilo would have liked to have her up here with him, but they were not yet married; the nuptials had been indefinitely postponed. Instead of planning his wedding, he was walking in his brother's funeral.

It was customary for family members to hold two days and nights of silent vigil over the white cloth-draped coffin before the funeral, and Hilo had slept no more than four hours a stretch in the days before that, so his exhaustion had taken on a kind of hellish quality. Every few minutes, the funeral gongs and drums would raise an awful din from the front of the hearse, calling down the attention of the gods to observe Lan's passage into the spirit world, and jolting Hilo to continue putting one foot in front of the other. It was said that one must not speak or sleep during the vigil because if the spirit of the deceased had any final messages to pass on, it would do so during that time. If nothing happened, that meant the loved one had moved on from the earthly realm and was at peace.

That was further evidence, in Hilo's opinion, that spiritual sayings were full of shit. Lan's ghost, if it was out there, was not at peace, and Hilo was certain it would have things to say to him if it could. *You're no Pillar,* it would say. *I was born for it, trained for it, and look at how it killed me. You think you can do any better? Grandda always said you were good for nothing but thuggery.*

"Shut up," Hilo murmured, though he knew it wasn't really Lan he was speaking to, only his own fears speaking in his brother's voice. Last night, in a moment of sleep-deprived, superstitious weakness, he'd laid his hands on the hilt of Lan's moon blade and strained his Perception out so far that dozens of auras and hundreds of heartbeats chorused in his mind like white noise. He hadn't felt the barest hint of Lan's presence. No spirit had appeared or spoken to him during the vigil, not even to say, *Don't worry, brother, you'll be joining me soon enough.*

They reached the cemetery at last. The hearse climbed slowly up to the burial ground where a new plot had been dug next to the green marble family monument where Hilo's father and other forebears were buried. Three Deitist penitents wearing white funerary robes were waiting to perform the final rituals. Hilo's mother was standing by Kaul Sen, who sat in a wheelchair by the gravesite, Kyanla holding a shade over him even though it was overcast. They had been driven here ahead of the procession. Kaul Wan Ria, fetched from the cottage in Marenia, had the bent posture of someone who had long ago stopped questioning or fighting the world; her grieving eyes were as dull as those of an old doll. The patriarch was motionless, his gnarled hands gripping the arms of the chair like tree roots sunken into clay.

Hilo embraced his mother, though she returned the gesture with limp arms and barely seemed to see him. Lan had been the most dutiful of her children, more than her other two put together. "I love you, Ma," Hilo said. She didn't reply. The gray in her hair stood out more stark than ever and she looked lumpy in shapeless white funeral clothes. Out of the entire family, the shock was perhaps greatest for her. Hilo doubted Lan had conveyed much to their mother about the situation between the clans in the city. Complicit in her ignorance, she was now enduring the greater part of pain, and Hilo was forced to make a mental note to himself that she ought to be moved closer to the family, or help hired in Marenia to better care for her.

He went next to his grandfather and knelt respectfully, clasping his hands and touching them to his head. "Grandda." He rose to his feet and bent to kiss the hateful old man on his forehead. As he leaned over, he half expected his grandfather to shoot out a claw-like hand and crush his windpipe in front of all the onlookers. Kaul Sen's fingers twitched but he merely glowered at his remaining grandson with vague disdain. Hilo moved aside, letting Shae step in to stand beside the chair and take their grandfather's hand. "Where's Doru?" he heard the old man grumble to her.

Hilo had been worried about his grandfather being here. Kaul Sen was even more unpredictable now. What might he say? Would he loudly denounce Hilo in public, or start ranting about how wonderful his son Du had been? Now though, Hilo relaxed a little. It was good that Grandda was here; in the wheelchair he looked frail and confused. Clearly, just a broken old man—no longer the Torch of Kekon. There were those in the clan, Hilo knew, the old guard, who might've agitated for Kaul Sen to step back into the clan's leadership position. Now they would see that it wasn't possible.

Hilo took up a spot next to the coffin. As the other members of the clan arrived, he observed whether they came first to him to pay their respect to the new Pillar, or whether they went to offer whispered condolences to Kaul Sen. Most came to him, as custom dictated. Some did not. Enough for Hilo to know his position as Pillar was far from universally accepted.

He kissed Wen chastely on the cheeks when she came up with Tar. She was lovely even in the white face powder that signified mourning and washed out the normal glow of her complexion. She slid her hand into his briefly as his lips touched her face. "Don't mind those old men," she whispered, as if reading his mind, or more simply, noticing how he glanced at the cluster of guests who had not yet come and addressed him as Pillar. "They haven't accepted reality yet."

"Some of them are powerful," Hilo replied quietly. "Some are councilmen."

"Councilmen are useless in a war," Wen said. "The Lantern Men don't need regulations or tax breaks right now; they need protection. They need the clan's strength. Look at all the Fists here, how they rally to you. Everyone else in the clan sees that too." She squeezed his fingers, then went to stand by her brothers.

Hilo scanned the crowd until he spotted Anden standing off to the side. He caught his cousin's eye and motioned for him to come stand with the rest of the family. Anden hesitated, then walked over. He looked wrecked with grief, the poor kid, his eyes rimmed and his face almost as drawn and pale as Lan's drowned corpse when Hilo had first laid eyes on it.

Hilo said gently, "What are you doing alone over there, Andy? You belong over here with us." Anden's face twitched like it was being barely held together, but he nodded mutely and took up his place next to Shae.

The gongs and drums sustained a final crash of noise that made Hilo's head hurt, and then fell silent, as did the crowd. The senior penitent, a Learned One, glided forward and began to lead the long, low chanting recitations that would usher Lan's spirit to the afterlife, where it would reside peacefully until the long-awaited Return, when all of humanity would be admitted back into the fold of Heaven to reclaim their lost kinship with the gods.

Hilo tuned out after a few minutes. He moved his lips to echo the chants in all the appropriate places, but he had never had faith in things he could not see or feel with his own formidable senses. Deitism, indeed all religion, made a complicated story out of truths that were simple but hard for people to accept.

Jade was a mysterious but natural substance, not a divine gift or the remnants of some heavenly palace. The Kekonese were genetically fortunate, like the first monkeys with opposable thumbs, but that was all; people weren't descended from the gods and they wouldn't return to being gods. People were people. The power of jade didn't make them better or closer to godliness; it just made them more powerful.

Hilo studied the somber crowd. It was populated with influential Lantern Men—business owners, corporate executives, judges, politicians. They were here with white envelopes of special tribute money to defray the cost of Lan's funeral and to publicly proclaim their continued allegiance to the clan. At this point it was a gesture, not a promise. The true strength of their commitment would be revealed over the coming weeks and months. It depended on what happened next, on which way the clan war turned.

Hilo glanced left and right, at his family arrayed around him at the front of the gathered mourners. Today he was putting on a display for the clan—Shae as Weather Man, the fearsome Maik brothers as Horn and First Fist, his fiancée, and his talented teenage cousin, all standing together. A confident public declaration that the younger generation of No Peak was still strong, that it would ensure the clan had a future. He hoped that for now, it would be enough.

The sermon ended with several more murmured refrains of *let the gods recognize him* and then everyone faced the coffin and watched as it was lowered into the earth. Hilo would have to stand and accept the condolences of lingering well wishers for some time. He wished he could lie down on the ground and pass out instead. Shae, who'd kept vigil with him, stood erect, staring ahead, one hand supporting their mother's arm. Kaul Sen looked slumped and lost in his chair. People began to mingle and converse in hushed tones. It was all extremely depressing.

"Here comes Chancellor Son," Shae whispered at him.

The ruddy, overweight politician approached and placed his white envelope tactfully in the collection dish by the coffin. "Kaul-jen," he said gravely, turning and raising his hands in a salute but not, Hilo noticed, holding it for long or tilting into any semblance of a bow. "My heart is unspeakably heavy for your loss."

"Thank you for being here to mourn with us, Chancellor," Hilo said.

"Your brother wasn't Pillar for nearly as long as he deserved. He was a reasonable and wise leader who always thought of the needs of the country and never forgot a friendship shown to the clan. I never had anything less than the greatest respect for Kaul Lan. He will be greatly missed."

"He will," Hilo agreed, making the effort to keep his face neutral, for it could not be clearer that the Chancellor was pressing a message upon him and was already, with his shrewd gaze, making unfavorable comparisons between the old Pillar and the new. Son conveyed himself with the smooth words of a diplomat, but Hilo didn't need Perception to sense that the man's wariness and ambivalence emanated all down the line of Lantern Men here today. They relied on the clan for protection and patronage, and when they looked at Hilo, they saw his obvious youth and violent reputation.

After today, Shae would tally the monetary contributions and then he'd have a better idea of where he stood, how much he needed to worry. As much as he wanted to take comfort in what Wen had said, Hilo knew that it didn't matter how many loyal Fists he had; if he lost the support of the Lantern Men, if they began to defect to the Mountain, then he would lose the clan. He turned, with reluctance, to politely greet the next one who followed on Son's heels to deposit his envelope and pay respect.

When at last the line of guests had finally thinned and the crowd began to disperse, Anden came up. "Hilo-jen," he said tentatively, "I have to talk to you." The teen's face was contorted, as if he were in physical pain. When he spoke, his words were rushed, his expression that of a man pleading forgiveness for some terrible crime. "There's something I didn't tell you when I should have. If only—if only I'd—"

Hilo drew his distressed cousin aside. "What is it, Andy?"

"Lan had me run errands for him before he died. He had me go to this place and pick up packages and bring them to him without telling anyone." Anden's agonized whisper was wound as tight as a wire. "Lan was acting strange when I saw him last. Angry, not like himself, and his aura was different, too sharp. The packages—they were vials, Hilo. Vials of—"

Hilo seized the lapel of Anden's suit and pulled him forward. He gave a single, sharp shake of his head. "Don't say it." His voice was low and angry.

Anden fell silent and stared at him, frozen.

Hilo's expression was chiseled from stone. He leaned in and spoke near Anden's ear. "Lan was the first of this family, the Pillar of our clan. The Mountain killed him and I'm going to make sure they pay for it. And no matter what, I won't have anyone sullying my brother's memory or casting doubt on the strength of the family. *Ever.*" His grip on Anden's lapel tightened as he drew back enough to lock gazes. "What you just said to me now—have you said it to anyone else, at school?"

"No," Anden said, eyes wide. "No one."

"Don't ever mention it again."

Anden throat moved but no sound emerged. He nodded.

Hilo's fingers loosened and his fierce expression melted. He straightened out the front of Anden's suit jacket and put his hands on the teen's shoulders. "It eats at me too, Andy—what else I could've done. I should've paid more attention. I should've had guards following him that night. It doesn't matter now; what happened has happened and we can't change it. It wasn't your fault, not in the slightest."

Anden did not look at him; he swiped his eyes with the back of his hand. Hilo hated seeing him riddled with sorrow and guilt like this. He asked softly, "Do you need some time off? Do you want me to talk to the Academy?"

Anden shook his head at once. "No, I want to graduate on time."

"That's good. Lan would've wanted that." Hilo tried to give his cousin a comforting smile, but Anden still wouldn't look up. The teen nodded and pulled away, retreating toward some Academy classmates standing with their families a short distance away. Hilo let out a tired breath as he watched his cousin go. He hadn't meant to speak so harshly, but Anden would be taking oaths soon, coming into the clan at a time of war—it was important that he understand. In a Green Bone clan, legacy was crucial. Lan's authority had rested on the legacy of his grandfather and father, and Hilo's would rest also on his brother's. The clan was like a body: the Lantern Men were skin and muscles, the Fists and Luckbringers like heart and lungs, but the Pillar was the spine. There could be no weakness in the spine, or the body could not stand, it could not fight. Lan had been ambushed by their enemies and had fallen as a warrior—there must never be any doubt of that.

Hilo said to Tar, "Get the rest of these people out of here. I want to be alone."

Tar and Kehn ushered the remaining guests gently but firmly back down to the cemetery gates. Shae bowed her head for a long moment. Her lips moved as if she was saying something silently to Lan's coffin. Then she turned and walked away, guiding their mother's slow steps. Wen came up to Hilo and put a questioning hand on his arm. "Go with your brothers," he told her. "I'll follow." She did as he asked.

Kaul Sen remained by the open grave with Kyanla standing patiently behind his wheelchair. "He was a good boy," the old man said finally. "A good son."

Suddenly, Kaul Sen began to weep. He cried with the silent, ugly face of someone who was embarrassed to do so, who thought tears were for the feeble. Kyanla tried to comfort him, handing him tissues from her purse. "Ah there, there, Kaul-jen, it's okay to cry, we're all human, we all need to cry to feel better, even the Pillar." Kaul Sen took no notice of her.

Hilo looked away. Seeing the old man weep made his chest heavy, as heavy as a ball of lead. His grandfather was an insufferable tyrant, but his life had been more tragic than anyone deserved. All his military and civic achievements, public accolades, and decades of rule over the family and the clan could not compensate for the fact that he'd buried his only son, and now his eldest grandson.

When his grandfather had broken down in dementia and been sedated days ago, Hilo had instructed Dr. Truw to remove and lock away some of the old man's jade. A few stones from his belt to start. The doctor said it would help; it would make Grandda less likely to hurt himself or others, it would dull his senses, slow his metabolism, make him more calm. When he awoke, Kaul Sen did not seem to even notice his missing jade—a sad sign in itself—but Hilo did. The Torch's once indomitable, unmistakeable aura was already a shadow of what it had once been. Loss of jade only made it more apparent. Seeing him like this now, Hilo knew with abrupt certainty that his grandfather did not have long to live. There would be another Kaul family funeral soon—though he wasn't going to wager on whose it would be.

Hilo knew he was the least loved of all his grandfather's progeny, but he made himself go to Kaul Sen's side. "It's all right, Grandda," he said quietly. "You made the clan stronger than any one of us." He crouched next to the wheelchair. "Don't worry, I'm going to take care of things. I'm not Du or Lan, but I'm still a Kaul. I'll make things right, I promise."

He didn't know if his grandfather heard him or cared, but the old man stopped weeping and dropped his chin to his chest, closing his eyes. Hilo had Kyanla push him back to the car.

Hilo stood alone by Lan's grave at last. And even though he didn't believe in Heaven or ghosts, there were things that needed to be said.

"Your jade, brother. I had it sewn under the lining of the coffin. No one took it from you, and no one else will ever wear it. It's yours." He was silent for a minute. "I know you don't think I can do this, but you didn't leave me any choice, did you? So I'm going to prove you wrong. I won't let it happen;

I won't let No Peak fall. If there is an afterlife, when you see me again, you tell me if I kept the oaths I made to you."

• Chapter Thirty-Seven •
THE WEATHER MAN'S PARDON

Shae went to the Weather Man's house, where two men kept Yun Do-rupon under constant guard. The two men were junior Fingers who would be no match for a senior Green Bone, but they did not need to be, not when their captive no longer possessed any jade. One man stayed by the front door to keep people away, and one stayed inside to keep Doru from getting out. They carried handguns only, not even their talon knives, so their prisoner had no chance of getting his hands on a jade-hilted weapon.

When Shae approached, the sentry said, "Hilo-jen said no one's to go in." Even these junior Fingers referred to Hilo in the familiar, as if they were his personal friends.

"This is the Weather Man's house," Shae said. "I'm the Weather Man, so this is my residence. The man in there is a temporary guest, and I intend to speak to him." When the Finger still hesitated, Shae said, "It'll be better if you were to simply report me to my brother rather than get in my way."

The Finger considered his position relative to hers, and let her in. The inside of the house was dark even in the middle of the morning. All the blinds were shut and the ceiling fan circulated warm, stuffy air that smelled of cloves and musty sweaters. Doru did not throw anything away; the house was filled with uncoordinated furniture, houseplants, and all manner of random gifts accumulated from decades as Weather Man—statuettes and little ornate boxes, colorful vases and carved paperweights, throw rugs and ebony coasters. In one corner of the living room, by the window, the other guard sat in a chair, looking bored. Doru was lying stretched out lengthwise on the sofa, a wet, folded towel over his eyes. "Is that you, Shae-se?"

"Doru-je—" Shae caught herself. "Hello, uncle Doru." The former Weather Man was no longer entitled to the suffix he'd held most of his life.

Doru lifted the towel from his eyes and shifted his lanky limbs, sitting up slowly and gingerly, as if he was unfamiliar with his body and suspicious it might break. Without his jade, he looked gaunt and creaky. The former Weather Man licked dry, thin lips and squinted at Shae, as if making sure it was her. "Ah," he breathed, leaning his head back and closing his eyes as if already exhausted merely from moving. "How did you manage, Shae-se? Going through this by yourself, so far from home?"

She had been young and healthy, better able to endure the headaches, crushing fatigue, and panic attacks of jade withdrawal. Doru was nearly as elderly as her grandfather. She couldn't help wondering if a quick death wouldn't have been a kinder fate for him than this humiliating ordeal. "It gets easier, after the first two weeks," she told him.

"I know, Shae-se." Doru sighed. "This isn't the first time I've been jade-stripped and imprisoned. At least this time I'm in the comfort of my home instead of a Shotarian torture cell." He moved his fingers in a *no matter* gesture. "I don't expect it to last as long though. Come closer, I can't hear you that well anymore. Sit down and do tell me why I'm still alive."

Shae picked her way over to the armchair and sat down across from the man. "Lan's funeral, uncle," she said. "It was yesterday."

Water gathered under Doru's papery eyelids and slipped out the corners of his eyes, tracing thin tracks down the sides of his face, like estuaries seeking a route through a landscape of wrinkles. "Why him? He was always such a good, thoughtful man, a dutiful son. Ah, Lan-se, why were you so foolish? So good, and so foolish?" Accusingly, "You could have let me come to the funeral. Hilo could have given me that one courtesy."

"You know he couldn't have."

"How did it happen? Poor Lan-se, how did he die?"

"He was ambushed on his way home from the Lilac Divine. Drowned in the harbor." Shae was surprised she could say the words.

Doru shook his head emphatically. "That can't be. It must have been a terrible mistake. That was never the plan, no, never."

A chill anger pumped through Shae's veins. "Why did you betray us, Doru? After so many years, why?"

"I only ever did what I thought was best. What Kaul-jen himself would want. I would never betray him, for anything or anyone." His face sagged with regret. "Not even his own grandchildren."

"You're not making any sense. Are you saying Grandda wanted you to conspire with the Mountain against us?"

"A good Weather Man," Doru said, "can read his Pillar like his own mind. Kaul-jen never had to ask me to do this thing or that, he never had to say, 'Doru-jen, what should I do?' *I* always knew what aim he was moving towards, even before he saw it clearly himself. If he said, 'We must capture this town,' I knew he meant to disrupt the shipping lines. If he said, 'We should talk to so-and-so,' I knew he meant to buy them out, and I should begin to make the preparations. I saw and did the things Kaul-jen did *not* ask. Do you understand, Shae-se?"

"No," she said.

"Kaul-jen only ever made a few mistakes in his life that he regretted. When he and Ayt were partners, the One Mountain Society was strong—strong enough to liberate a nation! You were born after the end of the war, Shae-se; you cannot appreciate or understand what that means. It was *peace*, not war, that divided us into clans, turned us into rivals for territory and business and jade. Your grandfather, I can tell he is heartbroken that he and Ayt would leave such a legacy of strife. I tried to fix what he wished he could fix. I tried to bring the clans together again."

"By covering for the Mountain while they mined jade behind our backs? By colluding with their Weather Man to sell us out? I examined the KJA and Treasury records. You were lining your own pockets."

"What do I need more money for, at my age?" His long face wrinkled in disdain. "Ayt's daughter means to combine the clans. She will do it peacefully, or she will do it by force. She is a stronger, more ambitious, more cunning Pillar than Lan ever was—Heaven forgive me for saying so. Many times, I tried to convince him to negotiate for a merger, but he refused to consider it. He had pride riding on one shoulder and the voice of that wolf Hilo on the other."

Doru's voice was fading, as if his energy was leaving him. "I agreed to obscure the Mountain's mining activities in exchange for money—money I put back into the clan. I strengthened our position in businesses where we're strong—real estate, construction, hospitality—and began to divest out of areas where the Mountain held the advantage—gambling, manufacturing, retail and so on. They would grow wealthier and more powerful, but we would be stronger as well, a better fit, two pieces of a broken puzzle—Lan would see reason and realize a merger was the only peaceful, sensible solution."

Shae closed her eyes for a long moment. "Did you know they would try to kill Hilo? That they would murder Lan?"

Doru shook his head emphatically. "Not Lan, *no*—let the gods recognize him. Hilo, I could do nothing about him. He was working at cross-purposes, stealing back the businesses I surrendered to the Mountain, stalking the borders and escalating fights. Fists are like sharks you know, it takes only a little blood in the water to stir them to a frenzy. The feud on the streets grew like fire; the Mountain became impatient. I knew they would decide Hilo had to die. I knew this, but I said and did nothing. So it doesn't trouble me that it's Hilo who will put me to death soon."

When Shae looked at Doru, at his papery hands and neck, she thought of her friend Paya, who she hadn't spoken to in years. It wasn't Paya's love of music, her skill with numbers, or her talent in Lightness that Shae remembered. It was the shock of a dozen filthy photographs spilling from a manila envelope that wormed into her mind. Shae could not bring herself to speculate on what else she'd find if she searched this cluttered house. Doru had been a presence in the Kaul family for all of Shae's life, he'd been like an uncle to the Torch's grandchildren, but he'd abused his position as Weather Man in so many ways even before he'd begun secretly undermining Lan. Whatever pity she could find for Doru now, she didn't disagree with what Hilo would surely say: "*He went against the clan. A Weather Man doesn't go against the Pillar. He has to die; there's nothing to be done about it.*"

Except that Hilo had not yet given the order to have Doru executed. He might be merciless to enemies, but Hilo was soft-hearted within the family. Shae suspected he was putting it off, not eager for it to be one of his first acts as Pillar. With Lan's funeral behind them however, it would be soon. Perhaps even today or tomorrow.

Shae made up her mind. She gathered the words she'd wanted to spit for some time and shifted forward to the edge of the chair. "You disgust me, uncle Doru. I don't need to tell you why. In my opinion, you've lived too long already, protected by Grandda's friendship no matter what you did.

I wouldn't shed a tear for you myself, but I'll keep you from execution, if you'll help Grandda." Her words thickened, and she paused. "All he does is sit in his room. He was so frail at the funeral, and he's barely spoken since then. When he does speak, he asks for you."

Doru's head had rolled back onto the sofa, but he was listening. She could see his eyes moving under his thin eyelids, and his throat bobbed as he swallowed.

"His mind is going," Shae said. "The doctor says he needs familiar people and routines. If you would play chess and have tea with him in the mornings, like you always used to, I know it would be of comfort to him. If you swear to take no further part in the clan business, I'll talk to Hilo. I'll convince him to let you keep your life, if you'll agree to help Grandda now, near the end, when he needs you."

She suspected she would have to fight Hilo hard for this, and so early on in their partnership, no less. But she was willing to do it. She was losing her grandfather, so soon after losing Lan. To all the solicitous clan members who'd crowded up to acknowledge Hilo as Pillar at the funeral yesterday, it had been obvious that Kaul Sen's will to live was fading fast, even faster than his jade aura as he was slowly weaned off the stones he'd won and worn over the decades.

It was heartbreaking irony that she'd spent the last few good years of her grandfather's life in a faraway country, and all she would get from now on were fleeting occasions of lucidity that came and went like flashes of tropical rain. He'd loved her most of all his grandchildren and wanted so badly for her to return to the clan, but now that she had, he didn't even know it. She could accept that, but she wasn't ready to let him go, to watch his body wither into a shell and his mind blow away like dust. "I want what's best for Grandda," she said to Doru. "That's even more important than clan justice. Do you agree, uncle?"

Doru lifted his head from the sofa. His skull swayed as if it was too heavy for his neck. The man's eyes were sunken but still shiny and dark as marbles. "I will always do what Kaul-jen needs of me."

"We'll tell Grandda you've had health problems—early symptoms of the Itches. That's why you're without jade. There'll be a guard present, and you're forbidden to speak of any clan business. That's the only way this can happen, and if you break the rules, I won't protect you from Hilo a second time."

"I can't swear on my jade any longer," Doru said with bitter humor, "but you have my word. I know my position, Shae-se. I did my best to steer toward a better outcome for us all, but I failed. Lan is dead, and Hilo is Pillar. I live only on his mercy, and yours I see, and if I can be of simple company to Kaul-jen for the short time we both have left, that is more than enough. You've nothing to worry about from me."

Shae nodded and stood up. It seemed inappropriate to thank him when she was the one promising to spare his life, and also inappropriate to apologize for his situation, so she merely said, "Good, then."

Doru laid his thin, fragile body back down on the sofa. "I get tired so easily now. I can't tell if it's this old jadeless body or the ache in my heart." He pressed the damp towel back over his eyes and went still, though his voice still rasped. "You may hate me for my weaknesses, as I know you do, but I could never wish any ill on you, Shae-se, and I never will. The only thing that makes me glad for my fate is seeing you—so strong, so clever and beautiful, with your jade on. It took murder and war to bring you back, but do you remember? I always said to your grandfather that you would some-day replace me as Weather Man."

• Chapter Thirty-Eight •
THE LANTERN MAN'S DILEMMA

The Twice Lucky had been doing excellent business for months, and as it was located right off the freeway not far from a territorial border, Mr. Une was alarmed but not entirely surprised when two heavily-armed Green Bones from the No Peak clan showed up in the morning and sat at the closed bar, playing cards on the countertop and watching the front door. The restaurateur went to see if he could offer them anything to eat or drink. "Are you expecting trouble, jen?" he asked.

"Maybe," said one of the Green Bones, a man with a short beard, whose name was Satto. The other was a much younger man named Caun. "The Horn thinks there will be. We need a phone, to call him if there is." It took Mr. Une a moment to remember that the men were no longer referring to Kaul Hilo, but to Maik Kehn.

Mr. Une brought out the phone from his office and plugged it in behind the bar. "Should I close for the day?" he asked, growing more nervous by the minute.

Satto said, "It's your choice. No need right now."

There was, indeed, barely any need, as business was very slow. Normally, lunch hour on a Fifthday was packed, but yesterday had been the funeral procession of the murdered Pillar, Kaul Lan, let the gods recognize him. Everyone expected that today, the clans would be back at war with a vengeance, and Janlooners were wisely deciding to stay home whenever possible. Mr. Une had heard that some businesses in disputed neighborhoods had reduced their hours, or like the Dancing Girl in the Armpit, closed for the day altogether. Mr. Une's father, however, had kept the Twice Lucky open almost every day, even during the Many Nations War when both Shotarian soldiers and Espenian bombs threatened to shut it down permanently, so the restaurateur was on principle disinclined to let any threat disrupt business.

He began to reevaluate his stance shortly after midday, when a phone call came in and the voice on the other end asked to speak to Satto. By this time, the two Green Bones had availed themselves of the lunch buffet and were looking bored. The few other diners in the Twice Lucky had seated themselves far away, and kept glancing at the two men nervously. When Satto hung up the phone, he said to Mr. Une, "Tell the customers to leave. The Mountain's attacked the Docks. They're on their way here." Caun was taking the liberty of shutting and latching the wooden blinds.

"Wh-When will they arrive?" stammered Mr. Une.

Satto shrugged. "Fifteen minutes perhaps."

Mr. Une went around personally to all the tables. None of the customers objected; they cleared out of the Twice Lucky at once, some taking their unfinished meals in takeout containers, many of them leaving generous tips on the assumption that Mr. Une would soon be needing the money for repairs. Mr. Une sent the most junior employees away as well. The rest of the staff shut away all the pots and pans, dishes, glasses—anything breakable that they could secure. They waited until all the patrons were out, as was the expectation in these sorts of circumstances, then they went into the break room or kitchen and sat on the floor. Mr. Une remained out front, alternately patting his brow with a cloth and wringing his hands. "Is it only the two of you?" he asked. "Not that I doubt either of your abilities, jen, but surely—"

At that moment, three other Green Bones from the clan—two men and a woman—came through the door, breathing hard and sweating, as if they'd run here from another location. Mr. Une's relief at the arrival of reinforcements was quickly shattered when the woman panted, "They've taken almost everything south of the General's Ride. Gont's leading the attack himself." The moon blade in her hand was wet. Mr. Une's stomach gave a protesting shudder. "They'll be here any minute."

Caun, standing by the door, swung his head toward the street as if he'd heard a sudden noise that Mr. Une had not. "They're already here." The Green Bones drew their weapons and ran out the door to defend the building. Mr. Une gave a bit of a squeak and hurried in the opposite direction. He dove behind the bar just as the sound of squealing tires, slamming doors, and gunfire erupted in front of the restaurant.

The initial spray of bullets peppered the entrance facade and broke three of the Twice Lucky's front windows—Mr. Une groaned thinking about the damage—but after that the gunfire ceased. In a contest for territory, it was to no one's advantage—either the attacking or defending clan—to badly ruin potential tribute property or kill bystanders. There was shouting outside, sounds of steel on steel, a scream of pain, the screech of another car arriving and additional muffled noises of fighting. Mr. Une thought he might have heard someone yelling, "Fall back!" but it was obscured by two more gunshots.

After that, there was silence. Mr. Une didn't dare to breathe.

Just when he'd mustered the courage to stand up to try and see what was happening, the front doors burst open and a huge Green Bone who could only be Gont Asch, Horn of the Mountain, strode in. Three of his warriors followed close behind, their eyes bright and wild, their faces and clothes speckled with blood. Gont stood in the foyer, surveying the empty dining room floor. "A very nice place," he said. He turned his head toward the bar. Mr. Une had ducked back down and was stifling whimpers with his sleeve. "Come out, my friend," Gont called.

Hesitantly, Mr. Une stood up. Gont motioned him forward. Swallowing, the restaurant owner forced himself to put on his most professional, solicitous manner and approach the posse of men. As he neared them, he glanced toward the front door and was horrified to see blood on the glass and the lower half of Caun's body lying in his field of view. He jumped like a squirrel when Gont said, "Where is your staff?"

Mr. Une tried to speak, but found it difficult, so he pointed toward the kitchen and back room. "Bring them out," Gont said to one of his men. Mr. Une gave another start when the front door opened and two other Mountain Green Bones entered, dragging a mostly limp Satto between them. They deposited him in front of Gont like cats offering up a slain rat. "Jade for our Horn," said one of the Mountain warriors, saluting Gont. "A worthy victory, this. The Twice Lucky is one of No Peak's jewels."

Satto struggled to his knees and spat on Gont's shoes. "My blood for my clan. Hilo-jen will tear the jade from your cold, dead—"

Gont brought his moon blade down with such swiftness and force that

Mr. Une did not have time to let out a sound before Satto's head rolled across the carpet and came to a stop at the foot of the hostess podium. "All of you fought well; divide his jade among you," Gont said to his men. "Go tell Oro not to bring out the staff until the bodies are cleared; no need to frighten them." The Horn sheathed his blade and sat down at the nearest table, looking around and nodding. He eyed the board with the day's specials written in chalk. "Is the lunch buffet still open?" he asked.

The question snapped Mr. Une out of his shock. "Y-yes, Gont-jen. Though it's been put away and it might not be as hot and fresh as it would be if you'd come two hours ago..." He trailed off in awareness of how ridiculous that sounded.

"I am told that this is a favorite dinner spot of my enemy Kaul Hilo," Gont said. "And that the crispy squid served here is particularly excellent. Regretfully, I have never had the opportunity to dine here. Such is the unfortunate reality of being a Green Bone in this city." Two of his men passed by, carrying Satto's headless body.

"I'm flattered that the Twice Lucky's reputation has reached you, jen," Mr. Une said hastily, sweating profusely. "Please, allow me to bring you a plate of crispy squid so that you can finally taste it for yourself."

"I would like nothing more," Gont said. "Also, bring me your ledgers."

Mr. Une hurried to do both. Ten minutes later, the Horn of the Mountain put a piece of squid into his mouth and chewed. His subordinates watched curiously. The remaining staff of the Twice Lucky had been collected from the back and gathered around as well. They stood in a silent, fearful semi-circle behind Mr. Une. Gont's heavy brow furrowed; he swallowed, then raised his hands and applauded. "Truly, the reputation of the Twice Lucky is well deserved," he said. "The crunchiness is perfect, the flavoring is so unique...and there is just the right amount of spiciness. I would gladly eat this every day." Despite himself, Mr. Une beamed at the praise. Behind him, the kitchen staff let out sighs of relief.

Gont continued eating as he turned to the black ledger book Mr. Une had set before him and opened it. "How much tribute do you pay to No Peak?" he asked.

Mr. Une told him, and Gont nodded slowly as he examined the books. "Your business has been doing better than that lately, and we're in a time of war. You'll pay one and half times that amount to the Mountain clan." He gestured to his Fists to take chopsticks and help themselves to the squid as well, which they eagerly did. "Now, my friend, swear your allegiance and tribute, and you'll be open as usual tomorrow."

Mr. Une's mouth opened and closed a couple of times before he mopped his brow and said, "Gont-jen, I've been a Lantern Man in No Peak for more than twenty years. My brother and my nephew are also Lantern Men loyal to the Kauls, my sister-in-law is a Luckbringer, my cousin is a Finger in the clan. Would you not allow me to leave here honorably?" It was well-engrained custom that if one clan took over another's territory, jadeless business owners and workers would be allowed to switch allegiance or leave without consequence; that's what had happened at the betting houses on Poor Man's Road that the Kauls had conquered just a few days ago.

"That would not be acceptable in this case," Gont said. "The Une family has run the Twice Lucky for as long as it's existed. It would be a travesty for it to continue without your able management and culinary vision at the helm."

Again, Mr. Une found himself flattered. The Horn of the Mountain had a rumbling, well-enunciated baritone voice that made him seem most reasonable. Perhaps it would not be so bad to be a Lantern Man in the Mountain; how different would it be, really, paying tribute to one clan versus another? Yet, never in all his years had Mr. Une seriously contemplated the Twice Lucky being taken by another clan. No Peak had always been so powerful here, Kaul Hilo's patronage so ironclad. The war might yet turn again and the restaurant revert to No Peak. It was safer not to betray anyone.

"Please, Gont-jen," Mr. Une said, clasping his hands together and saluting repeatedly, "The Twice Lucky is my family's legacy, but I must refuse."

Gont considered this. He wiped his mouth with the cloth napkin and stood. "Very well. I understand your position." He turned to his men; two of them had already departed, presumably to push on further into the Docks or wage battle elsewhere in the city, but three remained. "See to it that all the staff members are brought out of the building," he said. "Then burn it to the ground."

Mr. Une's face froze in horror. As Gont's Green Bones moved to obey, the restaurant owner cried, "No, Gont-jen, I beg you!" The old man stumbled to his knees in front of the Horn. "I-I pledge allegiance and trib-ute to the Mountain clan. I raise the light of my lantern to guide the way of its warriors and call upon their protection." His voice trembled in its haste. "For the love of the gods, *please*."

Gont raised a hand to halt his men. "I gladly accept your pledge, Mr. Une. I would've been very disappointed if this had been the one and only time I enjoyed your crispy squid." He stepped around the quavering Lan-tern Man, and strode toward the door, leaving his Fists in charge. "The Twice Lucky is only the beginning of what we'll take from No Peak. What we cannot take, we will destroy. When this war is over and the Mountain is victorious, there will be one clan in Janloon, as there was before, and then there'll be no need for good Lantern Men like yourself to worry."

• Chapter Thirty-Nine •
STEERING SHIP STREET

Shae stood in front of the large windows in Doru's corner office, looking out at the commanding view of the city. Being in this office made her skin crawl. It exuded Doru's presence. Everything from the old brown leather chair imprinted with his body shape, to the ivory fountain pen on the desk, to the open bag of betel nuts in the desk drawer reminded Shae that she was in the old man's domain, one he'd occupied for nearly as long as she'd been alive.

Her stomach was a mess of hard knots. She could not recall ever being more nervous in her life, not even on the first day she'd walked into a large classroom full of Espenians. When she'd knelt before Hilo swearing to be his Weather Man, she'd understood intellectually how difficult that would be, but grief and guilt had carried her through the days of the vigil and funeral and it was only now that she truly felt with full force the seeming impossibility of what lay before her. Whatever misgivings the clan might harbor about Hilo as Pillar, they were certainly even more doubtful of her as Weather Man. Doru had been an accomplished war veteran and businessman with decades of experience; she was a twenty-seven-year-old woman who'd been away from Kekon for the prior two years and never held a position of high authority in the clan. If she couldn't command respect and begin capably running the Weather Man's office immediately, investments would quickly go south and Lantern Men would defect in droves like rats off a sinking ship. She could lose this war for No Peak faster than anything her brother did or did not do.

Shae rarely smoked except on social occasions, but now she lit a cigarette to calm her nerves. What she most needed was the public support of the two men Lan had pegged as the logical potential successors to the

Weather Man's post: Woon Papidonwa and Hami Tumashon. The clan had to see that these credible men were behind her. Woon would be arriving any minute now. Shae remained standing by the window and did not turn around even when she Perceived Woon's aura exiting the elevator, escorted by Maik Tar.

Tar knocked on the office door, then opened it and said formally, "Kaul-jen, I've brought Woon Papi to you like you asked." Shae felt an approving twinge of gratitude toward her brother's lieutenant—clearly Hilo had briefed him well. She took her time stubbing out her cigarette and turning around. "Thank you, Tar," she said, and the Fist departed with a salute, closing the door firmly behind him, leaving Woon standing just inside.

"Woon-jen," Shae said, coming around the desk and motioning the former Pillarman toward the ugly dark green sofa in the sitting area of the office. Woon sat without a word. Shae casually filled two glasses of water from a pitcher on the side table and placed one of them on the coffee table in front of Woon. She noticed that his hand shook slightly as he took it. She lowered herself into the armchair opposite him.

"My brother spoke well of you," she said. "He trusted you and considered you a good friend, an old friend all the way back to the Academy."

Woon didn't answer, but in that instant Shae saw written plain on his face the depth of sorrow and shame he felt, and also the legitimate fear for his own life. Woon had failed Lan. He hadn't known his Pillar had gone out that fateful night, hadn't been there to protect him personally nor taken the precaution of ensuring that his bodyguards stayed with him. After Maik Tar had ordered Woon to get into the car this morning, the man would've spent the next twenty minutes believing that Kaul Hilo had ordered his exile or execution.

Finding himself in the Weather Man's office instead of kneeling on the side of a forested stretch of road seemed to have confused Woon, but after drinking the glass of water Shae gave him, he recovered enough to look up with a self-loathing hope in his eyes. "I don't deserve to live, Kaul-jen."

Shae said gently, "Lan would've forgiven you." She felt, as much from the involuntary pulse of emotion behind the man's aura as the look on his face, the effect her words had on him. She went on in a soft but firm tone, "If the clan is to win this war and avenge Lan, we can't afford to lose anyone needlessly. Neither Hilo or I can take Lan's place, we know that. Together we stand a chance, but you were Lan's Pillarman. You knew him well, and you know the business and the politics side of the clan better than either of us. Failures must have consequences, it's true, but there are other ways to atone."

Woon's face was flushed with remorse over his own relief. "What do you want me to do, Kaul-jen?" he asked in a whisper, and Shae knew that she had handled this correctly. Woon now believed she had plucked him from Hilo's justice for some more noble purpose that Lan would have wanted.

"I know Lan had plans for you to take on more responsibility in the clan, perhaps to become his Weather Man after Doru. Hilo has named me to his side, but I can't do it alone. Help me run the Weather Man's Office, as my Chief of Staff. That's a term I picked up in Espenia, for a role much like Pillarman but with more visibility, more decision-making power. Hilo will understand. Be my right hand, as you were my brother's. Will you do this, Woon-jen?"

Woon's eyes brimmed, and he nodded with his face lowered. "Yes. It's what Lan-jen would've wanted me to do," he said simply.

"Good," Shae said, relieved that this first conversation had gone as planned. "We have a lot to do, but we'll start tomorrow. Go home today, but start thinking about what steps we'll need to take to insulate our businesses. Before you go: who do you think should be made Master Luckbringer?"

Woon thought, then said, "Hami Tumashon."

Shae appeared to consider this, then nodded. Even if Woon had given another name, it would've been good to demonstrate that she was already leaning on his counsel. Still, she was glad he had pointed to Hami.

When Woon had left, Shae drained the rest of her water and leaned her head back against the armchair, preparing herself for what she expected would be the more difficult second conversation. The door opened and a woman who looked as young as Anden edged her head inside tentatively. "Kaul-jen?" she ventured in a high, girlish voice. "Is there anything you need?"

Through the half-open door, Shae could hear the normal chatter of muted conversation in the halls and the ringing of telephones. The Financial District was not technically neutral, but the banks and professional services headquartered in the skyscrapers of Ship Street were less susceptible to being taken over and controlled at the point of a blade. Those clan members who worked here—lawyers, accountants, and other Luckbringers of similar schooling—waged war in an entirely different way from Fists and Fingers, so business continued in spite of the violence raging just across the freeway. "Yes," Shae said, eyeing the girl and making a note to herself to move the unfortunate creature to a new job, one in which she would not have to dress in such a way and remind Shae of her uncle Doru's predilections. "Call facilities management. I want this entire office cleared out and new furniture brought in. And send in Hami Tumashon when he arrives."

She seated herself at Doru's expansive desk and was looking through the papers in his inbox when Hami knocked and came in, saluting her shallowly. "You asked to see me." The man's voice was carefully neutral, but his eyes were faintly narrowed with skepticism.

Shae put down the document she was studying. "Come in, Hami-jen," she said, gesturing to the chair in front of the desk. When he sat, she offered him a cigarette, which he declined. Hami was a brusque man in his late thirties. He'd been a respected Fist before a relayball injury gave him a permanent limp and turned his career path toward corporate law. He wore more jade than the average man on Ship Street and there was a certain proud and solid quality to his aura.

Hilo had assured Shae that Hami was a clan loyalist who could be trusted, though perhaps her brother's assessment was a reflection on the fact that in recent years Hami had clashed with Doru and his career had stalled as a result. Shae suspected Hami might have played a key role in helping Hilo find evidence of Doru's betrayal. She did not, however, delude herself into thinking that this meant the man held any desire to answer to a woman a dozen years his junior, regardless of whether she a Kaul or not.

Shae said straight away, "I'm in a difficult position and the Pillar has told me that you're the one I need to talk to, because you always speak honestly even when it doesn't serve you to do so. A strange quality for a lawyer, I might add." She saw Hami's eyes widen slightly at this. She'd gotten his attention. He might be honest, but he also knew how to reserve judgment and he appeared to be doing so now, waiting for her to continue.

Shae settled back in Doru's padded chair and spoke as if she were reluctantly bringing the Luckbringer into her deepest confidence. "Hami-jen, I didn't expect to have to sit in this office for at least another fifteen years.

I returned from studying in Espenia not long ago. I was supposed to run some of the clan's companies to get operational experience. Some of the easier, stable businesses that still have room to grow—in real estate or tourism, perhaps. Along the way, I could live life, travel, maybe meet someone and get married. I'm the youngest Kaul and so my grandfather always gave me more freedom."

"And now you're Weather Man." It was said matter-of-factly, but the upward twitch of Hami's mouth betrayed that he found this ironic and amusing.

"And now I'm Weather Man." Shae's voice hardened and she knew Hami would Perceive the true resentment and vexation crackling through her aura. "Betrayal, murder, and war have a way of ruining one's plans."

She sensed the man's wariness. Perhaps the senior Luckbringer had expected her to be an entitled girl playing at being an executive, someone he could begin to undermine or manipulate as soon as she began to order him around with insufferably false confidence. He was not as certain now.

Shae said, "If I thought it would serve the clan, I would ask the Pillar to put someone else behind this desk. But my brother is no fool. He knows how deeply Green Bones value lineage. In a time of war, having another Kaul in the leadership reminds everyone of the Torch and the victories of the past, and *that* reminds people that the clan is strong—that Kekon is strong. With the clan under attack, my personal preferences mean nothing."

Hami spoke a touch impatiently. "Why have you asked me here?"

Shae laid an expectant gaze on him. "Because I need you to tell me the truth. How difficult will this be? What must I do right away to secure the confidence of the staff and Lantern Men so this place doesn't fall apart and the Mountain doesn't sweep in and swallow us? Because if I fail, it will be the end of the No Peak clan."

Hami regarded her with what Shae sensed was tentative respect. She'd reminded him that she was and always had been the Weather Man in waiting—trained by Doru, educated at one of the best schools in Espenia, favored by the Torch—merely prematurely installed. And now she was being entirely honest about her credibility challenges. She was astute to have sought his advice at once, a fact that could not help but flatter him. Shae waited for his response.

After a moment, Hami cleared his throat and said roughly, "You'll need the senior Luckbringers on your side, the ones who really hold the relationships with the Lantern Men. You should hold a staff meeting as soon as possible. If you're going to make major changes, make them quickly while you're in this grace period when people are waiting to see what happens in the street war."

Shae nodded in agreement. "I do intend to make changes. I've learned enough to know that some of Doru's actions weakened this clan. Too many of No Peak's investment decisions were made by him alone; we've been cautious and reactive, waiting for Lantern Men to come to us instead of seeking out opportunities. It's put us a a bad position relative to the Mountain." She knew this was what Hami believed as well, but she treaded carefully now, not wanting to press the point and appear to be mining his discontent. "How many people in the Office would you say are loyal to Doru and might be a problem if they remained in their current roles?"

"Fewer than you would think," Hami said, and Shae saw the gleam in his eye that told her she'd touched upon their shared dislike for Yun Dorupon with just the right amount of force. "Yun-jen has not been popular recently; many people thought he should've retired five years ago. Most of his staunchest allies are old enough that they can be made to retire gracefully with a clan stipend. We'll find stronger support among the divisions that he under-resourced or gutted—Luckbringers that saw good businesses go to the Mountain. They'll be eager for change."

Shae noted Hami's encouraging use of the word *we* and asked with absolute bluntness, "Who was the leading candidate to be the next Weather Man before Lan-jen was killed and the Pillar appointed me?"

Hami's jaw tensed, but his honesty prevailed. "Woon Papidonwa."

"My brother's Pillarman," Shae said thoughtfully, as if considering Woon for the first time. "A good man, respected throughout the clan, though perhaps a bit staid. I'll make him my Chief of Staff." Let both men believe she had taken their counsel in appointing the other. "The current Master Luckbringer, Pado Soreeto—is he loyal to Doru?"

"Yes. He's been Master Luckbringer for twelve years."

"He's fired," Shae declared. "You're Master Luckbringer now, Hami-jen. Assuming that you're willing to take on the challenge of leading the clan in a time of difficulty, with the same clear-sightedness you've shown me today."

Hami did not look surprised by the sudden promotion, but he hesitated. Shae waited for his reply without betraying her anxiety. Her worry was that Hami would resign; not from the clan itself, of course, that was nearly impossible for a Green Bone of his level, but he was certainly free to seek a livelihood outside of the Weather Man's office—operating one of the clan's businesses or going to work for a prominent Lantern Man. A step down in status perhaps, but the money could be better. His departure might start a chain reaction of desertion. She had played her cards well, however; after another moment's thought, Hami said, "I would be honored, Kaul-jen."

"The honor is mine," she said, and offered him the first smile she'd given that day. "As you've already advised me, we have to move quickly, beginning with an announcement to the entire senior staff tomorrow. Can we meet again later this afternoon? We need to go into that meeting with a strategy."

Hami nodded and stood up. The dubiousness he'd so obviously carried into the room with him had been replaced with a mildly bemused sense of eagerness to get to work. "We'll be ready." He saluted her more deeply than he had upon entering, then strode out of the room. When he was gone, Shae closed her eyes and let out a long breath. Two down, several thousand to go.

The next afternoon, while workers while tearing apart her office, carrying out Doru's desk and chairs and bringing in new furniture, Shae walked into a long boardroom crowded with the senior Luckbringers of the Weather Man's office. She'd done her makeup to look older and pulled her hair back into a tight knot at the back of her head. She wore a conservative navy skirt suit but the neckline of her blouse accentuated her two-tier jade choker, and her loosened jade bracelets hung at her wrists. Not all Luckbringers wore jade, and those that did usually wore less than military members of the clan, but a strong display of green meant status and respect everywhere on Kekon, and the top floor of a tower on Ship Street was no exception.

Shae took stock of the people staring at her. Most of them were men, and all of them were older than she was. Woon sat on her right hand side, Hami on her left. Shae placed her hands firmly flat on the polished wooden table. "I wish I could begin by saying how excited and pleased I am to be here, but that would be a lie. I'm here because my brother, let the gods recognize him, was murdered." An uncomfortable stillness fell over the room. "Our territories are being taken, our tributes stolen, our businesses are under attack. The Royal Council has called for an audit of the Kekon Jade Alliance, which will show that we are being robbed of our fair share of jade. We're educated people here. We work in offices and make phone calls and balance books. But at the end of the day, we're clan."

Silence from around the table, though some people nodded.

"Yun Dorupon served the Torch faithfully for a long time. I respect him for that. But the truth is that we've fallen behind and as a result, have become prey to our enemies. For the clan to endure, we have to make No Peak strong again, stronger than even my grandfather envisioned, because this war against the Mountain threatens not just our clan but our country." Shae nodded toward the windows that looked out over the city. "The clans control the economy of Kekon. If the Lantern Men, the Royal Council, the Espenians, or the public lose confidence in No Peak's survival, they'll lose confidence in the stability of the nation as a whole. Two and half decades of exponential growth could come crashing down. We can't let that happen. That's why I ask for your commitment in no less a way than the Horn asks his Fists for their blood."

Shae inclined her head toward Woon and Hami in turn. "These two men, who I don't need to introduce to you, have given me that commitment. I'm privileged to have their loyalty and experience on my side. Woon is my right hand, he will be the Weather Man's Shadow. Hami will be Master Luckbringer, effective immediately. He has a few words to say about what will happen next."

Hami said, "We'll be evaluating all the senior positions over the next two weeks. Part of that will involve a detailed accounting of the past activities of the Weather Man's office. Over the coming weeks and months we'll be making personnel changes as well as reaching out to Lantern Men to recruit new Luckbringers. If you don't feel you can continue in your role under these new circumstances, the clan will accept your resignation and provide you with a retirement stipend for your service. Decide by the end of the day."

Shae could sense consternation and disgruntlement from some around the table, but as Hami had predicted, it was less than might be expected. People were used to showing respect to, or at least not challenging the Pillarman, and Hami, whose prior criticisms of Doru were secretly supported by many, capably commanded attention with his Fist-like intensity. With two of the most respected men on this side of the clan flanking her, Shae could feel the Luckbringers' reservations about her slightly tempered. At the very least, there was no open disagreement as Hami and Woon outlined the rest of Shae's immediate agenda.

By the end of the day, as she sat slumped in a stiff new chair in her disassembled office, Shae felt as if she'd pulled off a minor miracle. She hadn't lost the Weather Man's office in the first forty-eight hours. Word of her initial success would get around to the Lantern Men and they would give her the benefit of the doubt. For a while. It was the best she could've asked for.

Her predecessor's scent still lingered faintly under the smell of new upholstery and wallpaper, but the other signs of him were gone. Glass cases of old mementos, dark, thickly padded leather furniture, and heavily fringed drapery had been replaced by cushioned bench seating, open shelving, and copper globe lamps, some of it still wrapped in plastic or not yet placed in their final positions. The phone sitting on the floor rang. Shae picked it up and answered it. The agitated male voice on the other end demanded to talk to Yun Dorupon.

"I'm afraid that's not possible," Shae said.

"Don't give me that," the man on the other end snapped. "You tell him this is the Minister of Tourism calling from the Royal Council. I just returned from three weeks out of the country, only to find that the entire city has become a Green Bone battleground! Did you know this is being reported in the *foreign news*? Other countries are putting out travel advisories for Kekon. This is madness. Where is Yun-jen? I need to talk to him."

"Yun Dorupon is confined at home due to health issues that have unfortunately forced his resignation," Shae said. That was the story she and Hilo had concocted to prevent rumors of treason within the clan from getting out beyond the top levels of No Peak.

"His resignation?" the Minister fairly shouted. "Who's the acting Weather Man, then? Put me through to him at once."

"You're speaking to her," Shae said. "I'm the Weather Man. My name is Kaul Shaelinsan, and if there's anything further you wish to say, say it to me."

A stunned silence emanated from the phone receiver. Then a mumbled curse, a click, and the hollow drone of the dial tone.

Shae set the receiver back into its cradle and swiveled the chair around to stare out the darkening windows. She'd had Doru's locked filing cabinets opened before they were moved out, and on her shiny new desk were tall stacks of folders detailing all of No Peak's operations. She turned back around, pulled off one of the top folders and opened it on her lap. The evening was young and she had hours of work ahead of her.

• Chapter Forty •
BEING THE PILLAR

Hilo did not like to use Lan's study; it didn't suit him. So formal, and with so many books—did Lan really read all of those books? But he couldn't bring himself to change the room either, so he held his meetings at the patio table in the courtyard.

The Maik brothers looked like as tired and unwashed as infantrymen who'd just trekked in from the front line—stubbled faces, clothes bloodied and dirty, weapons stained. Hilo had managed to shower and change, but he suspected he didn't look much better. He'd spent all night in the Armpit. After winning Poor Man's Road, he was not about to let any of that district be retaken. The fighting had spilled into Spearpoint and Junko, but at dawn, No Peak still held the whole of its previous territory. That wasn't the case elsewhere in the city.

Hilo tore apart a bread roll and ate it as he regarded the silent Maiks. At last he said, "Neither of you wants to talk first, so it must be bad."

Kehn said, "We've lost the southern part of the Docks. Three of our Fists and eleven of our Fingers killed yesterday and last night. We took some Mountain jade too, but not enough. Gont and his men are camped out in the Twice Lucky."

Hilo said, "Which of our Fists?"

"Asei, Ronu, and Satto."

The Pillar's face twisted. The Maiks felt his aura flare like a flame. They looked at the ground as Hilo threw the rest of the roll back onto his plate and wiped a hand over his mouth. Softly, he said, "Let the gods recognize them."

"Let the gods recognize them," the Maiks echoed.

"What of Mr. Une?" Hilo asked.

"The owner of the Twice Lucky?" Kehn snorted. "Turned."

Hilo sighed through his nose. He suspected Gont had given the poor man a choice between switching allegiance and something far worse, but the unwelcome truth was that if the Twice Lucky could be taken and a longstanding No Peak man like Mr. Une turned, none of the clan's holdings were safe. He scowled as he voiced his gloomy thought to the Maiks: "Even the best Lantern Man is like a squid that'll change into any color to save itself."

"We have to take it back," Tar insisted. "Gont is taunting us by sitting in there. From where he is now, he can push further into the Docks, or attack Junko or the Forge. The men who took Satto's jade are in there; we can take it back for him."

"And where would you pull from, to mount an assault on the Twice Lucky?" Hilo demanded. "We'd need the best of our remaining Fists and a small army of Fingers to face Gont head on. I know the Armpit can't spare any. What about Sogen? I sent you to win that district; is it done?"

"No," Tar said, chastised.

Wen came out and set a plate of cubed watermelon and a jug of mint water on the table for them. "Thank you, love," Hilo said. He cupped a hand on the back of her thigh as she poured them glasses of water. Wen was wearing a soft lime green dress and heeled sandals that accentuated her shapely calves. It was one of the only good things in Hilo's life these days, to have Wen in the Horn's house. It was Kehn's house now, so everything was still proper, but she was only a short walk from the main residence, and most importantly, safe behind estate gates. She smiled down at him, a little wanly, then drew away to let her fiancé and brothers continue to talk.

"We'll take back the Twice Lucky," Hilo said, changing his tone to let Tar know he was not truly angry with him. "But not now. Gont will be expecting an immediate counterattack. Even if we drive them out of the Docks, the cost will be too high." He shook his head. "We'll strike back at a better time."

"And when is that?" Kehn picked a mint leaf from his glass and chewed on it.

"You're the Horn now, Kehn," Hilo said, eyes narrowing. "You tell me. You figure it out, then you tell me, and I give you permission to act or not. That's how it was between me and Lan. I never went against him, but I didn't wait to be told what to do either. I made the calls that were mine to make; everything else I went to him to speak my mind and ask for what I wanted." He was in a sour mood now.

It was Kehn's turn to be chastised. "All right, Hilo-jen," he said. "You're upset with us, we can see that. We'll do better."

"You're my brothers; I'm making your sister my wife. I wouldn't be treating you like family if I wasn't honest with you." Hilo drained his water in a long swallow and pressed the cool glass to his forehead for a minute before setting it back down. "I'm making some changes. You know Woon has moved into the Weather Man's Office to help Shae. It's the best place for him, where he can be the most useful. Tar, I'm making you my Pillarman now."

Tar blinked. Then he blurted, "Have I failed you that badly, Hilo-jen?" He pushed back in his chair as if to stand up. His jade aura roiled with confusion. "I'm not a...*secretary*! I'm a Horn's man, I belong here on the greener side of the clan, you know that. You want me to make phone calls and maintain the gardens?"

"You won't be doing any of that shit." Hilo pinned the younger Maik to his chair with a glare of renewed impatience. "You'll have a staff to do that sort of thing. I need you to do other work for me. It'll be important work, and you'll answer only to me. It's not something I can have the Horn handling, not when he has his hands full as it is, fighting the war. You'll pick two of your men to help you—choose first rank Fingers who you trust to never let out a word in carelessness, the ones who're most hungry to wet their blades. That should give you an idea that I'm making some changes to the Pillarman's role."

Tar sat back, still confused, but mollified into temporary silence.

Hilo turned to Kehn. "Who will you make your new First Fist?"

Kehn scratched his jaw. "Juen, or Vuay."

"Which one?" Hilo demanded.

After a moment's hesitation, "Juen."

Hilo nodded. "Good." He looked about to say more, but all three men paused at the Perception of Shae's jade aura, crackling with frustration, as it bore down toward them from inside the main house. Hilo said, "I believe the Weather Man would like to talk to me." His mouth curved in a faintly sardonic smile.

"The joys of being the Pillar," Tar said, as he and Kehn stood up.

Hilo's smile vanished at once. "I never wanted to be Pillar. There are people who're going to pay for the fact that I'm in Lan's place. Don't ever forget that."

The Maik brothers glanced at each other, then obviously deciding they'd spent enough time on their captain's bad side today, they saluted him and withdrew.

Hilo felt his pockets for a pack of cigarettes and finding them empty, picked at the bowl of watermelon until Shae's shadow fell over him and she stood next to his chair, glaring down at him. "You have to meet with the Royal Council," she said.

"Sit down, Shae," he said. "You make me nervous, standing there with your arms crossed like I'm a bad puppy." Hilo filled his empty glass of water and pushed it across the table toward one of the empty seats, gesturing for her to sit.

Shae snorted. "If only you were as easy to fix as a bad puppy." But she sat down, crossed her legs, and took the glass. Hilo couldn't help smiling as he looked at her. Besides Wen living next door in the Horn's house, the only other thing he was thankful for was Shae's return. His sister had been like a shadow of herself, embarrassing for Hilo to even look upon; she'd made him feel guilty and angry every time her saw her, as if she were deliberately trying to shame him and the family with her every decision. The confrontation in her apartment building over Caun had irked him for days. Now the icy burn of her aura, its familiar strength and ferocity directed at him, was a bittersweet comfort to Hilo. If only, if *only*, it had come sooner.

"Did you hear me?" Shae asked.

"I have a favor to ask you, first," Hilo said. "I'd like you to find a job for Wen. Something in the clan, in a safe part of the city, where she can feel useful. Her job now, it's not good enough for her. She can type and do secretary things, but she can do more than that. It would make her a lot happier."

"This is what you want me to spend my time doing?" Shae asked.

"It won't take much time. Have Woon ask around; there are always Lantern Men needing good help. It's not urgent, but I know it's hard on her now, with me and her brothers gone all the time, and it not being safe to go out much." He glanced at the Horn's house, caught a brief glimpse of Wen's figure in the kitchen window.

"Fine," Shae said. "I'll ask around. Can we talk about the Council?"

Hilo felt suddenly tired. "What do I need to meet with the Council for?"

The Weather Man dropped her chin in incredulity. "The Council's the governing body of the country. It's shitting itself over all the violence and the disruption to business, foreign affairs, jade income, everything. Councilmen are calling the Weather Man's office nonstop. Chancellor Son is beside himself that you haven't gone to consult with him once yet. They expect to hear from the Pillar. Lan used to meet with them regularly; they haven't been able to reach you at all."

"I've been busy," he said dryly.

"Leading your troops," she said. "You're still acting like the Horn. You don't belong on the front lines anymore. That's Maik Kehn's job now."

"He needs my help."

"Then maybe you shouldn't have made him Horn."

Hilo himself had been harsh on Kehn earlier, but he hated to hear anyone he cared about criticized in their absence. He shot a warning glower at his sister. "Kehn is one of my best Green Bones; he'd die a hundred times over for this clan."

Shae sat unmoved. "He's an unimaginative soldier, you know that."

"I was Horn until last week, and it's *my* place to manage the Horn now, not yours." Coldly, "I'm really not in the mood to be lectured by my little sister. I didn't appoint you as Weather Man so you could question all my decisions."

Shae sneered a little. "You want my resignation?"

Hilo sneered back. "Dammit Shae, *why* do you have to bait me all the time?" He put a foot on the edge of the empty chair next to him and kicked it over. Its metal frame clattered loudly on the patio tile. Hilo slumped in his seat. She'd always been like this, always taken some cruel satisfaction in goading him, knowing that she could count on their grandfather to take her side. The angrier and more violent he became, the more she seemed to gain in favor—always the more clever and disciplined grandchild. Really, the way the two of them had fought as children, it was a good thing Lan had been there or they might have actually killed each other.

Neither of them spoke for a minute. Their jade auras grappled warily, prickling against each other like static charges. Finally, Hilo said, "We can't be going against each other, Shae, not anymore. I asked for your oath and you gave it, and that means you don't show me disrespect, and you don't do things like *that*." He stabbed a finger in the direction of the Weather Man's house. "Pardoning Doru without even asking me." He spat a watermelon seed in disgust. "*Doru!* He was supposed to be feeding worms months ago, but Lan was too soft when it came to Grandda's feelings. You're the same way now, letting that snake live just to keep the old man company."

"You agreed to give it a chance," Shae retorted. "I hate Doru even more than you do, but Grandda left his room for the first time in days this morning. I saw them from the window, Hilo. I was working all night, same as you. I saw Doru pushing Grandda's wheelchair into the courtyard to have their tea and chess at this very table, like they always do. He was smiling. Even without all his jade, he was smiling. He still has life in him. This is worth it, for Grandda's sake."

"Worth having a traitor living with us? Worth sparing two of my Fingers to guard him day and night? Doru's got nothing to lose. He's dangerous to us."

"He's an old man whom you've stripped of jade," Shae replied. "He went entirely against what Lan wanted, and that makes him a traitor and a bad Weather Man, but I don't believe he ever meant us personal harm." She did not flinch from Hilo's unconvinced glare. "You're angry at me, but you know Lan would've agreed."

Hilo was hardly overjoyed by this truth. It would be easier for all concerned if Grandda was too far gone for Doru to make a difference. "The point is," he ground out, "you did it without coming to me. You did what you felt like, without doing it *properly*, just like—" He caught himself, but Shae's face had already stiffened.

"Like what?" she asked coolly. "Like moving to Espenia? Like dating Jerald? Like taking off my jade without permission?" There was, to Hilo's great surprise, a sliver of hurt in her voice. "That's what you were going to say, isn't it?"

This whole conversation was leaving a bad taste in Hilo's mouth. Three of his Fists were dead—good men, worthy Green Bones, all of them. He should be bringing funerary envelopes to their families. He should be out

in the city where he was needed, where the war was being fought and decided, not sitting here, bickering with his sister. "I told you," he said quietly,
mustering all his remaining patience, "I've forgotten the past. When you
push me like you do, sometimes I forget that I've forgotten it. I won't bring
it up again. It's over. What matters now is that it's the two of us. You're my
Weather Man, and I'm grateful. So say what you came to tell me."

Shae studied him silently for a minute, as if trying to decide whether
to accept his words at face value. So cynical, his sister. Finally, she seemed to
give in; her jade aura drew in a pace and settled into a grudging hum. "The
Council is calling for a negotiated truce between the clans."

Hilo's lips curled over his teeth. "Truce? There won't be any *truce*. Who
agrees to a truce when his brother lies in the ground? Besides, what say does
the Royal Council of jadeless puppets have over clan affairs? This is a matter
between Green Bones, not politicians."

"The Royal Council is concerned with national issues. A war between
the two largest clans counts as a national issue, hence the Royal Council is
concerned."

Hilo frowned. "The Chancellor is a No Peak man. Shouldn't the Council be in our pocket? Don't we have enough Lantern Men who sit on it?"

"Yes, and they're not happy about being ignored. They're not Fists and
Fingers who'll do as you tell them to, Hilo. They're loyal to the clan because
of money and influence, not because of jade and brotherhood. If you don't
address their concerns, their opinions will spread to the other Lantern Men
in the clan. The Mountain has councilmen in their ranks as well, who will
report to Ayt that we're losing our sway. If it gets bad enough, our businesses will turn en masse, without Gont even having to shed another drop of
blood. On top of that, there are those on the Council who aren't clan affiliated, who will gain political power if the war drags on and public opinion
starts turning against all Green Bones."

Hilo tilted his head back and stared gloomily into the branches of the
cherry tree. Shae leaned forward and tapped hard on the back of his hand
to force his attention back to her. "And here's the most important thing to
consider. The Council is the political body that deals with the Espenians,
and all other foreign states and companies. If you ignore the Council, if you
make it appear toothless and incapable of maintaining order, what's to stop

the foreigners from deciding that *they* no longer have to deal openly with the government either? What's to prevent them from going directly to the one clan that's been accumulating jade and producing shine behind the backs of the others? That's not us, by the way."

"You've made your point," Hilo grumbled. "I'll meet with Chancellor Son and the Royal Council. What am I supposed to say to them?"

"That depends," Shae said. "What will it take for us to win the war?"

Hilo drew in a pensive breath and let it out again. He wouldn't consider anything a true victory unless Ayt and Gont were feeding worms and their clan in ruins, but he had to concede that a more attainable goal in the near term would be to win all the battleground districts and force enough crippling business concessions on the Mountain that it could no longer hope to conquer No Peak. "If our Lantern Men stay with us, and we hold our remaining territories until the end of the year, we'll be in a better position," he mused. "The class coming out of the Academy is bigger and stronger than what the Mountain will get out of Wie Lon this year. We'll have enough Fingers to fill in our gaps by spring." He sucked the inside of his cheek, then added in a less optimistic tone, "Things could go badly for us though, between now and then. The Mountain knows our situation. They'll spill a lot of blood trying to end this quickly."

Shae nodded. "They also won't want the war to go on long enough for the KJA audit results to be publicized and the reform bills to be enacted. Even if there's nothing to be done about the jade they've already stolen, if the public turns against them it will be harder for them to keep hold of disputed and conquered territories." The Weather Man took a swallow of water, staring thoughtfully across the courtyard as she spoke. "The Council wants to bring you and Ayt into a room to begin negotiations. Let them do it. Show them that we're willing to talk. It'll mollify the Lantern Men, keep them on our side, and it'll prevent the Espenians from taking any action so long as they think we might come to a peaceful resolution. The longer we hold out, the better our negotiating position will become. We can use the Council to stall until spring."

The Pillar sighed. "These sorts of things—the Council, the KJA, the Espenians, these *political* things. They're not for me. I never paid attention to them."

"You have to now," Shae said firmly, though her eyes held an unexpected hint of sympathy. "There's only so much I can do as Weather Man. You're the Pillar. We can win every battle on the streets and still lose the clan if you don't realize that the war is bigger than you think. Right now, Ayt is on a different level than we are. She's been working for months or years to gain advantage over us beyond city territory—producing shine offshore, circumventing the KJA and seizing jade… Unless we can rise to that level and beat her on it, we can't survive, much less destroy the Mountain." A matter-of-fact vindictiveness flattened her voice. "Not just defeat it, but *destroy* it."

Hilo tapped his fingers thoughtfully on the metal arm of the chair as he regarded his sister. At last he said, "I'm not bringing up the past against you, I promised just now I wouldn't, but tell me: who broke it off, you or Jerald?"

Shae sat up and stared. "What does *that* have to do with anything?"

He smiled, with an ease he hadn't felt for days. "I'm just curious."

"It was mostly mutual." She frowned, then quietly amended, "He did."

Hilo stood from his chair. A dozen aches and pains made themselves known throughout his body but he didn't lose his smile. "Figures," he said.

Shae slid him a dangerous sideways look as he came around the table and circled behind her chair. "What is that supposed to mean?"

"When we were little kids, I used to beat you up, but you'd never give in. Never. You'd spit in my face and only come after me later when I wasn't looking. You didn't let things go. Nearly bashed in my skull that one time, do you remember? Then in the Academy, you were like some kind of machine, you never let anyone see you sweat, least of all me. You scared the shit out of boys. You were always too smart, too dangerous, for some foreign water-blooded pretty face in a uniform, don't you know that? For his own sake, he figured it out before you did, is all." Hilo draped his arms over Shae's shoulders and hugged her, then spoke into her ear. "I *could* still kill him for you."

"Screw you, Hilo," she snapped. "I can kill my ex-boyfriends myself."

He laughed, half-expecting her to break one of his wrists just to make a point. When she didn't, he kissed her brow, then let go of her and walked back to the house.

• Chapter Forty-One •
FIRST OF CLASS

At Kaul Du Academy, Pre-Trials are held two months prior to the final Trials which occur at the end of the year before the arrival of the rainy spring season. Unlike the Trials, which span two weeks and are closed, secretive examinations administered by the Academy's schoolmasters, the Pre-Trials are a one-day, public affair resembling a sports meet. Though the six jade disciplines are the focus of the event, in true Kekonese fashion, competitive matches in poetry recital, speed math, and logic games, among others, are also held, attracting their own ardent followers and bettors.

A month ago, Anden had been excited about Pre-Trials, but now he saw it only as an obstacle before graduation, and appreciated it only insofar as it gave him something to focus on. He'd eaten his breakfast silently and mechanically in the dining hall that morning, unable to share in the nervous banter of the other year-eights around him. He'd consulted the posted schedule and given his morning events his best effort, but didn't linger after each one to find out his scores, nor did he join the crowd of classmates who congregated around the bulletin board in the Hall to see the updated rankings after each event. Ostensibly, the Pre-Trials were a condensed, low-pressure way for graduating students to prepare for the more arduous exams to come, but most year-eights—at least, those angling for a position in the clan, which was a majority of them—were as anxious about it as they were about the real tests at the end of the year. Family members came to watch Pre-Trials; so did clan leadership. It was typical for the Horn and his top Fists to be there, scouting which graduates they would take as Fingers. Senior Luckbringers would be observing the academic competitions. Schoolmasters would be either reasonably harsh, or sadistically draconian for the next two months depending on how their pupils performed today.

Anden could not muster the will to care. He barely spoke to anyone at lunch and left the hall as soon as he'd eaten, arriving early to wait his turn at the tower event. It was overcast, and cool enough that the participants wore gloves, and tee shirts under their uniform tunics, and their breaths fogged in the air. There was a slight wind, but it wasn't strong enough that Anden was worried about it. He craned his neck to see up to the very highest platform crowning the several that ringed the thick fifty-foot tall wooden pole. When he was called up, he rubbed the training band around his wrist out of habit, running his thumb over the jade stones. A bell sounded.

He ran to build momentum, then leapt, Lightly, platform to platform, using both arms and legs to catch and propel himself upward with each gathering and heaving of jade energy that it took to send his body up into air against gravity. The ground receded rapidly; the seconds elongated so that as he sprang from one narrow foothold to the next, it felt as if he dangled in space for so long that he might lose his grasp on Lightness and fall to a bone-shattering finale. His heart raced but his deep breaths were steady and he felt no anxiety. He didn't care if he won or lost. He didn't even care if he fell. He kept his eyes focused on the top platform and when he reached it, he heard the bell sound from far below and then a round of stomping applause loud enough for him to know that he'd gotten the best time of the day so far.

Up here the wind was stronger; it whistled in his ears. He could see so far out: not only the rest of the Academy grounds and Widow's Park, but all the way to the flat gleam of the reservoir and forested Palace Hill with the Kaul house in the north, and the quilt of downtown Janloon to the east—a patchwork of clay roofs and concrete buildings and steel skyscrapers. He wished he could sit, dangle his legs for a minute, imagine that the city was as peaceful as it looked from up here.

He came back down; it took only a little Lightness to descend. Dudo was bouncing on the balls of his feet near the base of the tower, ready to take the next run. "You won that handily," he said to Anden. "None of the rest of us can beat that time."

"I haven't been eating much," Anden replied, to be polite, though it was also true. Not that it would make any difference, and not that the Pre-Trials were the reason for his lack of appetite. He passed Dudo, took a towel from one of the volunteer year-sixes and wiped the sweat from his face. When he looked up, he saw Maik Kehn in the front row of the audience, and he began to look around, thinking for a moment that must mean Hilo was here too. Then he remembered that Maik Kehn was now the Horn, and no one expected the new Pillar to have the time to make an appearance here this year. Maik caught Anden's eye and nodded to him.

At this time last year, Anden had been one of the year-sevens watching from the back of the crowd. It had been a damp, cold day; Anden remembered rubbing and blowing into his hands, and stamping his feet to keep warm. Hilo had been here; he'd sat right at the front with Maik Tar. Anden had caught glimpses of his cousin chatting with Maik, remarking on one student or another, smiling and applauding and apparently enjoying himself a great deal. During the breaks, he stood up and stretched and wandered onto the field to speak with the year-eights. They treated him like a god in their midst, saluting him deeply, hanging onto his every word, but the Horn put them at ease. He clapped them on the backs and complimented their efforts, he joked about the schoolmasters and told stories of when he'd been at the Academy and the trouble he'd gotten into as a student. Anden had hung back, watching.

"You'll be up there next year." Lan had come up behind Anden, startling him.

"Lan-jen," Anden said. "I didn't know the Pillar came to Pre-Trials."

"I like to come if I can," Lan said. "At least to hand out the awards and say a few words at the end. I'll come for the whole day, when it's your turn." Anden had looked away, embarrassed that the Pillar would make any special effort for him.

"Did they have Pre-Trials when you were here?" Anden had asked.

Lan shook his head. "I was in the very first graduating class. Grandda and two of his teachers founded the Academy the year after the Many Nations War ended. I suppose it existed before that, but not as a real school, just Green Bones training students in basements and secret camps. There were only fifty of us that first year. We had the one building and that training field." He gestured around the Academy grounds. "When I come here now, all this seems new. Though I guess it has been sixteen years since I left. Time goes by fast, and things change quickly."

The Pillar's voice held a tint of regret, and Anden wondered if he was thinking about something in particular. He never found out; Lan's presence had been noticed and some Academy faculty members had come over to pay their respects. Anden had sidled away, to watch the year-eights enviously and wonder how, since he possessed neither Hilo's magnetism or Lan's gravity, he'd ever live up to being a Kaul himself.

Lan was not here today, as he'd promised he'd be. For Anden, that one simple fact drained all meaning from the spectacle. Pre-Trials seemed a hollow, shallow thing now, a pantomime he had to go through to get to the real goal: graduation, jade, a place in the clan, vengeance for what had been done to his family.

Anden's next event was knife throwing, in which he placed second to Lott, who everyone knew was unbeatable. His final event was Channeling, or as all the Academy students called it, the Massacre of the Mice. Life can only Channel into life, but offensive Channeling was too dangerous for students to perform on each other in this kind of competitive public setting. So at Pre-Trials the year-eights stood behind a table in the packed Gathering Hall and each was given a cage of five white lab mice. They were not allowed to touch the mice with anything but one finger, and the judges disqualified anyone trying to cheat by using Strength or Deflection on the small creatures. Various attempts had been made over the years to try to upgrade the popular event to be more exciting—who didn't want to see a man try to Channel into a bull? For practical and budgetary reasons, the proposals were always overruled.

Channeling was Anden's strongest discipline and he tried not think about how it was well known to have been his mother's as well. When the bell went off, he didn't bother to try and touch the mice with his fingers. They were too nimble for that. He hovered both hands over the cage, quickly Perceiving all five tiny throbbing lives burning like tea lights. He chose one mouse at random, focused on it, lifted his palm slightly and brought it down, Channelling in one short, accurate burst. He felt the mouse's small heart seize up and stop. A brief, electric warmth tingled up his arm as the animal's life escaped. Four more quick, strong pops of Channeled energy and Anden stepped back, hands behind his back to indicate he was done. When the bell went off, two other students in the round of eight had killed all their mice, but Anden had the winning time of the day.

He felt a little sad as the judge held up his cage to the applause of the spectators. The five tiny bodies had been alive minutes ago and now they were gone, so easily snuffed out. It was the way of all things, to live and die at the whim of more powerful creatures, but he didn't care enough about the Pre-Trials to feel as if he'd *had* to kill them. It was a foolish guilt; he'd surely won the First of Class award today—why couldn't he try to be happy, even for a little while?

"Congratulations," Ton said, as they walked out of the Hall.

"You looked as if you weren't even really trying," Heike added.

Other fellow students came up to offer him praise as the entire exhausted but elated group lined up in the central field behind the Gathering Hall, waiting for the presentation of awards and the final closing words from Grandmaster Le. With the weeks ticking down to graduation, they'd become more interested in Anden all of a sudden, more aware of the fact that he would soon be the highest-ranked Green Bone among them, likely their leader, and clearly favored by the fierce young Pillar.

Anden tried to nod and smile and say a few words of thanks here and there, but he felt strange and detached, almost apart from his own body. He'd been wearing jade and expending jade energy all day and after his recent solitude, the clamor of so many other auras was more than a little overwhelming. Ever since the funeral, he'd kept to himself, stuck to the routine motions of training and schoolwork. The other students were tentative around him, uncertain of what say to someone who actually grieved Kaul Lan as a person, not the Pillar whose death had ignited the revenge killings on Poor Man's Road and sent Janloon spiraling into a storm of clan violence. It was just as well they didn't try; he wouldn't have known how to accept their sympathy. All he knew now was that remorse had a natural limit. After a certain amount of time, it finished eating a person hollow and had to alchemize into anger that could be turned outward lest it consume its host entirely.

Anden knew he was to blame for Lan's death. He did not believe Hilo's reassurances to the contrary. But Lan himself was to blame as well. So too were Shae, and Hilo. He couldn't hate his own family for their failings, but he could hate those who'd made those failings fatal. He could hate Gam

Oben, whose final blow had done its deadly work after all. He could hate Ayt Mada, and Gont Asch, and the entire Mountain clan. And shine, that Espenian-brewed poison. He hated it.

Lan had been ambushed, they said, by Mountain clan members armed with machine guns, who, when they failed to shoot him, drowned him in the harbor. That's all Anden knew—all anyone knew, it seemed. Even the identity of Lan's killers was unknown. Whoever they were, and whatever had happened that night, Anden was certain they wouldn't have succeeded if Lan had been himself. If he hadn't been injured, unstable, drug-addled, as Anden had seen him. If Anden had gone to Hilo like he should have, or if he'd told Shae everything he knew that evening after the relayball game, maybe they would have convinced Lan to wear less of his jade until he was better, taken away the shine so he couldn't use it as a crutch, or at least known enough to make sure he wasn't alone that night…

"Emery." Someone nudged him. "Go on."

Anden looked up. Grandmaster Le had apparently already made his speech and announced the winners of the individual events, then called Anden's name. The Grandmaster was now waiting expectantly to present Anden with the First of Class award, his thin mouth slowly turning down in a scowl with each second of delay.

Anden hurried up to the front and touched his hands to his forehead while bending deeply and apologetically. The First of Class award was coveted because the reward was great—a single jade stud presented in a ceremonial green velvet box. It would be affixed to his training band and guarantee that so long as he received passing grades in the final Trials, he would graduate with four jade stones—the maximum anyone could receive at the Academy. Anden accepted the box, saluted again, and returned to his place. He felt no great triumph, just a sense of grim relief.

Grandmaster Le said a few other things about the upcoming Trials and the need for graduating Green Bones to be especially well prepared in this time of strife and uncertainty, then wished all the graduates luck and called the Pre-Trials to a close. The crowd began to break up. Families and groups of friends gathered for photographs. Anden turned to go back to his dormitory room but his classmates were milling together nearby and he caught the sound of Lott Jin's voice in the conversation.

"The Kauls are fooling themselves if they think they'll get many Fingers out of the Academy this year," Lott was saying. "Not when following the Horn means ending up as worm food."

"Well, no one thinks Maik's the Horn that Kaul was," Pau conceded.

Heike agreed. "Patrolling and collecting tribute is one thing. Even clean-bladed duels don't always end in death, not if someone concedes. But fighting enemy Green Bones with more experience and more jade, who want to pick the stones off your dead body? That's different."

"In good times, everyone wants to be a Finger, at least for a couple of years. You get respect for it, even if you don't win jade or make Fist. But in a real war?" Lott's voice rose, tinged with scorn. "They're going to find out that not everyone's as foolish and jade-hungry as—"

He didn't get to finish because Anden spun around and barged into the knot of his classmates. He couldn't say why he did so now—he'd heard talk like this before and kept quiet, but now his jaw and fists were clenched, the precious green box he'd just won was gripped tightly in one hand. The others students stood astonished as Anden rounded on Lott. "I'm sick of listening to you talk shit all the time." He was more stunned than anyone by the disgust in his voice. "Any coward more concerned with saving his own skin than defending the clan in a time of war doesn't deserve jade."

They were entirely taken aback. They'd never seen him this angry before, not in eight whole years. But Lan was dead, and things were different now. Different than they'd been in the Gathering Hall on the night of the typhoon, back when Anden had still believed that his cousins had everything under control and there was no need for him to speak up.

Even in grief Anden had dwelled on the fact that Lott Jin had said barely a word to him in weeks, had seemed to outright avoid him. Seeing Lott's mouth hang open in amazement now gave Anden a burning rush of cruel satisfaction.

Lott's mouth snapped shut. "Have I offended you, Emery?" He drew out the syllables of Anden's name in an exaggerated Espenian accent, emphasizing their foreign sound. "I didn't realize it bothered you so much to hear anyone question the clan or say a single word against the great Kaul family." Lott's eyes glittered. "You might be First of Class, but none of us have taken oaths or been given rank yet. You can't tell us what to do or how we can talk."

"We're year-eights," Anden shot back. "No Peak is depending on us. The lower years will be watching to see what we do. That kind of talk is bad for the clan. And you were having it out here in the middle of the field, where anyone could hear you." He meant it in a genuine fury; doubts were like viruses, easily spread from mouth to mouth. Did Lott think that he was the only one who ever feared for his life, or who wished things were not the way they were? It was arrogant for him to talk loudly as if he could walk away when others could not. Anden threw his reproach at the other student like a knife. "Your father's a Fist; you should know better."

"Don't tell me what I ought to know, and don't talk to me about my da," Lott snarled, and suddenly there was a dangerous charge in the air. They were both wearing jade today, and Anden felt the other young man's aura flare like a grease fire. The huddle of year-eights shifted nervously. Dueling was forbidden on Academy grounds and there were instructors nearby. Already, some of the other milling students and their relatives on the field were pausing to glance over at their group.

"Come on, now," said Ton, stepping partway between Anden and Lott. "We're all a little jade-addled from today. Maybe we were talking a little too freely. I don't think there was insult meant from anyone here, was there?" He looked pointedly at both Lott and Anden.

"I suspect there was," Lott said angrily, but then his gaze slid abruptly behind Anden's shoulder and he stopped. In the same instant, Anden felt the unmistakeable liquid heat of Kaul Hilo's jade aura wash over him.

"Andy." Hilo put a hand on Anden's shoulder and joined their circle as if he did it every day. "Kehn told me everything—said you were incredible today. All I caught was the awards. Had to come see you up there as First of Class, at least. Sorry I couldn't make it earlier." Hilo's lips rose in the lopsided insouciant smile he'd always possessed, but Anden could see that he'd changed. His youthful appearance was shot through with darker shadows that played around his eyes and mouth. There were angles to his face, and fresh scars on his hands. The Pillar's presence quieted the group at once, disrupted its direction like a boulder landing in the center of a small stream.

"I…I'm glad you could come at all, Hilo-jen," Anden managed.

Hilo said, "Introduce me to your friends, Andy."

Anden went around the circle. When they reached Lott, Hilo said, with great interest, "The son of Lott Penshugon? I'm sorry your father couldn't be here to watch you in Pre-Trials. I'm sure he wanted to come, but I'm counting on him to hold the Sogen district for No Peak." The Pillar appeared not to notice Lott's tense shoulders and rigid face, and said even more amiably, "I'll tell him how well you did. He says you can throw a knife even better than he does, and you're the sort that can carry his jade, I can see that already. You should talk to Maik-jen. Any time; no need to wait until the graduation ceremony to do it."

Lott's face and neck flushed. "Thank you, Kaul-jen." His jaw twitched as he saluted Hilo, his eyes jumping sideways to Anden for a suspicious instant.

"That goes for all of you," the Pillar went on, his eyes sweeping around the small circle of year-eights. "I've been telling Andy you're the biggest, strongest class to come out the Academy in years. I'm already old compared to you. You're the future of the clan and a credit to your families."

"Thank you, Kaul-jen," Ton said, and the others echoed him a mumble.

"Our blood for the clan," Dudo added fervently, dipping deeply in salute.

"Soon, my friend, but not yet," said Hilo lightly, tugging Dudo up by the back of his collar. "You've got two more months to be an Academy student. Not just a student, but a *year-eight*. It's practically your duty to make the lives of the lower years miserable and to get the masters to declare you the worst class ever by the time you leave. *Every* class does it. I'd tell you some stories from my year, but it's the night after Pre-Trials—why aren't you all racing off campus to get drunk by now?"

Several of them laughed, then thanked the Pillar again and hurried away with backward glances. Lott cast one final unconvinced look at both Anden and Hilo, then followed after the others.

Hilo walked with Anden across the mostly empty field. His voice changed, lost its lightness. "You and Lott's son were ready to have it out back there. What were you having words with him about when I arrived?"

"It wasn't important," Anden mumbled. As angry as he was at Lott Jin, he was hesitant to speak badly of him in front of the Pillar. But Hilo continued to wait expectantly for an answer, until Anden felt he had to respond. "He was saying the clan won't get as many Fingers as you think it will. That those who have a choice won't want to take such a risk during wartime."

"We won't get oaths from all of them, that's true. Maybe not even as many as we're hoping for. Is that why were you so angry?"

"It was the way Lott was talking, Hilo-jen. He was being disrespectful."

Hilo nodded in understanding. "You were putting him in his place, then?"

"I…" Anden wasn't sure. There was the faintest teasing suggestion in Hilo's voice and in the curve of his eyebrow. Anden was appalled to think that his cousin might suspect some other reason for his emotional outburst at Lott. "I had to say something."

"Andy," said Hilo sternly, "a lot of those boys who're your classmates now will be your Fingers later. You've got to learn: there's a way to discipline a man so he hates you forever, and another way to do it so he loves you all the more for it. To know what it is, you have to know the man. What do you know about your friend back there?"

Anden hesitated. What *did* he know about Lott Jin?

Hilo said, "I'll tell you what I know: his old man's a boor. As loyal and green as they come, lucky for us, but Lott Pen walks through life like he's begging for someone to start something with him. Always glaring, never a kind word to anyone. The sort of person who kicks dogs. No wonder his son mouths off and has such a gloomy face. Not sure how to be his own man, with a father like that. Not sure what to think of the clan."

They were walking in the opposite direction of the dormitories but Anden followed without a word. He had the feeling that Hilo was telling him something he thought was very important: valuable advice for a future Fist. Hilo said, "What you were saying to him just as I came up—it made your friend feel less than his da, and he couldn't handle that. He'd have taken any scolding or beating from you so long as he felt equal or better than his old man."

No one could deny that Kaul Hilo had a way with his people. It came from a genuine concern, and was a talent more mysterious to Anden than any jade ability. They passed through the entry gates and walked down to the parking lot where the Duchesse was parked. "People are like horses, Andy. Fingers and Fists too—everyone. Any old horse will run when it's whipped, but only fast enough to avoid the whipping," Hilo said. "Racehorses, though, they run because they look at the horse on their left, they look at the one on their right, and they think, '*No way am I second to these fuckers.*'"

It began to rain, lightly, a cold winter drizzle. Anden glanced anxiously at the sky and rubbed the outside of his arms, but Hilo stood with his hands in his pockets, elbows jutting loosely forward as he leaned against the Duchesse. "Sometimes, Andy, the people you think you can count on, they let you down in a bad way, and that's hard to take. But for the most part, you give a man something to live up to, and he'll fight to do so."

Anden had the sudden and distinct impression that he was being gently chastised for failing today, in his reaction to Lott and the other year-eights. If it hadn't been for his cousin's appearance, he'd have antagonized the very students Hilo was depending on to join the ranks of No Peak in the spring. Anden dropped his eyes; he was well aware that he too had been given something to live up to. "You're right, Hilo-jen." It wasn't enough to be a Green Bone, even to be First in Class—he had to be a *Kaul*.

"Don't look like that," Hilo said. "Like you think I'm disappointed in you when I'm not. We all have to learn. You stood up to another man and demanded respect for the clan. That shows your heart was in the right place, and that's what matters. Now, let me see the new green you got for being First in Class."

Anden handed his cousin the small green box. Hilo opened it and removed the single round stone, the size of a shirt button and twice as thick, mounted with a simple metal clasp. He held the piece up and studied it. The jade was a flawless, vivid translucent green, edging nearly into blue. Even in the low light at the end of a cloudy day, it seemed almost to glow in Hilo's fingers. The Pillar made an appreciative noise in his throat and for an instant, Anden felt an insensible anxiety, a wild, irrational possessiveness, the sudden desire to seize back his prize.

His cousin smiled as if he could read this instinct in Anden's face or in his aura. He reached out and took Anden's left wrist. With a deliberateness that was almost tender, he loosened the leather training band and set the fourth jade stone into a vacant grommet next to the three others. He closed the clasp over the leather so it sat snugly against Anden's skin, then adjusted the band's buckle to fit. "There," he said, giving his cousin a playful tap across the cheek. "That's better, isn't it?"

Anden closed his eyes for a minute, reveling in the new energy that streamed like light through his tired muscles and frayed nerves. Even with his eyes closed, he felt as if everything was deliciously clear and heartbreakingly beautiful—the rain striking his skin felt as if it sizzled with sensation, there were a hundred thousand different notes of sound and smell and taste in the breeze, and his cousin's aura—the shape and place and quality of it—was clearer to him than sight. Anden laughed, a little self-conscious at grinning so stupidly. He could do Pre-Trials all over again, right now, and do better than he had before, he was sure of it. Every piece of jade gained was like an improvement on the *realness* of the world, the power he had over his own body and everything around it. He opened his eyes to see Hilo watching him with pride, but also envy. "Do you feel this way every time you get new jade?" Anden asked.

"No." Hilo glanced away. He put an unconscious hand to his chest. "You never forget your first stones—the first six or so. You remember the day you got each one, how you got it, what it felt like, everything. The ones after that add less and less. Every Green Bone levels off at some point. When you're carrying all the jade you're meant to carry, adding more doesn't make a difference. With some people, it goes the other way—it starts ruining them."

Anden's euphoria slid away at Hilo's words. *Ruined*. His mother, his uncle, now Lan—it seemed wrong, disrespectful, to think of them in that way, but what other way was there? Even the wondrous rush of new jade could not suppress the apprehension that rose in Anden—for himself, for others. He could see just a few of Hilo's jade studs in the space under the collar of his shirt and between the first two buttons, always left undone. But he knew that there was more adorning his cousin's torso, many dangerous trophies added in the last month alone. "That won't happen to you, Hilo-jen, will it?" he asked, unable to hide his worry.

Hilo shook his head a little sadly. "I don't feel anything anymore."

• Chapter Forty-One •
OLD WHITE RAT

The back of the Paw-Paw Pawn shop was one of a few places that Tem Ben could be found conducting business with those daring and foolhardy enough to be on the bottom rung of the black market jade trade. It was, Tem thought with satisfaction, a robust industry these days. The Green Bones were busy killing each other with enthusiasm, so criminals of all kinds were enjoying a reprieve. There was still the Janloon police to keep an eye out for, but really, all they did was fine petty crime, manage traffic, and clean up after the clans. They were civil servants, not fighters. Most possessed no jade at all. Nothing like the beautiful specimen Tem was currently examining under a 10X loupe. Under magnification, it displayed the characteristic uniform interlocking grain pattern that distinguished true Kekonese jade, the rarest, most valuable gem in the world, from all other inert green decorative rocks.

Tem frowned to keep his delight hidden from the twitchy Abukei man standing in front of his desk, chewing his bottom lip with crooked teeth stained red with betel nut juice. Tem waved a hand to gesture him back from blocking the light of the single overhead lamp. The Abukei man had good reason to be nervous; the jade he'd brought in was embedded in the hilt of a well worn talon knife. Lifting a Green Bone's weapon was a far greater offense than river diving—almost certainly fatal if one was caught. This shifty, ropey man didn't look like an experienced or cunning thief. Tem suspected that, like the other cut jade specimens he'd seen lately, this particular piece had been taken from a corpse. Green Bones were diligent about collecting the jade from their fallen enemies but in a chaotic street war, sometimes things were overlooked in haste, weapons were lost, fast scavengers could get lucky.

Tem was curious but his stated policy was no questions asked, and he stuck to it. He moved the loupe away and blew out sharply into his thick mustache. "There are some imperfections," he lied. "Twenty-five hundred dien." The stone was worth almost twice that much, but the man was eager to get rid of the knife, Tem could tell.

"Is that *all*?" the man wheedled, clearly suspecting that he was being cheated. "I've made nearly as much as that for river rocks before. This is a real talon knife."

"Jade is more plentiful these days," Tem said. "Twenty-five hundred."

It was still more money than the man had ever seen. He took the stack of bills Tem counted out for him and left, looking unhappy. It wasn't as if he had much of a choice. With Three Fingered Gee feeding the worms, and Little Mr. Oh having seen the excellent wisdom of retiring from the business, a jade thief in these parts would have to trek clear across the city to find another reliable buyer.

Alone in the pawnshop's back room, behind the glass cases of watches and jewelry and the wall of secondhand televisions and speakers, Tem Ben caressed the hilt of the wickedly sharp talon knife and grinned at his purchase. He unwrapped an Ygutanian toffee in celebration. He could not find them anywhere in Janloon and had to have a friend mail them to him. There were times when he missed his adopted country, but he had to admit winters here were far more pleasant, and there were lucrative opportunities on Kekon. It was fortunate that Ayt Mada understood the value of stone-eyes like him and rewarded him accordingly. Another year or two of this and he could live like a king in Ygutan. The Pillar had even promised there would be clan work and good money for him in Ygutan once he returned there. Of course, his family still considered him an unspeakable embarrassment, but being filthy rich was the best sort of revenge.

The bell over the front door rang as someone entered. The shop was closed to regular business; another jade seller perhaps? Tem leaned over to the peephole in the wall, which gave him clear line of sight to the front of the shop. A man in a short tan coat and billed hat stood at the front, barely moving, as if he were listening for something. Casually, he turned around and locked the door with gloved hands.

In an instant Tem knew the man was here to kill him. The jade carver slid open his desk drawer and extracted a loaded pistol—a Ankev semi-automatic with enough stopping power to take out an Ygutanian steppe bear—and pointed it at the entrance of the back room as he dropped the talon knife into a satchel of rolled money. Quietly, with the bag in one hand and the gun in the other, Tem backed away toward to the pawnshop's back door. He turned the knob and pushed. The door held firm. Tem shoved it hard with his shoulder. It budged slightly but stopped again; there was a metallic clanging sound from some obstacle barring the door from opening.

Fear swept over Tem. He dropped the bag and put his back to the door, the Ankev hefted and ready, waiting for the man to round the corner. *If he's a Green Bone, wait to shoot. Wait until he's too close to Deflect. Empty the whole magazine. If he avoids the first shot, the others will get him. Steel won't stop an Ankev. Nothing stops an Ankev, not one man, no matter who he is.* And Tem was an excellent shot.

He couldn't hear the man's footsteps. Indeed, the pawnshop was disturbingly quiet. Sweat trickled down the side of Tem's face but he didn't move. He waited. Still, nothing happened. Then suddenly, loud crashing erupted from the front of the shop as several heavy things hit the floor. Glass shattered. Tem stood rooted; was the man searching for something? Searching for jade? Was it his talon knife Tem had in his satchel? The carver took a sideways step toward the peephole and leaned down—

The wall next to him exploded in a spray of splinters and plaster. A man's fist punched straight through the thin interior drywall and seized Tem's wrist in a crushing grip of immovable Strength. Too late, Tem realized all the noise had been the sound of the Green Bone clearing the stacks of televisions and electronics from in front of the wall separating them. The seemingly disembodied arm protruding from the wall gave a violent twist and broke Tem's wrist the way one might dislocate a chicken wing joint. The stone-eye howled as the Ankev pistol clattered to the floor.

The hand released him. Tem fell back against the desk, holding his limp wrist against his chest and scrambling to pick up the fallen pistol with his left hand. The wall came apart in a cloud of white dust as the Green Bone smashed a hole large enough to step through. Tem raised the pistol; it shook as he tried to steady it with his broken hand. Whimpering with pain, he pulled the trigger. The enormous handgun kicked violently in his weaker grip and punched a hole above the back door.

The Ankev was yanked from Tem's hands. The man now holding it squatted down in the small space and brought the butt of the heavy metal weapon down twice like a hammer, shattering Tem's kneecaps. The carver screamed and rolled on the ground in agony. "*You shit-licking pig fucker!* I'll kill you! *I'll fucking kill you!*" he shrieked in Ygutanese.

His tormentor pulled over the desk chair Tem had been in minutes before and sat down. He put the Ankev down on the table and took off his cap, beating the plaster flakes from the felt. He brushed at the shoulders of his jacket, and finding that ineffective, he took the jacket off. After shaking off most of the debris, he laid the jacket over the desk on top of the gun. Then he rolled up his sleeves and waited until the stone-eye stopped screaming and lay gasping, eyes rolling with hate.

"You know who I am?"

"You're one of those whoreson Maiks," Tem said.

"That's right," said Maik Tar. "And you're Tem Ben, better known these days as The Carver." He pulled a rectangular black object from his jacket pocket. Tem saw that it was a portable cassette tape recorder, like the sort that a journalist might carry. Maik wound the tape to the beginning. "You've had a good run," he said. "Taking out the two other buyers on this side of town—that took some thick blood and style."

"I'm a *stone-eye*," Tem protested. "The clan let Gee and Mr. Oh run their businesses for years, and now you're going to kill a stone-eye over a little river runoff? Where's your precious Green Bone code of aisho, you *cur*, you fucking louse."

"Hey, if you'd stuck to buying river stones, it would've been different. Kaul Lan wouldn't have sent anyone after you, not a stone-eye, not when it might piss off the Tem family for no real gain. You take a carver off the streets, someone else fills his spot anyways, right?" Maik set the tape recorder on the corner of the desk. "But now that Lan-jen is dead and we're at war, it's time for an overdue chat. You're not just a stone-eye carver with bad Ygutanian fashion sense. You're a White Rat."

A White Rat: a clan spy and operative. Green Bone code against murdering enemy clan members with no jade didn't apply to White Rats. "My family's cut me off; I'm not part of the Mountain. You can't break aisho on a *hunch!*" Tem poured sweat.

"Oh, it's no hunch, so don't waste your breath on denials. We've had eyes on you for months. Did you really think you could piss inside No Peak territory and that we wouldn't smell the stink?" Maik peered inside Tem's satchel, rummaging through the cash and pulling out the wrapped talon knife as if unerringly questing out the nearby jade. He unfolded the cloth and whistled. "War time is good for carrion eaters, obviously." He took the knife and tested the edge with his finger, then laid it next to the tape recorder. "This can go the fast way, or the slow way, but in any case, you're going to tell us everything about the Mountain's activities in No Peak territory, starting with where you send all the jade you get your hands on. I've already got a pretty good inkling, but I want you to tell it for posterity. So be sure to speak clearly." He pressed the record button.

Tem Ben spat. "Tell your master Kaul Hilo to go fuck himself."

Maik's eyes narrowed into slits. He hit the pause button on the recorder, set it back down on the table, and picked up the talon knife instead. "The slow way it is."

• Chapter Forty-Three •
NEW WHITE RAT

As usual, it was near midnight when Shae returned to the Kaul house from the Weather Man's office. Woon dropped her off at the front, then drove the car around to the garage. He truly was the Weather Man's Shadow—never leaving the tower on Ship Street any earlier than she did, acting as her near-constant bodyguard as well as her Chief of Staff. She'd manipulated him in a time of grief to secure his loyalty but could not regret it, being too grateful for his expertise and the unflagging ethic he now displayed. She wouldn't have made it through a week as Weather Man without him.

Shae took the front steps slowly and tiredly, feeling, as she had before, a mixture of strangeness and homecoming. She'd broken the lease on her one-bedroom place and moved into the Kaul house before Hilo even asked her to. It was the only sensible thing to do given the war and her position as Weather Man. The Horn could no longer spare the manpower to give special protection to her apartment in North Sotto. The Kaul estate was secure and living here was the only reliable way of finding the Pillar when she needed to.

So she'd packed her belongings, told her landlord to keep the furniture for the next tenant, then taken a last walk around the neighborhood. She'd bought a meat bun from the corner bakery and lingered to enjoy the smell. She'd admired attractive window displays along the street. She'd noticed the faint tension and the slightly faster stride of pedestrians after they passed the newspaper stand with headlines about the clan war.

Then she'd gone back to her apartment one final time and called the regional director at Standard & Croft Appliance to explain that, due to family circumstances that would no longer allow her to travel abroad for work, she was regretfully declining his offer of employment.

She'd found that apartment herself. She'd gotten that job offer herself. They had been small but deeply personal victories. She hadn't lived in her apartment for long, nor had she mustered much excitement for the job, but she felt the loss of both.

She couldn't move into the Weather Man's house; Doru was still imprisoned inside when he wasn't spending time under guard with her grandfather. She didn't think she could ever live in that place, unless it torn down and rebuilt to eliminate any lingering presence of the man. So, ironically, she was back in her old bedroom. Not that she spent much time in it.

Shae paused with her hand on the door. Stretching out her sense of Perception, she could tell that her brother was not home. He had also moved into the main house so the Maiks could live in the Horn's residence. It felt to Shae sometimes, when she and Hilo were both present, that they were children again, sleeping down the hall from each other, passing each other in the kitchen, their auras buzzing up against each other like live wires. Neither of them touched Lan's room.

"Shae-jen."

Shae turned to see Maik Wen standing on the driveway behind her. Wen was wearing a fleece robe over a loose shirt and lounge pants, and beach sandals on her bare feet. She must've hurried down the connecting path when she'd seen Shae's arrival from the window of the Horn's house.

"Wen," Shae said. "Is something wrong?"

"No." The other woman came up to Shae with swift, graceful steps. "I couldn't sleep and wondered if you'd be kind enough to join me for a cup of tea."

Shae said, "Another time maybe. It's been a long day and I don't think I'd be very good company right now." She turned back to the house.

Wen put a hand on her arm. "Not even for a few minutes? I always see you come home late, then sit in the kitchen with a stack of papers for another hour before going to bed. Wouldn't you like a change of scene, for once? I've been redoing the house and have been desperately wanting to show it to another woman."

Shae had seen Wen come to the main house. Sometimes she was there waiting for Hilo, sometimes she seemed to be leaving when Shae was arriving or arriving when Shae was leaving. The two women exchanged nods or niceties in the kitchen or the hallway, but hadn't yet had a conversation of more than twenty words. More often than not Shae found herself resenting Wen's presence. She'd squirmed while trying to fall asleep at night, struggling to block out Perception of the blazing energy spill from her brother's lovemaking down the hall.

The idea that Wen paid any attention to Shae's habits at all surprised her enough that she hesitated and turned toward the other woman. Wen took this as acquiescence; she gave Shae a warm, enigmatic smile and looped a hand around her arm. She seemed a physical sort, just like Hilo—always connecting through touch.

"Our brothers aren't home yet. I wouldn't be surprised if they're having a drink together right now. Why shouldn't we do the same?" Wen asked.

Shae told herself to be polite. "All right, since you insist." She let Wen walk her over to the Horn's residence. They looked odd together: Wen in her robe, feet slapping in her sandals, Shae in conservative business attire, black pumps crunching on the pebble path through the garden between the houses.

Wen said, conversationally, "This garden's my favorite part of the entire grounds. It's so well designed—full of variety but not at all cluttered—and there's always something blooming no matter the time of year. At night, it smells heavenly. Of course, the houses are impressive, but the garden is particularly beautiful."

Shae, who'd never paid much attention to the garden, nodded and said, "Yes, it's nice." Lan had enjoyed it, she knew. She kept walking, allowed the thought of her brother to run its familiar, brief course through grief and anger, before she urged it to dissipate.

Wen glanced at Shae. "I didn't want to move here at first, either. Hilo and I had arguments over it. My apartment in Paw-Paw wasn't much, but I'd set it up the way I liked it and I was paying the rent myself every month. To be honest, it was romantic to have Hilo coming to me in my place. I was afraid of feeling like an intruder here, worried that the family would look down on me." She straightened slightly, lifted her chin. "But what's the value of silly pride compared to doing what's best for the people one loves? Moving here was the right thing to do. I don't regret it at all. Though it'd be nice to have company—everyone is out most of the time."

It was the most Wen had ever said to her, and Shae was surprised by how personal the woman was being, and how perceptively she'd picked up on Shae's own reluctance to live on the family estate. She wasn't sure if Wen was trying to empathize with her or advise her. She decided to respond simply. "I know Hilo appreciates having you here."

They reached the lit front stoop of the Horn's house. As Wen opened the door and stepped inside, Shae couldn't help tugging her right earlobe behind the woman's back. Stone-eyes weren't *really* bad luck, she scolded herself. They were merely genetic recessives, like albinos. Jade immunity wasn't a karmic punishment, even if Wen *was* a bastard, like everyone assumed she was. Nevertheless, the stigma persisted. Shae believed there was a more logical explanation for why Green Bones shunned stone-eyes: no one liked to be reminded that jade ability, like life itself, was a crap shoot. It was possible to have a Kekonese Green Bone bloodline behind you and still be born no better than an Abukei.

Wen had indeed transformed the house. Shae remembered it had been a sour-smelling place with green shag and outdated wallpaper. Hilo's fiancée had put in bamboo flooring and bright lighting, woven rugs, and new furniture and appliances. The walls had been redone in light colors that made the space seem much larger. Shae could still smell the lingering odor of fresh paint mingling with rose oil fragrance. The throw pillows and drapes were color coordinated in rich burgundy and cream tones. There were decorative black rocks and white silk flowers in a glass dish on the kitchen table. Wen went into the kitchen and started the kettle boiling.

"I can't believe it's the same place." Shae was genuinely impressed.

"*I* can't believe Hilo lived in it for so long, with it as hideous as it was," Wen said. "Now that it's presentable, he doesn't even come over because he says it's Kehn's house and he doesn't want to disrespect my older brother." She measured rolled tea leaves into a pot, then glanced around with a shrug. "Kehn and Tar are barely here anyways, and they wouldn't care if it was a cave with straw on the floor."

Clearly, Wen had put a great deal of time and effort into renovating this house for no one's enjoyment but her own, even though she'd be moving out of it as soon as she and Hilo were married. Shae's first, bitterly envious thought was: *she must have a great deal of time on her hands.* And then, with chagrin, she remembered she'd promised Hilo that she'd find a new, more challenging job for Wen somewhere in the clan. She hadn't done that. Not being a high priority, the task had slipped her mind.

No doubt Hilo had promised his fiancée it would happen. That must explain Wen's eagerness to talk to her this evening. Shae sighed inwardly as she took off her shoes and slid onto a bar stool at the kitchen counter. "Hilo told me you're hoping for a job change. I've been meaning to ask around the clan to see what's available. Things have been chaotic as you know, but I'll get to it this week. Is there anything in particular that you're looking for? A secretarial position in a different company?"

To her surprise, Wen appeared indifferent. "My mother told me that a stone-eye needs to have practical, useful skills, like typing. That way, I'll always be employable." She warmed the teapot and cups with boiling water, poured it off, then poured again and steeped the tea. "Most people aren't terribly concerned about bad luck when it comes to low positions in the office that don't involve customers or large sums of money. I can type a hundred words a minute, you know." A droll smile lifted the corners of her mouth. She turned to search in the pantry.

"I take it that's not what you want to do," Shae said.

Wen turned back around with a bottle in hand. "Espenian cinnamon whiskey," she declared. She poured tea into two cups and added a splash of liquor into each. "It goes remarkably well with the smoky flavor of this gunpowder tea. I wondered if you'd developed a taste for Espenian drinks while you were there."

Dirt cheap keg beer was more the speed with the student population in Windtown, but Shae nodded her thanks as she took the cup and sipped, finding that Wen had been right about the flavors. *What does this woman want from me?* It was clear Wen had something on her mind; she'd thought about Shae a lot more than Shae had thought about her. Or was Wen this perspicacious with everyone?

She'd never been comfortable with Maik Wen. She could put aside the fact that Wen was a stone-eye. More difficult was admitting that she harbored lingering resentment that it was acceptable for Hilo to be with a stone-eye woman but intolerable for her to date a foreign man. If anyone had bothered to see past Jerald's Shotarian blood and Espenian uniform, they'd have learned he came from an honorable family. The Maiks, though, had a bad reputation.

The way Shae had heard it back at the Academy, years ago Wen's mother had caused a scandal by getting pregnant and running away from her No Peak family to join her boyfriend in the Mountain clan. Some years later, Maik Bacu was accused of a grievous offense against the clan and executed. No one in No Peak was certain what had happened over there, but rumor was that he'd murdered an influential Lantern Man he'd suspected of sleeping with his wife. The widow took her two young sons and the daughter in her womb, and fled back to her relatives in No Peak, begging them to take her back in. They did so with Kaul Sen's grudging permission, but the Maik sons were pitied and fatherless, and when Wen proved to be a stone-eye, the family's disrepute was cemented. *You can't trust the Maiks,* Shae had overheard her grandfather say. *Impulsive and faithless on both sides of the bloodline.*

Hilo dismissed all that: "Fatalistic bullshit. No one's destined to become their parents." Befriending and trusting the Maiks when others wouldn't had turned out to be a great boon for Hilo. It frustrated Shae that could never tell if her brother was calculating about these things. Did he think that marrying Wen would cement Kehn and Tar's loyalty? Or had he fallen for her without considering any of that?

Shae regarded the other woman. Wen was not exactly beautiful, but Shae could see why Hilo found her alluring. She had a soft but inscrutable poise, an understated presence that drew the eye without ever appearing to be asking for attention. In conversation, she had a gentle intensity, and apparently few things escaped her notice.

Wen came around the counter to sit on the bar stool next to Shae. Touching Shae's knee, she asked solemnly, "Shae-jen, you're the Weather Man. What job can you give me that would be the most helpful to the clan right now?"

Shae had not been expecting the reversal. She pressed her lips together; she didn't like being caught by a question she thought she probably ought to know the answer to. "Helpful in what way?" she asked.

"Helpful to you and Hilo," Wen said. "Helpful in winning the war."

Shae swirled the tea in her cup. "The war is between Green Bones."

"That's what Hilo says," Wen replied. "Though it makes no sense to shield me by saying that. If the Mountain wins, they'll kill my fiancé. My brothers are his Horn and his Pillarman, not to mention the sons of a Mountain traitor—they'll die as well. I may be a stone-eye, but I have everything to lose in this war, everyone I love.

"Should I waste the Weather Man's valuable time by asking her to find me an inconsequential job photocopying and typing memos in some minor Lantern Man's office?" Wen raised her eyebrows. "Should I take such a job happily?"

Shae thought of other women who'd inhabited the Kaul house—her grandmother, her mother, Lan's wife Eyni. "You're going to be the wife of the Pillar," she said to Wen. "No one expects you to work, much less be part of the clan business, especially since you're a stone-eye."

"Expectations are a funny thing," Wen said. "When you're born with them, you resent them, fight against them. When you've never been given any, you feel the lack of them your whole life." Wen had finished her tea. She took the bottle of whiskey, poured a straight shot into her cup, and tipped it back. Shae glimpsed in the single, swift motion a hidden sharpness to Maik Wen. She realized she did not know the woman at all.

The Pillar's future wife said, "Let me work for you, Shae-jen. On something that'll help us win this war."

"There are positions in the Weather Man's office," Shae said slowly. "However, I don't think you have the educational background I'd need for them…"

"What's the most useful role a stone-eye can play in the clan?"

Shae knew the answer; indeed the disquieting thought had already occurred to her, but it was a long moment before she met Wen's eyes and replied. "White Rat."

Wen said, "Could you use a White Rat, Shae-jen?"

The woman was leading her into dangerous territory, Shae could see that now. She followed cautiously, as if stepping through a bog. Stone-eyes could safely and discreetly handle and transport any amount of jade without exuding an aura. Unlike the Abukei, who were suspect and discriminated against, stone-eyes blended in as ordinary Kekonese civilians. As a White Rat, a stone-eye could be very useful indeed, as a spy, a smuggler, a messenger, or a thief. Another reason to distrust them.

"You're too well known," Shae said.

"Only by my name, and only in No Peak. No one in the Mountain knows who I am or would recognize me. They know my brothers, but I don't look like my brothers." She was unflinching about her uncertain parentage.

"Hilo would never allow it."

"Never," Wen agreed. "He couldn't know. I'd have to have another job as well, a simple one, as cover. I'm sure you could come up with something."

"You're willing to lie to your future husband," Shae said, not able to mask her astonishment. "And you're asking me, as Weather Man, to go against the wishes of the Pillar. I'd be putting you in danger if I did this. Aisho would no longer protect you."

Remorse gathered in Wen's full lips and dark eyes. "Shae-jen, did you become Weather Man to please the Pillar, or to save the clan?" She smiled sadly to say she knew the answer and turned her face away, her voice falling slightly. "Hilo's brilliant as Horn. He's honest and fierce, and his men revere him. If heart alone could win the war, we'd already be victorious. But he was never meant to be Pillar. He's not farsighted or politically shrewd, and all the jade in the world won't change that."

She turned back to Shae, who sat nonplussed by Wen's flat assessment. "He knows he needs your help. If I can be of use to you as a White Rat, I'll be doing everything I can to help the family survive. He insists he loves me too much to let me get involved in the war in any way…and I love him too much to obey."

It must be at least one o'clock in the morning but Shae was wide awake and her mind had begun chewing at fearful possibilities. She looked around the renovated surroundings again, slowly. It had taken Wen a few weeks to completely change the house, to put together a skillful artifice of sights, smells, and textures, all working together to create a pleasing, polished appearance for the formerly ugly but honest residence of No Peak's most savage men. She realized now that she had misjudged Maik Wen, had seen her warm, pliable, sensual demeanor and overlooked the Green Bone core beneath the stone-eye stigma, forgotten that she was sister to the ferocious Maik brothers. She'd resented Wen before; now she was uneasy.

She thought: two strong-minded women in a man's world, if they do not quickly become allies, are destined to be incurable rivals. Going around

Hilo was something Shae was accustomed to, but this, she knew, he would not forgive.

She'd have to think about this more and proceed carefully.

Wen took Shae's empty cup from her and stood. "I've taken enough of your time and kept you from sleep tonight, Shae-jen." Without shoes, Shae realized, Wen was taller than her, with curves that years of hard training had sloughed off of Shae.

The Weather Man stood up. "Thank you for the tea, Wen. We'll talk again soon." She made her way to the door and put on her shoes. The delicate fragrance of winter flowering plum blossom swept in from the garden when she opened the door. She paused in the doorway, turning back for a second as the light in the hall elongated her shadow across the stoop of the Horn's house. "I think," she ventured, "that it's possible my brother has better taste than I've given him credit for."

Wen smiled. "Good night, sister."

• Chapter Forty-Four •
RETURN TO THE GOODY TOO

Bero thought about the tunnel beneath the Goody Too. He thought about it a lot, and whenever he thought about it, he was filled with bitter rage. Janloon was at war over the death of Kaul Lan—*his* doing!—and there was jade being won and lost on the streets everyday, but Bero was nowhere nearer to a single pebble of it for himself. Instead, he'd been forced to flee and hide, like a roach before a bright light.

He hadn't fled far. After stumbling through the darkness for what felt like an eternity, wondering with each step when his flashlight batteries would run out and leave him to wander blind until he collapsed and died, Bero had felt a breeze on his face. A faint breeze pungent with the smell of the harbor—sea salt and boat fumes, fish and wet garbage. The breeze preceded a distant circle of evening light, which Bero ran toward as if running toward his own dead mother. As Mudt had promised, the tunnel let out under an escarpment near the wharfs of Summer Park. In heavy spring rains or a summer typhoon, the tunnel would flood, but in the dry winter season it was an excellent smugglers passage. Dirty and exhausted, Bero paid for passage on a small private ferry, but he did not take Mudt's advice to flee far from Janloon.

For weeks, he'd laid low on Little Button. The island was only forty-five minutes away by ferry boat, and it wasn't officially part of Janloon, though on a clear day Bero could see the city from across the strait. Little Button was its own municipality. For centuries, there'd been a Deitist monastery here, before the Shotarians had turned it into a labor camp, and now it was a touristy sort of place with a restored Deitist temple, a nature preserve, and a quaint town full of little shops selling overpriced knick-knacks and hand-made items. Bero hated it.

It was, however, a good place to not be recognized. Full of Janloon day trippers and foreign visitors, it was easy enough to get a motel room and nurse the injuries to his body and his pride in glum solitude, watching television, eating takeout food, and plotting his return to the city. Little Button was run by a minor family clan that was a tributary of the Mountain, but from what Bero gathered, it was largely left alone by the Janloon clans. Just to be safe, he moved to a new motel every few days, so no one would start noticing him.

From the news, Bero knew that the city was a patchwork of street violence and there were parts of the city where it wasn't clear which clan was in charge, if any. The Mountain had taken a good chunk of the Docks but No Peak still held the Armpit and had conquered most of Sogen. Fishtown was anyone's guess. Bero had been gone for more than a month. In all this chaos, surely no one was still looking for him. On a clear morning, he went down to the marina and took the ferry back across the strait.

Bero blamed Mudt and the goateed Green Bone for his situation. They'd set him up. They'd promised him jade and then reneged on him. They'd never intended to bring him in. The more Bero thought about it, the angrier he grew. Also, he thought about the tunnel under Mudt's store and the hidden boxes he'd been too hurried and panicked to inspect or steal. Again, he kicked himself. All his misfortunes came from haste. What was in those boxes?

He knew where to get the jade that was rightfully his: from Mudt himself. He didn't have the Fullerton anymore, which was a shame, but he had plenty of money, and although civilian ownership of handguns was technically illegal in Janloon, conditions of disorder in a clan war ensured that the street sale of them was common. It took Bero one afternoon in the Mountain-controlled side of the Docks to get his hands on a decent revolver. His plan was to hold Mudt's son hostage at gunpoint until Mudt paid with his jade. If that didn't work, he would kill Mudt and take the jade.

An unexpected sight met his eyes when he got to the Goody Too that evening. The store was dark and the building was boarded up. The store's large banner had been torn down and there was no sign of anyone in or around the place. Bero wandered suspiciously up to the window and peered through. It was a mess inside. The place had been ransacked. Shelves were empty and fixtures were tipped over. Most of the merchandise was gone, but what remained was scattered on the ground and already picked through—useless stuff like old magazines and sun hats.

Bero kicked the front door and jiggled the padlock angrily. He looked around. The street was empty. This part of town was so close to the border between Junko and Spearpoint that apparently no one in their right mind wanted to be loitering on it. He pounded the sidewalk-facing windows, which shook in their frames. A homeless man on the corner, the only other person in sight on what was typically a busy intersection, called out, "Haven't you heard? Mudt's dead, keke!"

Bero turned around. "*Dead?* Who killed him?"

The man grinned a toothless grin from under his blankets. He shrugged and giggled. "He did! Walking around with jade, you're killing yourself!"

Bero found a heavy rock and broke one of the Goody Too's windows. It made a gods-awful amount of racket, but there was no one but the hobo nearby to take notice. As Bero kicked in the glass and climbed gingerly into the ruined store, he was fuming with a peculiar mixture of disappointment and hope. So Mudt was gone, and his jade with him. Someone had beaten Bero to it. That was just to be expected, wasn't it? Always, something would happen; fate would shine on him, it would dangle what he desired, then it would snatch it away. Lucky and unlucky, that was him. And now, maybe bad luck would turn to good again. Maybe. Maybe.

The closet in the back of the store was open. The drawers of the wheeled filing cabinet were open and the contents pulled out and dumped in the mad search for cash and valuables, but the thing itself hadn't been moved. His heart in his throat, Bero leaned his weight against it and pushed it out of the way. He felt around in the dark to find the break in the carpet. When he rolled it back, he found the trap door he'd escaped through five weeks ago.

Bero closed the door of the closet and blocked it with the filing cabinet. He pulled the chain of the single bulb overhead, flooding the small space with yellowish light. Bero tugged at the metal ring of the trap door; it lifted with a heavy scraping sound and a small cloud of dust. Queasy with anticipation, he descended warily down the steps into the tunnel.

It was still there, boxes and crates, untouched by the scavengers who'd torn through the rest of the store. Bero took one of the top boxes and set it on the steps. He cut the packing tape with a pocketknife and gaped at what he'd found.

Then he stared back at the small tower of containers. How had Mudt hoarded all this? Surely it hadn't all come from the goateed Green Bone, who'd only brought him the one small box that first night Bero had seen him. Mudt must've been a dealer. A grin spread across Bero's face as he pulled one of the small sealed bottles out of the open carton in front of him.

Shine. A lifetime supply of shine. All of it, now his.

His hands shaking with eagerness, Bero scooped up as many vials as he could fit into his pockets. Then he replaced the half-empty box on top of the others and with an avaricious backward glance, climbed back out of the tunnel into the store. He dropped the trap door into place, rolled the carpet over it, and moved the filing cabinet back to exactly where it had been over the entrance to the secret tunnel. Bero turned out the closet light and stepped back out into the demolished store, his pockets laden and his mind galloping. This building would probably be taken over by someone else soon. He would have to move his treasure trove to somewhere safe that he could more easily access…

A noise behind him and a flashlight beam falling across his shoulders made Bero jump and whirl in the dark. He scrabbled for his revolver and brought it up into the face of a boy, thirteen or fourteen years old. Mudt's son.

"What are you doing here?" Bero shouted.

"I thought you might be him, coming back for me." The boy's voice was high and strained. He held a cheap, folding talon knife in his fist; his knuckles were white on the handle. The flashlight beam stayed on Bero as the two of them stared at each other.

"Who's coming back for you?" Bero's finger hugged the trigger of the revolver. He didn't want this kid telling anyone he was back in the city, or getting the idea that his dead father's store of shine belonged to him instead of Bero.

The junior Mudt trembled, shaking the weak flashlight beam, but there was wild hatred in his voice as he spat, "*Maik*. He killed my da. Maik Tar killed my da and if it's the last thing I do, I'm going to kill him!" Tears sprang into his eyes.

Bero's finger was still curled but now he hesitated. Slowly, he lowered the revolver. "It's hard to kill a really powerful Green Bone," he said.

"I don't care, I'll do whatever it takes!" Both the flashlight and the talon knife dropped to the teenager's side and he stood nearly panting, glaring at Bero with flushed cheeks and maddened eyes, as if daring him to say otherwise.

"I've done it before," Bero told him with a thrill of pride. "I've killed a Green Bone. No one figured I could do it, but they were wrong, all of them."

The other teen's eyes widened with greedy curiosity. Whenever he'd seen the younger Mudt before, Bero had paid him little attention. He'd always seemed obedient and unremarkable. He was skinny and his hair was greasy and his face had a rat-like quality. But he wasn't as much of a pussy as either Sampa or Cheeky had been.

It wasn't good to do things alone, Bero decided. Fate was like a tiger encountered on the road; best to divide its attention. When things had gone most wrong for Bero, someone smaller and weaker had always been there to draw the bad luck to themselves.

"I'm not scared of Green Bones," Bero said. "They're the ones who are scared of us, you know. They killed your da because they're afraid of people outside the clan having jade. What we need is some jade of our *own*, keke."

"Yeah," said Mudt fiercely. "Yeah, that's right."

"And I know where to get it."

Mudt's flashlight beam came back up. "You do?"

• Chapter Forty-Five •
A SHARED JOKE

Hilo surrendered his weapons to one of the uniformed Green Bone guards standing at the entrance to Wisdom Hall. The guard was a young woman whose jade aura hummed with intense concentration as Hilo approached. The members of Haedo Shield were purportedly trained to an especially high level of Perception to detect signs of murderous intent. She would have to relax her standards for Perceived hostility if she was going to let anyone into the building today, Hilo thought, smiling to himself as he unstrapped his moon blade, unbuckled his talon knife, and unholstered his gun, placing them side by side on the table in front of the metal detector. It wasn't that he doubted the guard's abilities or didn't understand the sentiment behind leaving weapons outside the negotiating chamber, but both were pointless measures. There was plenty of jade being collectively carried into the room on people's bodies. The Green Bones in attendance could easily kill each other barehanded if negotiations broke down.

They would not though, not with a penitent in the room, and there were three of them present in the meeting chamber where the mediation between the clan leaders was scheduled to take place. Apparently the Council thought it wise to arrange triple the spiritual insurance. The penitents stood quietly in the corners of the room, one man and two women, their shaved heads bowed and hands folded in the sleeves of their long green robes. Acts of violence were forbidden not just in any Deitist temple but anywhere a penitent was present. They were in direct communication with Heaven, so the belief went; the gods would know who had gone against the Divine Virtues and struck first. Heaven's spies, as it were. Not only would the sinner's soul be damned, but on the day of the Return, his entire family line—ancestors, parents, children, and descendants—would be refused entry into Heaven and be forced to wander the empty earth in exile for all eternity.

Yesterday, Hilo had suggested to Shae that it would be worth risking whatever theoretical metaphysical reckoning would befall them in the afterlife, if the two of them could kill Ayt Mada right where she sat across the table from them.

Shae had turned a stunningly cold look on him. "The gods are cruel, Hilo," she said, as if she knew them personally. "Don't tempt them with arrogance."

There were two doors in the chamber, so he and Ayt did not even enter through the same hallway. Hilo went into the room and sat down in the end chair, nodding to the dozen members of the Royal Council who lined either side of the table and comprised the official mediation committee. They looked officious in dark suits and held expensive pens over yellow legal pads in leather folios.

Four of the committee members belonged to No Peak—stern-looking Mr. Vang, white-haired Mr. Loyi, horse-faced Mrs. Nurh, and smiley Mr. Kowi who had a head shaped like a turnip. Hilo recognized each of them on account of Woon's briefing the previous evening. The diligent former Pillarman was proving to be a great asset in the Weather Man's Office. Hilo was glad to have spared his life. He did not blame Woon for Lan's death, any more than he blamed himself, but it was good to see the man turn his remorse into effort for the clan.

Of the other politicians in the room, four were loyal to the Mountain. The remaining four were not clan affiliated. Hilo hadn't even known there were councilmen who had no clan allegiance, ones who might be bought. "There are fifteen independents out of three hundred," Shae had enlightened him. "Try to remember these things."

The seat at the other end of the table was empty. Ayt had not arrived yet. Hilo checked his watch. He leaned back in his chair and smiled at those assembled, apparently at ease as he waited. "Ayt-jen must've stopped to key my car."

A nervous chuckling from some around the table. Mr. Loyi half-smiled and Mr. Kowi laughed out loud, but Vang and Nurh looked unimpressed. Most of the people in the room, regardless of clan, regarded Hilo with a mixture of nervous respect and cloaked disdain; they didn't know what to make of the wolfish young Pillar. Hilo didn't particularly care for them either. Puppets behind puppets.

In the seat slightly behind and to the left of him, Shae's aura grew a little louder in his mind and she rapped a pen on the arm of her chair, as if in a warning reminder that they were here to improve their standing with the Council, not worsen it.

Silence descended abruptly over the room. The politicians that had been chatting quietly noticed and straightened back to the table expectantly. It took Hilo a second to realize that the change was in reaction to him. He had gone entirely still, his gaze resting unfocused on some middle distance as his Perception stretched beyond the walls. Ayt Mada and her Weather Man had entered the building and were making their way toward the room. His enemy's jade aura was dark, dense, and molten, like lava flowing inexorably closer, building in heat. It exuded a calm, unrelenting malice directed unmistakably at him, and as she could no doubt Perceive him where he sat, the intensity of their long psychic stare was such that Hilo felt there was almost nothing left to say by the time Ayt entered the room a minute later. Everything that was going to happen today had already happened. The rest would be meaningless talk.

As he had expected, Ayt's physical appearance was of little note in comparison to the impression left by her aura. She was dressed in black, with a cream-colored blazer and no handbag, jewelry, or makeup. She strode in, appeared faintly amused by the waiting crowd, and settled into the chair opposite Hilo on the other end of the table. Short, slick-haired Ree Tura took the seat behind her left shoulder.

"Good afternoon, councilmen," Ayt said.

"Ayt-jen." The politicians beholden to the Mountain nodded in her direction. They paid her respect, that much was clear, more than the No Peak councilmen paid to Hilo, whose lips twitched slightly, his eyes still fixed on the other Pillar. With Ayt's entry, the room changed. Where there had been businesslike anticipation, now there was a tension preceding something inevitable. The air held the quality of a taut bowstring, of the blade before it falls, of the space between hammer and pin. Even the suits in the room with no ability in Perception sensed it easily enough.

The chair of the committee, a woman named Onde Pattanya who was one of the few independent council members, was brave enough to stand up and start the meeting. She cleared her throat. "Respected Green Bones, and fellow members of the Royal Council, we meet in Wisdom Hall today, in good faith and in the spirit of the Divine Virtues, under the watchful eye of the gods—" she glanced meaningfully at the penitents in the corners, "—and under the auspices of His Heavenship, Prince Ioan III." She inclined herself toward the portrait of the sovereign on the wall.

"May he live three hundred years," the room murmured in dutiful chorus.

Hilo quelled a smirk as he glanced at the oil painting on the wall. It depicted a stately, heavy-browed young man in the traditional long-robed garb of Kekonese nobility, sitting on a wide, cushioned chair with one hand resting on the sheathed moon blade across his lap and the other holding a fan of palm fronds, representing the monarch's role as warrior and peacemaker.

It was an archaic symbolism. The moon blade was traditionally a Green Bone weapon; Hilo was quite certain the prince had never drawn a real one. Members of the Kekonese royal family were forbidden from wearing jade, an edict codified in the national constitution after the throne was reestablished following the Many Nations War and independence from the Empire of Shotar. Hilo had seen the prince, who was considerably less majestic in real life, during public festivities at New Year's and other major holidays, and there was a large framed photograph in the Kaul house of the monarch bestowing Hilo's grandfather with some royal honor for national service. Prince Ioan III was popular as a symbol of Kekon's unity and history, but he was a figurehead, a man who lived a comfortable, state-funded life of ceremonial duties. His splendid portrait was in the room but he was not. He merely gave his blessing to the Royal Council, which represented the people and passed the laws. Ninety-five percent of the Council members held clan affiliation and were funded by powerful Lantern Men, who were themselves tributaries of the clans. Real power in Janloon, and by extension the entire country, rested in the clans, in the two Pillars whose hatred for each other pervaded the length of the room like a pungent odor.

"Let me begin," said councilwoman Onde, "by applauding Ayt-jen and Kaul-jen and their Weather Men for taking the important step of being here, and signaling their willingness to resolve differences through negotiation instead of violence. I speak on behalf of the entire Royal Council in expressing my sincere hope that we will soon reach an agreement that will return our city to a state of peace. We are scheduled to meet here for five days, but all of us on the committee are committed to staying as long as necessary to assist in reaching an agreeable outcome. Of course," Onde put in with an optimistic smile, "if we conclude early, all's the better."

Hilo thought glumly about all the time that would be wasted—time in which he was kept away from the critical battles that were being fought throughout the city. While he was in here, Kehn was in sole command of the war, and while Hilo had faith in his Horn, he would be deluding himself not to admit that Gont outclassed the Maiks as a strategist and fighter. Ayt could afford to sit here; Hilo could not.

"We'll begin with an opening statement from each side," said Onde. "By coin toss, the Mountain will proceed first. Ayt-jen." She sat down and picked up her pen.

Ayt let a pause settle, just short of uncomfortable, before she said, in a clear, even voice that reminded Hilo of an Academy lecturer, "I'm deeply saddened that the rift between the two great clans of this country has led to bloodshed. However, my father—let the gods recognize him—impressed upon me the responsibility that Green Bones hold, to protect and defend the common people. When those who depend on us for protection are threatened, we have no choice but to respond."

She held a hand out to her Weather Man, who immediately placed a sheet of paper in it. "For some time now, No Peak's overly aggressive tactics have harmed respectable citizens and businesses. For the enlightenment of the committee, Ree-jen has listed merely a few examples." Ayt glanced at the paper in her hand. "Construction on the Reign of Luck Casino was delayed for three months due to sabotage which was explicitly ordered by the Horn of No Peak at the time…"

Hilo listened silently to Ayt's extended list of grievances. He kept his expression mild and unchanged, but impatience and anger built inside him. He could reply to every single one of the accusations. Yes, he'd ordered his Fists to disrupt the construction of the Reign of Luck Casino, but only because the building contract had been outright stolen from No Peak. Yes, he'd allowed his men to cripple those three Mountain Fingers—because they'd vandalized and terrorized a string of No Peak properties. Ayt went on with an accounting of old sore spots, some stretching back two years or more, none of them material to the war now.

When Ayt finished, Councilwoman Onde thanked her and reminded everyone there ought to be no discussion until No Peak had had a chance to respond. Onde turned to Hilo and asked if he was ready to make his opening statement. For a moment, Hilo considered declining the invitation and leaving the circus before it could continue, but Shae loudly rustled the paper she reached forward to place on the table beside him. Hilo glanced down at it. The Weather Man and her Shadow had prepared different speeches depending on what strategy Ayt employed—whether she began with grand statements, specific demands, or vague accusations. Hilo picked up the paper.

"I'd like to applaud and thank the Royal Council for recognizing the need for this meeting. As active citizens and members of the community, we Green Bones want peace and prosperity for Janloon as much as anyone else." The words sounded stilted and unnatural in his mouth and he skipped over some of the speech. *Does Shae really expect me to say all this?* He continued reading, reciting a list of No Peak's opening demands of the Mountain: withdrawal from the Docks, surrender of the Armpit, cessation of SN1 production, and consent to being subject to an outside inspection of financial records and jade inventories. The last one was so outrageous that Hilo had to fight a smile at Ree Tura's look of outrage, though Ayt herself seemed unsurprised and didn't react.

"Thank you, Kaul-jen," said Coucilwoman Onde. "I am encouraged by the clarity and forthrightness expressed by both Pillars in their opening statements. A solid basis upon which to build our discussion." Onde was likely one of the only individuals in the room to think this could be true. The clan-affiliated politicians on both sides of the table appeared more nervous after hearing the superficiality of the speeches, sensing it to be a sign that their Pillars had already come to an understanding without words. "As the issue of territorial jurisdiction is the most pressing in terms of contributing to the ongoing street violence, I suggest we begin there," Onde said brightly.

After several hours, Ayt made a show of conceding that the Mountain would hold its position south of the General's Ride and not press further into the Docks or the Junko district. In exchange, Hilo stated to the Council that there would be no further attacks on Fishtown or Spearpoint. Meaningless agreements. The Mountain *couldn't* push further into the Docks; Hilo knew they don't have the manpower. Just like he knew No Peak couldn't hold Fishtown or Spearpoint, even if he went after it. Neither of them was particularly valuable anyways. The Armpit and Sogen were the worst battlegrounds and there'd been no movement toward agreement in either. Kehn was installed with eighty warriors in Sogen right now.

Tellingly, no mention had been made by either side of the assassination attempt on Hilo, the murder of Lan, or the massacre of twenty-one Mountain Green Bones on Poor Man's Road. A room in Wisdom Hall was not where those grievances would be accounted for. Hilo stared across at Ayt as they both stood up to leave. *This is a joke. A joke we're sharing.*

The second day of negotiations did not progress much further than the first. During one of the fifteen-minute breaks, Hilo took his Weather Man aside. "This is an orgy of pigs in shit," he said. "A complete fucking waste of time."

"If we walk out now, it'll look like we broke off negotiations and No Peak will be held at fault for continuing the war," Shae insisted. "The way those suits in there see it, the Mountain took Lan and we took from the Mountain in return. In their minds, that settles the blood score between the clans and we ought to talk the rest of it out and get back to life as normal." She cut him off before he could reply with any derisive exclamations. "Remember why we're here. We need to show the Lantern Men and the Royal Council that we made an effort at peace. The way Ayt is stonewalling, we'll have their sympathies when we lay everything out on the last day."

Shae had obtained early results of the formal audit on the KJA and she planned, on the fifth and final day, to use them as leverage against the Mountain, and failing that, to disclose them and make it clear to the Council that the war was about far more than clan vendettas, that the Mountain's actions went against Kekonese law and values. Hilo admitted that it was not a bad plan. Either they would come away with enough concessions to put them in a tenable military position until spring, or they would hold the moral high ground and thus, hopefully, the support of the clan's Lantern Men and the public. Nevertheless, Hilo felt all these things were ancillary factors; they would not substantially change the outcome of the war and he chafed at the task of playing through this farce for the benefit of the spectators.

He returned to his place in the room. It was growing increasingly infuriating to Perceive the smugness of his opponent's thick jade aura, to catch the occasional twitch of amusement on her lips. They were in on this together, the placating and assuaging of the politicians and the businessmen, the self-importantly modern Kekonese who liked to tell themselves that there was no need to solve disputes in the old way, the way of the clean blade under the judgment of Old Uncle. A belief both Pillars knew to be falsehood.

Ayt was playing her part more willingly than Hilo, however, because she was good at it. Far better than him, a fact she lorded over him with every word and gesture. She'd been Weather Man before she'd become Pillar and knew how to come across as a seasoned and articulate businesswoman. She was using that advantage now, to taunt and provoke him, to make him seem like nothing but a young hoodlum. The contrast between them made these jadeless stooges forget that Ayt Mada was the most powerful Pillar on Kekon on account of having killed her father's Horn, his First and Second Fists, his Pillarman, and his youngest son. At times, the thought made Hilo chuckle.

The second day ended with so little change from the previous that even the relentless Onde seemed discouraged. Hilo was impatient to get to a phone, to find out if one of his Fists, Goun Jeru, who'd been ambushed and badly injured just before dawn, had survived the surgery room. He and Shae said little to each other, parting ways outside of Wisdom Hall. Shae stepped into a car waiting to take her back to the Weather Man's Office on Ship Street. Hilo found it amusing that for someone who had put on such a show of eschewing clan trappings back when she'd first returned to Janloon, his Weather Man seemed to harbor no qualms about wielding them now. Which merely proved to Hilo that his sister had been fooling herself the whole time and ought to have known better, ought to have come around before she'd been forced.

Hilo looked for his driver and the Duchesse in front of the reflecting pool but instead saw Maik Tar waiting in one of the clan's nondescript cars. When he got into the passenger seat, Tar turned down the radio and offered him a cigarette. Hilo noticed that the Pillarman's sleeve was speckled with dried blood; his eyes were ringed from lack of sleep but gleamed with a triumph that made the texture of his aura scratchy with repressed excitement. "How'd it go?" Tar asked. "Same as before?"

"Worse. A shame the penitents are still there."

"You could bring me in," offered Tar. "I'm not going to Heaven anyways."

"How's Goun?" The unhappy shift in Tar's aura answered him immediately. "Fuck," Hilo said quietly. Goun had been a classmate of his, a skilled fighter but also a funny man who put people in a good mood and could always tell a story. Hilo ought to have seen him before he died, ought to have gone in person to break the news to his parents and sister. Instead, he'd been mincing words and pandering pointlessly in Wisdom Hall.

A wave of rage boiled up Hilo's neck and into his face. "Fuck! *Fuck* the gods! Fuck Ayt and fuck Gont with a sharp stick, *fuck them.*" He slammed his head against the headrest and punched the ceiling of the car, denting it.

Tar dangled his cigarette out the open window and waited until his Pillar had calmed down. "Let the gods recognize him, poor bastard," he said at last.

"Let the gods recognize him," Hilo agreed in a deadened voice.

"It's not all bad news, though," Tar said, and waited with some obvious smugness for Hilo to ask him what redeeming thing it was he'd made a point to come in person to share. Tar was like a kid sometimes, eager to please, prone to both tantrums and overexcitement, possessing a curious combination of boldness and insecurity. Ever since he'd gotten out of the hospital, he'd seemed desperate for a chance to prove himself and displace the embarrassment of his injury. Redesigning the Pillarman's role for Tar was a stroke of personnel genius that Hilo was quite proud of.

Still, as he was in an awful mood over losing Goun, Hilo did not at once indulge the man's eagerness. Instead he asked, "Has Kehn been to Goun's family?"

"I don't know," Tar said. "I haven't talked to him."

"Who's managing Goun's Fingers?"

"Vuay or Lott, as far as I know." Tar sounded a little surly now. Goun had been his classmate too, but Tar seemed only mildly bothered by his death. He cared for only a few people in the world, though these people could ask anything of him.

Hilo gave in. "What's giving you such a hard on, that you have to tell me?"

After Tar had explained everything, Hilo stared out the window, his burning gaze resting unfocused on some middle distance as the fingers of his right hand drummed lightly and rapidly on one knee. "Drive," he told Tar. "Let me think about this." After a while longer, he declared, "Tomorrow's going to be different. A lot different. You did good, Tar," and his Pillarman smiled in satisfaction at the praise, touching the new talon knife on his belt.

• Chapter Forty-Six •
HONEST TALK

On the morning of the third day of mediation, Hilo arrived early at Wisdom Hall with Shae to meet with Chancellor Son Tomarho, who had been requesting a meeting with the Pillar for some time, with increasing pique. "Kaul-jen, come in. How're the gods favoring you?" Son asked, ushering them into the office.

"With their usual sadistic sense of humor," Hilo said. "You?"

The politician appeared to stifle an involuntary reaction to Hilo's casual blasphemy by lowering his ruddy face beneath a stiff and shallow salute. "Ah. Well. Well enough, thank you." Hilo was under the distinct impression that Chancellor Son Tomarho did not like him. A year ago, he'd refused Son's request that he break up the workers' strike on the Docks by force, and at Lan's funeral the man had shown only the minimum of respect to the new Pillar. The fact that Hilo had now ignored him for several weeks while he concentrated on the war could only have exacerbated the man's dislike. Indeed, the way Son was looking at him now, with an obviously forced smile that did not hide the coldness of his scrutinizing gaze, confirmed what Hilo suspected: the Chancellor saw himself as man of political refinement and distinction, someone existing above the unfortunate but occasionally necessary savagery of certain parts of the clan. Son looked at Hilo and saw youth and muscle—someone who ought to be taking orders, not giving them, and certainly not attending Wisdom Hall as Pillar.

It was difficult for Hilo to behave in a rational and civil manner toward people with whom he did not share any personal warmth. Their status or importance in the eyes of others had little bearing on him. He knew this was a weakness on his part; indeed, placing personal feelings over more politic considerations had led him into trouble before and earned him his grandfather's ire. When Hilo and his siblings were children, Kaul Sen had beaten Lan infrequently and Shae not at all, but his middle grandchild had been whipped for causing trouble with instructors at the Academy, for breaking the arm of the son of one of his grandfather's own business partners, for being seen around the city everywhere with the Maik boys.

Doing his best to quell both an instinctive resentment toward Son and a sense of general discomfort with the pompous formality of the oak-paneled office, Hilo let himself be gestured into the seat across from the Chancellor's wide desk. Shae positioned her chair slightly behind and to the left of his. He was glad she was present because she appeared more at ease than he felt. The Chancellor sat and gestured to his aide to bring refreshments, then turned to Hilo with that same painted-on smile.

Hilo said, "Well, I'm here. What do you want to talk about?"

Son's smile wavered visibly. "Kaul-jen," he said, recovering it with admirable speed, "I appreciate that you're a very busy man. Leading the clan as Pillar in this time of difficulty is no doubt all-consuming. I dare say as much work as running a country." The rebuke was delivered with a casual thrust but it was clear nevertheless. Son was the functional head of the government and not pleased with having been kept waiting by a twenty-eight-year-old street fighter who'd come into the clan's leadership unintended.

Hilo replied with a casual jab of his own. "I hope none of *your* political opponents are trying to take your head off with a moon blade." He nodded in thanks at the aide who put a cold glass of anise-scented tea in front of him. Trying hard to bear in mind what Shae had told him about the importance of the Royal Council and the clan's need for political support and legitimacy, Hilo changed his tone and said more seriously, "I'll admit I have a lot to learn about being the Pillar. My brother—let the gods recognize him—didn't have a chance to prepare me for it. Our enemies saw to that and I haven't been off my feet since. I apologize if I've been disrespectful by not meeting with you sooner."

Hilo's sincerity seemed to appease Son somewhat. "Well, the most important thing is that you've been sitting down with Ayt Mada and the Council's mediation committee. As Chancellor, I couldn't be part of the committee myself, but it's making progress, I hope? A negotiated peace is, after all, what we're all hoping for."

With great difficulty, Hilo kept the sneer off his face by lifting his glass and draining half his glass of tea. Chancellor Son's eyes flicked down to the sight of Hilo's hand, the callused knuckles covered with recent scabs, and was less successful than his guest in not betraying his contempt; his mouth twitched, wobbling his jowls for a second, before he said, "The sooner the clans can resolve their differences and return our city to normal, the better. For the sake of the people and the country."

"The Mountain murdered my brother."

Son Tomarho cleared his throat uncomfortably. "A terrible tragedy that will never be forgotten. However, I would venture to say, based on my experiences with Kaul Lan-jen, that *he* would've placed the ultimate good of the clan and the nation foremost in his mind, ahead of any personal desire for vengeance."

"I'm not Lan." And suddenly, having said these words aloud, Hilo relaxed. A smile returned. "The Lantern Men and the Royal Council will have to accept that."

The Chancellor frowned for the first time. "The Lantern Men of No Peak, while they are unwavering in their loyalty and allegiance to the clan, are naturally concerned for the safety of their communities and the hardship that's being imposed on them."

"You mean the increase in tribute payments," Hilo inferred. "It's true we've had to raise tribute in order to fight the war. The Weather Man can speak to that."

It was not the most graceful way to give Shae permission to speak, but Hilo was losing patience for the niceties. Besides, he'd been Perceiving for some time Shae's aura bristling with anxiety that he would fuck this meeting up, and he might as well let her say her piece. Shae leaned forward at once and said, "As you've said, Chancellor, war between the clans has disrupted business. No Peak is obligated to provide financial aid to our Lantern Men whose property has been damaged or whose livelihoods have been affected. When Green Bones are killed, we pay for their funerals and provide for their families. When they're injured, there are medical bills to account for. Unfortunately, the Mountain has a substantial financial advantage over us as a result of manufacturing SN1 overseas and appropriating jade outside of the purview of the Kekon Jade Alliance. The official audit results haven't been released, but I can provide you with all the proof you require." She inclined her head and concluded firmly, "No Peak needs the full support of its Lantern Men right now and we've raised tribute only so far as necessary on those who can bear it. If you wish to see the details of how we've calculated the new rates, I'd be more than willing to share them."

Hilo was impressed; his sister sounded like a real Weather Man. Chancellor Son leaned back in his chair, crossing his well-padded arms. "I don't doubt your math, but the reality is that increased tribute is a hardship for even the most loyal clan members. It will be seen as particularly poor thanks for those," and here Hilo had no doubt Son was referring to himself, "who've been tirelessly driving, on Kaul Lan-jen's mandate, the passage of bills legislating inspection and reform of the KJA."

"Fuck the KJA," said Hilo. "What happens there doesn't matter."

Son Tomarho's face went momentarily blank. "Kaul-jen," he said at last, completely nonplussed, "your brother—let the gods recognize him—believed strongly in establishing ownership safeguards around the national jade supply—"

"My brother was trying to prevent war. Now we're *at* war. Whoever wins is going to control the city, and the Council, *and* the jade supply. If the Mountain takes over No Peak to become the single most powerful clan on Kekon, do you really think Ayt's going to give a sick dog's wet shit about your legislation?" Pushing back from the table, Hilo stood up and stretched, stiff from a host of recently acquired minor injuries.

Surprised but following his lead, Shae stood up with him, but Chancellor Son remained seated, apparently at a loss for how to respond. Finally, he rose to his feet and said, with no remaining trace of his practiced geniality, "So you mean to disregard the concerns of the Lantern Men, then? And to dismiss the efforts of the Council?"

"Not at all," said Hilo. It was true that he was not Lan. He did not have Lan's gravity nor his diplomatic acumen, he couldn't handle this the way Lan would've handled it, but he'd dealt with disgruntled subordinates and unhappy Lantern Men before, on his side of the clan. "The clan would be worthless without its Lantern Men and without people like you, Chancellor," he said. "But I'm starting to think that after so many years of peace, some people have forgotten why they pay tribute. I've always been taught that back during the war the Lantern Men were patriots who risked their lives to help Green Bones, because Green Bones protected the people when the country was in danger.

"We're at war again now, and the country will be in danger if No Peak falls to the Mountain. *If one clan controls jade.* Isn't that what Lan was afraid of when he came to you?" Hilo fixed the Chancellor with a penetrating stare. It was not unfriendly, but there was a predatory quality to Hilo's stare that made many people flinch or lower their eyes when subjected to it, and the Chancellor was no exception.

"I can see you don't like me much," said Hilo with cool amiability. "But I'm the Pillar, and you're the highest politician in the country with ties to No Peak. We're clan brothers, of a sort. We both want to win this and come out alive."

Son's eyes widened. "I want what's best for Kekon, Kaul-jen. And that's peace between the clans. That's why I moved immediately to form the mediation committee."

"The mediation's a fucking farce," said Hilo. "You'll find out why soon enough. So we've got to win this thing. And that means the Lantern Men have got to *be* wartime Lantern Men. They've got to stick their necks out for the clan. Prove that allegiance that they're always going on about when they come asking us for this or that. They've got to pay the higher tributes—and *you* have to make sure they do it."

Chancellor Son burst into a coughing, nervous laugh. "There are thousands of Lantern Men in the clan. You're deliberately making decisions that risk a mass defection from No Peak. You can hardly expect that *I* ought to be held responsible—"

"What's that number again?" Hilo turned slightly over his shoulder toward Shae. "How many companies make up some large percent of the clan's business?"

"The twenty-five largest No Peak affiliated entities account for sixty-five percent of the clan's tributary income," said the Weather Man.

Hilo turned back to Son with satisfaction. "Right. So what the big dogs decide is what matters. All the little dogs will follow. The Son family is one of the big dogs. It has to go to the others and convince them to fall into line. Make them see that they might have to suffer a little right now, but it's so the clan can win. People are people, whether they're Lantern Men or Fists, jaded or not; they'll run when they lose hope but they'll put up with any hardship if they think they'll come out on top in the end."

Son tugged at his collar, which he abruptly seemed to be finding too tight for his bulging neck. "There could well be many Lantern Men who would rather defect to the Mountain than commit themselves to No Peak under such...*unyielding* terms."

The Pillar appeared to consider this. "You wouldn't be one of those people, would you, Chancellor?" he asked quietly. "If the Mountain destroys No Peak and takes the city, I'll be dead. My entire family will be dead. *You're* the one who'll live with what happens afterward."

Hilo could see the wheels turning in the politician's head. Jaded or not, one did not rise to power in Janloon without a great deal of shrewdness and a powerful instinct for survival, and Chancellor Son was well aware of the fact that he was far too closely and publicly tied to No Peak to survive politically in a city ruled by the Mountain. Son had orchestrated the KJA reform bills and the financial audit meant to expose the Mountain's illegal activities. His daughters ran a No Peak tribute business and had married into the clan; one of his son-in-laws was a Luckbringer and the other was a mid-rank Fist. His political and business allies would be targeted by Mountain-affiliated rivals. There was no escape for Son Tomarho, any more than for the Kauls.

Hilo saw all these thoughts writ in the Chancellor's deeply resentful silence and he felt compelled to walk around the huge desk to the man. Son seemed slumped into his own bulk, making no effort to move away and only tensing in a half-hearted way when Hilo laid a hand on his ample shoulder. "My grandfather and my older brother had great respect for you," Hilo said solemnly. "So I have respect for you, even if I can see on your face that you don't respect me as Pillar. Normally, I wouldn't put up with that, but I'm willing to forgive it because of course I understand: why would you accept me after years of dealing with Lan? There's one thing I'll say though: so long as I live, I'll never turn my back on a friend. Ask any one of my Fists, anyone who knows me, even my enemies, and they'll tell you if what I say is true. You're already an old friend of the clan, so if you're willing to forget my disrespect in not coming to you earlier, I'll gladly forget your slights to me. If we survive this together, we'll be like brothers-in-arms. What a laugh that'll be, won't it, two men as different as us? But the clan needs both of us to stand firm now."

Son drew a breath into his large frame and blew out loudly. When he turned to look at Hilo, he wore the dignified expression of a veteran statesman making an unfortunate but unavoidable decision and girding himself to face the inevitable storm to follow. The Chancellor might not be pleased or willing, but at least Hilo could see the man's reluctant regard, his grudging reassessment of the new Pillar. "I am loyal to the clan, and you've made your position quite clear, Kaul-jen," Son said, with a touch of bitterness and admiration. "I believe we have a mutual understanding." And he brought his clasped hands up to touch his forehead, inclining into a salute.

"What was that?" Shae hissed as they walked from Son's office down to the mediation committee's meeting room. "That wasn't what we'd planned."

"It went fine." Despite having achieved what he wanted with Son, Hilo was not smiling as he strode down the marbled hallway with grim purpose. He resisted the urge to append some smug remark to his sister about what had happened. You didn't need to speak sweetly and offer patronage at every turn to these people. You had to be honest with them and show that they had more to gain from your friendship than your enmity. Did she think his Fists obeyed him because they were rewarded with favors or cowed by threats? No. Mutual survival was the basis of brotherhood and loyalty, even of love.

"What is it? What haven't you told me?" Shae whispered urgently as they reached the doors of the meeting room. She could Perceive his cold fury and aggravation. He didn't answer her, merely pulled open the door and strode in; she'd know soon enough.

The meeting with the Chancellor had delayed them; they were the last to arrive. Ayt and Ree were already there, Ayt conversing formally but amiably with two of the councilmen that Hilo knew to be Mountain loyalists. Hilo dropped into his chair without apology for the tardiness. From across the room, the other Pillar turned her head toward him, unable to avoid Perceiving the ferocity in his aura. Others in the room shifted uneasily, sensing the change as well. The first two sessions had been expectedly tense. This was different. Something had brought Hilo to a true temper.

Councilwoman Onde cleared her throat. "As we're now all present, let's begin where we left off yesterday." She seemed uncertain of how to proceed and flipped nervously through the copious notes on her yellow legal pad. "We were discussing the financial terms of a peace agreement between the clans." Onde glanced at Hilo but hesitated to call on him. Instead she turned to the Mountain Pillar and said, "Ayt-jen, I believe you were about to make a proposal at the close of our session yesterday."

Ayt Mada wore an expression of complacent curiosity as she regarded Hilo. It was clear that something she had said or done had gotten to him, and she seemed eager to discover whether her foolhardy young rival would finally explode and make a spectacle of himself. Ayt laced her fingers. The loose sleeves of her silk blouse slid down her forearms, revealing snaking coils of jade. "Yes, Chairwoman," she said, "I was explaining that No Peak's offenses against us over the past year have been so costly that it is only reasonable we discuss reparations."

Reparations! It was too perfect; Hilo leaned his head back and laughed.

No one else at the table seemed to think his outburst of mirth and contempt was appropriate. The No Peak council members stared at him aghast and he could feel Shae's aura raking him with disapproval. "Kaul-jen," said councilwoman Onde, with nervous admonishment. "Ayt-jen has brought up the very valid and serious issue of financial settlement. Your response suggests you're dismissing the idea as humorous. The committee would appreciate it if you would elaborate on your position calmly."

Hilo leaned forward, a forearm on the table, the other hand pressing against the arm of his chair so he nearly rose from his seat. The room froze as the amusement on Hilo's face transformed into menace. In a soft, flat voice that carried in the frightening silence, he said to the other Pillar, "Enough bullshit, Ayt. You're a thief. *A jade thief.*"

It was the worst sort of insult between Green Bones, to suggest a person did not deserve the jade she carried, that she'd come about it dishonorably. For a second, Ayt's face went entirely still and her eyes burned with a light that appeared as if she'd fly out of her seat to snap Hilo's spine. Then with impressive aplomb, she turned a calm face to Chairwoman Onde. "It appears Kaul-jen has no respect for these proceedings."

"Don't talk to them!" Hilo barked. "You'll talk to *me*." For the first time, he saw Ayt regard him in a tense assessment that held something other than contempt. "The Mountain is behind the discrepancies in the KJA's records. Don't lie to my face, *thief*. You've been taking jade above quota from the mines all year."

Behind him, Shae sucked in a breath. Her jade aura flared and bathed him in shock and recrimination. *What are you doing!* He could sense her shouting at him in her mind. Their trump card, their biggest charge against the Mountain—he'd thrown it down more than two days early, without waiting for the audit results, without clearing it with her or gathering the support of No Peak loyalists on the Council. He'd ruined her plan; they'd lost the potential leverage of using the public disclosure of the audit results as a bargaining chip against the Mountain. Shae was furious. He could tell she kept herself silently in check now only because the Weather Man speaking out in this public forum without the Pillar's cue would only make them look worse.

Ayt, however, had recovered her poise. He was acting impulsive and desperate, as she'd expected. Nodding at something Ree Tura whispered quickly into her ear, she said, "Councilmen, I've offered up genuine territorial and business grievances. Kaul-jen throws out one preposterous, unfounded suspicion. Whatever the reason for the purported accounting discrepancies in the KJA, I'm sure the audit will reveal them to be due to unintended negligence rather than malice. This accusation is a distraction."

Hilo threw his hands up to gesture at the entire room. "*This* is a distraction. There's no mediation that can happen here." He pointed at Chairwoman Onde, who shrank back slightly. "You want peace? All of you want peace? There's only one kind of peace the Mountain will accept: one clan in power. In complete control of both jade and shine. *Gold and jade together.* Tell me if that's the peace you want."

The people around the table were shifting uncomfortably. Among the No Peak councilmen, Mrs. Nurh sat open-mouthed, Mr. Loyi was frowning. Mr. Vang and Mr. Kowi were looking from Hilo, to Shae, to each other, in stunned indecision of how to handle the situation. They had not been consulted on any of this.

"Kaul-jen!" said Onde with admirable authority, "I must ask you to—"

Ayt interrupted, her voice like steel. "The Mountain is the largest clan in the country. We have a reliable and adequate supply of jade and we hold nearly half the votes on the board of the KJA. Why would we need to steal what we openly control?"

"What a good question." Hilo tilted his head, scratching his jaw as if genuinely perplexed. "Maybe you aren't stealing it for yourselves. Maybe you're finding some other use for that jade that you don't want other Green Bones to know about." Shadows darkened his face. "Smuggling it on the black market through people like Tem Ben the Carver. Putting it in the hands of water-blooded crooks, like your informer Mudt Jindonon, who runs crime rings in No Peak territory with the Mountain's blessing. And with *jade*." The word came out as a snarl. Hilo rose slowly from his seat. "How many untrained, jade-fevered, shine-addicted gangsters are running around in the city, spying, thieving, wrecking havoc in the territory of other clans on the Mountain's orders, in exchange for jade they have no right to wear? How big are the Mountain's ranks, when you include them in the count?"

Ayt's body remained motionless but her head drew up in slow malevolence, neck lengthening like a rearing viper. Her aura burned with murderous intent. When she spoke, it was entirely without the practiced professionalism she'd shown earlier. It was like a sharp blade being drawn delicately across flesh. "How do you come up with such elaborate stories, Kaul Hiloshudon?"

Hilo reached for his breast pocket. Everyone flinched, except for Ayt, who made no move as Hilo pulled out a black cassette tape. "The stone-eye Tem Ben told it to me. He and Mudt are feeding worms at the bottom of the harbor now." He tossed the tape on the table. It skidded to the center and lay there like an explosive device no one would touch. Hilo leaned his hands on the table and spoke in a whisper. "I found two of the weeds you planted in my yard, thief, and I'm going to find the others. The next time we meet, it won't be in this room and there won't be any *mediation*."

Hilo turned and walked out the door. For a second, Shae remained seated, then he heard her stand up and follow him silently out. Neither of them spoke.

The phone call came two days later. "Ayt-jen wishes to meet with you alone," said Ree Tura from the other end of the line. "Somewhere neutral and private."

"What assurances do I have?" Shae asked.

Ree's slightly nasal voice lowered, as if he were leaning forward. "I'm speaking as one Weather Man to another, Kaul-jen. We aren't thugs. Choose the time and place."

After a moment of thought, Shae said, "The Temple of Divine Return. In the back of the sanctum, tomorrow night." She hung up.

• Chapter Forty-Seven •
HEAVEN IS LISTENING

Shae arrived early at the temple the next evening. She walked silently into the sanctum and knelt on a cushion in the back corner. The Deitist house of worship held a different quality for her now than it had when she'd come here a few months ago. Jade made it different. That other time felt like a distant half-waking dream for so many reasons. Now it was clear to her that what felt like stillness and silence to the ordinary person was in reality a constant crooning musical hum of energy, filling the sanctum, radiating into the marrow of one's bones. The six cross-legged penitents, in perfect stillness, radiated powerful auras that filled her Perception as completely as if she were staring into a floodlight that blotted out the center of her vision, leaving only the dim periphery untouched. As blinding as they were, the auras of the penitents were calm, as if they were harmonized in the same deep dream-filled sleep, their breathing as gentle as the wind rustling the prayer cards and leaves of the devotional trees in the courtyard.

The last time Shae had knelt in doubt and indecision and prayed in the temple, she had not truly believed that she would be unequivocally answered by forces beyond her control. Bathed in the energetic resonance surrounding her now, Shae shivered inwardly, for she no longer doubted that this was a holy place, a place where the gods might be paying attention.

That did not mean it was a kind place; indeed it was more dangerous than any other. Anything said or even contemplated in here would be heard by the penitents, might reach the ears of Heaven. Shae touched her head to the ground three times. She whispered, "Yatto, Father of All, I beg you recognize my brother, Kaul Lanshinwan, gone from this earth to await the Return. He was a follower of Jenshu, whom we call Old Uncle, and though he might not have come to this temple much, he had humility, compassion, courage and goodness—more of the Divine Virtues than any Green Bone I know." Shae closed her eyes and fell silent. She would have said more, she would've pleaded consideration for her grandfather, and for Hilo, and even for Doru, but she couldn't afford the time for contemplation and mourning, not tonight. She was here to learn what information she could from a deadly enemy. She needed to be clear in mind and prepared in body.

Ayt Mada's entrance into the sanctum interposed on the edges of Shae's Perception like a spear of red heat parting the slow energetic thrum of the temple, a harsh chord sounding over a low melody. Shae waited, focusing on her own composure, not betraying her unease. Ayt did not pause or look around the sanctum. She went straight to Shae and knelt on the cushion beside her. Ayt did not look at the other woman, nor did she touch her head to the ground as was religious custom.

"You should know," she said, "that I did not order the death of Kaul Lan."

Everything about Ayt Mada—her speech, her movements, and her aura—bespoke directness and control. During the time Shae had been in her presence in Wisdom Hall, she'd gathered that, beyond jade ability and training, it was constant unsentimental decisiveness that enabled Ayt to overcome all the male rivals in her clan. Even her pauses always seemed deliberate, never a symptom of hesitation or uncertainty. She let one of them rest between herself and Shae before speaking again. "I had no reason to want your eldest brother dead. He was a reasonable man. Overshadowed by his grandfather, perhaps, but nevertheless, an intelligent and respected leader. Sooner or later he would come to the proper conclusion, I was confident of that. We would've negotiated an agreement between our clans and avoided all this unpleasantness."

Shae found it hard to speak from fury that made her vision waver. "My brother lies cold in the ground. You expect me to believe you didn't put him there?"

"Any Green Bone in the Mountain would've been proud to win Kaul Lan's jade. No one has claimed that accomplishment. Doesn't that strike you as odd?"

"The taxi driver that picked him up from the Lilac Divine said they were followed by men in a black car. Someone knew his habits and was waiting for him that night. Several people on the street heard gunfire down by the pier, and there were countless bullet holes near the place his body was found. Two unregistered, damaged Fullerton machine guns were found on the dock—hardly the sort of weapon carried by common criminals in No Peak territory. The men who killed him were working for the Mountain. You lie if you deny it." She was grateful, and mildly amazed, that she was able to state all this with the matter-of-fact self-possession of a true Weather Man. "The Pillar is the master of the clan, the spine of the body, without which nothing moves. Unless you mean to convince me that those men were acting against your orders, how can you sit here and say you didn't kill him?"

"You're correct, Kaul-jen," Ayt said, surprising Shae with formal address. "I'm responsible for his death—but I didn't whisper his name. I intended to send a message deep into No Peak, to impress upon Kaul Lanshinwan the realization that going to war with the Mountain would be unwise and ultimately futile. In doing so, I intended to avoid the war, or at least shorten it. Things didn't go as planned."

"Because it was Hilo you wanted to kill."

"Yes."

For a second, Shae allowed herself to contemplate with morbid curiosity the idea of an entirely different unfolding of tragedy. Hilo's death would've been a terrible blow to Lan, but Ayt was not unreasonable in suspecting that the Pillar's sense of pragmatism and responsibility would've ultimately won out over desire for vengeance. Without a strong Horn to rely on, Lan most likely would've acceded to terms of peace rather than risk the entire clan in a disadvantaged war.

Shae brought her attention back to the moment at hand. Possibilities that lay in the past were illusions, closed doors, as meaningless as unfulfilled intentions. "You asked to meet with me," she reminded Ayt. "It wasn't merely to try and convince me that you only wanted to kill one of my brothers instead of both."

Ayt said sharply, "This war is pointless and destructive to both our clans. The audit of the KJA was childish and unnecessary; it invited the Royal Council and the press to come snooping into Green Bone matters. Is that something we really need when we can solve these issues quietly between us? The politicians have gotten it into their heads to try and pass some bureaucratic legislation, or form some oversight body—for what ultimate benefit? We may even attract international attention, and the last thing the country needs is more self-serving foreigners meddling in our affairs."

"You brought it on yourself," Shae replied. "The Mountain has been blatantly breaking the rules of the Kekon Jade Alliance. Doru has been covering for you."

"Doru is a far-sighted man, loyal to Kaul Sen and the ideals he stood for," Ayt said. "He realized that neither of the Torch's grandsons could replace him and that an alliance was inevitable." She turned to Shae with eyes that held the coldness that came from absence of doubt. "It is exactly that, Kaul-jen—inevitable."

"An alliance?" Shae said. "Why not just call it what it is? Destroying your enemies. Complete power in the city and monopolistic control of the country's jade."

Ayt studied her with such cool consideration that Shae felt in that moment a flutter of fear, like a moth in her ribcage. Ayt was not much larger than her physically, but that meant next to nothing when it came to a contest of jade ability. This was a woman who'd killed before her father's funeral and did not bow in a temple of the gods. Perhaps she would even strike in the presence of a penitent. If she wanted to kill Shae now, there was nothing to stop her. Shae forced a calming awareness into her body, deliberately noting the relaxed state of each muscle and joint. Ayt was so close she would Perceive fear with no effort, no matter how composed Shae's face.

At last Ayt spoke, as if she were lecturing a stubborn student. "You're an educated and travelled woman, not like those who've never left the country. Consider what's happening outside Kekon. Tension between Espenia and Ygutan grows day by day. The world is dividing into camps, and both sides covet the jade found only on this island. What kind of fortune did the Espenians spend to create SN1, so they could equip their elite soldiers with jade? The Ygutanians are playing catch-up, but they certainly want no less. I'm told they've been researching how to make their soldiers more naturally resistant, more like us. The Shotarians did the same thing years ago—brought Kekonese and Abukei women to secret facilities to be raped and impregnated, in an attempt to create a Shotarian army with natural jade resistance.

"We're a small country with a precious resource. If we don't take the right actions, we'll find ourselves at the mercy of imperial powers again. The only way for us to resist the foreigners in the long-run is to be united as one clan again."

"United by conquest, you mean. First you had to weaken No Peak. You might have tried to negotiate an upfront alliance with Lan, but instead you colluded with Doru and supplied jade and tip-offs to gangsters within our territories."

Ayt was unmoved by Shae's anger. "It's as you say. The Pillar is the master of the clan, the spine of the body. There can be only one spine. Kaul Lan was a proud man; he wouldn't have willingly relinquished control of his clan, certainly not while he had the strength of his Horn behind him. And Gont Asch and Kaul Hilo couldn't be in one clan any more than two cocks could share a henhouse. We had to establish supremacy in the streets before an honest and productive conversation could begin."

"Where is the additional jade you've been taking from the mines?"

Ayt astonished Shae by answering at once. "We're selling it to the Ygutanians. The contract is entirely secret of course, because of Kekon's public alliance with Espenia. But we know the Ygutanians are already acquiring jade through the black market. No matter what we do, how strictly we crack down, smuggling remains a problem. The potential profit for smugglers is so high they cannot be dissuaded even with death penalties. If we offer the Ygutanians a reliable supply, we'll destroy the underground trade. There will be less crime on Kekon, and far more profit to the clan. We'll be supplier to both sides of the mounting conflict. We'll ensure our security and protect our income no matter which foreigners prevail."

"That's why you're also starting to produce shine." Shae could not help but admire the simplicity of it now. "You can't sell that quantity of jade to the Ygutanians without also promising them the shine to go with it."

"Factories on the mainland manufacturing SN1 quickly and cheaply. Not the sort of stuff we'd ever want here on the island, but good enough for the foreigners. The Ygutanians have so many people they treat them as expendable anyways."

How much money was the Mountain already bringing in from its secret contracts, Shae wondered. Siphoning jade from the national coffers, selling it to foreigners, trafficking in shine…it must be millions of dien. Tens of millions.

Ayt's voice took on an edge of excitement. Shae sensed in the heavy texture of her aura a driven and deadly tenaciousness, like that of some purebred hunting animal that once set to quarry would rather run until it falls dead than give up the chase. She angled to face Shae directly now, and said, "If we introduce a reliable supply of cheap SN1 into the market, sales of jade go up and we profit. If we shut off the spigot, foreign governments will have to contend with jaded people going mad, unable to control their powers, dying of the Itches. With that kind of market power, we Green Bones will retain rightful control over jade—and we'll have the wealth and means to protect the country, as we've always done."

Shae was silent for a moment before answering. "It really is, Ayt-jen, a visionary and cunning strategy." She meant it; Ayt was truly a higher level Pillar, not satisfied with merely continuing her father's legacy but intent on altering the path of the clan and the country as whole. A formidable successor to the Spear of Kekon.

Under Ayt's leadership, the Mountain clan would build an international empire of jade and drugs. It would eliminate or subsume its rivals until one clan ruled Kekon. The country would foment global tensions and profit by spreading the availability of jade and shine to millions of people beyond its borders, with Green Bones sitting at the apex of a burgeoning jade pyramid they controlled.

"I share with you all my plans in complete honesty," Ayt said, "because I can see you're an intelligent and ambitious woman. There are few enough of us in the world of Green Bones, the world of men. I know that you were the top graduate at the Academy and the favorite of Kaul Seningtun, and yet you were obscured by your brothers. You discovered the clan was an insular, constricting place. That's how you came to work for the Espenian military, and afterward, why you left Kekon."

Heat climbed up Shae's chest and neck at Ayt's presumptuous but essentially accurate description. How had Ayt learned these things? She was indignant yet strangely flattered that the Pillar of the Mountain had thought to dig into her past in an attempt to find the right leverage to use on her.

"I see some of my younger self in you, Kaul Shae-jen. If I had known you would return to Kekon and wear jade again, I'd have approached you much earlier. Let the two of us resolve this feud. Your brother is a dangerous, foolish man-child driven by pride and bloodlust; he would fight to the last man on principle alone. It's what he knows how to do." Shae knew what was coming next. "Usurp him. End this senseless war. Ree Tura is near retirement and I tire of him regardless. I would make you my Weather Man. Weather Man of a great clan; Weather Man of Kekon itself."

"You overestimate me, Ayt-jen," Shae said, hearing something pitted and sour scrape in her voice. "I've been gone from Kekon for years and am still an outsider in my own clan. The Luckbringers and Lantern Men accept me grudgingly. All the Fists and Fingers of No Peak are loyal to my brother."

"There's no reason for them not to remain so. We can arrange things simply between us. Make it appear honorable. Kaul Hilo can fall in battle as the war hero he clearly wishes to be. There'd be no taint of treachery for you, no worry of vengeance from his followers. Afterward, you'd be acting with full legitimacy."

Shae nodded. An ambush then, getting Hilo alone at a place and time of their choosing. This time the Mountain would see to it that the assassination plan was better, foolproof. How easily Ayt spoke of all this, as if necessary fratricide was no less difficult to arrange than any other business transaction. *Truly, she doesn't fear the judgment of either men or gods.* Shae's stir of unbidden admiration tasted acidic in her throat. Ayt was a stronger woman than she.

Shae glanced in the direction of the penitents, who still sat unmoving, their auras unperturbed by the content of the conversation they might be exposing to Heaven itself. *Is anyone listening?* Perhaps, Shae thought with sudden heaviness, the penitents meditated in vain. Jade-enhanced senses and the power of Perception endowed Green Bones with so much more nuance and clarity about the world around them, but it didn't, in the end, offer up any great truth, any proof of the gods or hope that people could ever be anything more than what they were. Was Old Uncle Jenshu paying attention now? Did he grieve what had become of the legacy of honorable warriors? The Return couldn't be further away than Green Bones plotting murder in the sanctum of the temple.

Ayt had seen clearly Shae's ambition and resentment, had seized upon her rivalry with Hilo as an opening. Shae understood what that said about her: if the way to redemption was through the Divine Virtues, she was no closer to Heaven than the woman next to her. She turned to Ayt now. "You say you see your younger self in me," she said. "I see in you the kind of Green Bone I don't want to become. Jade meant something once. I'm not an oath breaker. I won't betray the memory of a slain brother, and sell the life of another for power." She stood up, wondering as she did so if she'd just sealed her own death. "I want no part of the Kekon you envision."

Ayt remained sitting for a few seconds. Then she rose to her feet and faced the younger woman. Her expression was unchanged, but her aura swelled with unmistakably ominous intent and despite herself, Shae took an involuntary step back.

"I despise it when my hand is forced," the Pillar said, adjusting one of the coils of jade on her arm. "Ayt Yugontin brought me, a girl that should have died, out of a war orphanage and trained me to be the strongest Green Bone in the Mountain clan. Yet when he grew old, he couldn't bring himself to name me his heir. He feared a backlash from the inner circle of men in the clan who would fault him for naming a woman his successor. The Spear of Kekon, who was never afraid to die fighting the Shotarians—he was afraid to name an adopted daughter to rule his precious clan.

"The man I call my father, the one to whom I owe everything—*he* forced my hand. Before his body was cold, I had to kill his closest comrades—Green Bones I valued and respected—for the position that should have been mine without question. With his dying breath my father could have prevented bloodshed, but he didn't. Such is the cowardice and short-sightedness of even the most well-meaning of men."

The expression of disappointment on Ayt's face held a frightening calm as she said to Shae, "I've offered you an opportunity which you've spurned. Don't worry, you naive and idealistic girl, I won't kill you now. I want you to remember, when you see your brother's jade torn from his mangled body, when your clan lies in ashes, that you could have prevented it but didn't. *You forced my hand.* You'll remember."

Ayt turned and swept from the sanctum, the wake of her passing stirring the holy room like a hot wind carrying the promise of drought and punishing devastation. Then she was gone, and the temple was once again harmonious. The penitents sitting in the circle had not stirred. Alone now, the strain broke through Shae's control. Her heart began racing and sweat beaded on her face. She sank back down onto the cushion.

Heaven help us. My clan, all Green Bones, all of Kekon.

• Chapter Forty-Eight •
READING THE CLOUDS

Hilo was furious at his sister. He stormed into the main Kaul house and found her at the table in Lan's study with Woon. Unlike him, she seemed to enjoy retreating in here, though he'd never seen her sit in Lan's chair; he would've forbidden her from using the room if she'd done that.

Both Shae and Woon were waiting for him silently when he barged through the doors; it would've been hard not to Perceive his approach. He swept an arm across the table, scattering papers everywhere, involuntarily Deflecting Lan's empty chair into the back wall and books off the bookshelves. Hilo placed both hands on the table and leaned over his Weather Man.

"Doru escaped," he said.

Shae paled, understanding the disastrous import at once. The traitor would flee straight to the Mountain, taking with him everything there was to know about No Peak's business secrets, not to mention knowledge of the Kaul estate and its defenses.

"You made me keep him alive, you convinced me he wouldn't be a threat. I shouldn't have listened to you. I should've killed that snake!" Hilo's face was flushed, his eyes bulging. His hands clenched and unclenched as if desperate to wrap themselves around Doru's absent throat.

Woon pushed his chair back from the Pillar nervously but Shae merely stared at her angry brother in astonishment. "How did he do it?" she asked.

"Om's knocked out with a broken jaw and Nune is dead; the old bastard snapped his neck. They were just kids, those Fingers! New enough to jade that they could go without it. How that withered scarecrow Doru could've—" Sudden realization swept across Hilo's features. A muscle in his cheek twitched. "Grandda." He whirled and strode back out of the study, nearly dizzy with fury. *"Grandda!"*

Shae leapt to follow him. He ignored her as he prowled up the staircase and flung open the door to their grandfather's room. Kaul Sen sneered at him from his chair by the window, a look of smug vindictiveness painted on his wrinkled face. His eyes, so often weary and vacant these days, danced bright and cruel. "Don't you know how to knock, boy?" he demanded in a raspy bark.

"*You.*" Hilo eyes moved up and down, scanning the old man in disbelief. "You gave Doru jade. You *gave* him *your* jade."

"And why shouldn't I?" Kaul Sen shouted. "You're taking it all away from me anyways, you impudent wretch! You think I don't notice? *This* is all I have left." The patriarch pushed his blanket to the floor and flung open his robe to reveal the sagging pale flesh of his torso over a belt now liberated of most of its stones. It looked like an antique item, the belt, weathered and empty, something that belonged in a thrift shop. "It's *my* jade. I'll give it away if I want, to whomever I want!"

Hilo was at a loss for words. He'd made sure there was no jade in Doru's house and that neither of the guards had any on them that might be stolen. The former Weather Man might have betrayed the younger Kauls, but he wouldn't *take* jade from the Torch any more than he would slit his only friend's throat. The idea that Kaul Sen would *give away* his jade had never even crossed Hilo's mind. "You've lost your senses," he said. "You've no idea what you've done."

"I set Doru free," said his grandfather with a vicious smile. "*He* doesn't have to stay trapped here, putting up with such humiliation. The way you treated him! The best Weather Man there ever was, a hero of the country! And you stripped him of his jade and locked him up like an animal, just like you're doing to me. *Disgusting.*"

Hilo took several trembling steps toward the old man in the chair, too enraged to even give voice to all his patricidal thoughts. Shae went defensively to Kaul Sen's side, her aura churning with agitation. She shot her brother a warning look. "*Hilo.*"

Hilo stopped a few feet away, the knuckles of his fists white. His voice, when he spoke, was a whisper of loathing. "No one in this family could be Pillar after you, could they Grandda? Not Lan; certainly not me. No one but the great Torch of Kekon. You dragged at and questioned Lan's every step, and you'd laugh to see Ayt Yu's daughter claim the jade off my body. Stay in this room then, until you *die*."

He spun and left, slamming the door behind him. He came across Woon standing at the bottom of the stairs, and forgetting, in his aggravation, that Woon was no longer Pillarman he said, "Call Dr. Truw. I want that man sedated and the rest of his jade locked up. When Om's awake, tell him he's to guard Grandda's room from now on. No phone calls or messages—if Doru tries to contact him, I want to know."

On the front steps of the house, Hilo sat down and lit one of his remaining Espenian brand cigarettes. They were getting hard to find. The upsurge in crime and violence was disrupting the flow of imported goods. Business was bad overall.

Why had he been so stupid? So soft-hearted? And Shae, always standing up for the old fiend. Dr. Truw had told them that Kaul Sen was sliding into dementia as his jade tolerance waned, that he was no longer cognizant of all his actions, but Hilo thought his grandfather's spiteful personality was simply more transparent now.

He draped his arms over his knees and felt weariness slowly crawl over the lingering anger. It had been a bad couple of weeks since he'd made his stand in Wisdom Hall, since No Peak had declared peace to be impossible and committed the city to war. There had been some visible victories: the release of the KJA audit results had reflected badly on Ayt, and with Chancellor Son leading the charge in publicly condemning the Mountain and wielding his influence, No Peak's most important Lantern Men were maintaining their allegiance, waiting to see what happened next.

What was happening was that Gont was winning the street war. The Mountan had apparently decided that there was no point holding back now. It didn't matter if No Peak held political or public sympathy if all its soldiers were dead. Even with his own network of spies, Hilo had underestimated both Gont's genius for urban warfare and the extent to which the Mountain had dug into No Peak territory by cultivating street gangs and mercenary agents that rose up to attack the clan within its own districts.

Shae came out of the house and stood behind him. "I'll find Doru." Her words were stiff. "You're right. It was my mistake. I spared his life, and it'll be my responsibility to correct that."

"He's long gone," said Hilo, "And he won't be easy to get to again."

"I'll get to him," she promised.

Let her try. He would set Tar to the task, and wagered his man would get it done first. "It'll be too late in any case," he said without turning. He couldn't muster the energy to maintain his anger at her. "We have to assume everything Doru knows, the Mountain now knows. They'll know which of our businesses are most valuable, which ones are weak, how much money and jade we have, how long we can hold out in the war." He ground out his cigarette.

"Then they'll soon know it's not long."

He looked over his shoulder at her, then turned back around. "So it's bad."

Shae said, "Tourism is down over fifty percent and that's hurting us far more than it's hurting the Mountain. Some of their strongest sectors, like retail, are actually doing better in the war—people are stocking up on supplies, and they're motivated to buy things now instead of waiting, in case a business isn't there tomorrow."

Woon, who'd joined Shae by the door, added, "With the KJA suspended, mining and jade exports have stopped, so we have no income coming in there."

The Mountain would be feeling the loss too, but they'd been hoarding jade and would have greater reserves. Shae said, "We're trading jade in the street war, but if they keep taking more from us than we're taking from them, we'll deplete our supply. We still need to make Fingers out of the Academy's graduating class in two months."

"What about the minor clans?" Hilo asked. "Can we get anything from them?"

Shae said, "The Short Tent clan and Six Hands Unity have lined up behind the Mountain, no surprises there. Stone Cup has sided with us—they hardly have a choice, given their dependence on the construction trade. The Jo Sun clan and Black Tail clan have made noises of support, for all the good that'll do us. Lip service is appreciated but you can't wring much juice from a grape." There were roughly a dozen smaller clans on Kekon; some held sway in certain towns elsewhere on the island or were entrenched in specific industries, some were independent and some were tributaries of the major clans, but none were even a sixth the size of either the Mountain or No Peak. "The rest are acting like Haedo Shield and staying clear, no doubt waiting to send bouquets of dancing star lilies to whoever prevails," Shae added.

Hilo stood up reluctantly and said, "Talk in the house." They went inside and though it still wasn't his favorite room, he went into Lan's study because it was private. Shae and Woon came in after him. The books and papers he'd scattered were still strewn all over the floor. Hilo stepped over them and fell into one of the armchairs, motioning for Woon to shut the door behind him. "Tell me how long can we last."

Shae said, "At this rate, we'll be in the red in six months. That's even if our Lantern Men stay with us, which they've done so far. It could be a lot less than that. It doesn't matter what Son Tomarho says, and it doesn't matter if people think Ayt is a crook. Once they sense we're bound to lose, they'll blame No Peak for dragging out the suffering of the city. They'll start reneging on tributes and looking to the victors."

"And the Mountain? How long can they stay at war?"

"We don't know, but longer than us," Woon said. "If they're producing shine in Ygutan like they say, that's an entirely separate and lucrative income stream."

"It's worse than that," Shae said. "They're smuggling jade to the Ygutanian government through secret contracts. That's how they're using some of the supply they've spirited away from the mines—to get in bed with foreigners on the other side. Between that and the shine factories, my guess is their coffers are just fine."

Hilo raised a puzzled expression to Shae. "How do you know the Mountain has secret contracts to sell jade to Ygutan? Is this for sure?"

Shae sat down in the chair opposite him and crossed her legs, lacing her fingers over one knee. "The Weather Man reads the clouds," she said. It was an old saying, meaning it was the Weather Man's job to know things, to cultivate secret sources of information in order to stay one step ahead of everyone else. A smile crept to Hilo's face upon hearing his younger sister cite such a hidebound clan adage reminding him that a good Pillar did not question his Weather Man's methods or sources too closely. *Like a duck to water.* Just as he'd always suspected.

Shae did not return his smile. "We need two things, and we need them *soon*, Hilo. We need money. And we need to turn around the street war. If

I can get us the first, and you and Kehn can get us the second, we might survive the year." She gaze dropped for a second, then rose again. "We also need to plan for what happens if we don't."

She was right to bring it up, but Hilo slouched further down in the chair, leaning his head back and closing his eyes. "Not now, Shae. We're not there yet."

"We may be soon," she said.

"I said not now," Hilo repeated. "Leave me alone for a while."

After a long moment, he heard his sister rise. She and Woon collected the spilled papers from around the room, then exited wordlessly. The door clicked shut behind them. Hilo remained motionless with his eyes closed.

He considered, with a dispassionate calm that was quite unlike him, the possibility that he was outmatched. If he failed and was killed—they were the same thing, as one would lead to the other—No Peak would likely perish with him. He would be the last Pillar of his clan.

If there had been a more fitting leader upon Lan's death, he would've stepped aside—kept the position of Horn for which he was better suited and done his best to win the war in that way. But there had never been any choice. Shae could not be the Pillar. Certainly she was smart and carried her jade well, but the clan would not accept it. She was the youngest, a woman, and she was no Ayt Mada, who had been the eldest and still came to power only by slaughtering all potential rivals. Shae would not do that, nor did she have the necessary common touch, a force of character or charisma that would compel other Green Bones, the powerful Fists in particular, to gladly offer their lives to continue fighting the war under her command if Hilo were dead. No, Hilo thought despondently, his sister was a study in aloof and self-sufficient competence, an able business leader but not a Green Bone Pillar. She would want the position even less than he did.

There were no other heirs to the clan leadership. Anden was a Kaul by adoption, but he was too young, not even jaded yet, and of mixed blood. Ayt would probably have him executed nevertheless, to be on the safe side. The Maik brothers were the sons of a disgraced Mountain Fist—they'd never be accepted as the head family of No Peak, if there was a No Peak clan to be head of by that point. Kaul Sen had had an older sister, and Hilo's mother had two younger siblings of little note, so there were some second- and third-removed family cousins scattered throughout the clan, none of them with the name or upbringing of a Kaul, none prominent or accomplished enough to lead.

Hilo was accustomed to the idea of death, but contemplating the extinction of his family, of his entire bloodline and the clan it had built, shook him deeply. He thought about how he might join Lan in death knowing he'd left unfulfilled the vengeance he'd sworn, and despaired that he hadn't had enough time to marry Wen and give her any children. He thought about these things, wallowed deeply in the pain of them for a short spell, then slowly turned his mind back to the present.

He wasn't dead yet. A man could be shot or stabbed, he could be fatally wounded, spurting his life out upon the ground, and still have a few precious minutes to bring down his enemy. Hilo had seen it before. Adversarial, opportunistic cunning was a Horn's strength, and Hilo was a natural Horn. Anything could happen in a battle. The right person with the right opening and the right weapon—that meant everything.

Now, he thought after some time, *I can plan for death.*

Chapter Forty-Nine

OVERTURE TO ADAMONT CAPITA

The ferry crossing was located in a part of The Docks now under Mountain control. Gont's Fists and Fingers patrolled the area, on the lookout not only for any counterattack by No Peak, but for thieves and smugglers who might take advantage of the change in territorial oversight to step up their activities. When Maik Wen walked up to the gangplank of the ferry, one of Gont's Fingers stopped her and asked to see her ticket. "You're going to Euman, miss?"

"Yes, jen," Wen said. "My grandmother was born in Shosone." A small fishing village on the western coast of Euman Island, now a tourist town catering to both Kekonese vacationers and Espenian servicemen. "She wanted to be returned and laid to rest there." Wen dropped her eyes sadly to the blue funeral urn cradled in her arms. She was dressed in a simple white sweater and a long white woolen skirt and her face was brushed with white powder. Her heart was beating slightly faster than usual, but surely it was normal for anyone stopped by an unfamiliar Green Bone from a recently conquering clan to be a little nervous, even if they had nothing to hide. This young man with the jade studs in his ears wouldn't Perceive anything out of the ordinary.

"Let the gods recognize her." Looking deeply embarrassed, he handed her ticket back and said, "I'm afraid I must ask you to open the top of the urn."

Wen sucked in a breath of indignation. "*Jen*," she protested.

"There're many criminals these days," the Finger said apologetically. "We have to check everyone's bags as they board, for weapons and contraband."

And jade. Euman had many miles of unguarded coastline and most intelligent smugglers would rather risk being caught by the Espenians than by Green Bones. Jade scavenged in a clan war and ferried out of Janloon by boat could find its way to the Tun mainland or the Uwiwa islands. Wen cast a look of deeply convincing insult at the Mountain Finger, but let her gaze drop quickly. She lifted the glazed lid of the vessel and allowed the man to peer inside.

If he touched the urn or took it from her to examine it, all was lost. They would not kill her, not right away. The Mountain would find out who she was and use her against Hilo. Wen thought, *I'll hurl myself over the edge of the gangway into the harbor.* Both she and the urn would sink to the bottom.

The young man said, "Go ahead, miss. Forgive my disrespect to you and your grandmother." He stepped aside to let her board the ferry. Wen replaced the lid of the funeral urn and walked up the gangway onto the deck of the ferry. Her face, resettled in an expectedly solemn expression of filial mourning, betrayed none of her relief, just as her body exuded no jade aura. She saw the Mountain Finger tug his right earlobe as she passed, but it was to ward off any spiritual ill will he might have accrued from examining the remains of the deceased, and not because he knew was a stone-eye. Wen held the urn closer to her chest. She no longer cared how heavy a stigma of bad luck she carried, not if it shielded her and served a purpose. Her deficiency was like a misshapen object, undesirable and unattractive in isolation, that made perfect sense when set in the right place.

The other people on the boat—commuters, day trippers, tourists—kept a considerate distance as she took up a seat near the bow. The ferry whistle blew shrilly and the vessel pulled away from the dock. With satisfaction Wen watched the waterfront recede. She could've chartered a private boat instead of risking this ferry crossing, but then there would be a record with the Maik name on it, one that might be examined if she was stopped and searched by a coast guard patrol. This was more anonymous, the personal risk worth the potential gain.

When Wen disembarked at the small harbor on Euman Island an hour and a half later, there was a car waiting for her. Shae had arranged it for her ahead of time. Euman Island, like Little Button, was not part of Janloon proper, but while Little Button was a minor independent municipality,

Euman was essentially run by the Espenians. As soon as the car began driving through the small town streets, Wen saw shops with signs written in two languages, currency exchange booths displaying the current conversion rates between Kekonese dien and Espenian thalirs, shiny foreign chain stores and restaurants, and most conspicuously of all, Espenians on the streets, in and out of uniform.

Wen felt as if she'd arrived in another country, someplace that was a hybrid of Kekon and what she imagined Espenia would be like. Of course, one often saw foreigners on the streets of Janloon, but nowhere near as many as there were here. Euman Island held twenty-five thousand Espenian military personnel, a fact that most Kekonese seemed content to ignore so long as they remained ensconced on this rocky and wind-blasted volcanic stump of land. The clans did not control this place, but so close to Janloon, they were far from without influence. The driver of the plain grey sedan that picked Wen up opened the door for her respectfully and did not ask any questions during the drive.

Wen rehearsed what she would say when she arrived. She had not, to her great regret now, learned much Espenian prior to this, and as the car drove past airfields and vistas dotted with silos and wind turbines, she spent the quiet minutes rolling the unfamiliar sounds around in her mouth, repeating what Shae had instructed her to say.

"Sir, what is your name?" Wen asked the driver.

The driver glanced over his shoulder at her. "Me? My name is Sedu." Mr. Sedu was a ruddy man with a short beard and callused fingers. Wen never forgot a name or face and she filed Sedu away in her memory. According to Shae, the man was the son-in-law of a Luckbringer who worked directly under Hami Tumashon and could be counted on to stay quiet. "What do you do, Mr. Sedu?" Wen asked, giving him a smile warm with true curiosity.

"I'm an electrician," said the man.

"Is that a good business to be in?"

"Ah, pretty good," Mr. Sedu said, relaxing somewhat. Wen suspected that when he'd been told to pick up a representative of the clan at the ferry dock and speak of the task to no one, Sedu had imagined he would be driving an intimidatingly high rank Green Bone such as Hilo or one of Wen's brothers.

"Do you do a lot of work for the Espenians?"

"Yes, a lot," Mr. Sedu said. "They have many facilities here and are always needing work done. I have three apprentices now and I am looking to bring on a fourth. The Espenians pay well, always on time and in thalirs."

"You must be very busy. I appreciate you troubling to drive me."

Mr. Sedu made a dismissive motion, any remaining tension leaving his shoulders. "It's no trouble. One should always provide a favor when possible. Different foreigners come and go, but the clans will always be here."

Wen smiled. "Do you speak Espenian well, Mr. Sedu?"

"Enough to get by. Not as well as my daughter. She wants to go study in Espenia, but I wouldn't trust her to live alone in that country. Espenian men, they do whatever they want, and there are no repercussions."

"Will you practice a little Espenian with me now, as we drive?"

An hour later, Mr. Sedu's car pulled up to a gate set in a tall chain link metal fence topped with security cameras and signed with large, red anti-trespassing notices. Behind the gate was a sprawling cluster of low, grey-green buildings. The flag of the Republic of Espenia whipped loudly in the island's stiff breeze. Mr. Sedu stopped the car before they reached the guard box.

Wen got out and walked the rest of the way, holding the blue cremation urn in front of her and breathing slowly to keep calm. Euman's relentless wind tugged at her clothes and at the stern knot in which she'd imprisoned her hair. She'd been less afraid when she'd faced the Finger back at the ferry dock. From here on in, her success depended entirely on the accurate judgment of Kaul Shae. And while she did not doubt the Weather Man's intelligence, Wen did not fully trust the Weather Man herself. Hilo's sister had turned her back on the family and left Kekon before. What was to stop her from doing so again?

Wen had come too far now and had no choice but to put her faith in the other woman. The ongoing clan war was already courting the risk of Espenian involvement; this was No Peak's chance to make a move before the Mountain did. "The Espenians aren't afraid to fight," Shae had said, "but if there's one thing I know about them, it's that they believe anything they want can be purchased."

A guard with a pistol holstered at his waist came out of the box as Wen approached. He began to ask her a question, but Wen stated firmly, "Colonel

Deiller. Please, I speak with Colonel Deiller. I come from Kaul Shaelinsan of the No Peak clan with a message for Colonel Deiller of Espenia."

Colonel Leland Deiller, the commanding officer of the Republic of Espenia Seaborne Infantry at Euman Naval Base, was enjoying a rare moment of quiet at his desk after a morning spent on the phone. In the nearly four years he'd been in this post, he'd never before seen so much attention trained on the island of Kekon. His superiors in Adamont Capita were focused on containing and deterring the growing threat from Ygutan, so as long as Kekonese jade regularly made its way over the ocean, the top brass was satisfied. That was no longer the case, and Deiller was suddenly getting concerned calls from top generals and even the Secretary of the War Department.

There was a knock at his door. His executive officer, Lt. Colonel Yancey, thrust his angular face into the office. "Sir, I think you need to come see this."

Yancey filled him in as they walked. "A woman showed up an hour ago. She asked for you by name. Claims she's an emissary of Kaul Shaelinsan."

That was a name Deiller had not heard for some time. "Kaul as in the Janloon clan family," he said. "This woman was sent by the granddaughter?"

"That what she says."

"I thought Kaul Shaelinsan left the country and emigrated to Espenia."

"Apparently she's returned." Yancey stopped outside the door of a small meeting room. "You want me to pull everything we have on her?"

"Do that," said Deiller. They entered. The woman sitting in the chair was dressed in Kekonese mourning attire and held a stone cremation urn on her lap.

The colonel glanced at his XO questioningly, then back at the unexpected visitor. "I'm Colonel Deiller, the commanding officer here."

"My name, Maik Wenruxian," said the woman, in broken but understandable Espenian. "Kaul Shaelinsan of the No Peak clan sends regards."

Deiller said to Yancey, "Can we get a translator in here?" He turned back to the woman. She would've been checked for any weapons and gone through the metal detector to get in here, but nevertheless, his eyes fell suspiciously on the urn she was carrying. "And what exactly do you mean by that, Miss Maik?"

The woman stood up and removed the lid of the ceramic vessel. To the colonel's utmost surprise, she tipped the contents onto the table. A stream of gray and white ash poured from the mouth of the container. "What in the—" Deiller exclaimed, and then he stared as chunks of green rock tumbled from the urn. They clinked together, landing in a dusty pile on the mound of powder that had concealed them. The woman emptied out the last stones, then set down the urn and gave a small, smug smile at their flabbergasted expressions. "Jade."

Yancey whistled. "Must be worth a goddamn fortune."

"Call Gavison in here. Tell me if those rocks are real Kekonese jade."

The translator, Mr. Yut arrived. His eyes nearly bugged out of his head at the sight of the jade on the table. Deiller said to the woman, "Explain why you have so much jade and how you got it here." Mr. Yut translated his question.

"As the Kekon Jade Alliance is under investigation for financial irregularities, all mining and export operations have been suspended, including official jade sales to the Republic of Espenia. We appreciate that this is inconvenient." The woman paused to let the translator catch up, then gestured toward the gemstones spilled on the table. "The No Peak clan has its own stores of jade and the Weather Man would like to discuss establishing a confidential arrangement that would ease this sudden disruption to the supply."

Deiller's eyebrows rose. Disruption was right; ever since clan warfare had erupted in the country's largest city, the military analysts in A.C. had become increasingly concerned that whichever clan prevailed might assume near absolute political power. That could mean existing contracts with the Republic of Espenia being reneged upon or unfavorably renegotiated. Kekon was vital to the ROE's military and political strength in the region: it hosted several Espenian military bases, was a rapidly growing and modernizing economy with historical hatred of Shotar and Tun, and most importantly, it possessed the only supply of bioenergetic jade on Earth. Deiller had already been on several calls with his superiors to discuss the potential for military action to secure the mines on Kekon if things went further south.

"Can you prove you're a representative of the clan?" Deiller asked.

The woman's watchful gaze and the white powder on her face made her seem even more coy and aloof than the usual Kekonese female. She inclined her head and said, "Kaul Shae asked me to tell you that the cormorant can still fish."

At that moment, Dr. Gavison came into the room. He pulled on lead-lined gloves and used metal tongs to pick up one of the green rocks and examine it under a small loupe. He did this with several stones. "Bioenergetic mineral structure all right," he declared. "Raw Kekonese jade."

"Miss Maik," said Colonel Deiller. "If you'll please wait here."

The woman nodded and sat back down. "I wait."

Seated in his office behind closed doors, Deiller asked, "How did she transport that much unsecured jade? She's not one of the aborigines."

"She must be nonreactive," Dr. Gavison said. "It's a naturally occurring but uncommon genetic trait. The Kekonese call them stone-eyes."

Yancey handed a file folder to the colonel. "I pulled what we have on Kaul Shaelinsan. She graduated from Belforte Business School in Windtown last spring. Not only is she back in Janloon, she became second in command of the clan when her eldest brother was assassinated a couple of months ago."

Deiller flipped through the pages in the file. There were records and photos of Kaul Shaelinsan from five years ago. As a local informant to the ROE, she'd done a few impressive and useful things for the Espenian military, provided information that would've been difficult or impossible to garner otherwise. Deiller had crossed paths with her only once, but he recalled her as an alarming individual, a young woman wearing more jade than a whole Navy special ops team. It had made him wonder if the ROE couldn't recruit more of these killers to their side.

"Sir, did you notice her code name? Cormorant.'"

"The cormorant can still fish." Deiller said, repeating the emissary's words. He recalled now that Kaul's work for them had caused some commotion at the time; orders had come swiftly from diplomatic higher-ups to terminate her status as a human intelligence asset. That wasn't to say ties couldn't be renewed if circumstances had changed. "What of this Maik woman? Do we know anything about her?"

"Nothing," said Yancey. "Except that she has the same family name as two of the top clan members. The Maik brothers are considered the closest advisors and strongmen of the second Kaul son, who's now the leader of the clan. If she's telling the truth, she's probably a sister or a cousin."

"She's got to be high up in a Janloon clan to have access to that kind of jade," said Gavison. "That's not stuff that gets smuggled by criminals—that's high quality, near flawless, bioenergetic Kekonese jade, one of the most valuable substances in the world. The amount she poured out of that urn is probably worth a couple hundred million dien, twenty or thirty million Espenian."

"How much jade are we losing out on every month with this government suspension?" Yancey wondered. "What's the long-term risk to the supply?"

Deiller frowned and turned to his executive officer. "Make sure Miss Maik is comfortable and that jade is secured. I don't want this getting out, so have a talk with Mr. Yut as well. I need to make a call to General Saker in A.C."

• Chapter Fifty •
THE GREEN BROTHERHOOD

The severed head of Lott Penshugon was delivered to the Kaul estate in a vegetable crate. Hilo's howls of rage rang through the courtyard.
No one, not even Shae, dared to try and comfort him. It was the third of
his Fists who'd been ambushed, murdered and beheaded in the past three
weeks. Lott Pen had not been a pleasant man in life, but Hilo counted him
as one of the clan's most tireless and fearsome lieutenants, a man who, with
the right word of encouragement, would do anything Hilo asked of him
without question.

The loss of each good Fist—Lott, Niku and Trin most recently, but
also Goun, Obu, Mitto, Asei, Ronu, and Satto—felt to Hilo like a personal
wound delivered by Gont Asch directly. The methodical bastard was bleeding out No Peak, killing each of Hilo's men before he came to Hilo himself.

It was some hours before Lott's jade-stripped, bullet- and blade-torn
body was recovered and reunited with his head. It was Kehn Maik's job to
go in person to pay respect and funerary money to Lott's family, but this
was one responsibility of the Horn that Hilo refused to relinquish. When
the two of them arrived, Lott's wife fell upon the ground with noisy sobs.
To be honest, Hilo was not entirely sure if the weeping wasn't as much
relief as grief—he didn't imagine Lott would've been an easy man to live
with. Kehn pressed the white envelope into her hand, assuring her that her
husband had given his blood to the clan, and the clan would always see to
the family's needs. She need not fear her children ever going hungry or
homeless.

Hilo saw four children: a toddler, a six-year-old boy, a girl of about
ten, and Lott's teenage son—Anden's classmate from the Academy, standing
blank-faced with his younger siblings huddled around him, still in Academy

uniform from having rushed home upon news of his father's death. Hilo knelt in front of the small children.

"Do you know who I am?" he asked them.

The girl said, "You're the Pillar."

"That's right," Hilo said. "I'm here to tell you that your father's dead. He died because he swore an oath to me, to defend the clan against its enemies. That's often the way of our kind, to die in this way. I lost my father before I could walk, and I lost my older brother only a few months ago. It's okay to feel sad or angry, but you should feel proud as well. When you're older, when you've earned your own jade, you can say, 'I'm a son or daughter of Lott Penshugon' and other Green Bones will salute you with respect, because of today."

Then he stood and spoke to Lott's son. "Are Trials over at the Academy?"

The young man roused his attention to Hilo slowly, as if emerging from a waking stupor. "Yes," he said at last. "They finished yesterday."

Hilo nodded. The graduation ceremony wouldn't occur until after New Year's Festival week, once final ranks had been determined and graduates had declared which oaths they intended to take, but excepting ceremony, the boy was a man now, the head of this Green Bone family. "I'm sorry you won't be celebrating the end of Trials, or the New Year." Hilo's voice held an undercurrent of sympathy, but it had the rough tone he would take with any of his own men under formal circumstances. "A representative of the clan will be here soon, to help arrange your father's funeral. If there's anything you need from us, Lott-jen, anything at all, you call the Horn directly, and if you can't reach him, you call the house and leave a message for me."

The young man's face moved in a brief contortion. He hadn't missed the way Hilo had addressed him as a fellow Green Bone and a member of the clan. He glanced over at his collapsed mother and down at the small siblings huddled around him. Hilo watched the youth's eyes, which had been full of scorn and resentment during their first encounter, slowly clear of their stunned confusion and resolve into dark acceptance, into blackness of purpose.

"Thank you for your generosity, Kaul-jen," he said, speaking like a man, and he raised clasped hands to his head, bending deeply in salute.

As they left the house, Hilo said to Kehn, "That young man is our brother now. We have to take care of him and bring him up right in the clan, like his father would've wanted. Start thinking about how best to do it. Maybe put him under Vuay—he's a good mentor."

Hilo's specific beliefs about what was required in a leader of Green Bones could be traced to a day some thirteen years ago, when the Maik brothers had been ambushed and set upon by a pack of six Academy boys and Kehn had had his cheek badly broken.

Hilo had not taken any special notice of the Maiks before then. Even though he and Tar were year-four classmates, they were not friends. The Maik brothers had few, if any, friends. They stuck together a great deal, as everyone was aware that they came from a shameful family. One day, a snide remark caused Tar to attack and beat another boy, and even though he was punished by the instructors, the boy's friends, Hilo included, took it upon themselves to wait until they had a chance to catch the Maiks off Academy grounds.

The brothers put up a ferocious defense. Hilo hung back; the boy being avenged, Uto, would later become one of his Fists but was not at the time a close friend of his, so Hilo felt it was rightfully the place of others to take the greater share of the feud. After a while though, he felt the Maiks had been through enough. The fight continued only because Tar had not suffered much. Kehn, two years older and larger, had taken the brunt of the attack and delivered impressive damage in return.

Kehn's refusal to yield cost him; he was finally struck so hard that he fell moaning to his knees with his hands over his damaged face. Tar's eyes clouded over with rage and he pulled a talon knife from seemingly nowhere. This caused all the boys to stop. Up until now, unspoken rules had been followed—only fists and feet were involved and there'd been no pinning or beating on the ground. The appearance of a knife signaled that the fight had turned potentially deadly, and it put all of them at risk for expulsion from the Academy. A ripple of uncertain menace went through the group.

Hilo did not like how things were going, so he called out, "We're done."

At that time, he held sway with the group, but not so much that they obeyed him in the heat of a moment like this. "We're *not* done," Asei retorted. "We have to teach these two a lesson. They can't be trusted."

"Why do you say that?" Hilo asked curiously, for he admired the Maik brothers now after seeing how well they fought and how fiercely they defended each other. He envied the bond they had, and with a pang felt that it was something he lacked, not having a brother of a similar age. Lan had graduated from the Academy the year after Hilo entered.

"Everyone knows it about them," Asei insisted.

"I'm not done, either," Tar snarled. Behind the upraised talon knife, his eyes were as wild as an animal's. Hilo suspected he did not care if he was expelled for murder.

"If we're here on account of Uto, then we're done," Hilo said, still speaking to Asei. "If you've got some other grief with the Maiks, you should've said so earlier. I don't know of any myself, does anyone else?"

"That's easy for you to say," retorted another boy, who was cupping a hand to his bleeding nose. "I didn't see you doing much of the fighting, Kaul; the rest of us did it for you and *we've* still got grief all right." A moment passed before anyone seemed to realize that the boy, Yew, had said something wrong. A dangerous light had come into Hilo's eyes.

"All right," he said at last, and though his voice had gone quiet, he was easily heard in the alleyway's sudden silence. "I can't argue with Yew; I shouldn't suggest what we ought to do if I haven't suffered as much as the rest of you. And it's also not fair that Kehn and Tar should have to keep fighting two against six when they've already been punished and can't help that their family is hated by everyone.

"I'll fight the Maiks; if the two of them can beat me, that'll settle the matter for both Tar and Yew here." Hilo shrugged out of his jacket and handed it to Yew. "No one else jumps in, or I'll have words with you myself, another day." Everyone looked skeptical, though also undisguisedly eager; this was a good matchup. The Maiks were fearsome and Kehn was large, but they were both tired and injured. Hilo was fresh, and he was a Kaul—no one who wanted to stay in the good graces of that family would dare to really hurt him, but the Maiks had no reputation to lose.

Hilo looked at Kehn's battered face and Tar's maddened one. "Put away the talon knife," he said, as simply as if he were asking Tar to close a window. "I'll give you three blows to even things up. I won't answer the first three. After that, I will."

The Maiks did not argue. The first three blows—two of Kehn's huge fists to the stomach and a third to the face—nearly knocked Hilo unconscious. He climbed to his feet, wheezing through tears of pain, and began to fight back. At first, the circle of onlookers cheered and jeered, but they quickly fell silent. The trio of fighters were having a difficult time—all three were soon staggering exhausted as if drunk, and none of them bore real hatred for the other side—yet they kept battling on through a bullheaded, adolescent sense of perceived honor. In a matchup of jade powers, Hilo would've prevailed, but in a blunt physical contest he could not hope to win. The Maik brothers had fought together too many times, and Kehn was too strong.

In the end, seeing Tar gasping and barely able to stand, but readying to hit him in the mouth again, Hilo broke into a bloody grin. He bent over, coughing with laughter that rattled his bruised ribs, and Tar, after staring at him nonplussed for a second, began to laugh himself, until he fell against the brick wall. Kehn scowled. As half his face was frozen from his injury, he looked like a ghoul as he went, not first to his younger brother, but to Hilo, and offered him a hand to help him upright. The three of them left holding each other up, the other five boys shuffling bewildered a respectful distance behind them, and returned to the Academy, where Hilo and the Maiks were assigned to clean the Academy's toilets together every day for the next three months.

Looking back now, Hilo shook his head at the stupidity of fifteen-year-old boys, but after that, no one spoke badly of the Maiks to their faces, not unless they wished to challenge Kaul Hilo, which they did not.

With the death of Lott senior, Hilo was not optimistic about No Peak's chances of holding Sogen. Most of it was already lost and the violence was spilling into Old Town, which only a few weeks ago he would've counted as a No Peak stronghold.

He strategized gloomily with Kehn in the car as they drove to the Cong Lady, which had become one of the clan's primary meeting locations and was constantly occupied by the Horn's men. Hilo personally preferred the food in the Double Double, but there was fire damage to the kitchen and no point in repairing it during a street war when they might lose the property again. They arrived to receive another terrible shock. One of the Fingers rushed through the door and down the front steps as soon as they stepped out of the Duchesse. "It's Eiten," the young man gasped, his face a sickly hue. Trembling, he led them into the betting house and down the stairs.

The silent crowd of Fingers in the hallway parted, pressing against the walls as Hilo and Kehn came through. Eiten was lying, moaning, on a black leather sofa in the basement lounge. Both of his arms were missing, chopped off, the stumps at the shoulders cauterized. Someone had brought Dr. Truw. The portly Green Bone physician was bent over, hands on the man's chest, Channeling into him. Eiten wept, "No, stop, get off me," twisting his armless torso to try and shake the doctor off. As Hilo stared down, shaken at the sight, Dr. Truw stood and wiped his perspiring brow. "That should keep him alive until he gets to a hospital. An ambulance is on the way."

"Hilo-jen," Eiten sobbed, and Hilo crouched next to him. "Help me, please. He wouldn't give me a clean death, wouldn't even give me the respect he at least gave Lott and Satto. He sent me back alive to give you a message."

Hilo bent near Eiten's face. "What was Gont's message?"

Eiten's grey eyes burned with fury. He looked as if he'd spit if only he could sit up. "I don't want to say it, Hilo-jen. It's insulting, not even worth you hearing."

"That disgraceful piss drinker crippled you for this message," Hilo said. "Tell me what it is, Eiten. I promise on my brother's grave I'll take Gont's jade for you."

Still, the man hesitated, his bloodless face slick with sweat. "Gont says he'll give you until the end of New Year's Day to surrender yourself. If you do, he'll grant you a death of consequence, on your feet and with a blade, and let your family bury you with your jade. The rest of No Peak will be spared if they can choose allegiance to the Mountain or exile from Kekon." Eiten drew a difficult breath. "If you refuse, Gont promises to keep sending you the heads of your Fists, and he'll do worse to Anden and Shae-jen than what he's done to me. He means to burn the Torch's house to the ground and destroy the clan completely."

Eiten saw murder sweeping across the Pillar's eyes and he lifted his head in sudden urgency. "End my life, Hilo-jen, and take my jade for the clan.

I'm useless to you now. I'm a Green Bone, a Fist of No Peak. I can't live like this. *Please…*"

Kehn made an inarticulate noise of agreement behind the Pillar.

Hilo's fog of wrath cleared long enough for him to lean forward and place a hand on the man's brow. "No, Eiten. Right now, you're humiliated and in pain. You shouldn't make the decision to die in this state. All you're missing are your arms. There are good prosthetics these days; the Espenians make them. You still have a sharp mind, and your training, and your jade abilities. And a wife—you have a beautiful wife, and a baby growing in her belly. You shouldn't die if you can help it."

"She can't see me like this," Eiten sobbed. "I can't let her."

Hilo turned to Pano, the Finger who'd brought them in. "Go tell Eiten-jen's wife that he's been hurt. Make sure she stays at home, until he's ready to see her. Get her whatever she needs, comfort her that he'll be all right, but make her stay at home. Go now."

He turned back to Eiten as Pano rushed off to do as he asked. "You should live to see your child be born. And wouldn't you like to be alive when I tear the jade from Gont's body, on your behalf?" Uncertainty slackened Eiten's face. Hilo said, "A new year is around the corner, so I'll tell you what: give it one year, so you can see these good things coming to you. At the end of this next year, if you still want to die, come talk to me. I'll honor your wishes myself, without question. I'll see that you're buried with your jade and that your wife and child are taken care of."

Tears rolled from the corners of Eiten's eyes and pooled under his head on the black leather under the bright lights of the casino. "Do you promise, Hilo-jen?"

"On my brother's grave, just as I said."

Slowly, Eiten's breathing eased. His jade aura calmed, the shrill spikes of desperation and pain ceasing. When the ambulance arrived, Hilo stepped away to let Dr. Truw and the paramedics take the man away. Kehn went out to speak to the ambulance driver to make sure the Fist was taken straight to Janloon General in the Temple district and not any of the lesser hospitals. When Kehn returned, Hilo asked everyone else in the room and the hallway to leave. They did so in a solemn hush.

Hilo poured two shots of hoji from behind the bar, and put one of them

in front of Kehn. "Drink," he said, and downed his own glass. The liquor
burned his throat and warmed his stomach, settling his taut nerves. When
Kehn set his glass down, Hilo said, "Shame on you, Kehn. It was a good
thing I was here."

Kehn was taken aback. "What did I do?"

"You would've killed Eiten like he asked."

"It seemed the merciful thing to do. It was what he wanted."

"To make his wife a widow and for his child be fatherless? No, what he
wanted was his dignity. I promised him that. Now we don't have to bury another Fist. We've lost too many people as it is." He rested his forehead in his
hands for a moment. Nine of his best Fists slain, and one horribly maimed.
Dozens of his Fingers dead or crippled. Hilo looked up at Kehn. "I expect
you to honor my promise to Eiten if I'm not alive to do it. You need to tell
Juen about this, Vuay too, so one of them can honor it if *you're* not alive."

Kehn nodded, but he looked frustrated. It was unlike him; he was usually stalwart even in dire situations. It was Tar who would show his emotions,
who would vent on behalf of both of them. Now, however, Kehn's soldierly
composure was visibly fissured. He understood all too well how badly the
war was going and how that failure could in large part be laid at his feet.
The elder Maik's tired face was rigid with the baleful desperation that Hilo
remembered so well from that first memorable encounter when they were
both teenagers. "I wouldn't have thought of saying what you did to Eiten
just now," Kehn said in a gruff voice. "I can't do what you do, Hilo-jen."

"You have to learn to be the Horn. I'm giving you a hard time, I know.
If Lan were here, he'd be tearing into me for everything I'm doing wrong
as Pillar."

"But he's not here," Kehn said, and Hilo heard the resentment, realized
that Kehn saw the difficulty inherent in his position so long as every jade
warrior in the clan still looked to Hilo as the true Horn when he entered
the room. There was nothing to be done for it though, not with the stakes
so high. He had confidence that given autonomy and time to find his footing, Kehn would be more than capable as Horn, but Hilo was also grimly
aware that he couldn't afford to step away right now. A wartime Horn needed not only the respect but the love of his men, needed empathy in addition
to cunning and resolve. As No Peak's position became increasingly dire, it

became more and more important that the Green Bones saw him among them and kept faith.

"Soon I may not be here either," he said somberly.

Kehn's head jerked up, the frown on his face sharp. "You're not thinking of giving in to Gont's threats?" When Hilo didn't answer, alarm began forming on the Horn's face. "Like Eiten said, it's an insult, not worth listening to. Does Gont actually think you'd hand yourself over like a sheep to the butcher? We've killed many of theirs, and he's trying to scare our Fingers with what he did to Eiten."

"Maybe," said Hilo, but he didn't think Gont was so superficial. No, the man must be aware of the important fact that Shae had told Hilo and that Kehn did not yet know: based on respective clan resources, the Mountain would eventually win the war. But it would take time and be bloody and costly to both sides. The Mountain would be a weak and gutted victor by the end, perhaps unable to manage all its territories or maintain the support of its Lantern Men and the Royal Council. Smaller tributary clans might break away. The jade smuggling and SN1 manufacturing businesses Ayt had built would be at risk from takeover by criminals and foreigners.

"He's trying to force an end to this," Hilo muttered. Even if the Mountain was better financially girded for prolonged war, it had to be worried about losing the support of the people in its districts. Ordinary jadeless citizens need not fear being active targets of Green Bone violence, but sometimes there were collateral casualties, and property and economic damage were inevitable. Once the Academy graduates joined No Peak in the spring, the conflict would surge further, and the city would suffer more. On top of that, given public censure from the audit of the Kekon Jade Alliance and the pending passage of oversight legislation, the Mountain surely wanted to secure victory soon. Once it did, Chancellor Son would be out of power, and Ayt Mada could pressure the Royal Council to drop the issue.

Look at me, Hilo thought wryly. *Actually thinking about all the political bullshit.* Perhaps he *was* learning, gradually, to be a Pillar after all. Too little, too late, though. Politics moved slowly and blades moved fast.

"Gont won't intimidate us with crude savagery," Kehn insisted, pouring them both another shot of hoji. "Every Green Bone down to the lowest Finger would give his life for you, jen. Gont wants a quick victory? He won't get anything of the sort."

Hilo had never shied away from any fight, and he was willing to wage a long and brutal war if that was what was required to overcome his enemies. But if defeat was on the inevitable horizon, then he held no pointless desire for any more of his Fists or Fingers to lose their limbs or their jade. He would value a clean death for himself and his loved ones. It was, in truth, not so bad a trade Gont was offering him.

The idea of dying for the clan was not rhetoric to Hilo. The clan was an extension of family, in some ways more family to Hilo than his own kin. He had never known his father. His mother had loved Lan; his grandfather had loved Shae. Hilo had found his place in the world among peers—that was where his expressiveness and daring were valued. Now the clan was relying on him in a very real and personal way: Kehn and Tar, his other Fists like Juen and Vuay, poor Eiten and Satto and Lott who deserved their vengeance, all the way down to the Fingers like Pano and that kid, Hejo, who'd unflinchingly risked his life by going into the Factory at Hilo's command, and future clan members like Anden and Lott's son. He asked them all to offer up their lives for the brotherhood; he would never ask less of himself.

Hilo swirled his glass and drank, then took the bottle and put it behind the bar before Kehn could reach for any more. A Horn could never afford to have his wits addled. "Kehn," Hilo said, "if I die, you'll want to avenge me and take back my jade from Gont or whoever kills me. That's natural, but I don't want you to do that. I'd rather you took care of Wen. Make sure she has a good life, a good home. That's more important to me, even if you have to leave Kekon, even if you have to turn."

Kehn was aghast. "I would never swear oaths to the Mountain. *Never.*" And Hilo remembered it wasn't just loyalty to him that drove the Horn's vehemence, but the fact that the Mountain had executed Kehn and Tar's father and cast his family into disgrace. The Horn's voice shook as he said, "Why are you talking like this, Hilo-jen?"

Hilo said, "I just want my wishes to be clear." Then he walked to the door. "We need to talk to the guys upstairs, they're waiting for us. And then we'll drive to see Eiten's wife before we go to Sogen to sort out who will take Lott's place there."

• Third Interlude •
BAIJEN'S TRIUMPH

In Kekonese religious mythology, Old Uncle Jenshu, the One Who Returned, had a favorite nephew named Baijen, who remains the country's most well known and revered ancient hero. Stories of Baijen, the courageous Green Bone warrior, have been told to Kekonese children for hundreds of years, and more recently, comic books and films have recounted his adventures and deeds. Unlike his divine uncle Jenshu, however, Baijen remains a mortal champion and is not worshipped as a god.

According to legend, when Baijen was finally slain in furious battle against his greatest foe, the invading Tun General Sh'ak, he was recognized by the gods for his valor and accorded a place in Heaven. From his vantage point in the divine realm, Baijen looked down upon the Earth. He witnessed his remaining men fighting and dying in his name, and saw that his people were on the verge of being conquered. He watched, helpless, as his beloved grief-stricken wife prepared to throw herself from the cliff before the oncoming army could reach their mountainside home.

In a panic, Baijin begged the gods to allow him to return to earth for one night and give up his place in Heaven to another. At first, his request was refused, but Baijen was immovable in his pleas. He wailed and beat his head on the steps of the jade palace, refusing to be deterred until Yatto, the Father of All, taking pity on him, agreed.

The fallen warrior fell at the feet of the gods and wept in gratitude. That very night, he returned to earth, sweeping over the battlefields littered with bodies, and entered the tent of the Tun General. He burst in upon his shocked enemy and, laughing in triumph, killed him where he stood in his underclothes.

In accordance with the pact Baijen had made with the gods, the soul of

General Sh'ak flew to Heaven. Baijen, the savior of his people, was left to roam the earth as an exiled spirit for all eternity.

Green Bones have an old saying: *Pray to Jenshu, but be like Baijen.*

• Chapter Fifty-One •
NEW YEAR'S EVE

Preparations for New Year's week were muted in Janloon; the city expected few out of town visitors this year, and locals were not in a festive mood. The two major clans, which normally each donated a considerable sum to public celebrations and charitable events during this season, were too besieged to arrange anything except minor community functions in their largest and most securely held districts. On every New Year's Eve day in Janloon that Shae could remember, the Kaul family, led by their grandfather and later by Lan, would be out in public in the Temple district, lighting fireworks, handing out candy coins to children, and accepting a stream of well wishes from Lantern Men. This year, she and Hilo sat alone at the patio table in the courtyard of the Kaul house, where they'd spent all night in discussion.

There was almost nothing left to talk about now. Shae watched the rising sun smear the clouds with streaks of red over the roof of the house. In forty-eight hours, she might be the short-lived Pillar of a clan in its death throes. Her duties at that point would be relatively simple: see to the proper burial of her brother, the safety of her remaining family members, and a somewhat orderly transition of power in exchange for a swift and honorable death for herself. Minimizing further bloodshed would be the most difficult part. There would be those who'd rather fight on, no matter how hopelessly. She was in possession of sealed letters from Hilo to each of his top Fists in his own handwriting, should it come to that. She'd leave the more difficult conversation with the Maiks to Hilo.

After a spell of silence, Hilo said, "I haven't thanked you for giving Wen that new job."

"It was nothing," Shae said. "She gave me a good idea of what she wanted." Wen's official new job was working for the Weather Man's office as a design consultant on real estate development projects. It required a fair amount of travel.

"I'm glad to see the two of you getting along," Hilo said.

"I've gotten to know her better."

Hilo smiled faintly. Shae thought he looked weary and a little distant. How these past months had shaved away at the boyishness of his face, damaged the ease and openness of his manner. He said, "The family was hard on you at the time, but now I'm glad for your Espenian connections. I don't know how you pulled it off, but however you did, I'm grateful." He squinted into the sunrise. "You said we needed two things to survive: money, and a military victory. You delivered the first one, faster than I could get the second. You always were one up on me like that."

She still wished they could think of something else, some other way. She did not like or approve of Hilo's decision. It was awful on many levels and she'd told him so several times, but in the end he was the Pillar, and also the Horn, in spirit if not in title, and she had no basis on which to argue, no superior plan or more cunning ruse, like she'd had on Poor Man's Road. This might be their only chance, and in the end, she agreed they had no choice but to take it. "This is a terrible gamble," she said.

"So was you meeting with Ayt."

Shae's face jerked up. When he saw that he'd unbalanced her, the smile on Hilo's face broadened and he looked more like himself.

"Have you been *spying* on me?" Even now, he could surprise and aggravate her with his arrogance. "Having Caun follow me around again?"

Hilo's smile fell off his face. "Caun Yu is dead. He was killed at the Twice Lucky when Gont and his men took it."

Shae stilled. She tried to connect the face of her handsome young neighbor to Hilo's deadpan words, and realized that the vague sorrow she felt was the barest portion of what Hilo carried; in recent weeks he had seen many of his Fists and Fingers killed. "Let the gods recognize him," she said quietly.

Hilo nodded, his eyes sad. "I haven't had anyone following you," he assured her. "Just a lucky guess, is all, though I see I'm right. I figured Ayt would contact you, that she'd try to convince you to kill me." He shrugged one shoulder. "It makes sense. It's what I would do if I were her."

Shae sat back. "You never brought it up. You weren't even worried?"

Her brother laughed a little. "Ah Shae, if you decided to betray me, what could I do? What's the point of life if you can't even trust your own kin?" He kicked her foot under the table, a teasing, childish gesture. "For you to hand my head over to the Mountain, you must really hate me. I must be such a terrible brother that I'd deserve to die. So there was nothing to be done about it."

That was the way it was with Hilo; it always came down to the deeply personal for him. Shae stood up. "I need to move; I'm stiff from sitting so long. Do you need to go, or will you walk in the garden with me for a few minutes?"

"A few minutes," he said, and got up to accompany her.

Wen was right, the garden was the most beautiful part of the Kaul estate, and she'd never really paused to appreciate it. The morning light was slightly foggy, illuminating the still pond and the late winter blooms: bright pink cherry tree blossoms draped over dense shrubs laden with sprays of small white berries. Hilo crushed one of them between his fingers. "If you play your cards right, Ayt might let you out," he said. "Exile wouldn't be so bad for you. There's plenty you could do elsewhere." Faint bitterness in his voice. "I'd feel better about it."

Shae thought of the meeting she'd had with Ayt Mada in the sanctum and how it had ended. "No," she said with grim confidence, "I don't think that will happen." By dramatic and inexorable steps, she'd given up her chance at that other destiny; she'd hovered, gazing through that open door, and then she'd turned away. She was surprised to find, even faced with the probability of ruin and death, that she felt no great regret. At first, her decisions had been about herself, then they had been about honoring and avenging Lan, and in the end, they had been about more than that. She could say to the gods on the day of the Return that she had finally been the Green Bone she'd wanted to be: seeking if never achieving the Divine Virtues, but true to family and country and aisho.

She and Hilo kept walking, in a more companionable silence than she suspected they had ever before shared in their lives. She didn't want to break it, but then she pictured Lan sitting on the stone bench in front of the pond, watching the lazy carp and the rainbow sparrows that flitted on the birdbath rocks. She might not have another chance to settle her mind on this.

"There's one last thing I need to ask you," she said to her brother. "Ayt told me she didn't order Lan's death. That no one in the Mountain has claimed responsibility." She waited. "Hilo…where is Lan's jade?"

Hilo's gait did not break but his steps slowed, until he stopped and turned to face his sister. His face, bathed in shadow from a passing cloud, was suddenly unreadable. "I buried him with it."

Shae closed her eyes. When she opened them again, she felt them prickling with unexpected tears. So Ayt had been telling the truth. No Green Bone would've left jade on the body of a slain foe. Her brother had not been killed by an enemy warrior. "His death was an accident," she whispered in anguish.

"*It was no accident.*" Hilo's voice was cutting. He took a step toward Shae, his aura flaring harsh and bright in a tempest of sudden emotion. She'd never seen him look more dangerous than he did in that single step. He spoke with slow, deathly intensity. "There were two machine guns on the pier, and a dead man, a teenager. Ayt and Gont sent at least two men after Lan that night. One of them got away, and if I'm still alive when Tar finds him, I'll force a jade stone down his throat and bury him alive to die slowly of the Itches. Don't doubt, not for a single second, that the Mountain killed our brother."

"By sending a couple of jadeless thugs?" she cried.

Hilo's breaths were growing hard, as if he'd run some great distance. He took hold of his sister by the arms, his grip fierce, though she didn't resist, only stood limply, staring at him. "Lan was weak that night, Shae. He'd been badly hurt by Gam in the duel at the Factory, but he didn't let on. He was carrying too much jade, trying to stay strong in front of the clan. I ordered an autopsy done, that I never told anyone about. There was shine in his blood, Shae, too much of it. *Shine!* Lan hated the stuff, he would never have taken it, but he must've thought he had no choice."

He released her abruptly and stepped back, his eyes deep pits of implacable hatred. "The Mountain always intended to conquer us. They broke us down, threatened and hounded us, ruined a good peacetime Pillar like Lan. It doesn't matter what happened that night, they're the reason he's dead. I'll risk everything tomorrow to set straight that score."

"You misled me that day," Shae said, but there was no anger in her words, only bitter grief and acceptance. She felt, strangely, that it all made sense in a perfect and terrible way. It only confirmed in her mind that the will of the gods was a conspiracy of many things; people laid the tracks of their fate yet were helpless at the same time. They'd all played their part in this—them and their enemies. "The Mountain didn't even know Lan was dead when we attacked Poor Man's Road. We were the ones who came down from the forest first; we slaughtered twenty-one unsuspecting people."

"Misled you?" Hilo's eyes were pits. "Never. You came back on your own, Shae, without a word from me, and thank the gods you did. As for those people—they were Green Bones. No Green Bone is unsuspecting of death."

• Chapter Fifty-Two •
FROM NOW UNTIL THE LAST

That afternoon, Hilo went into the house and changed into his best suit. On his way out, he paused in front of the closed door of Kaul Sen's room. Om saluted and stood aside to let him enter, but Hilo didn't go in. He stared at the blank door, Perceiving his grandfather's slow but steady heartbeat beyond it, his raspy breath, the weak texture of his aura, so shadowy now that he was down to almost no jade at all. The old man was napping in his chair. *He's tolerable when he's asleep,* Hilo thought.

As stunned and enraged as he'd been and still was, Hilo admitted that the act of giving jade to Doru to enable the traitor to escape was the most *himself* that the Torch had been in months. Sneaky and subversive, unbending, righteous in his principled fury. Right now, it wouldn't surprise Hilo if the patriarch claimed the final victory and misfortune of outliving all his grandchildren. Hilo put a hand on the door, but could think of nothing to be gained from going in. He turned and went down the stairs, exited the house and crossed the short path over to the Horn's residence.

When Wen opened the door and saw him dressed so formally, she backed away from him and put her hands to her chest, bending as if in pain. She trembled as he stepped in the house and put his arms around her. "You've decided to go," she said.

"Yes," he said. "We have to be married today."

Even though he'd prepared her for this possibility, she let out a desolate noise and sagged against him slightly. "This isn't how I'd imagined it at all."

"Me neither." He pressed the side of his face to the top of her silken head and closed his eyes. "I was imagining the biggest banquet and the best food. A live band. And you, looking lovely with your hair done up and walking with your hand on my arm, in a long green dress. Or red, I like red just as well. I'd especially like it if the dress had a high collar, in a traditional style that's elegant and modest, but then also had a slit up the thigh to show off what a sexy piece you are."

"I already picked out the dress," she warned him.

"Keep it hidden," he said. "Don't show it to me yet. We might still have everything we planned for—the banquet, the guests, the music—everything. Later."

"We will," she said. "You'll come back after you've done what you need to."

He smiled and kissed her on the brow, touched by the certainty in her voice. "I will," he said. "But no matter what, you'll be safe. Shae has Espenian connections; I don't know how she managed to do this, but she's arranged visas for you, your brothers, Grandda, and Anden. She'll get all of you out of the Mountain's reach."

"Kehn and Tar won't go," Wen said.

"I've ordered them to. They can't stand the idea of running, but in this case, they're sure to die if they stay. Better to live for a chance to settle the score later. You'll have to remind them, and hold them to my orders, if it comes to that."

"If it comes to that," Wen said. "I don't think it will."

"I don't think so either," he assured her. "It's still important though, that we get married today, just in case."

"Just in case," she agreed. She rubbed the gathering of tears from her eyes and stepped out of his embrace. "I'll get changed. Give me a few minutes."

He sat down in the front room and waited, thinking, as he looked around, that this really was a nice house, that he would've enjoyed living in it with her, the way it was now. Wen returned a few minutes later, wearing makeup, a soft, pretty blue dress, and a pearl necklace and earrings. Hilo smiled and stood to offer her his arm, and they went out into the courtyard to be wed.

Judge Ledo, a man well trusted and paid by the clan, had been summoned to officiate the marriage. Kehn and Shae stood as witnesses. The civil ceremony took only a few minutes, not the hour or more of chanting that would've been involved under Deitist tradition, but the legal marriage vows still harkened to the Divine Virtues.

I will practice humility: putting my beloved before myself, expecting no praise or reward, for now we are joined in all things.

I will practice compassion: giving gratitude for my beloved, suffering when they suffer, for now we are joined in all things.

I will practice courage: protecting my beloved from harm, facing all fears from within or without, for now we are joined in all things.

I will practice goodness: offering freely of myself to my beloved, honoring and caring for each other in body and soul, for now we are joined in all things.

I make this pledge to you and you alone, under the eyes of the gods in Heaven, from this moment until the last one of my life.

Wen's expression weakened, fighting tears, as Hilo repeated after Judge Ledo, reciting the final words. *From this moment until the last one of my life.* How long would that be? Hilo felt the vows settle into him, binding him with a different power than the clan oaths that had directed his entire adult life. Already he felt a curious compulsion to try and reconcile the two sets of pledges, sensing the impossibilities he'd encounter in the attempt. Gazing at Wen's lovely, trusting face, he was struck with remorse that he couldn't, even with the consuming love he felt for her, promise not to break her heart. Because there were times a man couldn't be loyal to a brother and compassionate to his wife at the same time. A jade warrior couldn't truly be joined in all things with his beloved, not when he'd promised his blood to the clan.

Wen took a steadying breath and said her vows with a strength that made him admire and appreciate her all the more. Kehn stepped forward to tie their wrists together with strips of cloth, right to left on each side as they faced each other, and Shae placed the cup of hoji in their joined hands. They both drank from it, then poured it on the ground to call forth good luck. Judge Ledo pronounced them married.

Hilo knew it was a poor wedding for the Pillar of the clan. He was deeply sorry for having robbed Wen of the grand and joyful occasion she deserved. But the important thing was that she was his wife now, and if she became his widow tomorrow, she'd have everything he'd promised to leave her. The Mountain couldn't touch assets bequeathed to family members through wills. Wen would have enough to start up a new life, a safer life, in Espenia. And for now at least, he was her husband, and that made him happy, happier than he'd been in a long time.

He took Wen to the main house and up to his room, where he shut the door and undressed her and made love to her. They kept the soft lamp light on and took turns guiding each other, not speaking in words but with the silent brushing of skin across skin, the contact of fingertips and mouths, the merging of breathes. Hilo ached to stretch this oasis of time to its breaking point; whenever he crested toward climax, he denied himself and turned his attention to Wen instead, until she was spent with pleasure and whispering sweetly for him to give in. At last, with fierce desperation and quivering reluctance, he found release, and afterward tried to stay awake long enough to burn the merciful moment so indelibly into his mind that he could certain it would be the last thing he would remember.

• Chapter Fifty-Three •
BROTHERS IN ARMS

Anden arrived at the Kaul house late in the evening on New Year's Eve. The Academy had let out for the holiday week and throughout the day students had been departing campus to spend the break with their families. Anden had been slow to pack his bags and leave. The Pillar had spoken to him at length the day before, so he knew what to expect when he arrived, but for much of the day he hadn't felt ready to face what lay next. Instead, he walked the grounds of the Academy, trying to soak in the feeling of the home that he would soon be leaving. For many years, he'd thought of the Academy as a place of necessary hardship and tribulation, of sweat and chores, of modest meals, little leisure, and unsympathetic masters. Now, though, he realized that it was a haven, a refuge where Green Bone honor was an untainted goal, the only place where a person could wear jade and practice the jade disciplines in true safety.

The two weeks of final Trials had passed in a blur. After so many years of preparation and feverish last-minute studying and training, the conclusion of academic and martial testing had seemed almost anticlimactic to Anden. He'd been most worried about his science and math exams, and they'd been the first ones in his schedule. After that, there were no major surprises. He improved marginally on most of his scores from Pre-Trials, especially Deflection. On the last day, he wore his jade and fought four of the Academy's Green Bone teaching assistants in a row over thirty grueling minutes. By the end, he was exhausted and battered but still standing, panting but ready to continue. It was not for nothing that Hilo had beaten him and taught him to always get up again.

The Masters made notes on their clipboards and nodded in dismissal. Anden had saluted them and walked out of the testing hall with barely more pride and triumph than he might've felt after completing a menial chore like washing the floor. *At least that's over with.* He would graduate, that was the important thing. These tests weren't real. The real ones were yet to come.

When he got to the Kaul house, Anden went straight into the courtyard where the Pillar was sitting at the shaded table with the entire family. They were finishing up a New Year's Eve dinner, and the delicious smells made Anden's mouth water: roast suckling pig, seafood soup, spicy shrimp in sauce, pea shoots with garlic, fried greens. Anden only got food that good once or twice a year, but it was a modest holiday meal for a family like the Kauls, who in the past had hosted expansive public New Year's feasts. Anden stopped to take in the scene. His cousin Hilo was sitting at one end of the table in a black suit, his back to Anden. Wen leaned close directly on his left, her hand on his leg as if to hold him in place in his seat. Shae sat at the other end. Between them on one side were the Maik brothers, and on the other sat Kaul Sen in a wheelchair with Kyanla poised nearby. There was an empty seat and place setting saved for Anden.

For a second, Anden stood, the poignancy of the moment burrowing into him with a pain that made it hard to take another step. The picture was incomplete; Lan was missing from it and so too was any sense of joviality. The voices were muted, the postures tense. Even from a distance, the gathering had the feeling of a funeral vigil rather than a New Year's family feast. Only Hilo seemed remotely relaxed or happy. He brushed aside Wen's reach for the teapot and refilled the cups around the table himself. He helped himself to another serving of roast pork, said something light-hearted to Tar, who nodded but didn't smile, and he wrapped an arm lazily around Wen's waist.

Hilo looked over his shoulder at Anden. He smiled and rose from his seat to walk toward him. "Andy, you're late. There's barely any food left." He embraced his cousin warmly, then led him to his place at the table, next to grandfather.

"Sorry, Hilo-jen," Anden said as he sat down. "It took me longer than I thought to get out of the Academy. And the traffic was bad. New Year's week after all."

"You should have called me to send a car." Hilo shoved Anden's head in mock admonishment and doled food onto his plate. Contrary to what

Hilo had said, there was still plenty of it sitting on the table. "The Trials are over; you're not a student anymore. You don't need to be riding around on a bike or taking the bus."

"Congratulations on the end of Trials, Anden," Shae said.

"Thanks, Shae-jen," Anden said, not quite meeting her eyes.

Their grandfather seemed to rouse from picking at the small morsels of food on his plate. He turned his wizened head toward Anden, his eyes suddenly narrowed and piercing in their intensity. "So you're one of us now. Mad Witch's boy."

Anden froze with a spoonful of soup poised in midair. He set it back down in his bowl, sickly warmth climbing into his throat and face. Kaul Sen said, "I hope you carry jade better than your ma. Ah, she was green all right, a green lady monster—but she went out worse than even her father and brothers." He leveled a bony finger and shook it at Anden. "I said to Lan, when he brought you here: 'That mixed-blood boy is like a cross between a goat and a tiger—who knows what he'll be?'"

Hilo stared at his grandfather and spoke in a voice so lethal Anden cringed at the sound. "Kyanla, I think it's past Grandda's bedtime, don't you?"

Kyanla sprang up. "Come, come, Kaul-jen," she fussed, hurrying to pull his wheelchair from the table and take him back into the house. "Time to rest."

"Mind your jade, Mad Witch's boy," Kaul Sen said in parting.

The table had fallen silent. Hilo let out a long sigh and threw his napkin onto the table. "He's not well," he explained to Anden apologetically. "Losing jade tolerance does things to old people, up here." He tapped the side of his head.

Anden nodded mutely. Kaul Sen had never been cruel to him. When Anden had been seven years old, the man had seemed like a god, and as recently as a year ago, he'd been strong and hale. He'd said to Anden, "You belong in this family, boy. You'll be as powerful a Green Bone as my own grandsons."

"Ignore him," Hilo said now. "Go on, Andy, *eat*. The rest of you stop looking so damned gloomy. This is a happy night: Andy's finished the Trials. I'm a married man. It's warm, spring is on the way, it's New Year's Eve. You know what they say about the first day setting your luck for the rest of the year. Don't start it in bad spirits."

Anden forced himself to chew and swallow. He felt terrible; he'd made things worse by arriving. Putting on a weak but heroic smile, he said, "Congratulations on your wedding, Hilo-jen. You look especially beautiful tonight, sister Wen."

"Now that's more like it," Hilo said. "Thank you, Andy."

Wen smiled thinly, but Anden thought she was studying him with a particularly anxious expression. Her brothers, sitting opposite Anden, seemed the most unhappy tonight. Kehn and Tar had not spoken a word since Anden's appearance, and when they glanced at him, it was with something approaching resentment. Anden avoided meeting their eyes. It was the place of the Horn and the Pillarman to protect the Pillar with their own lives; they could hardly be faulted for begrudging Anden his part in what would happen tomorrow.

Hilo said, "You know what we should've had today? Candy coins. We always had candy coins on New Year's Eve when were kids, didn't we Shae?" And gradually, limp conversation returned. Anden ate as quickly as he could manage, not wanting to prolong the suffering around the table.

Kyanla returned to clear the dishes, and the family stood slowly, lingering for a minute, glad for dinner to be over, yet reluctant to leave. Shae came over to Anden and put a hand on his arm. It seemed a deeply apologetic gesture, and Anden knew what she was apologizing for. With Shae so close, he could feel the jade on her, the slightly brittle prickle of her aura, a sensation that had been absent when he'd sat across from her over dinner at the barbecue house a seeming eternity ago.

"I was wrong," she said in a low voice. "I didn't listen to you. I…"

"I know, Shae-jen," he said. "You don't have to say it."

"What you're doing now, I didn't want Hilo to ask it of you. I argued with him about it, told him he was putting you in a terrible position, but he's convinced it's the best chance of saving the clan. I'm sorry I couldn't talk him out of it."

"I understand," Anden said. "It's my choice."

Hilo whispered something to Wen, who nodded and departed with her brothers. The Pillar said, "Come with me, Andy. Let's talk inside."

"Should I bring my bag into the guest room?" Anden asked.

"Leave it. We'll bring it in later." Hilo led him, not into the main house, but toward the training hall. When they got there, he flicked on the lights and they blazed to life over the long wooden floor. Anden shuddered inwardly, remembering the last time he'd been in here, the last time he'd seen Lan alive. Hilo slid the door closed and turned to face Anden. The relaxed manner he'd displayed at dinner was gone, replaced with an equally familiar dangerous intensity. It amazed Anden that his cousin could move between the two states with such speed. "You've had a chance to think about it some more," Hilo said. "You think you can do what I'm asking?"

Anden nodded. He felt, suddenly, as if this was the moment of true commitment, this was where his entire existence had been leading. The Pillar was counting on him, and him alone, in the clan's time of need. "I won't let you down."

"I know you won't, Andy." Hilo looked stricken for a moment. "We need to prepare for tomorrow, but we should do this right. I'm asking you to act on behalf of the clan, on behalf of me, and that makes you a Green Bone of No Peak. The graduation ceremony hasn't happened yet, but you're through the Trials, so you can take oaths. Do you know them by heart, or do you need me to say them with you?"

"I know them," Anden said. He knelt on the floor in front of his cousin and raised his clasped hands to his head. His voice came out strong and steady.

"The clan is my blood, and the Pillar is its master. I have been chosen and trained to carry the gift of the gods for the good and protection of the people, and against all enemies of the clan, no matter their strength or numbers. I join myself to the fellowship of jade warriors, freely and with my whole being, and I will call them my brothers in arms. Should I ever be disloyal to my brother, may I die by the blade. Should I ever fail to come to the aid of my brother, may I die by the blade. Should I ever seek personal gain at the expense of my brother, may I die by the blade. Under the eyes of all the gods in Heaven, I pledge this. On my honor, my life, and my jade."

Anden touched his head to the floor near Hilo's feet.

Hilo raised Anden to his feet and embraced him. "Brother," he said.

• Chapter Fifty-Four •
BE LIKE BAIJEN

Late in the day on the first of the year, Hilo and Anden drove into the Docks and arrived unmolested at the front of the Twice Lucky just before sundown. Hilo made Anden drive. "I want to make sure you don't damage my car on the way back," he said. It had been some time since Lan had taught Anden to drive on one of the family's old cars and the teen was so nervous behind the wheel of his cousin's prized automobile that he crawled the monstrous sedan like an old lady all the way there and Hilo teased him for it. "The Duchesse Priza is a fucking powerhouse and you're driving it like a pedal cart."

"You could've had Kehn or Tar drive," Anden protested.

"I couldn't," Hilo said. "You saw how upset they were last night."

Their arrival was anticipated. The Duchesse's slow approach had been seen and reported long before they got anywhere near the Docks, so when they pulled up in front of the Twice Lucky and Anden turned off the engine, the first thing Hilo saw was that the parking lot appeared to be clear of any real customers. Only a few large black cars like Gont's ZT Valor were parked in the side lot, and there was a small crowd of Mountain Green Bones gathered in front of the entrance to the restaurant.

Hilo waited in the car for a moment. He could Perceive the eagerness of the men outside, and the implacable aura of Gont Asch rolling like a black boulder through the interior of the Twice Lucky toward the front door. And most clearly of all, he Perceived his cousin's dread beside him, the rapid beating of Anden's heart, and he was impressed that the young man's face betrayed so little of his fear. Hilo put a hand on Anden's shoulder, rested it there for a moment, then got out of the car. He took off his jacket and laid it on the passenger side seat, then he shut the door and strode toward the gathered enemy. After a moment, he sensed and heard Anden get out and follow several paces behind him, his heartbeat still loud in Hilo's Perception.

Gont Asch stood before him now, in leather vest with moon blade at the waist, flanked by a dozen of his warriors. Hilo stopped a short distance away. For all their mutual enmity, the two men rarely faced each other in person, and for several minutes they stood regarding the other. No one else spoke or moved; they watched the unfolding exchange. At last, Hilo said, "You know, this is my favorite restaurant."

"I can see why," rumbled Gont.

"Have you tried the crispy squid balls?"

"I eat them nearly every day," said the Horn of the Mountain.

Hilo's left eye squinted and his lips pulled back in a tight grin. "I'm envious." He glanced up and down the line of seasoned Mountain fighters, certain some of them were wearing the jade of his slain Fists. "All right," he said. "I'm here. It was a low thing you did to Eiten, you fuckers." He spat to the side. "Any man who challenges me with a clean blade, I'd give him respect. But you stole a warrior's dignity to get my attention. Well, you have it now."

Gont paced forward slowly like an advancing lion. His voice was a cautious growl. "If this were a dispute of personal honor, the two of us would have matched clean blades long ago, Kaul-jen. But this is clan war. We are Horns who must do what we do, for our clans to prevail, is that not so?" He circled Hilo, measuring him with deep-set eyes. "I must admit, I did not expect you to come. I assumed I'd have to cut my way through every last Green Bone in No Peak to get to you."

"You still want a duel, I'll give you one right here and now," Hilo said, following the enemy Horn around with his eyes and Perception.

Gont gave a low, snorting chuckle. "That wasn't the offer. I'm not so selfish as to risk the outcome of a war on a single duel." He stopped in front of Hilo, his broad frame casting a large shadow across the space between them. "We both know the Mountain will defeat No Peak in the end. Why let your loyal followers throw their lives away for you? Why drag out the suffering of this city we both care for? If I were in your position, I would think to the selfless example of Baijen."

Hilo was silent. An invisible spasm coursed through him—he did not

want to die. He was certainly prepared to, but he didn't want to. He knew
Gont could Perceive the burst of conflicted emotions but he didn't try to
hide them. "You gave me certain assurances," he said. He nodded back to
where Anden stood, some distance behind him. "My cousin is here to make
sure they're fulfilled."

Gont drifted his eyes over to the teenager and motioned him over.
"Come here, Anden Emery." Anden approached, calmly but visibly reluctant. Gont gestured him closer and closer, until the young man was near
enough for the Horn to place a large, meaty hand on his shoulder as they
both faced Hilo. "Do you know what part you're to play in this agreement
between your cousin and myself?"

"He knows," Hilo said, his jaw stiffening at the sight of Gont's grip on
Anden's shoulder. "I trust him to stay out of it once it starts. He's to bring
me back to the family; I want to be in one piece and with every stone of
jade still on my body. If Anden returns safely and reports that everything
happened as you promised, my Weather Man will surrender control of the
clan. I've spoken to my Horn and written letters to all of my Fists ordering
them to lay down their blades and accept your terms. If you honor your
bargain, she'll give these letters to them. If you don't, all my Fists and Fingers will fight to the last man to bring the Mountain to its knees. You'd
destroy us but the victory would be hollow. Your clan would be crippled,
and the city in ruins." Hilo's words held absolute conviction; he meant what
he said. "We both know it could go that way, but neither of us is so selfish,
Gont-jen. That's why I'm standing here."

Gont nodded, a grudging respect in his eyes. He released Anden and said,
"I give my word that young Anden here won't be harmed or interfered with."

"One other thing," Hilo said. "I want *you* to finish it. I merit a clean-bladed duel and instead you give me *this*. The least I deserve in a death of consequence is to not go down in a careless, hacking mess. Do you understand,
Gont-jen? I want another Horn to give me a warrior's death."

After a moment, Gont inclined his head, a touch of dark humor in the
movement of his lips. "I assure you it would be my pleasure, Kaul-jen."

Hilo ran his eyes through Gont's men. They had followed their Horn,
inching closer in anticipation, but now they halted and shifted back, sensing the change in the set of Hilo's body, the settling of his shoulders, the

readiness in his knees. Hilo undid the next two buttons on his shirt and yanked the top of it wide open to reveal the long line of jade pieces studding his collarbone. "Come on, then!" He was suddenly impatient. He drew his talon knife, spun it around his index finger by the hilt ring before gripping it and dropping into the coiled stance of an experienced fighter.

"Gont-jen, show me which of your men is greenest with the knife!"

Anden stood off to the side, Gont's weighty presence hovering near him. He stifled a gasp as the three Mountain men circling Hilo closed in together. The scene became a blur of movement and slashing that Anden could barely follow. They were good fighters, these men that had stepped forward with their Horn's permission. They wore jade through their eyebrows and ears, around their fingers and wrists and necks. They moved with supple ferocity. Yet they must've known right from the start that in volunteering for this worthy task, they were likely to die. Kaul Hiloshudon was a feared talon knife fighter and now Anden understood why.

The Kekonese talon knife is a hooked, double-edged four inch blade used for slashing, puncturing, hooking, and controlling the joints. Anden had seen Hilo's weapon; it had three jade stones set flush in the handle and was made of the same Da Tanori steel as the best moon blades, but unlike the moon blade, which has always been the quintessential Green Bone weapon, the talon knife is the tool of the street fighter. Simple, jadeless versions abound in Kekon and youngsters in Green Bone families learn to handle it long before they ever touch any other weapon.

Hilo fought as if he didn't even have a knife. He never looked at his hands or his blade, didn't rely on leading only with the right side, never seemed tense in the arm or overly conscious of his weapon, the way anyone less comfortable would behave. He weaved and sidestepped and circled, deflecting his opponents' attacks and entering their space with his own— except that each contact he made was punctuated with flashes of steel. One fighter came at Hilo with a high cut; Hilo hooked the man's wrist, slashed across the inside of the elbow, slipped the blade over the other arm, and drove up, slicing into and around the man's neck like paring a piece of fruit.

It happened in a second. The man was not fast enough with his Steel to follow the flurry; the knife cut into his jugular and he fell with a bloody gurgle. Hilo was already moving on, his eyes blazing motes of fire. So it was with the next man as well; Hilo returned one slash with three or four of his own in fluid succession. The next opponent caught Hilo across the ribs and then across the back of the neck. On most people, the talon knife would part flesh effortlessly but Hilo's Steel was nearly as good as Gont's was purported to be—not so much in strength as in fluidity. A master of Steel could direct his jade energy in a nimble dance of tension and release, avoiding hampering his own movements, flexing a shifting shield of near invulnerability at an instant. Anden stopped breathing for a second as he saw the blade part Hilo's clothes, yet only a trickle of blood stained them. Hilo grunted as he repositioned and threw Strength into a left-handed strike to the throat. As expected, his opponent slipped and reacted, meeting the blow by Steeling into his upper body. With a quick step, Hilo went low and slashed the man across the femoral artery before stabbing into the back of the knee. The Green Bone buckled with a cry and Hilo matched it with a triumphant snarl as he drove the knife tip into the vertebrae of the man's neck.

"You're wasting my time!" he shouted, dancing away from the body. Sweat stood out on his brow and neck. "At this rate, Gont-jen, you'll run out of Green Bones! If I'd known fighting Mountain Fists would be this easy, I'd have come around here earlier!"

He's goading them on, Anden thought, despairing. The Mountain fighters who came forward now were not hesitant. They were infuriated by the deaths of their comrades and spurred on by the knowledge that even the best fighter is doomed to tire rapidly against multiple opponents. Anden forced himself to stand unmoving, to watch and not look away as the fight became a true melee. Hilo scrambled to stay out of the center of the storm. He slammed two men back with a Deflection as he took on a third. He leapt Light to avoid a simultaneous attack from two sides but was dragged back down. He Channeled into an attacker but before he could finish the kill, he was knocked to his knees by another man's Strength. Anden's breath grew shallow and panicked; his nails dug into his palms as glimpses of his cousin disappeared behind the blur of dark clad bodies and flashing knives.

Hilo's talon knife skittered across the pavement out of the circle of fighters, and Gont Asch bellowed, "Enough!" A few of his men, maddened with the fight, didn't obey at once, and Gont bellowed again, flinging his arm out in a wide, shallow Deflection that sent his own Green Bones staggering. When they parted, Anden saw that the Pillar of No Peak was on his hands and knees, blood flowing freely down his face and across the back of his shirt. There was a rattle in his breath as his shoulders heaved up and down.

Suddenly, Anden thought of the time Hilo had come to the Academy and handed him a beating just for the fun of it, to test what kind of a man he was, whether he was the sort to keep fighting no matter how outmatched. Hilo had beaten him so easily that day, toyed with him the way the way a large dog pins and nips a small one. At that time, Anden had never imagined he would see this: the most ferocious of the Kauls as helpless against his enemies as Anden had been against him. Gont strode forward. "Enough," he rumbled again. "You've taken enough Green Bone blood today, Kaul Hiloshudon of No Peak. You deserve your warrior's death." Gont reached for the hilt of his moon blade, and in that instant, Hilo propelled himself forward like a shot, tackling Gont across the midsection.

The two men crashed to the ground together. Hilo spat in Gont's face. "Did you think I'd offer you my neck like a duck on a fucking chopping block? I'm going to take you with me!" And he raised up just enough to gather his remaining Strength for a skull-crushing blow.

Gont blasted Hilo back with a Deflection that knocked the other man flat onto his back. Mountain fighters ran forward to attack again but Gont shouted, "Leave him!" as he sprang to his feet, remarkably fast and Light for a man his size. The Horn stalked toward Kaul, who rolled to his feet with a groan and attacked again. Gont fended off the weakened man's lunge and hit him across the face. Hilo fell but rose again, and again Gont dropped him, this time with a kick that buckled him across the ribs. Anden shook; his eyes, his throat, his chest burned. A wild and vindictively satisfied light had come into Gont's eyes, emerging from behind the heavy curtain of stony control. "You...are...so...*persistent*," he growled with each blow that sent Hilo staggering or collapsing, only to rise again. "You...don't know... when to stop."

With a heaving of Strength, Gont lifted the slighter man and hurled him bodily several feet. Hilo smashed into the asphalt and this time he didn't rise. He lay like a broken and torn doll, and his chest barely moved in a gurgling, rasping breath. As Gont drew his moon blade, Hilo's head tilted back and he cried out, "*Now!*"

Anden ran. None of the Green Bones were paying him any attention. He was a teenage student, merely a designated witness to this event; none of them had seen a weapon on him, or sensed even the faintest jade aura. The fear and anxiety they'd Perceived in him had seemed only natural. Now he sprinted, his heart a drum in his ears, and flung himself upon his cousin's prone and bloodied form. "*Andy,*" Hilo whispered, and reached out his hand, and from the inside of Hilo's left sleeve, Anden tore out a long string of jade and looped it around his closed fist.

Two days ago, Hilo had had nearly every piece of jade he owned removed and strung onto a thin cord that could be taped snugly against the inside of his left forearm—the arm not drawing attention with a talon knife. He left only the studs on his collarbone, the ones everyone saw, in their usual place. There was no difference in his aura; he still carried every one of his gems against his skin. Now, Hilo's body shuddered violently as his jade was ripped away.

Anden's world exploded in a rush of pure energy.

It was as if he'd burst out of the confines of his own body. He was everywhere and nowhere; he was crouched over his cousin, he was looking down on himself and Gont from above, he was *inside* the people around him, the pulse of their blood and the throbbing of their organs cavernous, surrounding him. His own body was a strange and limiting thing—an odd combination of systems and parts, organic matter, flesh twined around bone, skin and water and brain matter—and he was keenly aware that he was merely that, and much more than that. He was sensation itself, he was conscious energy, energy that knows and manipulates itself at will.

Never had he imagined such awareness, such ecstasy of power and feeling.

Last night, when they'd rehearsed how it would happen, Anden had tugged at the hidden jade without pulling it entirely off of Hilo's arm. They hadn't wanted to risk dangerously weakening themselves with jade rush and withdrawal. Even still, Anden had felt the tingly high of so much jade, more than he'd ever been in contact with before. That had been nothing compared to this.

"Don't make a move before I signal you," Hilo had said. "If I die before

I can call you, you might still have a chance, but only if Gont is close. He has to be close."

Gont was close now. Anden felt the hitch in the man's motion, the instant of complete surprise. Hilo had done a good job keeping all of the Horn's attention focused on him, and him alone, rousing his temper to obscure anything that might have made him glance back at Anden, even the split second of intent between Hilo's cry and Anden's response. The moon blade in Gont's hand swung down but there was indecision in it; the white length of metal fell so slowly, as if the air it parted was thick as honey, and Anden felt the bizarre urge to laugh when he realized Gont hadn't slowed down—it was Anden's perception of time that had elongated a thousandfold.

Anden could feel the man's jade aura like a tangible thing that could be grasped with both hands. Almost experimentally, he brought a palm up and felt his greater-than-self clutch the flow of energy, envelop it, burrow into the heart of it. Gont froze, and then understanding and alarm washed into his eyes. His legendary Steel poured up and around him. Anden felt his questing force being pushed back, sensed Gont's powerful aura battening itself in defense. Anden rose to his feet, the string of jade stones clutched in his fist, one hand still reaching out to his enemy, and *pushed*. His Channeling was like an iron spear. It tore through the outer layers of the man's Steel and stopped just short, met by impenetrable resistance, unable to go further.

Gont's eyes bulged. The moon blade quavered as if his entire body was locked in a paralysis of action and reaction. Anden felt his skin tingle with sudden climbing heat. Blood trickled from Gont's mouth and nose; shock and panic strengthened his Steel and Anden felt it expanding inexorably back against him. He could no longer breathe; the force building inside him was such that he felt his eyes and lungs would soon burst.

In that instant of desperate stalemate, Hilo pushed himself up in a surge of tenuous strength driven by supreme force of will alone. He grabbed Gont's talon knife from its hip sheath and sank it into the man's side. Gont let out a roar of pain. "Don't you remember?" Hilo rasped. "Baijen came back from the dead to kill his enemy."

Hilo collapsed to the ground. The remaining Mountain fighters sprang forward to help their Horn, to cut Anden and Hilo to pieces, but they were too late. The talon knife buried in Gont's side had created the needed opening. Gont's attention and Steel wavered and Anden Channeled with all his force, felt the unbearable pressure inside him release in a violent surge, lancing into the other man's body.

Gont's heart stopped, his lungs seized, the veins in his brain burst. Anden, unable to block out the cruel clarity of his Perception, shared in the sensation of death, felt every terrible spike of destruction as it tore through his enemy's body. Gont was dying; *he* was dying too. As the Horn fell, Anden sank with him, mouth open but unable to make a single sound. Then the storm of death crashed out and another wave hit: the blowback of jade energy rushing into Anden, like a wind sucked up by the angry god Yofo and shot out as an earth-scouring typhoon. The return energy rush from destroying a man as powerful as Gont Asch was indescribable. The light and heat of a thousand stars erupted in Anden's skull. His head rocked back and he screamed from the very pit of his soul in a terror of agony and ecstasy.

He was going to combust; he needed to expend this terrible boiling, this overabundance clawing under the surface of his skin, desperate to escape the confines of his flesh. The Mountain fighters rushing at him with upraised blades were like vessels into which to Channel the overflow. An outlet, a precious outlet. He didn't even need to touch them; it was as easy as snuffing the life from mice in a cage. He caught up two men in midstep. They clutched their chests, eyes and mouths wide with shock, blades clattering to the ground. He watched with curious detachment and greedy joy as they died.

The Green Bones that remained backed away. Anden registered their fear of him and heard himself give an odd giggle. He was a demon—a pale teenage monster drunk on jade energy and killing. *What happens when you cross a goat and a tiger?* Kaul Sen had wondered. An abnormality. Something terrifying and unholy. With a shudder, Anden's spine rippled. He flung his hands out sharply, fingers splayed, unleashing a Deflection that tore through the air and lifted three men off their feet, throwing them into the air before they tumbled and rolled to the ground. They scrambled up, staggering and limping, and staring back with wild alarm, they ran from him, the others following on their heels. Their footfalls thundered.

The barest sense of reality floated back to Anden's conscious mind, which felt as if it were curled in terror in a dark corner of his self. Hilo's unmoving form on the ground, the blood and life draining from his wounds. Anden had to…he had to get help…phone someone. He stared at the coils of jade in his right hand, and with a wrenching force of will as strong as if he was plucking out his own eyeball, he opened his fingers and let the string of gems fall. He stood up, took one step, and suddenly the entire world tilted and fell away into sudden blackness, and Anden sank, insensible, to the asphalt next to his cousin.

• Chapter Fifty-Five •
NOT FINISHED

Anden awoke in the hospital, hooked up to an intravenous tube and machines that beeped quietly. His head felt heavy and swollen, his eyes crusty. His throat was raw and his skin was tender, as if the entire surface of his body was a single bruise and it hurt to even shift his weight on the soft mattress of the hospital bed. For a moment, he couldn't understand why he was here, and then it came back to him all at once. His heart gave a panicked lurch and he was quickly bathed in sweat.

The remembered terror and euphoria of the jade he'd harnessed—*so much jade*—filled his mind completely. Nothing else seemed of any importance at all. Wonder and craving gripped him as he looked down at his pale bare arms lying on top of the white bed sheet. *He'd killed Gont Asch.* Horn of the Mountain, one of the most powerful Green Bones in Janloon. He'd felt the man's death as if it had been his own, and when the agony of it had passed through him, he'd reveled in the release of the man's life energy recoiling into his own. Such exhilaration. He'd killed those other two men too; their deaths had been satisfying, though not quite as memorable. Perhaps only the first kill was so intense? Or was it the strength and jade ability of the man he killed that made the difference?

Ah, *jade!* It was just as the penitents said: jade was divine. It came from Heaven and it could make men into gods. Anden licked his parched lips, wondering where the jade was now, when he would get to put it back on and feel that way again.

And suddenly, he wanted to cry.

He wasn't normal; he knew that. He'd always suspected such would be the case. The powerful but unstable Aun line mixed with foreign blood and jade sensitivity. Yet he'd been told, and he'd believed, that the rigorous training of the Academy would overcome his deficiencies. Discipline and jade acclimation created Green Bones who were powerful but controlled, not monsters that laughed with the pure sensate joy of reaching out and stopping hearts. Hilo had killed many times, but he was still sane.

Hilo! Anden's head pounded as he pushed himself up.

A nurse came in, a stout unsmiling woman who checked some read-outs on Anden's monitor. "Where's Kaul-jen?" Anden croaked. The woman didn't answer at first, merely released some medication into his IV tube. "Is he alive?" Anden asked.

"He's alive," the nurse said. Anden heard it as if through a gathering fog. Whatever was in the IV tube, it was powerfully sedating. In a minute, he was unconscious.

When he woke again, Hilo was sitting by his bedside. Anden gasped at the sight of him. It was as if the famous youthfulness of his cousin's face had been siphoned out from under his skin, leaving a scarecrow version of himself. Hilo's eyes were bruised, his cheek split and stitched, and one wrist was splinted. Despite this, upon seeing Anden awake, he smiled broadly at once, his sunken eyes dancing with warmth. "You did it, Andy." In a rush of affection, he bent over Anden, seized the top of his hair and kissed him on the brow. "You sent the Mountain running. You saved the clan, cousin. And my life, I'll never forget about that."

"How did we…" Anden swallowed, trying to moisten his mouth. He saw his eyeglasses on the table next to him and put them on shakily. "How are we alive? What happened after…?" It was difficult to form complete sentences.

Hilo laughed. He got up and filled a paper cup with water from the sink. They were in a private hospital room, Anden realized. Hilo moved gingerly, with little of his usual languid grace, as if he'd been taken apart and put back together and wasn't sure if all the pieces were accounted for yet. He sat back down and placed the water in Anden's hand, closing his cousin's fingers around the cup as if guiding an uncoordinated child. Unsteadily, Anden raised it to his lips and drank, grateful and embarrassed to have the Pillar of the clan sitting here and treating him so gently.

"Mr. Une, the owner of the Twice Lucky, saw what happened and phoned the house. Shae called Kehn and Tar—they were waiting in a building just across the freeway in Junko, less than five minutes away." Hilo paused to draw a breath, wincing at some unseen injury, but still smiling. "It's all good news, Andy. After the Mountain lost its Horn and half a dozen of its other top Green Bones, Kehn and our Fists swept in like a fire. They took back the rest of the Docks in a day." Hilo's face was bright with pride. "After he and Shae saw us to the hospital, Tar won us the rest of Sogen. Juen and his men pushed into Spearpoint and killed so many of the Mountain Fingers there that we don't have to worry anymore about losing Poor Man's Road. We turned the war. *You* did."

Anden tried to absorb this. "Does this mean Ayt's been defeated?"

Hilo cocked his head. "Andy, a Green Bone's not defeated until they're dead. Didn't the two of us just prove that?" He pressed his lips together. "The Mountain's an old clan, a big clan. We've hit them bad and forced Ayt to pull back. She'll have to name a new Horn—probably Gont's First Fist; I'm told he's still alive. It'll be some time before they can come back at us again. But Ayt's not finished." There was grimness in Hilo's voice, but a dancing optimism in his eyes, something Anden hadn't seen since before Lan's death. "But neither are we, Andy," he said, leaning in as if to share a secret. "You and me, we got Gont. We'll get her next."

Anden was confused; why was it so hard for him to feel happy right now? He was alive, Hilo was alive, Gont was dead, and No Peak had prevailed. He ought to be relieved, he ought to be in good spirits just as his cousin was. Instead he felt hollow and lacking, hungry not for victory or vengeance, but only for the awareness and power that had been so fleeting and transformative. Brief exposure to a large quantity of jade had carved his mind with indelible knowledge of what it was capable of. Everything else—family and clan included—paled in comparison.

"How…long have I been in here?" he asked.

"Five days," Hilo said. At Anden's look of alarm, he said, "Don't worry, you'll be fine. I was dancing closer to the grave than you, and you're younger and stronger than I am. Dr. Truw's been in here constantly for both of us. We should make him our personal family doctor."

Anden wasn't sure he could put his thoughts into words, but he had to try. "Hilo… I don't feel right. I feel strange, *empty*, like I don't care about important things anymore. Killing Gont—I felt it all. It was the worst thing I've ever had to go through, but I want to do it again." Anden's voice cracked in distress. "There's something wrong with me, isn't there? Am I sick? Is it the Itches?"

"Don't be silly," Hilo said. He laid a compassionate hand on Anden's shoulder and sighed. "Handling that much jade for the first time, under that kind of stress—it knocked you flat. You're especially sensitive, no question of that. We've been giving you regular doses of SN1 to bring the fever down, reset your system. The doctor says your brain scans are normal now, so give it a few more days and you'll feel like yourself again." He gave Anden a pat. "Don't worry, graduation is still a week away; you'll be out of here by then for sure. Neither of us is missing that."

Anden looked over at the IV stand, followed the clear tube to where it was taped to the inside of his arm. "I'm being doped with shine?" The poison that had killed Lan, dripping into his veins.

"Don't look so worried," Hilo said quickly. He flicked the hanging tube with a finger. "It's entirely controlled; there's no risk. Dr. Truw's been monitoring you the whole time. You'll be weaned to a low dose by the time you're out of here, and the doctor says we can talk about whether to keep you on it or try taking you off. He doesn't suggest going off it yet since you'll be getting your graduation jade soon. Better for your body to have that safety cushion for now. It'll help you."

Anden felt overcome with exhaustion. He leaned his head back and closed his eyes, his chest tight, the nonspecific desire to weep still building inside him yet unable to find release, mixing instead with the confused craving and the drug crawling through his veins.

"Just rest for now, Andy," Hilo said gently, and didn't say anything else after that. His hand still rested on Anden's shoulder and through the physical contact, Anden felt the familiar thrum of his cousin's jade aura, faint and muted, either by Anden's own dulled senses or because Hilo had not recovered enough to be wearing all his jade. All that jade Anden had held—it belonged to Hilo, who had so much he didn't even feel anything when he got new pieces. Anden lay still, but resentment and envy coursed through him like an infection taking hold.

• Chapter Fifty-Six •
GRADUATION DAY

In years to come, the city would recall the holiday week that came to pass as the New Year's bloodletting of the Janloon clans. Many referred to it as the vengeance of the Kauls. In some parts of the city it was nodded at approvingly, in others it elicited the nervous tugging of earlobes. What was apparent by the time the districts settled into a new stalemate was that neither clan would be enjoying a swift victory. Despite all doubts to the contrary, the youngest grandchildren of the Torch had fended off annexation and in so doing, solidified unquestioned clan leadership.

It was tradition for the graduating year-eights of Kaul Du Academy, who finished their Trials before the holidays but had to wait until the auspicious start of the year for final results and graduation, to spend the first week after the break performing back-breaking service on the campus grounds—a final lesson in the Divine Virtue of humility—before being allowed to take their oaths and receive their jade. Anden was still recovering in the hospital and not able to join his classmates in scrubbing paving stones, repairing fences, pruning trees, and guiding clueless year-ones from place to place. True to Hilo's prediction however, he was out of Janloon General Hospital two days before graduation, and well enough to attend convocation on an overcast spring day, gray with the threat of rain.

Word had spread that Anden had been the only one with the Pillar at the battle that had killed Gont Asch. When he arrived in formal Academy robes to line up in the Gathering Hall before the ceremonies, a deep hush preceded him wherever he walked. At the check-in table, Master Sain inclined his head with more respect than Anden had ever received from an instructor. "Emery. Stand at the end of the line. You'll be the last to enter." Anden knew that to mean he'd received the highest marks in the Trials, which, combined with First of Class standing in the Pre-Trials, had compensated for his only slightly better than average academic scores to place him Rank One.

Anden saluted and retreated to the end of the forming line. "Ton," he said in greeting. Ton startled before raising his hands in a salute. "Anden-jen," he said. "I'm glad to see you're well." There was a formality in Ton's voice, the tone of a Finger addressing a Fist, and Anden stopped, uncertain of how to respond. He wanted to correct Ton for addressing him as a Green Bone even before the graduation ceremony, but it was clear from the other teen's manner that he'd done it deliberately. Anden swallowed his growing discomfort and turned to nod hello to Dudo and Pau; both of them dipped into salutes.

Anden's gaze drifted behind them to Lott. A fleeting emotion, the dim shadow of an ache, passed through Anden's center, but that was all; he didn't have room for anything else. That part of him felt numb. Lott, who ever since his father's violent death, had a grim, hollow-eyed look about him, inclined his head toward Anden civilly. "Jen."

Anden turned and faced the front of the line, closing his hands within the long sleeves of his formal black robes. Two weeks of convalescence, healing sessions with Dr. Truw, and administered SN1 had done what Hilo had promised it would: Anden felt physically recovered, and more like himself than he'd been when he'd awoken in the hospital, distraught and parched with jade craving. Even so, it had been a mental struggle to work himself up to the event today, to prepare himself to stand before the staring eyes of not just his fellow students, but the entire clan.

"You're a hero, Andy," Hilo had said, but Anden didn't feel like a hero. He felt damaged and unsure of himself. He thought of the SN1 still circulating like a pollutant through his bloodstream. These people didn't really know what he was. A cross between a goat and tiger indeed—something unnatural and dangerous, something that could not exist without the aid of dubious modern science.

At the sounding of the drums outside, the one hundred and twenty-six men and thirty-two women who'd completed the full eight years of Green Bone training at Kaul Du Academy shuffled out of the Gathering Hall and into the main courtyard, filing neatly into rows directly in front of the low stage that had been set up facing the hundreds of folding chairs containing watching relatives and clan members.

Anden knelt on the pavers with his classmates under the tent that had been erected to shield against the threat of rain. As Grandmaster Le began speaking, Anden looked over his shoulder into the rows of spectators. He found the Kauls at once, sitting front and center. Hilo was in a sharp olive suit and black vest he'd bought just for the occasion; he looked much better, his face still scarred but no longer gaunt. He was clearly in good spirits, as he'd been on the car ride over, exuding the cheerful nonchalance that had almost disappeared from him in recent months. He had one arm curled around Wen's shoulders. Anden saw him tug her affectionately to the side of his body and pull the hood of her jacket over her head to cut the slight but damp wind. On Hilo's other side was Maik Kehn, and next to Wen was the Weather Man. Shae sat erect, in a dark skirt and blouse, her gaze serious and slightly preoccupied, but when she noticed Anden watching, she gave him a small smile.

He brought his attention back to the front as Grandmaster Le called forward the first group of students. All year-eights were required to declare their intended allegiances prior to final Trials, and these eleven graduates had elected to take penitent's oaths. A Learned One from the Temple of Divine Return mounted the few steps onto the stage to administer the oath of penitence. The students stepped forward and knelt. They recited the lines binding them to a life of religious service, then touched their heads to the ground before rising and walking behind their classmates. The next twenty-five students had committed their jade abilities to the healing arts; they were called forward to take oaths before a master physician of the College of Bioenergetic Medicine, where they would continue their training. Anden shifted, his legs numb, as a third group of eighteen graduates was called up before Grandmaster Le himself to pledge themselves to the honorable profession of teaching the jade disciplines. They would return to the Academy as assistant teachers the following week, with the hope of one day becoming masters.

At last, the remainder of the class, the large group who'd declared service and loyalty to the No Peak clan, came forward en masse to take their oaths. A ripple went through the spectators and graduates alike as the Pillar of the clan strode down the center aisle and mounted the stage with quick steps. Hilo turned and looked out across the crowd. Anden thought he looked pleased. Roughly a hundred new Green Bones for the clan, nearly two-thirds of the graduating class. Some would become Luckbringers, but a majority would start as Fingers, for Kehn and his Fists to command.

Everyone waited for Hilo to begin speaking the jade warrior's oaths line by line, so the gathered graduates could repeat after him. Instead, for a long time he said nothing while an uncomfortable pause lengthened. People began glancing at each other in confusion. Grandmaster Le cleared his throat impatiently, but Hilo shook his head. "Grandmaster," he said, smiling, and speaking loudly enough that the crowd could hear him, "I didn't appreciate this place enough when I was standing down there in those black robes, so let me take in this beautiful sight for a minute. I'm not a student anymore, so you can't even wallop me for holding you up." The crowd chuckled at this. *He's truly the Pillar now, and everyone knows it,* Anden thought. *And still himself, mostly.*

"Brothers! And sisters," Hilo shouted. "The Pillar is the master of the clan, but Pillars change and still the brotherhood survives and continues. You're taking this oath as much to each other as you are to me. So who knows the Green Bone warrior's oaths by heart and can lead his classmates in taking them first?"

This was not how the ceremony was supposed to go, but even Grandmaster Le didn't try to intercede when Lott stepped forward from the line. "I will, Kaul-jen."

Hilo nodded and motioned the teen onto the stage. Anden watched, his heart beating in his throat, as Lott walked calmly up the three steps and knelt before Hilo, who leaned in to whisper something briefly into his ear before stepping back. Anden caught a glimpse of Lott's bleak and determined expression as he raised his clasped hands to his forehead. "The clan is my blood, and the Pillar is its master," he began in a strong voice that carried clearly across the courtyard. And the voices of a hundred of his classmates rose up and echoed him: *The clan is my blood, and the Pillar is its master!*

As his lips moved, reciting the oath he'd already taken two weeks ago, Anden couldn't tear his eyes from the sight of Lott kneeling up there in front of everyone, hands raised and eyes lowered before Hilo's warm but penetrating gaze. A bewildered grief rose in Anden. He was certain this was never what Lott had wanted; he'd never wanted to follow in his father's bloody footsteps. It ought to be him, Anden, up there instead. The Kauls were *his* family, he'd already proven himself worthy of jade, everyone was acknowledging him as Hilo's protégé and a fearsome new force in the clan. And yet, he was stricken for Lott, and horribly, incomprehensibly grateful not to be on the stage, because it seemed, for a long, surreal moment, that Lott was him, that he'd taken Anden's place as he'd appeared when kneeling on the wooden floor of the training hall of the Kaul estate after New Year's dinner, and now Anden was looking at himself through someone else's eyes, seeing blood and jade and tragedy.

"On my honor, my life, and my jade," Lott finished, and touched his head to the ground. The other new Green Bones of No Peak repeated his words, closing the oath. As he had with Anden, Hilo drew Lott to his feet, embraced him, and with one hand on his shoulder, said something to him in a low voice that Anden couldn't hear. Lott gave a short, tight nod, then stepped off the stage to take his place back in the line. Hilo clasped his hands in sharp salute and raised his voice, addressing the new members of the clan. "I accept your oaths and call you my brothers-in-arms."

"Our blood for the Pillar!" someone shouted. A few other voices rose up as Hilo descended the stage. "No Peak! No Peak!" Anden began to turn to the crowd to see who'd started the chant, but Grandmaster Le, glaring disapprovingly, brought up his hands to demand silence. All the graduates, and many members of the audience, had grown up under the Grandmaster's strict rule, and instinctively fell quiet.

"Now," said Grandmaster Le with more than a touch of reprove at both the overly dramatic oath taking performance, and the crowd's reaction, "we must award these graduates the jade they've earned for their years of hard work, discipline, and training."

At the back of the stage was a table with four separate groupings of small wooden boxes. Every set of eyes swiveled eagerly to Master Sain as he took a box from the first pile and opened it. "Au Satingya," he read from the inside of the lid.

Immediately following final Trials every year-eight had turned in their training bands and the jade it contained. Now their jade would be returned permanently, possibly with fewer or more stones than they'd surrendered, depending on how they'd performed in the exams. Each pile on the table represented a level of accomplishment in the jade disciplines. Au Sati, who stepped onto the stage to polite applause, had earned one jade stone, strung onto a metal chain. Grandmaster Le lifted it from the box and placed it over Au's head. Au would become one of the lowest rank Fingers, or if he was bright enough with numbers, an entry level Luckbringer.

"Goro Gorusuto," said Master Sain, calling up the next graduate as Au saluted and stepped back off the stage. So it went, until the first group of boxes was cleared, and a larger grouping of graduates began coming up one at a time to receive two stones of jade each. For some of the young men and women graduating, the jade they were awarded today would be the only green they would ever wear. For others, it was merely the first of more to come, with jade passed down through families, awarded by superiors in the clan, or most prestigious of all, won in duels and battles.

When the higher-ranked students who'd each earned three stones began filing across the stage, Anden found himself so nervous he could barely watch. Dudo received his jade, then Pau and Ton, all of them breaking into smiles once they'd gotten past the Grandmaster and joined their fellow graduates on the other side. The collection of boxes on the table grew smaller. There were only a dozen or so boxes in the final pile containing the reward for the top students, the ones who'd earned the maximum of four jade pieces—as much jade as one would expect on a senior Finger or a junior Fist, more than most Kekonese and any foreigners could safely tolerate.

Putting on that much jade ought to be easy for Anden now, after what he'd been through. It would be a momentarily disorienting rush, like what he'd experienced during training, nothing like the powerful, crippling high he'd suffered in front of the Twice Lucky. And still, his fingers began to feel numb and chilled and his stomach clenched in craving and visceral reluctance. The Grandmaster began calling up the final students. An especially loud round of foot stomping applause greeted Lott as stepped up and bent his head for the Grandmaster. Anden could hear his fellow graduates nearby, already chatting, congratulating each other, discussing how they'd have their stones reset, whether they wanted thumb rings or eyebrow studs or other, more daring piercings. There was only one box left on the table.

"Emery Anden," said Master Sain.

The chatter died as Anden stood up. Suddenly he felt as if he was in a waking dream, a self-consciously fictive state in which he was doing something without believing that he was really there. His legs moved him forward, his shoes hit the steps, and when he reached the stage, he heard someone shout, "Kaul-jen!"

Applause broke out and other voices echoed the first. "Kaul-jen!"

Anden paused, thinking the crowd was shouting for Hilo. When he realized they were cheering *him*, heat flowed into his face. *They're saying I'm a Kaul*. A mixed blood orphan like him, and they were placing him alongside Lan and Hilo and Shae. It was the greatest flattery he could imagine, and he was mortified. Because it wasn't true; he wasn't like them. As Grandmaster Le lifted out the four jade stones on a silver chain, Anden stumbled back as if the box contained a venomous spider.

"No," he blurted.

Grandmaster Le frowned, his motion arrested. "What do you mean, *no*?"

"I don't—" Anden choked out. "I don't want to wear jade."

In all his years at the Academy, he'd never seen the grandmaster entirely taken aback, as he was now, his gray eyebrows like two bristly arches, his lined face locked into place. Master Sain and the other faculty members on stage looked at each other in bewilderment but none seemed to know what to say. A graduate refusing his jade? Such a thing had never happened.

Anden heard the stunned silence before the whispers of disbelief began to rise. He didn't dare fix his eyes anywhere but at his feet; he was disgracing himself, disgracing Hilo and Shae. Burning with shame, he clasped his shaking hands and brought them to his bowed forehead in a salute of deepest apology before turning and descending the stage without speaking.

He had never seen Hilo so livid with confusion and rage. The Pillar came straight for him as soon as Grandmaster Le brought the graduation ceremony to a quick and awkward conclusion. The crowd of watching clan members parted before Hilo in fearful haste. Hilo's fingers locked around Anden's bicep like talons. He dragged his unresisting cousin away from his fellow graduates, around the back of the stage, putting several feet of distance between them and the silent stares of so many others. Hilo spun Anden to face him. "What do you think you're doing?"

Anden tried to speak, but when he opened his mouth, he didn't know what to say. There seemed to be no way to explain what he'd done. Hilo's hand was still clamped around his arm, and through it, Anden could feel his cousin's jade aura shrilling like a swarm of infuriated hornets. "I'm sorry," he managed at last.

"You're *sorry*?" Hilo seemed unable to find words of his own for a moment. "What's this about, Andy? What's come over you? You made a fool of yourself in front of the clan, in front of all your Green Bone brothers. You made a fool of *me*."

"I'm not like you, Hilo," Anden burst out, anguished. Everything he'd feared about himself, every doubt he'd tamed with strict training and faith in the clan, every nightmare involving bloody bathtub water and his mother's screams had seemed in one instant to rise out of that small box on the stage, overwhelming even the horrible knowledge that he was ruining all that he'd ever wanted. "I'm not someone who should have jade, who was ever *meant* to have jade. If I start wearing it today, I'll only want more and more, as much as I had when I killed Gont. I'll become worse than my ma, the crazy Mad Witch, I know I will. I can feel it in my blood now, no matter what you say." He could barely breathe enough to speak. "You could dope me up on shine, on that poisonous Espenian stuff that killed Lan, but that's not how I want to live. I don't want to be what you're making me: a—a—"

"A what?" Hilo demanded angrily. "A Green Bone? A part of this family?"

"A weapon," Anden finished in a whisper.

Hilo released him with a jerk and stepped back. His face contorted in a baffling mix of emotions, foremost among them hurt, his eyes widening in deeply wounded surprise, as if Anden had pulled out a knife and cut him across the cheek. Behind Hilo's shoulder, Anden glimpsed Shae approaching, Kehn and Wen following her but stopping some distance away, holding back from intruding.

The Pillar took a step forward and raised his hands to seize his cousin by the shoulders. Anden flinched, certain for a second that Hilo would really hurt him now, but Hilo merely said, in a calm, forced voice, "This is my fault, Andy." He gave Anden a firm shake to force him to look up. "That fight—it was too much, too quickly. And landing in the hospital afterward, that was a scary thing. You scared yourself. I'm the one to blame, but I had to do it, because we needed you. I couldn't have done it myself, couldn't have saved the clan without you. We still need you."

Anden felt terrible guilt searing his face as Hilo said, in a quiet voice that was both entreating and reproving, "You humiliated both of us just now, but I know you didn't mean to; I'm not going to hold it against you. Let's go back out there together to find Grandmaster Le and get your graduation jade. It's what you worked for all these years. We'll forget this happened, and we'll do it right this time, build you up slowly. You're a member of this family, Andy. You were raised to be a Green Bone."

Anden felt his resolve quaver but then he shook his head vehemently. "I'm too sensitive to jade; it makes me too powerful. It makes me enjoy killing too much." He swallowed thickly. "The Mountain knows how much of a threat I am now. If I wear any green at all, Ayt will do whatever she can to have me killed, and I'll have to kill so many others just to stay alive…" His words were rushing out in a torrent of desperation. "And every time I kill, I'll enjoy it, more and more, and earn more jade, and all the shine in the world won't help me in the end, I know it."

Hilo threw up his hands. "The Mountain's wanted me dead for years! We live with death and madness angling for us but we do what we have to do, we deal with it! You think I had it any easier than you last week? I had to go through fucking jade withdrawal when I was most of the way to being a corpse, and still wake up to be the godsdamn Pillar." His voice rose; he forced it back down with visible effort. "Being powerful makes you a target, being a *Kaul* makes you a target, but a Green Bone never turns his back on his family or his clan." The light in Hilo's dilated pupils was dangerous. "Think about what you're doing, Andy."

Shae appeared next to them suddenly. She spoke in a voice that was low and resolute, and carried a current of cold reproach that she turned on her brother. "This is Anden's decision, Hilo. He's graduated and taken oaths; he's a man now."

"Who do you think those oaths are *to*?" Hilo demanded. "Those are *clan* oaths, made to the Pillar. They're what we live and die by. If you do this

Andy, you're betraying me." The grimace on Hilo's face was terrible. "How could you say I made you into a *weapon*? Like I didn't love you and treat you like my little brother, like you were nothing to me but a tool? *How could you say that?*" He took a step backward, shoulders trembling as if it was physically painful to hold himself back from murdering his miserable cousin where he stood. His face and voice turned suddenly cold and remote with scorn. "You do this and you're out of the family."

"*Hilo*," Shae hissed, looking as she would strike him. "Stop this."

"Hilo-jen…" Anden pleaded, his body turning cold.

"Get out of my sight," Hilo said. When Anden didn't move, he roared, "*Get out of my sight!* You ungrateful, traitorous mongrel, I never want to see you again!"

Anden stumbled backward, stricken, the force of Hilo's flushed fury strangling whatever words might have tried to escape his throat. He turned and ran.

He ran until he left the grounds of the Academy. He tore off his graduation robes and threw them into the dirt and kept running in his dress pants and thin shirt, muddying them as he scrambled through the forest of Widow's Park without regard for direction. He ran until tears blurred his vision and exertion scalded his lungs and legs. When he stopped running, he kept stumbling and pushing through the trees, as if he could escape what had happened, as if he could lose his shame in the woods.

When he emerged onto a main road, he saw where he was and he began running again. The cemetery gates were open for visiting hours and he panted his way up the gravesite-cluttered hillside, half sobbing, until he collapsed in a heap in front of Lan's headstone at the foot of the Kaul family memorial. "I'm sorry," he gasped, trembling, the wind chilling the sweat-soaked shirt to his skin. Fat raindrops had begun to fall, streaking the lenses of his glasses and plastering the hair to his head. Rain splattered the marble slab, darkening it from a whitish green to a color almost like dirty jade. "I'm sorry, Lan." Anden sat and wept.

When Shae showed up minutes or hours later, she was carrying a black umbrella, which she held over him, letting the rain fall on her uncovered head as she stood next to him gazing at the family's final resting place. "He would've been proud of you, Anden," she said matter-of-factly. "He was always proud of you."

• Chapter Fifty-Seven •
FORGIVENESS

The letter that was delivered to the Weather Man's office on Ship Street two weeks later held no return address, but Shae knew who it was from as soon as she picked it up and saw the tight, upright handwriting scratched across the outside in blue fountain pen ink. She sat down at her desk, fingering the corners of the stiff envelope, then tore it open and read.

Dearest Shae-se,

I can't tell you how much I regret having to betray your trust. I've always done as Kaul-jen commanded in all things, and I can still say that is true. I assume that you and Hilo are searching for me, and I expect no sympathy or mercy should we meet again.

Take care what you do now. Hilo may believe he has won, but a Mountain is not easily pushed into the sea. There's nothing I can do to change the fate of your brother and poor Anden, but my heart aches to think of anything bad happening to you. So consider this a sincere warning from your caring uncle: have a plan to escape Kekon quickly and on your own. Store away some money and use your Espenian connections so no one in the clan knows. A good Weather Man is always reading the clouds.

With fond regrets, Yun Dorupon.

Shae swiveled her chair around slowly to look out upon the city below. Springtime warmth hung in the thin smog over the steady hum of the freeway and the bustle of the harbor; the air conditioning in Shae's office came on with a noisy chugging sound. She felt, suddenly, very aware of herself, of the flesh and blood, breath and aura that comprised her physical being, sitting here in this office that had for so long belonged to the man who had written the letter in her hands.

She and her family were alive on a day she had thought, a few weeks ago, they would not be. No Peak had suffered, and was suffering still, but it hung on, tenacious—as Green Bones and their ways had for hundreds of years. She read the letter through once again, then held the corner of it to a cigarette lighter and watched it burn down in the ashtray. *I won't run, Doru, not this time—and I'm coming for you.*

Seventhday brunch service at the Twice Lucky was not as brisk as it had been in the past, but with the Docks back in No Peak control and violence on the streets having settled down, business was returning to the popular old waterfront establishment. Shae and Hilo sat across from each other in a booth situated away from the rest of the diners. Kaul Sen's wheelchair was pulled up to the end of the table. Kyanla, sitting next to him, adjusted the napkin in the old man's lap. Wen was not able to join them this morning. She was taking Espenian language classes several times a week at Janloon City College when she wasn't traveling as part of her new job.

Shae placed some sausage and pickled vegetables on her grandfather's plate next to hers. He mumbled something that sounded like appreciation and patted her hand. These were the moments she looked for now: small things. Reminders of the family patriarch she'd admired and loved, the man who'd insisted she be no less a Green Bone than her brothers. Kaul Sen's remaining fragments of lucidity might be as illusory and brief as the appearance of peace in the city of Janloon, but she appreciated both all the more for their fragility.

The Mountain had retrenched, shoring up defenses in Summer Park, Spearpoint, and the other southern districts which comprised its core territories. Rumor had it that Ayt Mada had appointed a new Horn. Not Waun Balu, Gont's First Fist, as Hilo and almost everyone else had expected. Instead, Ayt had traveled to Wie Lon Temple outside of Janloon and recruited one of her father's former warriors, Nau Suen. Nau had spent the last two years living an undemanding life as a senior instructor at Wie Lon Temple—a clan reward, it was generally suspected, for giving Ayt Mada's ascension as Piller his full and vigorous support, including slitting the throat of Ayt Eodo with commendable alacrity. He was said to be a master of Perception.

Shae tried again to enjoy the meal and put the war out of her mind for a brief spell. Across the table from her, Hilo plucked at the plate of crispy squid balls. "These make it all worth it," he said, a smile curving his lips but not reaching his eyes. He was trying to be cheerful, but Shae was not fooled. He had been beaten to within spitting distance of death by Gont and his men and many weeks later, he still saw Dr. Truw regularly and tired easily from the injuries he'd sustained, but that was not what ailed him. Her brother carried a cloak of hurt over him, a sullen resentment that often flared into anger or self-doubt. He'd saved the clan but lost another brother.

"You should forgive him," Shae said, "even if he can't forgive you yet." She considered the irony of these words coming from her mouth. There had once been a time when she'd been certain she never wanted to see or speak to Hilo again, and here they were, Pillar and Weather Man of the clan.

She hadn't been able to get Hilo to acknowledge any mention she made of Anden, and sure enough, her brother did not look at her or reply to this latest attempt. Shae kept trying; it was early yet. Lan had told her that after she left for Espenia, Hilo hadn't spoken about her for six months. "Don't you want to know where he is? Whether he's somewhere safe?" She'd at least made arrangements for that.

"No," said Hilo.

Any answer was progress; Shae didn't press further. After leaving her cousin broken-spirited but calm on the beach behind her mother's cottage, she'd spoken to Wen, who had spoken to Kehn, who had quietly sent two reliable guards to Marenia.

Mr. Une came up to their table, half bowed in a mincing shuffle. The left side of his head was bandaged with a thick wad of gauze. He carried a small black wooden box and his face was tight with a forced smile that did little to mask his extreme nervousness. "Kaul-jens," he asked, "is everything to your satisfaction?"

Hilo set aside his downcast manner and offered the restaurateur an expectant smile. "Mr. Une, you know how happy I am to be back in one of my favorite spots."

The owner of the Twice Lucky flushed and bent at the waist as he set the small black box on the table in front of Hilo, as if humbly presenting him with a special dish from the kitchen, except that the unopened box contained Mr. Une's left ear. A plea for the Pillar's mercy, for having turned to the Mountain. "I hope to continue serving you, Kaul-jen," he said, his voice trembling a little. He dabbed his brow as he bent to Shae and Kaul Sen as well, including them in his appeal.

Hilo put his hand on the box and gently set it aside. Mr. Une sagged visibly in relief; touching the box was a sign of the Pillar's acceptance. Hilo said, soberly, "All's forgiven, my friend. Sometimes even the most loyal and devoted men make mistakes when they're forced to make decisions under terrible circumstances."

"Yes, Kaul-jen," Mr. Une agreed wholeheartedly, clasping his hands to his head and touching his forehead repeatedly as he backed away. "Very true, indeed."

Shae noticed her grandfather's head beginning to droop. "Kyanla," she said, "take grandfather home. Hilo and I will be along later."

Kyanla dabbed Kaul Sen's mouth with a napkin and moved him back from the table. People fell silent for a moment as the wheelchair passed through the dining room. Some raised their clasped hands in respectful salute to the old Torch. When Kaul Sen and his nurse had gone, several people rose one at a time from their seats and came to where Hilo and Shae sat.

"Kaul-jens, we live near the Twice Lucky and it's our favorite place to eat, but we never came here while those dogs held it," said Mr. Ake, father of two Fingers. "We're so relieved there's peace in the neighborhood again."

A couple, Mr. and Mrs. Kino, whom Shae recognized as Luckbringers in her office, slipped an envelope under her plate. "To assist Mr. Une with his tribute this month," they explained. "We know the clan will help him with the damages to the windows and the carpet."

A palpable current of relief was growing in the dining room, where the ceiling fans spun through the muggy air blown in over the harbor where Kehn and his men patrolled. The patrons of the Twice Lucky had seen the restaurant owner's bandaged head, and they saw now the box sitting next to Hilo on the table, and were comforted that the Pillar was merciful and had renewed his endorsement. With the solidified confidence of the clan's Lantern Men, and the jade income from the Espenians, Shae allowed herself a stir of grim optimism. Perhaps Ayt's ruthless vision—one clan over Janloon—would come to pass, but not, Shae vowed, in the way the Pillar of the Mountain envisioned.

Hilo accepted all the respect paying with something approaching his usual relaxed good humor. Presently, he said, "Please go enjoy your food. My sister and I have business to discuss," and the impromptu line of clan loyalists dispersed and returned to their tables. The Pillar and his Weather Man were left alone to finish their meals and to speak on clan matters.

• Epilogue •
SO MUCH OPPORTUNITY

There'd been a man at the gravesite when Bero first went, a young man who stayed there a long time, but the second time Bero snuck into the cemetery with Mudt, it was at night and the eerie hillside was empty. He found the right place easily enough. Due to space considerations, most Kekonese were cremated and their ashes entombed. Not many families were afforded full burial plots and large marble monuments.

Kaul Lanshinwan had been laid to rest near his war hero father. Bouquets of spring flowers, bowls of bright, waxed fruit, and sticks of burnt down incense in small cups of sand had been left at the foot of the headstone by the clan faithful. Below the name and dates carved into the marble, there were only two simple lines:

Beloved son and brother.

Pillar of his clan.

With a violent motion, Mudt spat on the grave and made to kick over the items on the ground. Bero yanked him back and hissed, "Don't be an idiot. You want them to start guarding this place?" The boy pulled away from Bero's grasp but stopped trying to do damage. He stuffed his hands into his pockets and glanced around the moonlit cemetery with sullen unease. Grave-robbing was, after all, punishable by death.

Bero crouched down and ran his hands along the base of the monument. He pressed his palms to the grassy earth and brought his cheek so close to the ground he could smell the pungent odor of the moist dirt beneath the growing turf. Several feet below him lay the body of the man he'd killed, and Bero was certain that buried with him was *jade*. Jade that belonged by right to Bero. Now that he had the entire stash of shine safely stored away and the clan war had ebbed so Janloon was almost, it seemed for now, back to normal, he could think on how to make his luck again.

There was always opportunity in this city.